# The Rights of Desire

# The Rights of Desire

A Novel

André Brink

Secker & Warburg
LONDON

Published by Secker & Warburg 2000

2 4 6 8 10 9 7 5 3 1

Copyright © André Brink 2000

André Brink has asserted his right under the Copyright, Designs
and Patents Act 1988 to be identified as the author of this work

First published in Great Britain in 2000 by
Secker & Warburg
Random House, 20 Vauxhall Bridge Road,
London SW1V 2SA

Random House Australia (Pty) Limited
20 Alfred Street, Milsons Point, Sydney,
New South Wales 2061, Australia

Random House New Zealand Limited
18 Poland Road, Glenfield,
Auckland 10, New Zealand

Random House South Africa (Pty) Limited
Endulini, 5A Jubilee Road, Parktown 2193, South Africa

The Random House Group Limited Reg. No. 954009

A CIP catalogue record for this book is available from the British Library

ISBN 0 436 27462 0

Papers used by The Random House Group Limited are natural,
recyclable products made from wood grown in sustainable forests;
the manufacturing processes conform to the environmental
regulations of the country of origin

Typeset by Palimpsest Book Production Limited,
Polmont, Stirlingshire

Printed and bound in Great Britain
by Mackays of Chatham PLC, Chatham, Kent

The obscure moon lighting an obscure world
Of things that would never be quite expressed,
Where you yourself were never quite yourself
And did not want nor have to be
— Wallace Stevens

I rest my case on the rights of desire . . . On
the god who makes even the small birds quiver
— J. M. Coetzee

# One

# 1

THE HOUSE IS haunted. Which is why it was so cheap, long ago —
almost forty years ago; thirty-eight years and four months ago —
when we first bought it. Ghosts were not yet fashionable. Two
fixtures came with the house. The ghost of Antje of Bengal. And
the housekeeper, Magrieta Daniels. Who was in her early thirties at
the time. And after Riana's death — after all the years, after the birth of
our sons and the loss of my daughter, in the long twilight that follows
happiness and unhappiness, guilt and innocence, with nothing more
to hope for, no new surprise, no sudden moon, a landscape of the
mind as monotonous as my childhood plains of the Kalahari, and only
the intricate treachery of memory to keep one awake at night — she
stayed on to look after me. And after Antje of Bengal, of course, the
poor victim of her violent lover and master in the early Dutch days
of the Cape.

In those times Papenboom, no more than a halt between Rondebosch
and the Company's gardens in Newlands, a mere cluster of houses
surrounding a mill, a brewery, a bakery and a tavern of ill repute,
was almost two hours by coach from the settlement on Table Bay.
All that has remained is the name Papenboom Road, lost in a warren
of small oak-shaded streets below Newlands Avenue; and then this
house, more Victorian than anything else, squatting on the massive
foundations of the original Cape-Dutch mansion and with only a
stretch of boundary wall left of what was once, reputedly, an estate
of impressive dimensions.

We were happy here, Riana and I. The house was the sign of our
emancipation from the offensive air of entitlement of her parents,

who would never understand, or forgive, our decision not to move in with them on the wine farm in the Paarl Valley, the pride of seven generations of Hugos, worse than Southfork, Dallas. A daughter pregnant on her wedding day was, God knows, bad enough; a son-in-law blown up by the wind like a dust-devil from the heathen interior, with hardly a penny to his name and only the smell of books around him, added insult to injury; but that all the accumulated pride of a family of Boer aristocrats should – knowingly, willingly – be renounced in favour of what, in their eyes, could not but be a miserable suburban existence, was provoking the long-suffering understanding of the Almighty himself.

But we made it. And except for the loss of a girl child I'd never even known, a loss more piercing than anything else visited on me (but sooner or later one has to pay for one's sins, I suppose), we had a good life in this house. A life defined by it, unthinkable without it. How then can they now expect me to give it all up – the house, the memories, everything I need to know who I am – and exchange it, like a book in the library, for a room or a flat among total strangers in some retirement complex?

'But Dad, your health,' they said. Johann. And Louis. And their wives. 'But Dad, your safety,' they said. 'But Dad, you owe it to yourself to spend your last years in comfort and ease and peace of mind,' they said.

'For God's sake, I'm not old. I'm sixty-five.'

'Yes, but the heart attack.'

'It wasn't a heart attack, it was a bout of angina. People live with it for years. The doctor gave me all the pills I need. Enough nitroglycerine to blow up a truck.'

'Yes, but think of your neighbour, whatsisname.'

'Johnny MacFarlane. I know exactly what happened to him, it was a terrible thing. This country is going to pieces and no one lifts a finger to stop the crime. But that doesn't mean anything is going to happen to *me*. I can look after myself. And I have Magrieta.'

'Magrieta is also getting on. She's even older than you.'

'She's a very robust seventy. And she enjoys looking after me.'

'The house is falling apart. It's getting darker and gloomier every year. No one has touched the garden in ages. It's a wilderness.'

'I like it that way. Lots of places to sit and read where no one can disturb me.'

Hour-long, two-hour-long conversations on the telephone. Louis from Johannesburg; Johann from Sydney, halfway around the globe. Johann even dispatched Cathy to come and talk to me, knowing I have a soft spot for her. More than for my own children; but of course they're sons.

'Come on, Ruben, be reasonable.' She has always charmed me by calling me by my name. Given my age, and hers, it is disarming.

'What can be more reasonable than to want to stay in my own home?'

'If Magrieta could sleep in, we'd be willing to give it another thought.'

'You know very well Magrieta has at long last found a place of her own in Delft. How can I now expect her to give it up?'

'But Jesus, Ruben, *please* . . . ! Don't be so pig-headed. You can't live here on your own.'

'I'm not living on my own. I have my ghost to look after me when Magrieta's not here.'

'Oh come on! You can't be serious.'

'You've never taken time to get to know Antje of Bengal.'

'Nor do I have the slightest wish to. Will you please try to listen to me?'

'I've done all the listening I care to do. We've been over this too many times already.'

'Ruben, I've come all the way from Australia.'

She has a way of standing – a kind of ballet pose, head half-raised, chin jutting out, dark eyes smouldering, blonde hair tossed back, slim hands on slim hips – which must be calculated to melt all male resistance. But I held firm.

'That was your own choice, Cathy. Look, I love you very much, my dear. But emotional blackmail doesn't work with me.'

She was on the point of going out – we were right here in the study, among the books and papers, the sleeping cats, the tangled

leads of record player and amplifier and speakers and radio and PC
— when she suddenly turned round to face me again.

'What about lodgers?' she asked. 'You could take in a few
students . . .'

'No students in this house. Coming and going and boozing and
smoking and fornicating and playing loud music day and night. Thanks,
but no thanks.'

'Then what about a couple, Ruben? A respectable, decent, middle-
aged couple. There must be many of them looking for a good place
to stay. As long as you have *somebody*.'

'I'm too used to being on my own. My way of life is precious to
me. They'll be a bloody nuisance.'

'The house is big enough. You can let a few rooms at the back.
They needn't ever be in your way. But at least they'll be around
if you need them.'

I could see that she would not let go. After two days of nagging I
surrendered. She wanted to stay on until the matter had been decided,
but then — thank God — Johann phoned and asked her to come back, he
couldn't control the kids any longer. Even so, with her canny female
foresight, she waited for the advertisement to be published before she
left. Between Magrieta and me, I decided, we might find someone
suitable; and if we didn't, just too bad. At least I would have tried.

We've had two couples so far. The first we turned down without a
twinge of conscience. Middle-aged, real down-and-outs from Jo'burg.
Crumpled clothes, a battered cardboard suitcase, a smell of stale sweat
and hopelessness. He'd lost his job, she had no teeth. Everything about
them spelled trouble. I was relieved to find that Magrieta felt just as
strongly as I did.

Then a younger couple, in their late thirties, early forties.
Coloureds. They seemed quite decent people. Teachers, both.
Waiting to move into a house they'd bought in Athlone, but it
would take six months. Magrieta seemed keen to have them. But
I put them on hold. One can't be too precipitate in such matters.
Wouldn't like to invite trouble with the neighbours, upset the balance
in the street. So when they phoned back I said six months was too

short: given my state of health, I couldn't have people moving in and out all the time, too much upheaval. They quite understood.

Magrieta made it very clear that she disapproved. Didn't say anything, but she has her ways. Hoovering the passage while I was listening to music, rearranging the papers on my desk, closing books I'd left open, knocking her broom against the skirting boards. The first time she'd behaved like that was over thirty years ago, soon after Riana had lost the baby; the unfortunate episode with Alison. But this time was less serious, and I think we've both learned a bit of give and take. After a few days Magrieta resumed her quiet, efficient routine.

I'd just begun to relax, preparing to settle back into the predictability of my old ways – I'd given it a go, no one could accuse me of not trying; it didn't work out, so now let me be – when the third phone call came, a week after the others. Young woman, by the sound of her voice. An unusual voice, with a kind of liquid darkness in it, and hidden laughter, reminding me somewhat of Françoise Hardy in the sixties.

But I refused to succumb so easily. 'I'm really looking for a couple,' I warned her, hoping it would put her off.

She said, 'Please, can we talk about it? I'd like to come and see you if I may.'

'Well, all right, if you insist,' I grunted. I know I can sound very rude on the telephone, but I didn't want her to come with any unreasonable expectations. At the same time I was hoping she'd risk it anyway.

She'll be coming round tonight. Magrieta went home for the weekend. It has been raining all day, real old-fashioned June weather. The huge, heavy oak trees surrounding the house are glistening with wetness in the dark, black on black. I've had to set out the pots and pans and buckets for the leaks in the passage; every time it rains, for the last two years now, Magrieta nags me to get somebody in for the roof, but when the sun comes out one forgets. I should make a note for Monday. Any moment now, I think, unless the rain has put her off, the doorbell may go.

# 2

I'VE NEVER FELT much need of other people. Two or three good friends at a time have always been about as much as I could handle. Even at university, I remember, when there was an intervarsity rugby match, one of the highlights of the social calendar, I'd take a book with me to read during half-time, while the rest of the students around me went berserk on the stands. Riana was just about the only one who ever managed to coax me from my shell.

After I'd started working at the library there were colleagues, of course; and I became particularly close friends with one of them, Dougie Visser. There were also the members of the Music Club, and Riana and I had a standing arrangement with a few of the other couples to go out together, dining at this house or that, going to concerts, of course, or to films or plays. But after her death it petered out. It isn't easy for married couples to accommodate a man on his own; and without her constant encouragement I felt less and less inclined to go out anyway. There was one other widower in the group, Kobus Haarhoff, who continued for another year or so to accompany me to performances of the City Orchestra. But then, quite out of the blue, he met a woman he'd been engaged to for a while before his marriage and with almost indecent haste they went off to settle in her house in Ermelo or somewhere.

My world was shrinking. Yet as long as I could withdraw into my work at the library I cannot say it bothered me. Books have always offered me almost all I need. But then, without warning, that last, small, safe sanctuary was invaded too.

About a year after the last elections – that famous moment when we were supposed to become a democracy and our lives changed utterly for at least three months – a young man was brought to my office and I was asked to train him. 'Teach him all you know,' they said. He was bright, and he was black. Siphiwo Mdamane. We got along quite well, except he had the exasperating habit of wandering in at about ten in the morning, taking an hour off for lunch and leaving at four. Been in the Struggle, spent eighteen months in detention, wrote some poetry, missed out on university (*First Liberation then Education*), but now he wanted to get on with his life. Commendable. But whether that life should embrace librarianship, neither Siphiwo nor I was very sure.

Three months to the day after his arrival I was called in by a deputy-something in the Department of Culture to report on the new recruit. I told them he'd need about another year to find his feet. Two days later I was offered a package, with a very firm indication that I'd better take it or else. And Siphiwo Mdamane was given my job.

I had less than three years to go to retirement. Couldn't they just have allowed me to see it out? But the new Medes and Persians were not to be swayed. Dead wood had to make way for the previously disadvantaged – the new catchphrase. This particular branch of dead wood found itself wedged between a rock and a hard place, where it was causing an obstruction.

My former colleagues seemed embarrassed to look me in the eye, as if I'd suddenly been diagnosed with AIDS or something. Dougie Visser was the only stalwart who still came round regularly. At least once a week he would drop in, which gave us both the occasion (he had a very strict wife) to drink a little and complain too much. In the long run that became somewhat problematic. But at least he was *there*, a friend in need. Until God in his overrated wisdom saw fit to strike him down with a coronary. Dougie, the fittest man in the library, strong as an ox, who climbed Table Mountain every weekend and had a marrow-chilling swim in the Atlantic at Llandudno every morning, summer or winter. But they say God is no respecter of persons.

After that Johnny MacFarlane was the only man still available to trudge through the desert with me. I met him soon after he'd moved into Papenboom Road, the small and then rather derelict house at Number 23. That must have been eight or nine years ago. The sheer energy with which he set about knocking the place into shape impressed me; and one August afternoon, on my way to the café in Newlands Avenue, I stopped at his gate to watch, with nothing less than awe, the progress he'd made in the garden since the previous day. (Being such a wretched gardener myself I admire people who can grub and burrow with their bare hands in soil and make the wilderness bloom.)

I assumed he was busy at the back of the house, otherwise I wouldn't have stopped to stare so openly. But suddenly, like a mole covered from head to foot in black mud, he emerged from a hole he'd been digging. It was obviously meant for the young silver tree waiting at the side, leaves quivering with eagerness, in a black plastic container.

'Could you give me a hand?' he called.

I could hardly refuse. How could I foresee that such a simple action – stripping the plastic from the lump of soil and roots and handing him the sapling to plant in the mixture of soil and compost and phosphates and 2:3:2 and God knows what else in that muddy hole, not just with enthusiasm, skill and dedication, but with something I could call by no other name than grace – would lead to such a network of consequences that it would be past midnight before I finally repaired to my own house? And that was only the beginning.

After he'd planted the tree he matter-of-factly asked me to hose him down, which involved stripping every stitch of muddy clothing from his slight but sinewy body and contorting himself like some exotic dancer in the powerful jet of nearly freezing water. It took a considerable time before a recognisable human shape – surprisingly tanned for that time of the year, except for a strip of stark white round the middle – emerged from the layers of caked mud. Only then was I sent indoors for a towel, while he continued his savage whooping dance to get the circulation going again. By the time I came back he had turned a distinct tinge of blue, even through the tan.

He ran to the bathroom while, unbidden, I got a fire going in the lounge from a pail of pine cones, a pile of neatly stacked wood and a scuttle of coal. But he was still not ready to settle down. First he had to go back outside to wash his bundle of clothes and boots and put away his gardening tools in the garage. An almost obsessively tidy man, I soon discovered.

'Coffee?' he enquired, when at long last everything was to his satisfaction. It was more a statement than a question. That in itself turned out to be quite a process, as he roasted and ground his own beans. But finally we were seated with coffee and rusks (which, as I was to find out, he'd baked himself), and large heavy glasses of Pinotage. All that was lacking, I thought, was music. But he killed all my illusions on the spot.

'Not in my house,' Johnny responded laconically to my suggestion. 'Music is the most overrated noise in the universe. I have birds in my garden. That's all the sound I need.'

The end of a possibly worthwhile friendship, I promptly decided. Which must have been what he himself thought a few days later when I declined his offer to help me kick-start my own garden. That we could still become such good friends says something about the relationship.

Our coffee and wine that night was almost inevitably prolonged into supper, which he prepared with a minimum of fuss and a maximum of skill from the most ordinary-looking ingredients, all of them fresh. Vegetarian. And delectable. Afterwards, with a new bottle of wine, a Cabernet Sauvignon, he proposed a game of chess. It had surfaced earlier in our conversation that we both had a passion for it. Even though over the previous years, since Riana's death, I'd regressed to playing mainly against myself and losing most of the time. (From Johnny's amused chuckle I deduced that in similar circumstances he would generally come out the winner.) He'd hand-carved his set himself, from yellowwood and stinkwood. Strange and exquisite little figures derived from indigenous myths.

I drew white and proceeded with one of Fischer's more daring openings. Johnny's first few responses were straight from the book, but then he made a most unexpected move with one of his knights. I felt an almost forgotten, and almost sexual, excitement throbbing in my temples as I replied with a move as daring as his own. Nearly five hours later, when he briefly dropped his guard, I mated him with my queen. Pure luck.

A sequel was inevitable. Though I doubt that either of us at that stage realised just how close the friendship would become. A game of chess every weekend, and often on week nights as well, merely marked the outline of a soon-established routine. In the long run our conversations became much more important. They dealt with everything under the sun and a fair amount beyond it. He turned out to be as manic a reader as I. Much of it overlapped – philosophy, art, literature – but there were enough differences between us to keep the unexpected always hovering in the background, just as in our games of chess.

One of our favourite battlefields was religion. Johnny was a devoted Catholic, whereas I'd broken with the Church long ago. This just added salt and spice to our arguments. The discussions were always passionate and intense, but never vicious or personal. Like chess, they were a form of mental exercise, as strenuous as his regular bouts of jogging or his workouts in the gym.

Religion wasn't the only score on which we differed, either. In most respects we were chalk and cheese. I was much older than he, by at least a dozen years. And I have always been a man of books, while Johnny, in spite of his love of reading, was an outdoor person. A botanist at Kirstenbosch, his most meaningful relationships were with plants. A new protea, or even the commonest little vygie, could inspire him to the lyrical flights of a man in love. I came to suspect that this passion actually took the place of love in his life. For one thing, he never spoke about women. He might occasionally ask something about Riana, but he never seemed interested in finding out more about my married past. As it happened, I learned to keep my memories to myself.

His own love life, inasmuch as it existed, remained a closed book. Some of the neighbours, I discovered, began to whisper that he was gay. He often had young male visitors and I knew that one of his favourite indulgences was going on hiking trips – to the Cedarberg, through the Swartberg to The Hell, up into the Richtersveld – invariably accompanied by four or five youngsters. But, for all I knew, there was nothing more to it. He never spoke about it, I never asked. However much we shared, we both had regions of experience we chose to keep to ourselves; and the way in which we respected this choice in each other enhanced rather than diminished the quality of our friendship. Even more so when we both lost our jobs almost at the same time. 'Rationalisation' it was called, an abuse of language. There's nothing rational about it. A whole new vocabulary is proliferating unchecked around us.

In a way I suppose it was even worse for him: he was just fifty when it happened, I was nearly sixty-three. But in other respects he seemed to reconcile himself to it more easily, whereas I, much to Magrieta's consternation, became more and more brooding and annoyed with the world and myself. Johnny tried to get to grips with the change by going on more, and longer, field trips; and spending more and more time in the garden when he was home. If he'd cared for that kind of thing, Number 23 could easily have graced the pages of *Garden and Home*.

But then, of course, he died.

The event sent ripples of shock through the neighbourhood, the way a dog trembles after a beating. It had always been such a peaceful suburb, hardly anyone bothered to lock a door in the daytime.

Until that early evening in February this year. The way we heard it afterwards, Johnny had hired a youngster off the street that morning to help him dig in a pile of new manure he'd had delivered from a farm somewhere, and after working all day the gardener had asked him for a sandwich and something to drink. Johnny went into the kitchen to fix it. The youth followed. And then suddenly attacked him, wrenching from his hand the knife he'd been using to cut the bread, and demanded money. Johnny took him to the bedroom and gave him whatever cash he had, a mere sixty or seventy rand. The youth started dragging him from room to room, stabbing him all the while – the house was left in an unbelievable state – and eventually tried to hack through his throat. Left him for dead.

At some stage Johnny came round again. He couldn't phone as the line had been cut. So he dragged himself outside, along the street. From the trail of blood it seemed he tried to gain entrance at three or four different houses, but the gates were shut and he was too weak to open them. (Mine has been broken for years; but, of course, I was out that evening.) Then he began to crawl in the direction of Newlands Avenue, where he might hail a passing car, losing consciousness more times than he could afterwards recall. Even though he ended up in a bloody heap in the road no one stopped. Neither did I.

How could I have known it was he? I'd been to a book launch in Queen Victoria Street and it was already deep dusk by the time I came out of town. I was in a hurry to start reading the newly-published book, which contained among other essays the first fully researched account of Antje of Bengal, written by a young historian from UWC whom I'd put on the track (there's a rather pleasing dedication on the flyleaf). In Newlands Avenue I had to swerve sharply to avoid the bundle of rags in the road; had there been oncoming traffic there could have been a bad accident. My first thought was that it was an animal, a big dog, struck by a car; only in the moment of driving past did it turn out to be human, half-raising itself and shaking an arm at me. A drunken bergie, I thought. The only logical – rational – explanation in the circumstances. I drove on home, went inside to warm some soup Magrieta had left for me and settled in the study with my book. If the incident did return to me, I shrugged it off. How could anyone in his right mind be expected to stop – after dark – to deal with a drunken and possibly abusive vagrant on the road?

The next day the story broke. It seemed that it was nearly midnight before someone had stopped to help Johnny. A black man and his son, bricklayers, in a bakkie, on their way home to Kraaifontein. They'd loaded what they thought was a dead body on the back and driven it to Groote Schuur, where some signs of life were noticed by an otherwise lethargic guard. The staff in Casualty were busy – possibly having tea or playing cards – and it was another two hours before Johnny was attended to. All the time the bricklayer and his son waited patiently to hear the outcome, then assisted an orderly in telephoning the police and making a statement.

Quite miraculously, Johnny MacFarlane recovered sooner than anyone could have expected and barely three weeks later I helped him back over the threshold of Number 23. His throat was still heavily bandaged and he was in a wheelchair, but otherwise he seemed all right. He was reluctant to talk about what had happened, but in the circumstances I suppose that was not unusual. Which also made it easier for me not to refer to my encounter with the bergie in Newlands Avenue that night.

There were a few nasty rumours when in what the papers proudly announced, as always, as a 'breakthrough' the police arrested the youthful gardener and it leaked out that he'd accused Johnny of having 'interfered' with him. But that is beside the point, really. What came as a blow was that the accused was granted bail a day after his arrest, whereupon he promptly returned to Papenboom Road and finished off the job he'd botched the previous time. Mrs Lategan, who lives in Number 20, diagonally opposite Johnny MacFarlane's place, noticed a 'suspicious character' emerging from Number 23, his clothes spattered with blood, swigging from a bottle of brandy in his right hand and carrying a large box on his left shoulder. Good citizen that she is, Mrs Lategan phoned the police, who arrived with surprising speed and took Vuyisile Mthembu in again.

Three days later he was out on bail once more, although the amount had been raised from R100 to R500. And since Johnny MacFarlane is now safely out of the way one can only hope that Papenboom Road no longer holds an attraction for the tempestuous youth. For at least a month we all kept our front doors locked, but already we are drifting back into the peace and quiet we have always enjoyed.

# 3

WAS IT REALLY only on Saturday, the night before last, that she arrived, with dirty feet and a smudge on her cheek, an hour late? Her black hair, hacked off unevenly and very short, was plastered wetly against her small neat skull. She was wearing a large shapeless sweater that sagged down to her bare knees and massive clodhopper boots. She must have noticed the look I cast at the trail of mud across the doorstep and into the passage, for she stopped in midstride, apologised, and took them off, not without some effort, hopping on one foot at a time. Pretty feet.

Only then did she say, matter-of-factly, 'You're Ruben Olivier who placed the ad?'

'I am. And you, I presume, are Miss Butler?'

'Ja, I'm Tessa. Sorry I'm late. But the bloody Beetle broke down and I had to use my tights to fix the fan.' A sudden broad smile as she gestured down to her knees. 'I'm afraid this isn't the best of entrances, is it?' The smile turned more rueful. 'I meant to dress up properly, I promise you. I had everything laid out. But just as I was about to change I got a rather tiresome visitor, so I couldn't . . . Anyway, that's just too bad. Suppose I've flunked, haven't I?' She narrowed her huge eyes. 'Are you a philosopher?'

I couldn't help chuckling. 'What on earth makes you say that?'

She shrugged. 'You look – well, famous or something. Must be all that hair. You look . . .'

What was she going to say? Distinguished? Wise? Or simply unkempt, tousled, dishevelled, sloppy, gone to seed? ('My Rubinstein,'

Riana used to tease me. And that was even before my mane had turned white.)

'Sorry, I should have combed it for the occasion.' Involuntarily I pushed my fingers through the tangle, probably making matters worse.

Rivulets of rain ran down her face. 'Well, what *are* you?'

'Just a librarian. Was.'

'That's it, then. You do have a bookish look.' (Tania had said, that memorable afternoon, 'You have the body of a writer.' Whatever that might mean. But coming from her, and in those circumstances, I tried to take it as a compliment.)

I looked at her in the dull yellow light of the passage. The perfect roundness of her head, the small pointed nose, the rather arrogant chin, the unsettling frankness of her eyes. Colour? God knows. Like Madame Bovary's, I thought, they might be black, or blue, or green.

'Can I see the room?' she interrupted. Again the quick smile, this time perhaps with a touch of nervousness. 'That is if it's still available?'

'It's not let yet, but as I told you . . .'

'I promise you I won't make a nuisance of myself.'

'It's not that. But I really thought a middle-aged couple would be better for me.'

'I may not be quite as young as I look.' Mischief in her eyes, defiance perhaps; but behind it I could still detect anxiety.

'You can have a look,' I said uneasily, 'but I'm not promising anything.'

As I turned to lead her down the passage – past my study right, and the bedroom left – there was a sudden eruption of laughter behind me, like a subterranean watercourse that suddenly breaks out in a spring. 'What's going on here?' she asked, gesturing towards the assortment of containers along the floor.

'I'm afraid the rain always catches me unprepared. Magrieta keeps nagging at me, but when the sun comes out I forget to call the plumber. Or whoever one calls to fix a roof.'

'Is Magrieta your wife?'

'My housekeeper.'

'Oh.' She turned to the haphazard assortment of containers on the floor. 'We can set up a symphony orchestra,' she said, bending over the first saucepan to check the sound with a finger. It wasn't particularly melodious.

'Are you into music?' I asked.

'I strum a guitar from time to time. But I prefer listening.' She shook her head energetically like a dog coming from the water.

'Anything special?' Perhaps, I thought, this might be a test.

'I take it as it comes.'

I paused, then tried to prompt, 'Classical?'

'If it's not too heavy,' she said cautiously. 'Can I see the room now?'

I filed the information in my mind. 'Follow me.'

We picked our way past the multifarious obstacles in the passage. A rather unconventional sequence of rooms: the small guest bathroom right, then the main spare room and the large lounge dominated by Riana's gleaming black baby-grand piano, looming in the dark like a silent reproach; on the left the dining room with the huge twelve-seater yellowwood and stinkwood table inherited from the Hugo family, followed by kitchen, scullery and pantry. Haphazardly inspired by its original Dutch foundations, there's something unpredictable about the architecture of the place. A smaller transversal passage divides the front part of the house from the back, most of which is taken up by a cluster of bedrooms where our sons once ruled the roost, now turned into boxrooms. I opened the door to one of the two Magrieta had prepared to house our putative lodgers.

'This is huge!' she said as she stopped on the threshold of the first room, tentatively furnished as a study or a workroom. She walked through to the middle door. 'It's like a honeymoon suite. A fireplace! And look at the ceiling. My God.' She stretched her neck to stare up, narrowing her eyes as if she were short-sighted. The taut, vulnerable line of her throat. Then she approached the large brass bedstead in the bedroom, sat on the edge and bounced a few times.

'Made to last,' I said straight-faced.

'No two ways, I'll take it.' Another enthusiastic bounce before she collected herself. 'But of course it's still up to you.' She stood up, suddenly looking thinner than before, and she shivered. 'Jesus, it's cold.'

Which brought me back from wherever my thoughts had gone. 'Come through to the study,' I said, as if she'd trapped me in an indiscretion. 'I have a fire going. You look as if you need it.'

'Oh that's great. I'm freezing.'

I led the way back to my study, past the out-of-tune containers in the passage, and stood aside at the door to let her pass; she entered into the half-dark — as usual I had only the reading lamp on the desk burning — like a small girl arriving at a party, looking around at the disorder which I'd always found comforting. She stooped at a pile of records to flick through them. Again the slightly myopic narrowing of her eyes.

'You have a lot of these,' she said after a while.

'They tend to accumulate over the years.'

'You haven't changed to CDs?'

I shook my head, perhaps not without embarrassment. 'Too much of a bother.' I hesitated for a moment. 'And I'm actually rather fond of these.'

She gave a small indulgent smile.

'Shall I put on something?' I asked.

'If you want to.'

'Any favourites?'

'You have any Bob Dylan?'

'I'm afraid not.'

'No sweat. Just pick anything you want.'

The music gently insinuated itself into the room. A cat stirred. I turned the volume down.

She listened to a few bars, her head turned sideways. 'What is it?'

'Flute sonatas. Mozart.'

'Why not?'

I kept an eye on her, unwilling to pass or fail her straight away.

She was already over at the desk, inspecting it like an archaeologist at a new site. A nod towards the computer quietly humming in its pool of bright light. 'At least you have some of the mod cons,' she said, smiling.

'I had to learn the ropes when the library modernised a few years ago.'

'And nowadays?'

'I file research notes on it – history, literature, music, painting, that kind of thing. And I use it for e-mail. After years of fighting a valiant rearguard action I finally succumbed. But it's not plain sailing. In fact, it left me in the lurch again today.'

'What's wrong?'

'I must be doing something wrong, but it just gets stuck.'

'Can I take a look?'

'Do you know anything about computers?' I asked warily.

'It's my survival kit.'

'Well . . .' I was still hesitant. 'So many well-meaning people have already screwed it up.'

'Let me just have a quick bash. If it doesn't work, I'll leave it.'

'It's not really necessary. I . . .'

But she'd already moved in behind the computer. 'What programme are you using?'

Within minutes she was clicking and typing away at a speed that made me look on in a mixture of admiration and horror.

'Do be careful,' I ventured.

She didn't even seem to hear me. From time to time she asked a brief question, then resumed. Ten minutes, twenty, half an hour. Once or twice she muttered, 'Fuck!' More often she would nod with a brief look of satisfaction. 'Goody!'

I couldn't take my eyes off the fluid motion of her hands on the keyboard. Long fingers, delicate knuckles, but with no-nonsense square points, short nails. I found a phrase: lyrical hands. She'd make a consummate pianist, I thought. Accompaniment to the intricate patterns described by the flute in the background.

It came almost as a disappointment when she stopped. 'I think that'll do it.'

'You deserve a glass of wine,' I said.

'Love it.'

'Merlot?'

'Brilliant.'

When I came back from the kitchen, she was sitting on the floor in front of the fire, knees drawn up, the sweater pulled over them, down to her feet, showing only her toes. (A ring on one of them.) She looked up and stretched out an arm to take the glass. The fire highlighted her wide-apart cheekbones. In the narrow face, the cropped hair still clinging to her head, her luminous eyes were almost unnaturally large. With no hair to mask or distract, only essentials remained. There was something curiously reassuring about her presence, as if she belonged there, had always been there, a child of the house.

I sat down in my easy chair – old scuffed leather, once dark red, moulded by time to the contours of my body – seeing her looking at me intently across her knees.

'You must be lonely in this big house.'

In different circumstances the comment might have struck me as uncalled for. But in the intimacy of that half-darkness surrounding us, with my customary defences down, and coming with such unassuming candour from this girl with the hint of unsounded depths beneath her upfront beauty (how hard I'm trying now, in retrospect, to justify myself!), I did not find it offensive or out of place. And once I responded, of course, the chance to protest, or retreat, or even choose, was precluded.

'I savour my solitude,' I said.

'Is that why you wanted a lodger?'

'I didn't. My children made me do it.'

'Where are they?'

'One son in Australia. One in Johannesburg, also thinking of emigrating. Canada.'

'No daughter?'

'No daughter. Once . . .' I stopped and looked down at the glass cupped in my hands.

'Once what?'

'Nothing. I was just thinking.'

'She died?'

'No.' I resisted for a moment this invasion of my privacy which she seemed to take so blithely in her stride, then said into the gloom behind her, 'She never lived. I lost her before she was born.'

'Didn't you try again?'

'My wife couldn't. Not after the miscarriage. It went rather horribly wrong.'

'Are you divorced? Or did your wife die?'

'She died. Long ago. Eleven years.'

'You never thought of marrying again?'

I shook my head.

'What do you do for sex?' she asked.

I need an interpolation here. NOTE ON SEX FOR THE AGED WIDOWER. There are ways and means, I could have said to her, but of course I didn't. What would she know about it, this unmarked young woman from the turbulent night, this stranger with her cropped wet hair, huddled in her ugly sweater, exposing her toes to the fire like the small pink noses of kittens? The imaginings one resorts to, the inadequate memories, the occasional sordid measures to plot relief, courting nothing but repeated disappointment if not disgust. The late-night call, after hours of frantic hesitation, to an agency listed in the smalls, the humiliating catalogue, just answer yes or no: blonde or dark or redhead, busty or petite, dominating or submissive, exotic or local, whatever. Never the same one twice. It's like ordering takeaway pizza or pasta. The return call to confirm. The wait in the darkened house, the car at the gate, the seedy man with the knowing look delivering the merchandise, sign to confirm receipt in good order, real bargain, enjoy, enjoy, pick her up in an hour. The brief tide of the distant city noises – fire brigade, ambulance, police – flooding in, then firmly shut out again by the heavy teak front door. Only the bedside lamp burning, 60-watt and dimmed, dingy rather than romantic. The appraising look, the pretence of worldliness, the halting pleasantries, the glass of sherry perhaps, the perfunctory shedding of clothes, occasionally a fleeting endearing moment when there's a hitch which briefly individualises the encounter – panties caught on a high heel, a hairclip coming undone – the ever-unconvincing show of desire. Invariably the relief at rising to the occasion (one day, sooner rather than later, it too must fail), yet simultaneously the disgust at this mindless independence of the flesh. Afterwards the deft peeling off of the condom, a quick scuttle to the bathroom, the toilet flushing, a handbag snapping shut like a vagina dentata. Now what? Another glass perhaps? — Don't go, don't go, don't leave me alone; just get the hell out of here. — The single hoot in the quiet night street, there's Stan now. Or Joe, or Pete, one of the monosyllabic brotherhood. The door closing, the car pulling off. Darkness descending, fold upon fold. The house stirring accusingly in its sleep. Antje of Bengal gliding through the empty rooms, always just beyond the reach of sight. My own pale face caught in the bathroom mirror, disconcertingly old and close but distanced by the mottled glass. The ghostly shock of white hair, the belly beginning to bulge, the meagre shanks, Don Quixote stealing with ravishing stride to the bed of some noble lady bound to turn into a coarse peasant wench. Somewhere in the night the girl, whose name I have forgotten, or never asked, must be on her way to her next assignment, starting all over again; and I here face to face with what purports to be myself, yet not the same, not ever, not me. Back to bed and only now in retrospect can some passion be extracted from the memory, more charitable than the smooth professional performance of the body that so briefly pretended to be here and real. Supposed to induce sleep, but it brings only wakefulness, acute rediscovery of what went wrong, what never happened. The infuriating flesh, so shamefully insistent in its demands, poor fork'd creature. Try again, eyes closed in urgent animality, yes, yes, the better to clutch at elusive memory, no, no. What do you do for sex indeed.

Or, I could have said, I read. And that might have been closer to the mark. The deeply satisfying sublimation of travelling through the pages of books. Which never let you down, never say no, never offer a cold shoulder. And custom cannot stale their infinite variety. Oh, not that books are 'easy'! They may be very demanding, they may play hard to get, they may not open themselves to exploration unless you're prepared to offer everything in return. But if you do, how abundant the reward. Foreplay, fullplay, afterplay, endgame, all, the ultimate consummation devoutly to be wish'd. And then you dare to ask me what I do for sex?

\*  \*  \*

'That's a very personal question,' I told her tartly, still winded by her brazenness. I should have told her there and then to go. So why didn't I? I've thought about it so much since then, yet still cannot come up with any clear or coherent answer. Did I, perversely, *want* to be insulted, invaded? And if so, why? Or was it, simply, a night in which the accumulated desolation of months and years had reached a point where it would have given way to just about any appeal from outside? It was the first time since Johnny MacFarlane's death that I could open myself to anyone; with Cathy, I admit, I'd been tempted – but I'd been restrained by my suspicion of hidden agendas. And for at least a week before this evening I hadn't spoken to another human being apart from Magrieta (and the manager of the café in Newlands Avenue). Not that I necessarily missed it; one learns to talk – aloud – to oneself, as one starts conducting the music played on the hi-fi. But that night I was conscious of a kind of hunger in myself to confide in anyone prepared to listen; and ready to submit to any demand in return. However, even that might not be explanation enough. It was the girl herself, this improbable girl, blown in by the storm, unconscionable, obnoxious, outrageous, beautiful. (A chance to practise the scales of my adjectives.) The way she had of saying, quite calmly, the most preposterous things without – or so it seemed – any intention of being offensive. As if she were truly eager to find answers to her questions. As if the answers *mattered* to her. (Yet, at the same time, when – like this time – I denied her an answer, she would quietly drop it and move on to something else.)

I waited for her to apologise, but she said nothing. It probably didn't even occur to her that I might be offended. And something else happened to change the ambience. One of the cats, my favourite, the ginger who proudly goes by the name of Amadeus, entered, haughtily surveyed the scene and then undulated towards Tessa – something he'd never done with a stranger before, not even with Johnny – to settle on her lap. It was an acknowledgement, a sign of approval, a gesture quite out of the ordinary for that beloved, disdainful creature. And the way in which Tessa responded by leaning over to rub her nose in the cat's belly fur, before she sat back again to stroke the now voluptuously purring Amadeus, appeared to clinch the relationship.

For quite a while Tessa still didn't respond to me. Only after a long slow sip of the wine, dark as Homer's sea, did she speak into the fire. 'It would be good to make do without sex, wouldn't it?' She turned her eyes to me, bright in the half-dark. 'Tell me, does it sort of fade away when one grows older?'

I could feel my hackles rise again. 'I'm not old enough to tell yet,' I said stiffly.

She smiled. Then a sudden change of subject: 'Why did your sons chicken out?'

I felt an unreasonable need to protect them. 'They've got their lives ahead of them. They believe it's a dead-end here.'

'I would never think of leaving.'

'Johann, the one in Australia, is a doctor. He couldn't take it any more, the way hospital services are going down the drain, medicine stolen from the dispensaries, staff going on strike and trashing the place, leaving patients to die. That sort of thing.'

'And the other one?'

'Louis. He's a civil engineer. Started losing contracts because he refused to pay bribes.'

'There's also more money in Canada, of course.'

'Mainly,' I said, stung, 'he wants to go because his wife's best friend was hijacked on her way home a month ago, and raped, and then thrown out of the moving car. She'll never walk again.' When she didn't respond I added, deliberately provocative, 'They say one out of every two women in the country will be raped in her lifetime.'

'What makes *you* stay?' she challenged me.

'I've never tried to figure it out. I suppose one gets used to a place. Perhaps, in a way, you even love it. Which may be perverse, seeing how it's been treating us.' I gulped down some wine. 'Or perhaps it loves *us*.'

'That's a bloody sentimental thing to say,' she sneered. 'A country can't love you. At most it may need you. It's much the same as people.'

She drained her glass, then half-turned to hold it out to me. I reached for the bottle on the floor and leaned over to refill the glass without getting up. There was something quietly ceremonial about the moment. Inexplicably, I felt my hostility subside. I no longer cared even to feel offended. It was enough, for the moment, to accept her presence with all its quirks and unexpected probings and challenges, its shifts, its darts, its hidden liquid fire.

'Have you really never thought of packing up yourself?' she returned to her inquisition.

'You can't teach an old dog new tricks.'

'You don't look so old.'

'I'm sixty-five.' I couldn't keep myself from adding, 'Probably as old as your father.'

'My father is thirty,' she said with a straight face, a subdued tone to the rich darkness of her voice. She must have seen my perplexed stare, for after a moment she explained, 'He's just a rather faded photo on a wall.'

'I'm sorry, I . . .'

'He died when I was three.' She looked past me with solemn eyes. 'He was murdered. It was a terrible thing. We were staying with friends on a farm. They came in the night. The whole house was spattered with blood. If my mother hadn't run away with us we would all have been butchered.'

I stared at her in horror. 'It's unbelievable, it's . . .' It took a while to compose myself. 'How did you ever come to terms with it?'

'I'd rather not talk about it,' she said quietly. 'Even now, after all these years.'

'Of course. I didn't mean to upset you.' Groping for a way out I asked, clumsily, 'How old are you?'

Her mood changed; she grinned, though not with much joy. 'To me, thirty has always seemed like the end of the world. I suppose it's because he was thirty when it happened. I can't believe I'll have to face it in three months' time.'

'You may well have worse things to face than that.'

'At least I'll have a solid base here,' she said calmly.

It stirred up an edge of disquiet in me. 'Listen, Tessa . . .'

Matter-of-factly: 'You don't want me here, is that it?'

'Well, I told you I was really looking for a couple. I can't burden you with my needs.'

With a hint of sarcasm she asked, 'What *are* your needs then?'

'It's not what you're thinking!' I protested.

'What do you think I'm thinking?'

'I told you it has nothing to do with what *I* want or need. It's my sons who're worried about my living on my own. They believe it's getting dangerous. We had a murder in the street some time ago. I'm no longer all that young, and my health . . .' I flared up. 'That's what *they* say, anyway.'

'You want a housekeeper?'

'No. I told you I have a housekeeper.'

'A nurse then?'

'I'm not an invalid.'

'A companion?'

'I'm all the company I need.'

'You want someone to fuck?'

'This is outrageous.'

'Is it? We all need someone to fuck from time to time.'

To my annoyance – my disgust – I felt a tingling in my loins. I blurted out, 'Look, all I need – *they* think I need – is someone in the house when the housekeeper isn't around. In case . . . Let's just forget about it, right?'

'I won't cook, I won't keep house, I won't sleep with you. But I can be around.'

'Why would you want to stay here?'

'I have nowhere else to go right now.'

It is not easy to recall all the meanderings, the large, easy loops, the repetitions and variations and divagations, the sudden changes of direction, of our conversation. It lasted most of the night. At some stage I fetched another bottle, once she wanted a glass of water, twice I went to make her coffee and rooibos tea for me. (My heart.) On some of these occasions she accompanied me to the pantry and the kitchen, perching on a broad scrubbed shelf while she watched me, dangling her bare legs like a child in church. But through it all the conversation rambled on and I am at a loss to recapture it now, two days later. But I must try. I have no choice, if I wish to preserve it; even while it was happening I caught myself, as I so often do, thinking of how I would recall it afterwards, what was likely to stick in the mind, what might slip through the holes in the moth-eaten net of memory. As if I'm not wholly present while it is happening and can only try to recover it afterwards. Levinas says somewhere, 'The great "experiences" of our life have properly speaking never been lived.'

Even as a child it was like this. There were a couple of undoubted astral experiences, the unsettling impression of finding myself remote from where I knew I was, with a bird's-eye view of what was happening and of myself. Once, on a visit, with a clutch of school friends, to the 'Bushman cave' a mile from the farmhouse among the flintstone koppies, little more than an overhanging rock sheltering a tract of San paintings thousands of years old and obscured by layers of graffiti, I suddenly found myself on top of the outcrop, overlooking my own attempts at impressing my young visitors with knowledge half-gleaned from books or the stories of my old Griqua mentor, Outa Hans, the foreman on the farm. Another occasion was the afternoon in the dark, fragrant barn with the wise and radiant little Lenie among the stacks of lucerne bales behind Pa's broken-down implements – horse-carts, ploughs, a grey tractor, sheep shears, dip cans – when once again there was an unexpected shift to a vantage point on the high eaves where the red-eyed wood pigeons nested.

These experiences may have been extreme. But for as long as I can remember there have been gradations of the same sense of displacement. The way, I suppose, an actor is inevitably aware of both role and self, and the precarious interval between them. Where falls the shadow. Except in books. Except here in my study, or at work in my library in the city – before the axe came down – amid the reassurance of words.

We, my two older brothers and I, didn't grow up with books. We had the Bible, and a stray foxed volume of hunting stories from the turn of the century, and the *Landbouweekblad*, with pictures of Afrikaner oxen and tractors and farmers on horseback; and that was that. Books belonged to a world disconnected from ours. Our reality was the hard, masculine world of the farm, where I grew up with no women near by. That farm world was strictly defined and permitting of no exception: rain, for example, was excluded. It was unreal, imaginary, miraculous, not of the same order as the sun-blackened koppies on the endless veld, the brittle grass, relentless sun. I was three years old when I saw rain for the first time; and it was unbelievable. I ran outside like a mad thing, tearing off my clothes to feel the naked water on my naked skin, laughing like a small hysterical jackal, flailing my arms, kicking up spray from puddles, rolling in mud. Until my big brothers came out to moer me to my senses and drag me back inside. All night long I lay trembling with a joy which I was too small to understand, as I listened to the thunder rumbling outside and to the clattering on the tin roof; and, as it subsided, to the myriad sibilant whisperings of water, weaving their web of sound in my mind. When the sun came out the next morning only the signs were there, and in my memory the world had become a different place.

It was something I couldn't share with anyone except Outa Hans, who could tell stories about the rain. My brothers were not like him. They were enemies, and violent. There were rare moments when, to a small boy like me, they were fun, like when they had farting contests to see who could blow out a candle, or change the colour of its flame (blue, violet, sometimes green). But mainly they were the bane and terror of my youth. All they did was jeer at me or beat me up for sport. They would interfere with the few secretive friendships I did have. With small black boys on the farm. Or, most precious of all, little Lenie, who would sometimes come visiting with her parents from the neighbouring farm. She was my age, a sweet little wisp of a thing, but as tough as nails. My brothers were much older; but when they were around they never left us in peace. There was one awful day when I must have been about ten. Lenie and I were playing behind the sheep kraal wall when they came there for a smoke break. To my surprise they were singularly friendly with Lenie. I soon discovered why. They wanted her to lift her dress for them, which she did with a shrug and a smile. A yellow dress, in which she looked like a small bright nasturtium. But then they tried to coax her into taking off her panties. I don't think she refused because she thought it was wrong but simply because she didn't want to. At first they offered her bribes. A tortoise shell, a pocket knife, the skeleton of a small bird, a newborn lamb. These were followed by promises of things even I knew were preposterous: a hundred dolls, a hundred pounds, a hundred swallows in a cage. She just shook her head, backing up against the heavy stones of the kraal, which had been stacked with his own hands by my legendary grandfather Goliath before the birth of God. Lenie didn't look scared, just mildly surprised that such a negligible item of clothing could mean so much to anyone. Their mood changed, they became abusive, then threatening. They'd drown her in the cement dam, they'd string her up from a rafter in the barn. I was petrified. There was a moment, as they moved in on her and made to grab her by the arms, when it seemed she was going to give in anyway. And then, in a voice I didn't recognise as my own, I croaked, 'You don't have to do it if you don't want to, you know.' They turned on me. She ran away. They nearly killed me: one of them holding my arms pinned behind my back, the other laying into me with his fists and kicking me, and kneading me with a knee in the stomach and in the groin, until I vomited and blacked out.

Some weeks later, when Lenie came to the farm again and my brothers weren't there, we wandered across the veld in search of the small things we collected, and then she whispered something wetly in my ear and took me by the hand and led me to the barn, where with giggles and hot breathings she revealed to me what she wouldn't show my brothers.

It was as if I could see the thoughts taking shape in my own head: *Is that all? So what was all the fuss about?* Perhaps it was the sense of distance that made it seem so unremarkable. A body, even that first girl's body of my life, was no more than just a body.

Only months later, when Lenie was no longer there, I started going back to the barn on my own and transformed that discovery into something momentous. That was what turned the barn into a place of miracles. I collected it in my mind with my most precious memories: the day the rains came, swallows taking off for the distant north in the first chill of autumn, a sunset more glorious than any other, the pictures painted on the hollow rockface by people gone from the face of the earth.

It was the kind of wonder I later came to associate with books. Perhaps this happened because it was rain that first made me see the inside of the dusty little town library. I must have been about eleven or twelve, my brothers had already left school; and it happened during the holidays, for I remember the long ride in to town from the farm. Pa was in a hurry — he always was in a hurry when we went to town on the mule-cart or in the bakkie because he panicked when he found himself among people — and somewhere between the co-op and the railway station it began to rain; and because he knew it would be useless to try and drag me along to his other ports of call (including, most especially, as I knew only too well, the bar in the Queen's Hotel) he shooed me into the library. And forgot me there; and only remembered when he reached the farm, too late to drive all the way back.

When he turned up the next day, in a rage which he couldn't direct at himself and so vented on me, I was still there among the shelves. The previous afternoon the half-blind old lady who tended the library and smelled of ancient dust and sour quinces had never even noticed me, and had locked up and gone home; I'd only realised when it grew too dark to read. Even then it was no punishment. I settled on a broad window sill where a street lamp cast its dull pool of light from twenty yards away, and read and read until I fell asleep; and when I woke up in the dawn I continued from where I'd stopped.

Pa arrived in mid-morning to drag me out under the blinking eyes of the old librarian in the grey cardigan, her hair gathered in a bun held in shape by two knitting needles — one blue, one green — but I kicked up such a row that he had no choice but to let me take the book home with me. It was a children's edition of *Don Quixote*. I could barely read English, most of the book was well beyond my understanding; but the very strangeness of it, the mere rhythms and cadences of the language, cast a spell over me. *In a certain village of La Mancha, which I do not wish to name, there lived not long ago a hidalgo.* 'La Mancha'. 'Hidalgo'. Dear God. This was the meaning of magic. This made even the Bible sound true. *And God said, Let there be light, and there was light.* I rode out with that lean hidalgo across the plains of La Mancha as spare and fierce and open to the wrath and the abundance of God as the Kalahari. An emptiness that permitted of never-ending invention; a freedom informed by the word, conjured up by books. To read, to read, perchance to dream.

And forever since this has been the condition of my world; more acutely so since Riana died; and still more so in the consummation of solitude these last few years after I was so treacherously dumped by the library that had been my sanctuary from the upheavals outside. My library was – all libraries are – a place of ultimate refuge, a wild and sacred space where meanings are manageable precisely because they aren't binding; and where illusion is comfortingly real. To read, to think, to trace the words back to their origins real or presumed; to invent; to dare to imagine. And then to reread, a new Columbus let loose on endless worlds beyond unnamed seas. Every time I open the *Don Quixote* – every time I open whatever book already read – I'm stepping, like Heraclitus, into a different stream with new secrets, new initiatory rites, new mysteries and celebrations. Am I getting carried away? Transport is the business of books, the purpose of my world-without-end in which, as I make my notes in the margins, I can pursue Adam's first act of mastery: This is a meerkat, this a porcupine, this a young woman called Tessa. Small mnemonic markings on paper, through which I may later rediscover the sense that had eluded me the first time round. (Of course it may be unreliable: that is the key to it. Once, a year after Alison, I discovered the little scrap of paper torn from a notebook, on which I'd jotted down, some time that alien afternoon – my only record of that bright event – the cryptic phrase, *Alison's mole*. And I will never know what it referred to; nor has there ever been anyone I could have turned to for an answer. Some secrets, they say, can only be lived, never understood. It would have meant so much to know. It might have redeemed a day which has been haunting me ever since.)

And so, even while I was sitting on my trusted old chair, two nights ago, watching Tessa watching the fire, reading her as if she were a book, as I smelled the evaporating damp from her jersey and observed the occasional, defiant little flames reflected in her eyes,

I would be making my provisional mental notes to be jotted down later: 'lyrical hands'; 'luminous eyes'; 'wet-dog smell of wool'; 'glint of ruby in dregs of wine'; 'purring of invisible cats'. Will these, too, one day be relegated to the order of 'Alison's mole'? Remember, remember. Remember to look back on this later. Remember how it will look then, how it will be, will have been. I live in a liquid future perfect, in which her presence dissolves like a small, imperfect lump of sugar.

Now, as I write it down, I return to my question, 'Why would you want to stay here?'

And she says, obviously, 'I have nowhere else to go.'

'Where have you lived till now?'

'For the last month I've been sharing a garden flat in Kenilworth. Now my flatmate has decided to get married. No one ever expected that, they've been fighting like cat and dog, he's a fucking nutcase. But there you are. Margie just came home on Monday and said, "Pete and I got married this morning. He's moving in. Look, I'm terribly sorry, but I'm afraid you'll have to find another place."'

'She can't just throw you out.'

'We're friends, I can't make things more difficult for her. Besides, he's been making passes at me behind her back. It'll just make shit.'

'When must you move out?'

'He brought his things over this morning. I suppose I could hang in for a while. But the sooner the better. And anyway . . .' She brings the glass to her mouth, discovers that it is empty and holds it out to me again. 'Can I have a refill?'

'Of course.' I empty the bottle. And ask, 'You were saying?'

'Everything seems to be happening at the same time. You won't believe it.' She takes a gulp, puts the glass down, clutches her feet in her hands. And then lunges into a complicated story about an affair with a lawyer, offices in Claremont, lasted two or three years as far as I can make out. He even persuaded her to give up her job with an advertising company to become his firm's secretary.

'It was quite good to start with. Then, somehow, it began to get out of hand. Before I really knew how we got there he began to discuss marriage. He even gave me a real knuckleduster ring, all diamonds and rubies, too ghastly, but Brian thought it was important. Then, about a month ago, with the wedding date already fixed, he broke it off.'

'Just like that?'

'I think he was looking for an excuse, getting cold feet, the usual story. So he started ranting and raving about my seeing other men, he really went ballistic. The cherry on top came when he accused me of fooling around with his senior partner.'

'And you weren't?'

'That's a very male thing to say,' she snaps, her cheeks flushed with what must be indignation. 'Anyway, there were all these outrageous accusations, and instead of backing me up the partner just withdrew into his shell, so in the end Brian told me to fuck off and I threw the ring at him, and the diamond fell out and turned out not to be a diamond after all, and of course then I got fired from my job as well.'

'Couldn't you take them to court?'

'They're lawyers, for Christ's sake. And perhaps it was good riddance from both sides. Also, they did give me a handshake. Not exactly golden, but kind of cheap alloy.'

'So now you're out of a job too?'

A shrug. 'That's not too bad. I have something else lined up. Starting on Monday, in fact. I'll be handling the publicity at a new glossy mag, it's called *Woman*, you may have heard of it, it's all the rage, and full of possibilities.' A quick smile. 'So you needn't be scared that I can't pay the rent.' She turns her naked eyes to me. 'It's all up to you. Will you take me or throw me out?'

'Don't you have folks to turn to?' Clutching at straws. And why? Because I'm really holding out for the right couple? Because I feel threatened? By what? This waif turned up out of the pouring night, top-heavy in her ridiculously outsized jersey, hair glued to her head?

'They're in Port Elizabeth. My mother stayed on there after my father's accident.'

'I thought he was murdered?'

She hesitates, then continues smoothly. 'Well, he was murdered by accident. They were looking for someone else. Anyway, then Mom had to fend for herself. She took a job as a receptionist in a hotel, but that paid too badly. So she took to the bottle. And to men. Not that I blame her, mind you. But it was tough on us – me and my brother, Stephen, he was two years older – and in the end the Welfare people took us away from her and put us in a home for a few years. Even after we went back to her, she never cared much about us, only about her job and her friends.' As a result, I learn from the rather convoluted account she gives of her past, she and Stephen were very close. He used to be her ally and confidant, but then 'betrayed' her. Something to do with splitting to their mother a secret Tessa had entrusted to him in the greatest confidence when she was seventeen. This means that neither mother nor brother can help her out now, and even if they could she won't ask. Nor will she turn to friends. 'I've got to solve my own problems, right?'

She looks at me as if she's expecting me to press for more, but I'm afraid to ask: she may just answer. Her frankness is too disconcerting. Why, I ask myself, is she telling me all these things? To wear down my last defences? To 'test' me? To play the fool with me? Or, simply, to flow with her impulses?

'No chance of making up with the boyfriend?' I ask, to avoid the issue.

'You must be joking.' She sniffs. 'Actually *he*'s the one who's trying to make a comeback. Came round earlier tonight to Margie's place, just as I was getting ready to come over here.'

'*He* was the tiresome visitor?'

'Right. You wouldn't believe it, the way he carried on. Calling me cruel, pleading for another chance, roses at my feet, actually going on his knees, eating up the carpet. I won't ever understand men, I'm afraid. I mean, a month ago he threw me out, sold all my furniture, tried to wreck my life. Now he's grovelling to have me back. Enough to make one puke. I looked down at him and thought: My God, is this the man I used to worship? Now he just makes me feel shop-soiled.'

'Still, one can't just shake off a thing like that.'

'I suppose not. But overall, I must say I'm more relieved than anything else. You know, it's the longest relationship I've ever had in my life, it was getting scary.'

'What is it that scares you?'

'I don't know. Just the thought, I suppose, of sharing one's whole life.' Her untroubled eyes on me. 'For how long were you married?'

'Twenty-seven years.'

'Jesus.'

'You make it sound like a life sentence.'

'Perhaps it's a generation thing.' She shifts her position, folding her long legs under her, leaning back against the shapeless old couch which Riana and I bought at an auction; it was our first proper piece of furniture after the bed. We didn't even have a table at the time, only an old door on four short stacks of bricks. 'Would you say your marriage was a happy one?'

'Of course!'

'I always get sceptical when people say "Of course",' she comments quietly. A pause. She drops her head back to look up at the shadows on the ceiling. 'I don't mean to doubt what you're saying. It's just that, offhand, I don't think I know of a single couple among my friends that's truly happily married.'

'Just because your mother neglected you . . .'

'That has nothing to do with it. I'm talking about all my friends. They all start off like rabbits, then turn into cats and dogs. I sometimes wonder if that's their way of saying, "I love you." You know? Words no longer mean much, so they have to try other ways. Wasn't it like that with you too?'

'No,' I say firmly. 'We had our differences, obviously. But when she died, we were still as much in love as the first time we slept together.'

'Is that really true?'

'If anything, we were *more* in love at the end. You know, if one lives through so much together, shares so much, good times and bad . . .' I must be getting maudlin from the wine, never been much of a drinker. And there is simply too much gathered up inside me, for too long, to check myself, once I've yielded to the flood. Going back right to the beginning, when there was lust to keep it all together, Riana was an incredibly beautiful girl. But then, as we grew older . . . Bodies change, they sag, they grow slack. It's not so much that one turns to other things to sublimate disappointments of the body: it's rather a matter of finding the body beautiful in different ways. When you're young the idea of losing the firmness and the bloom of youth is too unnerving to contemplate. But when it happens to the two of you together you start shifting your definitions. A lived-in body that has suffered, that has endured, that has survived, has a kind of beauty you may not think possible from where *you* are now. Every line, every varicose vein, every fold of fat, every grey hair becomes a sign of what you've shared, of what you love.

How much of this did I say out loud to her, how much remained unspoken in my mind? I'm not sure it matters much. I must have said enough to irk her, for I can still hear her response.

'You sound as if you're trying to convince yourself.'

'You'll never understand,' I snap back at her.

How can she know what it is to wake up at night and feel the empty space beside you and know that nothing you do can change it, can bring the departed back? To live with this emptiness for years and years, unable to think of anything except what you've lost, feeling yourself grow feebler and lonelier every day, and hating every moment of it? If only it'd happen quickly, but it drags on so slowly you hardly notice it from day to day and it's only on the rare occasions when you can't avoid it, when there's a lapse in discipline and you dare face yourself – once every few months, once a year, it doesn't matter – you discover more signs of decay. One day it will mercifully be over, but it seems you never really *get* there. It's just this slow decline as you turn more and more into the kind of thing you've always hated, you've always feared. And all you can do is reach back more and more hopelessly, more and more terribly, to the past, to the thing you've lost, to the one thing that has made life worthwhile, to love. Every day a little more slips through your fingers. But you hold on, oh God, you hold on, because you know – so fiercely, so desperately – that once you were happy, oh yes you were, once you loved, and that must last you for however long you may go on dragging yourself through the emptiness. Tomorrow, and tomorrow, and tomorrow.

Again, I do not know how much of this I actually spoke. All I remember is that at some stage I broke off very suddenly, ashamed, bewildered. I mumbled something like, 'I'm sorry, that was uncalled for.'

'So you did love her,' the girl said quietly. 'You're right, I cannot understand it. But I guess I believe you.' Then she held out her hand. 'I think we need more wine.'

'I've had too much already.' I got up from the deep chair. This, too, was becoming more difficult, however imperceptibly. The slight strain in the lower back, the creaking knee joints. 'What about some coffee?'

'Let's have both. I'll go with you.'

# 4

ON THE WAY back from the kitchen she asked to go to the bathroom. I showed her to the small one next to the study. While I was coaxing the dying fire in the grate to life again, adding a few vine stumps, I could hear her pee next door. There was something unabashedly youthful about it. Ah sweet bird of youth, when even urinating can be exuberant, when nothing is tentative, when life is absolute. I found it homely too, a sound, banal as it might be, affirming a human presence. I hadn't heard it here for a long time. When the emissaries from the agency visit me they turn on the taps to drown out the sound.

The toilet flushed. I heard the bathroom door open. But Tessa stayed away. I poured her wine, and her coffee, and my tea, and was on the point of going to the passage in search of her when she came back, looking puzzled.

'I thought you were living here on your own?'

'Of course I am.'

She looked at me with a small frown between her eyes. 'I saw someone going down the passage. Could it have been the housekeeper?'

'Magrieta doesn't come in over weekends.'

She looked hard at me, then came past me to the couch and flopped down on it, swinging up her legs with a charmingly casual flash of the small white triangle of panties between her thighs; the sort of thing which the sex-starved hermit I'd become cannot fail to notice.

'You're kidding, right?' she said. 'I promise you I saw someone.'

'What did she look like?'

'It was too dark to see properly. But it seemed like a young woman or a girl. Small, slight, in a long dress, barefoot, wearing a doek or something. I said hi to her, but she didn't seem to hear me.'

'Then you've just met Antje of Bengal.'

'Come again?' She took a sip of coffee, then switched back to wine.

'I'll tell you what I know,' I said. 'Although there are several versions of it.'

Antje of Bengal had been brought to the Cape, with her mother Katrijn, on a Dutch slave ship from Batavia in 1696, when she was only about seven years old. Under the large wild fig tree on the Parade, where the slave auctions were held, she was sold to Anthonij Stalpaert, a baker in town, for forty rix dollars; her mother was bought for five times that amount by a free burgher at Klapmuts and as far as we know they never saw each other again. Eleven years later, when Antje was eighteen or thereabouts, her master died and the girl was auctioned off to Willem Mostert, the tavern keeper at Papenboom and the first owner of this house.

There was something fishy about this, but it is difficult to get to the truth as there is so little documentation. Even in the fullest and most recent published account of Antje's life in Geoffrey Dugmore's *A Sparrow for Two Farthings: Slavery at the Cape, 1657–1795* (Juta, Cape Town) there is little more than conjecture about this period in her life; but it would seem that Willem Mostert, a close friend of Stalpaert's, had met Antje at the baker's house quite a few years before he bought her. We know that on at least three occasions, in 1703, 1704 and 1706, Mostert had offered to buy the girl from his friend, the last time for the quite substantial sum of 250 rix dollars. But the baker, for reasons of his own, refused to part with the young slave. One gets the impression that after the last failed attempt to acquire the girl there came a break in the once warm friendship between taverner and baker; and this turned so bad that at the time of Stalpaert's untimely death at the age of barely forty-five there were rumours that he had been poisoned. By none other, it was whispered, than Willem Mostert, whose obsession with Antje had been kindled when the girl was barely nubile.

Be that as it may, in 1707, when the baker's estate was sold by auction after his wife had decided to return to Holland, Antje joined the household of Willem and Susara Mostert here in Papenboom. The couple already had six other slaves at the time, four females and two males, which suggests that they were fairly well-to-do people. But the money came exclusively from Susara's side, and this is important in view of what happened later. Because Willem, as far as we can make out, had been practically penniless on his arrival at the Cape in 1690 or 1691. There are no records at all of his arrival, which leaves one free to imagine that he made the perilous crossing from Holland as a stowaway. Once landed, aged no more than twenty-six, he must have scouted around for a while, doing odd menial jobs, including a stint with the baker Anthonij Stalpaert, before he made his first appearance in recorded history by hiring out his services to several free burghers in the outlying districts. As luck, or his uncanny sense of opportunism, would have it, he finally showed up on the farm of the affluent widow Susara Uytenbogaert, who was almost twice his age and a lady of substantial bulk. He must have used some irresistible powers of persuasion, for less than a year after his arrival on the Stellenbosch farm they were married. Soon afterwards, in 1702, he persuaded his wife to move to Papenboom, where her only son Diederik was the keeper of the tavern. The son had the good sense to die in a hunting accident on the slopes of Devil's Peak (does it take too dirty a mind to suspect that his stepfather was a member of the hunting party?) and Willem Mostert took over the tavern.

After Antje's arrival in the Papenboom household she was assigned sleeping quarters with two of the female slaves and the two men in an outbuilding where the stores were kept; the remaining two slave women slept in the kitchen in order to be at hand when their mistress needed them. We do not know when Willem started creeping out of the solid, canopied conjugal bed at night to meet Antje in the backyard and take her up to the attic of the outhouse, where they disported themselves. And we have no way of knowing, either, whether the passion was mutual or whether Antje merely submitted to the master's exercise of what he clearly regarded as his 'rights'.

Certainly the 'spirals of power and pleasure' cited by Nigel Penn in a different but comparable account ('The Fatal Passion of Brewer Menssink' in *Rogues, Rebels and Runaways*, David Philip, Cape Town) were much in evidence in the relationship between Willem Mostert and Antje of Bengal. From the brief, and soon abandoned, divorce proceedings which Susara instituted against her husband three years later (cf. Dugmore, pages 109–11) it transpires that over the years, even before Antje made her appearance on the scene, Willem Mostert had been in the habit of consorting sexually with most of his wife's female slaves; when confronted by Susara he had the audacity to respond, 'Do you still not know the Cape custom, that here we live by the Old Testament?' Her reply is not recorded.

Certainly, the relationship between Willem and Susara deteriorated appallingly. A barometer of the tensions in the household, as it transpired from evidence given by the Dutch Reformed pastor at the inquest four years after Antje's arrival in Papenboom, was Willem Mostert's increasingly provocative attitude towards his wife, whose only retaliation appeared to have been an alarming increase in size. No longer content to meet Antje in the outhouse attic, Willem soon transferred their trysts to the tavern section in the front part of the homestead; and subsequently to the attic right above the main bedroom. And when Susara complained to him in the mornings about the noises she'd heard during the night, his explanations ranged from the realistic (rats and squirrels) to the fanciful (witches' sabbaths, where the Devil consorted with young virgins). One thing that transpires from all this is Susara's obsession with the sinister underbelly of religion: her all-pervasive fear of the dark and of the supernatural, of the devil, and of hell. And Willem very soon discovered how to play upon this fear like a terrible instrument of music, reducing his wretched wife – by now a mass of blubber – to a permanent state of abject terror.

Within a few months even the witches' sabbaths in the attic were no longer enough to feed the curious excesses of the man's lust. The next step was to pour a sleeping draught into his wife's tisane at supper, wait for her to fall asleep, then lead Antje by the hand into the bedroom and copulate on the zebra-skin mat at the foot of the bed. Susara slept through it all. When that no longer tantalised the sense of danger he seemed to require for his couplings, he discontinued the nightly administration of the potion. From then on he appeared to derive a perverse satisfaction from tormenting his wide-awake wife with the sounds of his fornication only a step or two away from her. He always had an explanation ready. And, what is rather more amazing, his wife appeared to accept them all. For whatever reason, she must have been desperately afraid of losing him. But one night Willem went so far as to draw Antje into the bed itself, and this was too much even for the credulous Susara. When she overcame her terror of the dark and lit a candle, the two were caught in flagrante delicto, Willem wearing only a nightcap and a shift, Antje stark naked. Susara struck at her husband with a copper bed-warming pan. He warded off the blow and in his customary way lunged into a dazzling rhetorical performance to explain what had happened. Whether it was due to his eloquence or to Susara's pathological fear of facing the truth no one can tell, but he actually managed to persuade her that he had been awakened from a nightmare by the slave girl, who'd crept into the bed to summon him to an attempted burglary in the wine cellar.

Once again his wife gave way to his wave of unreason; but this time, in a pathetic assertion of independence, she moved into a spare bedroom at the back of the house, taking Antje with her. At night the door was locked, the key secured under her pillow. For a few days Willem pondered the possibilities, meanwhile assuaging his needs at odd times during the day by luring Antje into hidden corners of the house and outbuildings. He came up with an obvious, if daring, solution: Antje was asked to unlatch the bedroom window upon retiring at night, after which the two male slaves, Adonis and Cupido, would set a ladder against the high wall under the window. To add piquancy to the situation, they were instructed to remove it after Willem had made his entry and not to return before the first crowing of the barnyard cocks.

One night, presumably after a rather more rumbustious performance than usual, Susara dared to investigate. Confronted with the unseemly spectacle when she parted the heavy curtains to let in the light of the full moon, she picked up a chair and started belabouring the couple. Willem jumped through the open window, suffering no more than a sprained ankle, and leaving Antje to bear the brunt of her mistress's massive rage. Susara only stopped when the heavy chair was in smithereens. So severe was the beating that it resulted in a miscarriage – the first indication anyone had that the slave girl had been pregnant with her master's child.

Even a long-suffering woman like Susara sooner or later reaches the limits of her endurance, and for her this was it. At the first light of day she had a carriage inspanned and decamped, with two of her female slaves, to Cape Town, where she found lodgings with distant relatives of her first husband. Within an hour of her arrival she presented herself at the home of the Reverend Le Boucq, pastor of the Dutch Reformed Church, and when she emerged some time later the man of God accompanied her to the chambers of the Council of Justice in the Castle to institute divorce proceedings against her husband. This was serious, for as Penn points out (op. cit., page 37), 'Divorce was regarded as a very extreme step indeed.'

What must have concerned Willem was more than the disgrace of such proceedings (compounded by the fact that he was still, hard as it may be to believe, a deacon and stalwart of the church): he stood to forfeit everything he owned, including Antje, as it was all in Susara's name. As soon as he got wind of the new turn of events, and leaving the still suffering Antje to the care of her companions, he betook himself to town on horseback. Like Susara before him he first stopped at the pastor's residence, where he gave what must have been a startlingly different account of the affair, reinforced by a hefty contribution to the church coffers (filched, no doubt, from his wife's money box, whose lock had never posed any problem to his ingenuity). So successful was the venture that Pastor Le Boucq personally accompanied him to Susara's temporary quarters in order to plead his case. It is said that Willem literally grovelled on the floor before the formidable woman's feet, shedding a torrent of tears, offering her several baskets of presents and swearing by God and all his angels to mend his ways. He had been, he explained, possessed by the Devil; but thanks to the Reverend's promise to intercede for him with God Almighty he had every hope to be freed from those fiery clutches to spend the rest of his days beside the only woman he had ever truly loved, Susara Uytenbogaert. Of course, she accepted and the divorce proceedings were withdrawn.

But the event marked a turning point in Willem Mostert's checkered existence. Uppermost in his mind was now the resolve to kill his wife. Even apart from the need to assure a future with untrammelled access to Antje, he simply could not live with the now very real risk of losing everything he'd never had. The idea of murdering Susara may strike one as less extreme than the measures he dreamed up to effect it. Going well beyond everything he'd done before, he asked his wife's permission to undertake a trip to Cape Town accompanied by none other than Antje. Of course, that was not the way he presented it. What he said was that Antje's presence had become a burden to their marriage and that he wanted to take her to town at the earliest opportunity in order to sell her to the first agreeable bidder. This act of renunciation so moved the gullible woman that she would probably have given her blessing even if he hadn't offered to take Fatima, one of the older slave women, with them as a chaperone.

And so the couple went off on a honeymoon of two weeks, Fatima's collaboration having been secured with a promise of manumission. Under assumed names they stayed at an inn frequented by the sailors of visiting ships; when they were not engaged in the exertions of passion, Willem went visiting Pastor Le Boucq and other influential acquaintances (expounding, among other things, with a great show of agitation, on his wife's sadly deteriorating state of health, which included lapses into dementia), while the two women spent hours in the warren of rickety little stalls and hovels on the lower slopes of the Gallows Hill buying a fearsome assortment of potions and concoctions. Among the items later listed at the murder trial were delicacies like 'a powder and hair mixture', 'ground-up bones of the dead', 'skin shaved from the limbs of murderers hanged on the gallows', 'the ground umbilical cord of a strangled child', 'the excrement of tigers and wolves' – an unholy assortment collectively described by one historian as 'perhaps, primarily, a magical substance whose power derived less from pharmacology than necromancy' (Dugmore, page 114).

After a fortnight the threesome returned to Papenboom with their stock of exotic provisions. If Susara was shocked at seeing Antje back, Willem gave her the assurance, duly endorsed by Fatima, that it was only temporary and that he was expecting, any day, confirmation of a quite exceptional offer for the slave girl from a notable at the Cape whose name for the time being had to be kept secret. Susara's only condition was that henceforth Antje would have to be locked up at night in the attic, with a sentry posted at the door, an obstacle readily surmounted by strapping together two ladders which were held in position outside by Adonis and Cupido. This task was made even easier when the magic substances began to take effect within a week.

Susara was beset by the most terrible afflictions: headaches, vapours and cramps of every description. Showing commendable concern for his wife, Willem summoned Dr Junniaar Bronssvinkel all the way from town at least once a week; in between, frantic with worry for all the world to see, he would drive to town himself, accompanied of course by Antje, to fetch new medicaments. Susara's condition steadily declined. Soon she could no longer leave her bed, which Willem joyfully exploited by bringing Antje down from the attic as before and disporting himself with her, once again, in the very bed where Susara was convulsing and crying out in her own agonies.

When she mustered the strength to protest he would painstakingly explain that she was suffering from hallucinations, brought on by demons that possessed her. Even while still firmly ensconced between Antje's thighs he would make the sign of the cross over Susara's head, cover her eyes with a damp cloth held in readiness for the occasion, and pray loudly to God to be merciful to his poor suffering wife, all the while thrusting and bucking and cavorting at her side.

Five months later the poor woman mercifully expired, after four final days and nights of unbelievable pain and terror, accompanied by the frenzied and seemingly incessant coupling of the lovers. And then it was over. At Susara's funeral Willem had to be restrained from jumping into the grave. Three days later, after the guests had left — a funeral was a huge social occasion in those days — Willem went into the large empty house alone. For hours he sat in the deserted tavern, staring at a blank wall, not touching the tankard of bad beer on the

splintered oak table in front of him. When Antje came to him —
one can imagine her bare feet making subtle, sucking sounds on
the dung floor — he waved her away. His lust, to all intents
and purposes, had perished with the last breath of his wife.

It is hard to tell, at this remove, whether the end should have been
predictable or not. As Willem Mostert grew more irascible, keeping
the tavern locked up and refusing to see anybody, he was faced by a
rebellion among his slaves. Fatima was the first to remind him that
he'd promised to set her free. Had she chosen a better moment,
who knows, he might have reacted differently. As it was, he gave
her a flogging that went beyond even his own previous excesses.
Then the others, particularly Adonis and Cupido, confronted him
with their own demands of recompense for their assistance during
his courting of Antje. She made the mistake of siding with Willem
against her own. It was only a question of time before the matter
was reported to the Council of Justice.

The most surprising aspect of the whole case was that Willem
Mostert was never indicted, never even summoned as a witness.
Antje was the one hauled to court on the charge of murder, but
even when put to the torture she never breathed a word of reproach
against her master; the other slaves, charged as accomplices, did
make various accusations, which were, however, not taken seriously.
Officially, not a finger was pointed at the enigmatic taverner.
In fact, the Reverend Le Boucq personally testified, before the
case even reached the court, to Willem's exemplary concern for
his wife's health during her many months of debilitating illness.
His testimony was backed up by Dr Bronssvinkel. What other
dark transactions took place we have no way of knowing. All
we can tell for sure is that Willem was never charged. As one
perceptive historian succinctly explains it apropos of a similar case:
    'We may . . . assume that one of the state's ambitions was to
maintain the social and judicial distance which existed between
masters and slaves at the Cape. To place a member of the Cape's
élite in the same case as criminal slaves, and to judge this member as
a co-conspirator of these slaves, was obviously more than the Court

of Justice could stomach. To declare them as equals before the law would be to undermine the structures of inequality which bound the Cape's colonial society together' (Penn, page 56).

On a limpid blue-and-golden autumn day in March 1711 Antje of Bengal was tried, condemned and executed. Justice was summary in those times. Her fellow slaves were sentenced to punishments of various degrees, ranging from flogging to life imprisonment on Robben Island, but death was reserved for her alone. As Dugmore paraphrases it, 'she was condemned to be taken to the place of public execution, to be bound to a pole, branded with hot irons and then strangled with a cord until dead. Thereafter her head and right hand were to be removed and fixed on stakes at the entrance to the Castle, and the remains of her body fastened to a forked post and exposed until consumed by the air and the birds of heaven' (op. cit., page 116).

Willem Mostert was a member of the festive crowd that gathered on the Parade to watch the execution. Afterwards he withdrew to the home of Pastor Le Boucq, with whom he had found lodging and to whom it would seem he made some kind of confession during the same night (submitted during the subsequent inquest, with such emendations and corruptions and hiatuses as the man of God deemed fit to bring to it). Two days after Antje's execution, under cover of darkness, Willem managed to retrieve the dismembered parts of the broken, once beloved body, and returned to his home in Papenboom. That, at least, in the absence of hard evidence, is the consensus among the few historians who have shown interest in the sad affair. After Willem had divulged his intentions to the pastor, Le Boucq had tried – he later insisted – to dissuade the taverner, but to no avail.

A week afterwards, a traveller in need of fresh horses on the route from town to Constantia stopped at the house in Papenboom to find it open and deserted, the whole place pervaded by an ungodly smell. Too timid to investigate, the stranger went down the road to the brewery. From there a few slaves were sent out. They discovered Willem Mostert's decomposing body hanging on a riem from a massive transversal branch on an oak tree beside the house. There was no sign of Antje of Bengal's body.

Inevitably, in those superstitious days, there were soon rumours of a marauding ghost and no one showed any interest in acquiring what under normal circumstances should have been a coveted property. A year later, upon the recommendation of the Dutch Reformed Church council, the house was razed to its foundations. The estate was subdivided and the peripheral portions sold off. But the central plot remained vacant, in spite of its enviable location on a main thoroughfare in a leafy suburb of the rapidly expanding town. Only towards the end of the nineteenth century an elderly gentleman from England bought the plot and constructed on the old foundations a dwelling in the colonial Victorian style.

# 5

THE STRANGE GIRL in my study had stretched herself out on the old couch, propped up against an assortment of cushions, one leg folded under her, the other on an armrest. During my narration she'd twice topped up her wine glass. After I'd stopped talking she remained silent for a long time, staring into the dying fire. When she finally spoke there was an almost accusing tone in her voice.

'You really think the woman I saw in the passage was Antje of Bengal?'

'Who else could it be?'

'Have you ever spoken to her?'

'I've never even seen her myself, although I suppose I can say I've been aware of her presence. Which may or may not have been my imagination.'

'Then how can you tell she was the one I saw?'

'My housekeeper has seen her. Quite often, in fact. They seem to have regular conversations.'

She swung her legs off the couch (once again that unnerving glimpse). 'You're just trying to scare me off, right?'

'Why should I?'

She reflected. It showed in the perplexed frown between her eyes. 'I suppose it *could* have been a shadow or something,' she said after a while. 'Or just my imagination in overdrive.'

We were both silent for a moment. I was conscious of the irregular solfa tones from the containers in the passage, wet branches scraping against a window, a sound in the chimney. Something from Mrs Radcliffe. Or *Wuthering Heights*.

'Why don't you discuss it with Magrieta? In broad daylight.'

'Does that mean I can move in?'

'If you want to.'

With a shrug she bent over at the grate and quietly stoked the fire again, adding the last two bits of wood from the scuttle to the flickering embers. Then she returned to the couch and settled back into her previous position.

'It's a terrible story,' she remarked suddenly. 'I guess all those historians were men?'

'Why?'

'It's supposed to be Antje's story, but she hardly features in it.'

'That may be enough reason for her still to stick around,' I said lightly.

She took it more seriously than I'd meant it. 'You may be right.' It was one of those occasions when the weight of the unspoken is tangible below the spoken. In a sense, to me at least, Antje's absence was more real than anything around us, visible, in the half-dark study. Like an obscure moon illuminating our darkness from somewhere very far away, very long ago.

The girl helped herself to the last drops of wine. 'Do you think she had any say in it at all?'

'If anybody knows it will be Magrieta.'

'Men like having women at their mercy.'

'Not all men.'

'Willem Mostert did.'

'I wasn't just thinking of him.'

I saw the distortion of her face in the wine glass. 'No man will ever muck around with me again,' she said.

'You're talking about the lawyer boyfriend?'

She shrugged. In the gloom her eyes were shining like a cat's.

'Would you rather not talk about it?'

'It's not that.' She put her glass down. 'I very nearly didn't come here tonight, I was so cut up about it. You know, you think you know a person — I mean, it's been a couple of *years* — and then all of a sudden you realise you don't know the first thing. It's like they're someone totally different. In the beginning he was so considerate, all the old-fashioned stuff, God, flowers, presents, you name it. And then the things he said to me tonight, when the grovelling didn't work. As if I was the one who threw *him* out. Kicked him in the balls, he said, tried to castrate him, I mean, Jesus!' She raised her arms and rubbed her scalp vigorously causing the fuzz of short hair to stand up like a dark halo in the dull light.

'But it *was* good to start with?'

'It was wonderful.' Her eyes half-closed. 'He took me everywhere. When he found out I'd never been abroad he took me to see the world. Paris, Rome, Prague, Tokyo, Hong Kong, New York, you name it. It was unreal.' A deep contented laugh in her throat. Then one of her quick mood changes: 'Have *you* travelled a lot?'

'Not much. Especially not by way of holiday. Twice, with my wife, Riana, when the children were still at school and could be left with their grandparents. It was unforgettable. The concerts: Furtwängler, Kubelik, Gieseking, Rubinstein, Kempff, all in the flesh. The museums. Above all, the libraries. The British and the Bodleian and Trinity College. The Bibliothèque Nationale. Coimbra. When we got to the manuscripts in the Vatican, I thought: Now I can die happy, for my eyes have seen the glory of the book. In later years my trips were mainly for conferences, when the library sent me. But my really important travels . . .' I stopped. 'Sorry, I must be boring you.'

'Do tell.'

Now I was embarrassed. How would she react? But what the hell, I thought. I said, 'My real travels, the trips that mattered, have always been in books.' And of course now I couldn't hold it back any more. 'I went to Spain with Don Quixote – I still go every year in the summer – and to St Petersburg with Dostoevsky every winter. In between, I go to Paris with Balzac, or with Zola if I feel up to it. He can be a demanding travelling companion. Or to London with Dickens, who else? And naturally to Dublin with Mr Joyce. Or up to Davos with Mann, to Prague with Kafka, to Algeria with Camus, to Boston with Henry James, to a small distant planet with the Little Prince. I've been on some exhausting trips through Australia with Patrick White, or the northern wildernesses of Canada with Atwood. And of course I've gone whaling with Melville, and criss-crossed the face of America with Jack Kerouac, and later with Humbert Humbert, the poor obsessed bastard.' I reined myself in. 'I'm afraid once I get going . . .'

'I'd love to go on a trip like that,' she said, snuggling into the deep, warm recesses of her voice.

'Travelling is the perfect way of finding out if people are compatible.'

'I'm not so sure,' she commented. 'I mean, travelling with Brian was great. I was usually on a total high. Even so it didn't work out. It was only afterwards that I realised I could never relax and just be myself with him. Or perhaps one just grows older, your expectations change.'

'If you ask me, you need some time to sort things out.'

She settled more deeply into the cushions on the couch. 'I feel safe here,' she said in her unnervingly direct way. 'I don't think I've felt so safe in years.' Her eyes, steady and calm, studied me for a long time. Neither of us looked away. 'I don't know why, I don't even know you.' (Exactly, I thought. For all she knew I could be a sex maniac or a serial killer. Which made her trust as alarming as it was disarming.)

'I haven't spoken so freely to anyone in a long time,' I confessed.

The night was around us, the darkness and the rain, the distant city with its occasional disembodied rumblings and sirens, the long past, nameless dangers lurking and predators on the prowl; but all that mattered was this small space we so randomly and fleetingly shared. Our separate lives might continue afterwards, but for this moment we were here, with intimations of other more secret spaces which might or might not be explored.

She yawned, and stretched herself, and said, 'I suppose I should be going.' She couldn't know – or did she? – how much might be at stake on this edge between going and staying. Everything was indeed possible, there was past and present involved in it, and, who knows, future. But she made no move. It was not a choice but the absence of a choice.

I listened to the complicated drippings from the passage for a while.

'Would you like another cup of coffee?' I asked.

'That'd be great,' she said lazily. 'Would you mind if I waited right here?'

'Of course not.' At the door I hesitated, and looked back. 'You're not scared Antje might look in on you?'

She didn't answer; I wasn't sure that she'd heard me.

When I came back with her coffee she was fast asleep, drawn into a foetal curve on the couch, the cat at her feet, her hand lightly clenched against her mouth. For a long time I stood looking at her. I moved some stuff out of the way and put the tray down on a corner of the desk, then went to my bedroom for a blanket. Very carefully, so as not to disturb her, I covered her. I left the reading light on.

I didn't sleep at all that night, but it was good to lie awake. When I went back to the study in the morning with freshly made coffee she was gone.

# 6

No sign of her all yesterday, Sunday. Throughout the morose day —
brief periods of light drizzle, restless wind, interspersed with moments
of watery sun — I was waiting for the telephone to ring. Surely she
would at least call to let me know? As the day wore on the memory
became less and less reliable. Even as I stood beside the deserted
couch in the morning her visit appeared unreal, more unreal than
the phantom of Antje of Bengal flitting through the half-light of
passages and rooms. The mohair blanket with which I'd covered
her lay crumpled on the floor; the leather cushions still showed the
imprint left by her body. On the corner of the desk the tray with
cold coffee, unused cups. Empty glasses, two discarded wine bottles
on the floor in front of the fireplace. What evidence was that? I could
have imagined it all.

I reached for the blanket. Was there still, somewhere, a scent of
her lurking in a fold? The wetness of her cropped hair, the damp wool
of her jersey? Nothing. On an impulse I went to the front door. Muddy
tracks in the passage. A touch of reassurance, but hardly decisive.
Looking back, an intimation of loss briefly quivered inside me. What
chance had I missed? Yet it was barely disappointing. I've become
so used to hope frustrated, possibilities unrealised, opportunities
denied, that I've learned to take disappointment for granted even
before it happens. The best protection against hurt. And yet I had
been vulnerable the night before, perhaps without even realising it.

The girl too. Tessa. I tasted the name with the tip of my tongue.
Perhaps Monday, I thought. Perhaps tomorrow.

But in the morning there was still no sign of her. There were only the remaining telltale signs from Saturday night, and although I'd tried my best to remove them nothing can fool Magrieta. Who came in, as usual, at eight and started bustling about, making her presence emphatically known.

Magrieta has always been not so much erratic as inscrutable in bringing me coffee in bed in the mornings. (It is the only time during the day when I still drink it.) If it is tacitly understood to be part of her domestic duties, she usually makes her own decisions. This morning I waited until a quarter to nine. When there was still no knock on my door, while the din in the house was steadily increasing, I put on my dressing gown to go and make my own coffee. Magrieta was laboriously scrubbing the table (quite unnecessarily, as I had cleaned it yesterday), looming over it like a thundercloud. She was wearing her much-laundered green housecoat over one of her customary gaudy outfits: multicoloured floral dress, pink cardigan, striped red doek.

'Whole place is in a blerry mess again,' she said, breathing heavily from the exertion. I have never been able to establish if she is in fact asthmatic (it is risky to make any enquiries about her health as that invariably triggers an astounding catalogue of complaints) or whether being constantly out of breath is just brought on by obesity. Magrieta must weigh well over a hundred kilograms if she weighs an ounce.

'I did my best to clean up.'

She snorted. 'You a man, Meneer.' How many times over the years have I asked her to call me by my name? But it was no use. Magrieta straightened up with a great show of effort and rubbed the small – if that is the word – of her back. 'When men try to clean up they jus' make it worser.' Feigning nonchalance she asked, 'Meneer had guests?' She made it sound like an orgy.

'Just somebody enquiring about the rooms.'

'A woman.'

'Now what makes you think so?'

'Unless it's men using lipstick nowadays. On that glass on the washup.' She had left the *corpus delicti* in full view. 'Behind the sofa en all.'

'Sorry, I missed that one.'

'Young woman too.'

'Ag now come on, Magrieta.'

'I could smell her on the sofa. It's only young girls what use such scent.' She clicked her tongue and resumed her scrubbing. Out, damned spot. Without looking up she asked, 'She moving in with us now?'

'I don't know. We'll still have to see. I need your advice on it.'

'Thought we was going to look for a couple.'

'We haven't been able to find anyone suitable yet, have we?' The kettle was boiling. I put a teaspoon of instant in the mug and poured water on it.

'That coloured couple looked very all right to me.'

'But they could stay only for six months, Magrieta. That would have been very inconvenient.'

'Girls is trouble,' she said, nodding her head repeatedly, knowingly.

I played the only trump I had. 'She met Antje of Bengal,' I said, leaning back against the kitchen dresser to watch her reaction.

'Go on!' She stopped scrubbing to stare at me.

'It's true. She went to the bathroom and when she came back she saw Antje in the passage.'

'She got a fright?' She wiped her hands on the overall. 'I bet she peed in her pants.'

'She wasn't scared at all.'

'You tole her the story?'

'I told her. But I explained to her that you're really the one to ask. You're the one who speaks to Antje.'

She gave a contented chuckle. 'We spoke many times. Poor little Antje, she's a good spook. She been looking after this place like it was her own house. I was never scared of her, except that first time.'

I knew what was coming and braced myself for it; but Magrieta's good will was worth the effort.

Magrieta Daniels was still a young woman when she met Antje of Bengal for the first time. It was barely six months after she'd started working for the Benade family, who owned the house at the time. From the very first day she knew there was something 'wrong' with

the place. She'd always been sensitive to such things, even as a child.
Born with a cowl, her mother had told her. But mentioning it to Mrs
Benade just earned her a stern reprimand. She tried to control the
apprehension, tucking a New Testament into the front pocket of
her overall when she came to work. But then she heard from the
neighbours' servants that the place was indeed haunted. She began to
muster her courage to give notice – even though it was an awkward
time to do so, as she was preparing to get married to a man her
parents had chosen for her; money was scarce, she needed every
penny she could get for the gazat.

Her mother tried to persuade her: they were good Christians,
were they not? Even if the house was haunted they had nothing to
fear from ghosts, they had God on their side. Her mother went
so far as to consult a Slams in District Six, where the family were
living at the time; and after a certain sum had changed hands the man
produced a small sewn-up skin bag filled with mysterious substances,
which Magrieta was instructed to bury just inside the front gate. This
actually had the opposite effect: on the very first morning after she'd
buried the doepa she met the ghost in the transversal passage that
separates the front section of the house from the cluster of rooms
at the back. The figure of a young woman in a long dress, carrying
her head in her hands.

Magrieta promptly dropped the tea tray she was carrying. No
amount of coaxing could persuade her to return to that part of
the house. She wanted to get out, that very day, even if it meant
forfeiting the whole month's wages. That was when the lady of
the house made an about-face, presumably because she feared the
repercussions if this first-hand account of the ghost were to spread
through the marketplace. It was difficult enough to find good servants.
Magrieta was promised a raise, and shorter hours, and no work – for
the time being at least – in the back part of the house. She was sent
home early to recover from her palpitations.

As she left the premises through the back gate, somebody behind
her said, 'Please don't go.'

Magrieta turned round quickly and caught her breath. It was the
girl again, standing beside the greatest of the ancient gnarled oaks

in the garden. This time she had her head in the right place. And there was something so forlorn and supplicating in her attitude that Magrieta felt her fear evaporating.

'Who – who are you?' she stammered, keeping a safe distance between them.

'I'm Antje,' said the girl in an unusual accent. Never having heard Dutch spoken, Magrieta couldn't place it at all, but she had little trouble understanding. 'I must talk to you,' the stranger pleaded.

But Magrieta, still in a panic, fled down the shaded street, with only one thought in her mind: never to come back to that house. Even so, on the train home, her conscience began to trouble her. Had she really done the right thing? That poor girl had seemed so distraught, so genuinely anxious to speak to her. Suppose it wasn't even a real ghost?

Her mother, unsettled by the story, promptly took her back to the Slams. He had promised to protect them from evil and look what had happened!

To their amazement, the old man beamed. 'Allah is truly wonderful,' he said (which must have sorely upset that good Christian woman). 'This is a sign that it is not an evil spirit at all, but one that means well. If it wished you harm it would never have replaced its head. Now listen to me, girl. If ever it speaks to you again, you must not run away. Stand your ground, answer it, do whatever it tells you. If it wants to greet you, cover your head with a handkerchief.'

In trepidation, but with a curious boldness, Magrieta returned to her work the next day. For a week nothing more happened. She was just beginning to think that it had all been her imagination – perhaps a result of something she'd eaten; or God's punishment for the liberties she'd allowed her betrothed, Andries, to take with her body the evening before the visitation – when Antje returned. This time Magrieta was alone in the scullery, washing dishes. It was a day of gusty wind, a black south-easter, following days and nights of pouring rain. There was a voice behind her. She immediately recognised it.

'Magrieta.'

She started shaking all over.

'Magrieta, I am your friend.' Every word pronounced separately in that half-familiar, half-strange language, as if to make sure she would be understood.

'Oh my God,' Magrieta whispered.

'You must get out of this scullery right now. Run to the front door as fast as you can and out into the garden.'

'But . . .'

'Magrieta, run!'

Magrieta ran. As she burst through the front door on to the broad stoep she'd polished only the day before, she heard a tearing, crashing, juddering sound from the back. When she reached the garden she saw what had happened. The oak outside the kitchen window, hollowed with age – the very tree beside which Antje had made her previous appearance – had been blown over by the wind, its roots torn out of the soggy earth. It had crashed right through the roof, destroying most of the kitchen below. Where she had stood at the sink in the scullery was now only a mound of rubble.

She started walking backwards from the scene, until she reached the front stoep again, where she steadied herself against the railings below the fancy broekie lace of the curved veranda. She was too shocked even to cry. She was still standing there, chilled to the bone, when Mrs Benade returned from her shopping. All Magrieta could stammer was, 'Madam, she saved me. It was that Antje girl again.'

The woman ordered her inside and made her lie down on the floor (it wouldn't do to allow a servant girl on a bed), where she was given sal volatile, wrapped in an ironing blanket and left to recover. This was how Antje found her. That was when they had their first proper conversation. Many others followed; it became part of the daily routine. In due course Magrieta lost all the diffidence she'd felt towards her new acquaintance. And she was such a good worker that her employers were prepared to overlook the odd quirk in her character which made her consort with a presence no one else could see.

But it was only a year later, when Magrieta had been married for three months and had in fact just discovered that she was pregnant, that the relationship deepened into friendship. She was again on her own, this time polishing the Oregon pine floor in the dining room, when

Antje appeared in front of the long gleaming table, which remained faintly visible through the outline of her body.

'Magrieta,' she said (able by now to speak a more respectable Afrikaans), 'I want you to leave your work and go home.'

'But it's still morning,' she protested. 'The Madam will be angry.'

'We can work that out later. Right now there's more important things at home.'

'But what is it?'

'Just go and see.'

Her heart beating in her throat, Magrieta set off on the long way home: down to Newlands Station and into town, and from there to Hanover Street and up the incline to the little partitioned-off flat she and Andries were renting from a shyster landlord. No need to dwell on it. She found Andries and an unknown naked girl right there on the front-room floor just as he was tugging at his belt to take off his pants. Magrieta dealt with the intruder in a most summary manner; and after the girl had scuttled out, hair torn and face scratched, clutching an insufficiency of clothes to her breasts, she turned on Andries with a kitchen knife. He might well have lost all claim on a meaningful future had a hawker not appeared in the open door at that moment to offer them a bunch of harders fresh from Hout Bay harbour.

There were wild recriminations, and tears, and pleadings, and promises, ending at last in forgiveness. Things were never quite the same again — 'One thing I know now,' Magrieta would repeat in the years to come, 'a man is a man, en that's not a very smart thing to be' — but it is to be doubted whether Andries ever dared to cross the line again. She was very calm about it, confident that at the slightest possibility of a recurrence her faithful companion from the dead would be there to tip her off.

I have good reason to believe it. There was that single occasion, thirty years ago, three months after Riana had lost the baby when in a kind of madness I still find difficult to explain I brought Alison home. The lovely music student, over a weekend when Riana and the boys were away at her parents and Magrieta was home with her family in District Six. I'm not offering excuses. We knew it was wrong. But I was infatuated, and after those three months of rage and rebelliousness, blindness, pain, all I knew was that this was a chance I couldn't let pass, a last grasp at what had begun to slip away from me – all those melodramatic things one makes oneself believe in such an extremity. We had drunk too much, something which hardly ever happens to me; she seemed to want it as much as I did; and we began our feverish fumblings on the couch in the study, our desire too urgent to be displaced to a bedroom. There's one thing I'll never forget: Alison lying back on the couch, flushed, and stretching out a hand to clutch my rampant member while I undressed, and saying softly, 'You're so beautiful,' which no woman had ever said to me before, and as at last I knelt between her legs to enter her, Magrieta said from the door, 'Middag, Meneer,' and went past to the bedroom she used during the week.

When I knocked on her door that evening, she was asleep, or pretended not to hear. I spent the long night sleepless in a chair. The next morning I went to talk to her in the kitchen where she was preparing breakfast with a vigour that reverberated through the house. My head was throbbing.

'Magrieta,' I said, 'about what happened yesterday . . .'

'Is not my business,' she said firmly, emphatically breaking eggs into the frying pan.

'We must talk about it.'

'Is nothing to talk about.'

'I want you to understand.'

'Meneer must go to Miss Riana if there's talk you want to talk.'

'You're a member of the family, Magrieta.'

'I got my own family.'

'For God's sake, Magrieta!' I was really pleading now, but she kept her back to me. Some back.

'Meneer is taking the name of the Lord in vain.'

'At least tell me what you were doing here yesterday,' I stormed at last. 'You never come in over the weekend.'

'Antje called me back.'

'Don't be bloody ridiculous . . . !'

She shrugged in her infuriating way. And then settled into her provocative yet unassailable manner of cleaning the house. Very, very thoroughly and meticulously – especially my study, where she tackled every book, every separate piece of paper, as if to rid them, jointly and severally, of every stain or speck of scandal that might still cling to them.

I never risked incurring the revenge of Antje of Bengal again. In a sense, I thought, my own future was at stake.

'Antje of Bengal is very particular about who she appears to,' I reminded Magrieta. 'It must mean something if she showed herself to our guest.'

'She carried her head in her hands?'

'No. I don't think she wanted to scare Tessa.'

'So the name is Tessa.'

'Miss Tessa Butler. The friend she's been staying with is getting married, so she must move out.'

'When she coming?'

'We haven't finalised anything yet. When I came out yesterday morning she was already gone.'

'You came out where?'

'From my room, Magrieta. She slept here in the study.'

'We can't take in any jentoe from the street.'

'That is why I slept in my room.'

She grunted. Perhaps it was a sign of approval. 'En where's her parents now?'

'She has a mother in Port Elizabeth.'

'How old is she?'

'Twenty-nine.'

'Then why she not married?'

'She was engaged but the man broke it off.' This, I thought, might evoke some maternal sympathy.

'Rotter,' she commented. 'Men. They should all get their things cut off when they still small. Look at cats en dogs. It save a lot of trouble later on. How many times did I say that to Antje?'

'I'm afraid you came too late to help her.'

'But now she en me are together. En between the two of us we'll keep this house clean.'

'It's not as if you kept men out of *your* life, Magrieta. You were married three times.'

'It's different if husbands en wives stick together. Otherwise . . .' She shook her head. 'I'm not saying anything against Meneer, but men got trouble between their legs en then it's maar better to keep it in the family.'

'If Miss Butler comes back you can look her over properly,' I proposed. Adding with a straight face, 'Discuss it with Antje too.'

Magrieta was mollified. She even took my cold coffee mug from me and gently pushed me out of the way. 'Let me make you proper moerkoffie,' she said. 'This stuff is just mud.'

While she was setting up the percolator I sat down at the kitchen table and opened the morning paper to scan the daily menu of murder, mayhem, corruption and scandals, keeping an eye on her – this woman who'd been in charge of my life for nearly forty years, who'd helped Riana and me through good times and bad, who'd kept the house running like a ship through sometimes turbulent seas. It must have been harder on her than she'd ever let on, dealing not only with our lives but with the rough patches of her own: the deaths of husbands and children, the forced removal from District Six in the sixties, political upheavals and family squabbles. Her main concern, as far as we could tell, had always been our wellbeing, not her own. But on rare occasions, as on this Monday morning when she didn't know I was watching, something of what all this had cost her showed fleetingly on her face: the suppressed grief and anger, the disappointments, the weariness of which she would never speak. There was no way she would allow me even to broach it. Only the knowledge that, however invisible or remote, it was *there*, occasionally bearing down on a moment we silently shared.

She poured the fresh coffee and went about her business. I finished the cup, complimented her on it and withdrew to have my bath and get dressed. Afterwards I spent a few hours working in my study. But I was too restless to concentrate. The rain had stopped, the sun was back, one of those incomparably bright Cape winter days. But it wasn't the weather that made me go outside every ten minutes or so to inspect the garden, check for mail, even saunter a few yards up and down the glistening street under the black branches of overhanging oaks. It was she. The young woman. Tessa.

Look, I told myself, this was ridiculous. I should get a grip on myself. Even if she had left her footprints across my mind, in the no-man's-land I'd reached this was only to be expected: I was in an impressionable, vulnerable condition. Would I not have reacted in exactly the same way to any other attractive, young, streetwise, modern woman appearing from the rain that night? There was nothing to set her apart, was there? Nothing special at all. If she was anything, she was impudent beyond bearing, impertinent, insolent. She had no sense of boundaries – in what she'd presumed to ask me about my life, even in what she'd told me about herself. No woman in her right mind would confide so unreservedly in someone she'd just met. Or otherwise it was shameless manipulation. The oldest wile in the world. For God's sake, could I not see right through her?

The short answer was no.

She was *not*, and I knew it in my guts, a simple specimen of her generation – like any other, like all the others. But what was it, then? If I tried to discount (but how could I?) her unkempt beauty, her shop-soiled innocence, her eyes, the tone of her voice, that laugh – what else was there? Ah, but the blatant sexiness was blended with unselfconscious grace, with surprising control; if she seemed lost and bewildered, she was also coolly efficient and professional in dealing with my computer. All right, so she was cheeky, arrogant, bitchy. But I was prepared to take my chances that she was also gentle, generous, genuinely caring. I'd caught hints of both sides. It was like catching from a distance snatches of an unfamiliar but exciting piece of music, just enough to know you must hear more, must get hold of title and composer, must go out to buy the record. The lure of the unknown? Not 'the mysterious', because in a way there was no mystery; but possibly a kind of darkness, a melancholy behind the exuberance? The contradictory glimpses she'd offered, unasked, of her childhood. If any of it could be believed! This was getting closer perhaps: the sense that she was moving – dancing almost, lightly, playfully — along the edge of an impossible abyss. Knowing it was there, but defying it, defying even my awareness of it. What was true, what a lie? Did it even matter? There was something there that defied understanding, something by definition not explicable.

And where was she now? Had she really left for good? I couldn't believe it. Still, as the hours dragged past, it began to seem true.

Instead of taking my usual nap after lunch I drove up to the university, to the library, not so much to read as just to get away. I couldn't face the empty house now haunted by her memory.

When I came home it was half past five and already getting dark. Magrieta met me at the front door.

'There's a woman sitting on the roof,' she said.

# Two

# 1

So much can change in a short time. On the surface my life may not seem to be different, but I know that deep down nothing is the same. Tessa has moved in. She is around very seldom, but her presence has shifted relations in the house. There used to be two women around, if the ghost qualifies as one; now there are three. For most of the day she is at work at her magazine, which recently moved into an elegantly renovated old house in Claremont; I've driven past there, out of curiosity, after I'd obtained the address from telephone enquiries. Three times she has gone out in the evening, otherwise she works in the small bright circle of light cast by a slender anglepoise halogen lamp in one of the two interleading rooms she has taken (I offered, why not?, to let her have both for the price of one, they're empty anyway). With their own bathroom, they are comfortably apart from the rest of the house, which was a boon when the boys lived there. Sometimes we have a nightcap together, or she has coffee and I my rooibos tea, usually in my study.

In the mornings I see her off when she leaves in the smoking Beetle. In almost unnerving contrast to the girl I first met she dresses immaculately for work. Pencil skirts, tight-fitting slacks, striking yet understated tops, a minimum of jewellery (sometimes only a small detachable tattoo in the little hollow between her clavicles), impeccable make-up, the image of sophistication. The only incongruity about her appearance was the large plastic bag filled with bananas, oranges, several slices of bread and jam, packets of crisps, cartons of juice, which she initially carried with her in the morning. Magrieta was the first to object: if Tessa wanted to take food to work, she told me, we should get her a proper lunchbox, not this disgusting bag. After only a few days, in her pointed way, Magrieta quietly prepared what she termed a 'decent lunch' of roast chicken, potato salad, an apple and some trifle in a small carton, with cutlery and a neatly folded striped serviette, and a small stainless-steel flask of coffee, all packed in the enamel container with which she once used to dispatch me to my library in the mornings.

'What on earth is this for?' asked Tessa in surprise when Magrieta presented her with it.

'Miss Tessa can't go to work in the mornings with such a cheapskate plastic bag,' said Magrieta. 'What will people think of us if they see you coming from our house? En with such smart clothes en all.'

'But it's not for me, Magrieta,' said Tessa. Seeing Magrieta's baffled stare, she explained, 'There are some people who always wait for me near my office, so I give them food for their kids.'

'What kind of people?' Magrieta insisted.

'Just people.'

'Decent people?'

'Well, I suppose you could call them bergies.'

I tried to keep a straight face, watching them. I knew Magrieta.

She didn't disappoint me either. 'Those blerry good-for-nothings?' she stormed. 'Begging in the streets, it's just making trouble for everybody.'

'I've known them for years,' Tessa tried to softsoap her.

'En they still begging? So what good did it do them?'

After Tessa had left, an indignant Magrieta confronted me. 'I'm not making good food for a lot of bergies no more, Meneer. En in your lunchbox nogal.'

'But no one asked you to do it, Magrieta,' I pointed out.

'That one's jus' asking for trouble,' she muttered.

She obviously gave the matter considerable thought, resulting in a kind of compromise that both amused and pleased me. Magrieta restored my old lunchbox to the cupboard where it had spent most of its life and replaced it with a much-used Tupperware container that would do the job without bringing shame on our household. Tessa was free to choose her own food for her clients again, but as it turned out Magrieta happened to discover some useful, and often quite appetising, leftovers which she would add to the lunch when Tessa wasn't looking.

In a way, I suppose, this is indicative of how things have been working out at home. After giving it a while to settle into some kind of pattern I felt justified to send my sons brief and non-committal messages by e-mail: *I have taken a lodger. We'll have to wait and see how it works out, but at the moment it seems satisfactory for all concerned.* No need for them to know more, especially as regards the more personal angle.

After alerting me to the presence of the woman on the roof last Monday afternoon, Magrieta led the way to the side of the house, where a long rickety ladder had been propped up. I thought of Adonis and Cupido keeping watch while Willem Mostert was having his way with Antje of Bengal up in the draughty attic. I hurried past her towards the ladder.

'Where you going?' asked Magrieta, alarmed.

I was already halfway up.

'Your heart can't take such baboon tricks, Meneer,' she protested from below.

'Just steady the ladder.'

The moment my head emerged above the gutter I recognised her, on hands and knees high up on the roof, scuttling along the tiles. She was wearing jeans, a red sweatshirt, trainers.

'What on earth are you doing?' I asked. I felt like laughing with the sheer joy of seeing her, a prodigal daughter returned from distant lands.

'I saw a cat up here and thought it needed help, but it ran away. So I decided to check on the leaks.' She sat back, wiping sweat from her flushed face, squinting against the watery light. 'There's quite a few broken tiles, I think you should have them replaced.'

'You'll break your neck, young lady. I'll get somebody in. It's not your job.'

'If I'm going to stay here it damned well is.' A brief pause as she smiled, showing strong white teeth. 'I hope it's still OK with you?'

'Of course it is,' I said. 'I've been waiting for you to call.'

'Sorry, I've been up to my ears. And now I've brought lock, stock and several barrels.'

'Whatever you do, come down first. Magrieta can make us some tea.' I felt like celebrating.

I helped her to carry in her boxes, and suitcases, and bundles, and books, and armloads of loose clothing, and all the components of her computer, from the battered Beetle at the front gate. Which I would have noticed on arriving if I hadn't taken the side street to the garage entrance.

'Is this all?' I asked as I dumped the last box on her floor.

'There's a few bits and pieces more which I'll pick up tomorrow.'

'No furniture and stuff?'

'I told you Brian threw me out before I moved to Margie's flat. He kept almost everything.'

'I was worried about you all day yesterday,' I said.

'That's sweet of you.' She sat down on a bundle to survey her meagre possessions. 'But there was absolutely no need. My guardian angels are on duty round the clock.'

'When I woke up you were gone.'

'I should have left a note. I'm sorry. I had such a good time here on Saturday and I slept like an absolute baby.' The warmth in her deep voice was like a caress.

'Tea's ready,' said Magrieta at the door.

'You haven't met properly, have you?' I asked. 'Tessa Butler. And this is Magrieta Daniels, who's been a friend and a mother to me for almost a lifetime.'

'I hope I won't be a nuisance, Magrieta,' said Tessa. 'If I misbehave, just give me the boot. Or the strap, if you prefer.'

Magrieta's smile transformed her round face into a globe with lines of longitude and latitude. But she tried to give Tessa a stern line. 'Better not misbehave to start with,' she said. 'Now come en drink your tea before it get cold.' As we came into the study where she'd set down the tray she plunged straight into what must have been uppermost in her mind. 'Meneer tells me you saw our Antje?'

'There's a lot I want to ask you about her.'

'En she didn't scare you?'

'I was more surprised. I was . . . all sorts of things. But no, not scared. She seemed such a sad and beautiful young woman.' Was she playing up to Magrieta or was that really how she'd remembered the brief encounter?

Magrieta poured the tea, watching with approval as Tessa helped herself to sugar.

'Good,' she said. 'I don't trust people who drink bitter stuff. Me myself I take three. En four when it's coffee.'

I could see that she was aiming to settle herself on an armrest of the couch. 'Perhaps,' I said quickly, 'you can tell Tessa all about Antje tomorrow. I'd just like to discuss a few things with her first. If it's all right with you?'

Magrieta seemed disappointed, but quickly pulled herself together. And by the time she left for home she'd made us her special bobotie for supper.

But we didn't have the bobotie that evening, at least not for supper. My expectations of another long conversation with Tessa were rudely snuffed out when she appeared in the kitchen door, just as I was heating up the oven, and announced that she was going out. I'd already stacked the fire in the study and set out a tray with wine and glasses, banking on the feeling of impending celebration I'd had on the rooftop.

'Something wrong?' she asked.

'No, no, it's just . . .' I composed myself. 'This is your home now. Come and go as you please. I must still give you a key.' I went to get it. Her fingers brushed against mine when I handed it over and I wondered whether my face betrayed anything. My God, I thought, I'm sixty-five. I'm behaving like a twenty-year-old.

'I'll leave the stoep light on,' I said when I opened the front door for her. 'Do be careful. The world is not a safe place any longer. Especially not for young women on their own.'

'I'll be with friends, don't you worry.'

'Will you . . .' I fumbled for a moment. 'At what time will you be back?'

She smiled. 'Is there a curfew?'

'Heavens, no.' I felt caught out. 'Goodnight. See you in the morning.'

'Ciao.' And she was gone, alone, into the wild night with its distant hum of never-ending danger.

I didn't feel like having supper on my own, though I've been doing just that almost every night for eleven years, since Riana died. Ever since the news came that day I'd had this strange feeling of being disembodied, of having died myself, of surviving in limbo. Leftover time to kill. Said who? This evening the feeling was particularly strong. I put the bobotie in the fridge and made a slice or two of toast, which I washed down with tea. Then started wandering aimlessly through the labyrinth of the old house, not bothering to put on lights. I knew it all by heart.

In front of her door I stopped. I put my hand on the knob, then let go with a sense of self-reproach, and went away. Only to return again. This time I opened the door and turned on the light. She hadn't unpacked anything. All the boxes and bundles were still huddled haphazardly on the floor where we'd dumped them. No sign that she'd taken possession of the room yet. Detached both from her and from the room they'd been abandoned in, the chaos of alien objects conveyed no hidden meaning. Not even the rather battered guitar with a broken string. Beside it, on the bed, lay a glossy copy of her magazine. *Woman*. It seemed slick and sophisticated, incongruous among all the other stuff. With a sense of disappointment – but what, for heaven's sake, had I expected? – I turned off the light again. I couldn't even feel guilty about invading her space, for there had been nothing to invade. I felt as out of place as any of the boxes on the floor.

Annoyed by my lack of control, I returned to my study and tried to work, but found it impossible to concentrate. I studied all the objects accumulated on my desk over the years among the books and papers: a brass inkwell picked up at a flea market in Portugal, an olive-wood container for pens from Tuscany, a framed photograph of Louis and Johann as boys, small plaster busts of Mozart and Haydn, an assortment of carved boxes and ceramic containers of paperclips or rubber bands or drawing pins, paperweights from many places, a miniature reproduction of an early Sumerian writing tablet from the Louvre, Pa's robust pocket knife, the only thing I have of him, bristling with blades, a corkscrew, a screwdriver, a fierce-looking spike which he'd used to remove stones from horses' hooves. But nothing could hold my attention. I caught myself listening to every sound from outside, tensing at every car that passed. Two or three times, more, I went to the front door, opened it, ventured on to the stoep; once I walked down as far as the garden gate. Then, vexed with myself, I went back into the house, closing the door very firmly. To the kitchen for yet another cup of tea. This, too, would have to stop. Afterwards I had a long bath and put on my pyjamas and the threadbare but still cherished old dark-red dressing gown I've had for almost forty years. In its prime, babies had vomited over it during nights of colic or teething or earache; as it became more and more lived in it began to show the stains of innumerable substances: food and drink, Riana's tears and occasionally my own, medicine, toothpaste, pipe oil from the years I smoked, ink, lipstick, semen. It bears the inscriptions of my life more truly than any CV. I can wrap myself in it like a cloak, I can retreat into it like a hermit into his cave. Ensconced in it, that night, I withdrew to bed to read, but it soon bored me. Another cup of tea? No, just a glass of water this time. And back to the study to put on a record. Haydn's *Creation*, which never fails to draw me into its spell. The cosmic explosion of orchestra and chorus on 'And there was light'.

This time, too, it proved infallible. I turned the volume up — the garden is big, the neighbours well out of earshot — and felt the old sense of expectation as the third part approached. The sublime dialogue between Adam and Eve.

The music was so overwhelming that she was in the room before I realised she had come back.

'Wow,' she exclaims, unbuttoning her long black coat. 'Some sound you've got here.'

I get up quickly to turn it down. 'Sorry, I didn't hear you come in. What time is it?'

'You weren't waiting up for me?' she asks accusingly.

'Of course not.' I feign indignation. 'I was working and listening to Haydn.' And then shrug. 'Oh well. I couldn't let you stumble into a strange place on your very first night, could I now?'

'It's very sweet of you,' she says, as she has done before. 'But you really mustn't do this. Please. Will you promise?'

'Had a good evening?' I ask.

'It was all right.'

'No . . . problems?'

'Oh no.' She finally wriggles out of her coat. Everything she wears is black — sweater, slacks, boots — except for a long scarlet scarf, which she deftly unwinds and drops on a chair. Then she shakes her head vigorously, brings her hands up to run her fingers through her hair, and then stops abruptly, smiling as if surprised. 'I keep forgetting that I cut off my hair,' she says.

'Is that a recent change?'

'Just before I came here on Saturday.' She goes over to the cold fireplace. 'Burning all my bridges, you see.' She turns back, something theatrical in her pose, a glint of defiance in her eyes. 'Brian was absolutely furious. He was infatuated with my hair.'

'In times of war people tend to cut off the hair of women who sleep with the enemy,' I remark impulsively. 'Perhaps you reminded him of that.'

'Do *you* like short hair?'

'I haven't given it much thought. *You* look good with it. Especially the way you have it trimmed now.' I wonder briefly whether I should check the impulse, but then let go. 'Actually, you're beautiful,' I say. And immediately feel embarrassed.

But she is laughing — not the full, exuberant explosion of the first night, but with the same submerged richness of sound.

It is this, perhaps, more than anything else, which prompts me to go past her to the fireplace. The matches have been there since I stacked the fire, hours earlier. And I light it without waiting any longer.

She does seem surprised. 'Isn't it too late?'

'It's never too late for a fire.' I remain bent over it until the first tentative flickerings steady into licking tongues. 'And a glass of wine?'

Unbidden, she goes to the couch and leans back, briefly closing her eyes. 'This is good,' she says. As if summoned, Amadeus enters in a quiet, dignified ripple, unceremoniously jumps on Tessa's lap and is acknowledged, as before, with a face nudging his pale marmalade underbelly. While I pour the wine Tessa sits up to unlace her boots and draws her feet in under her. She accepts the proffered glass, takes a long slow sip and turns her eyes to me, the wetness of the wine still on her lips. At that moment, without warning, I feel a stirring of desire, and quickly gulp down some of my own wine and go to my own easy chair.

It is like being drawn into a play, the same play we were in two nights before, except we know it better now, the words come more easily, we seem more prepared to trust each other and so to probe more deeply with the words we've been given, naming new things, unnaming others, bringing to life what has been, until now, mere possibilities huddling in the shadows as yet untouched by the fire.

'I like it here,' she says again. 'You know, I thought yesterday, and earlier today, that perhaps it was wishful thinking rather than memory. I was wondering whether it could really be as cool as I remembered it and now I know it is.' She raises her glass in mock-seriousness. 'Thank you, Ruben.'

And again we talk. Without plan or premeditation, allowing the words themselves to lead us wherever they wish; and there is a kind of curiosity, in me at least, to see where it will go next and how far. What Laurence Sterne would have called a sesquipedality of a conversation.

She talks about her evening out with the editorial staff of the magazine. 'I think we'll be going places,' she says. 'All of them women in their twenties and thirties. The energy is bouncing right off the walls, just my kind of scene.' The intriguing little frown as she studies her wine. 'But somehow I'm already not sure I'm going to stay there long.'

'Why? Are they too go-getting for you?'

'I may be something of a go-getter myself, make no mistake, darling.' The offhand way she uses the term has nothing ambiguous about it. But I cannot help wondering how it would sound if she really meant it. 'No,' she resumes, 'I can handle the rat race. And

I can live with the lofty ideals and stuff. But I have a nasty feeling they're being dishonest about it. What they really want is the money, success, glamour, whatever. Which is fine by me. But then don't pretend you're fighting a moral cause. In my experience, which is more or less zilch, nothing can be as immoral as a moral cause.' Already her glass is empty. 'What gives me the creeps is the way it reminds me of my mother. All holier than thou, but all she really wanted out of life was the big bucks. I suppose one can't blame her – after my father cleared out and she was left with two small kids to look after.'

I find myself groping for a moment. 'I thought you said your father got killed?'

'Did I?' She doesn't seem put out at all. 'I was speaking meta-phorically.'

'Let me get this straight,' I say. 'He just left?'

'Right. Went off with a bitch he used to teach at university. Maths. Everybody said he was brilliant. But then this little student got the hots for him and off they went. Quite a scandal because she was only eighteen or nineteen, so her parents went to court and he had to skip the country. Never heard from him again.'

There is a brief silence. Before it can lengthen into something problematic I ask, 'So you had to grow up without him?'

'Just as well, I think. I certainly never missed him. If I missed anything it was a mother. I had an abundance of fathers.'

'How come?' I ask, bemused.

'Well, you see, when that bastard upped and left us, we had almost nothing. Mom had to find ways and means of keeping us going. And she didn't have any qualifications, they got married too soon, she left varsity without finishing. So we were practically living off charity.'

'That was when she got the job at the hotel?'

'No, she actually went to work at an estate agency. Learned the ropes in no time, and she was a shrewdie. Between you and me, she also knew how to turn on the charm – she was a beauty all right. Anyway, she got a few lucky breaks and started her own agency. Today she's *the* name in the Eastern Cape, I promise you. Problem is, she was a driven woman. Like, possessed by the fear of losing everything again. So she never let up, never really had time for me or Stephen – he's my brother. In fact, we were hampering her and she never allowed us to forget it. We were part of the burden my father had left her with. When I was a teenager I'd do *anything* just to let her notice me. But she was so much the hard-nosed business woman she couldn't be bothered.' A wry chuckle. 'I did some pretty weird things in the process, I can tell you. Sometimes I think it's a miracle I didn't end up in jail or something.'

'Was that after the children's home?'

She narrows her eyes. Suddenly she bursts out laughing. 'Was that what I told you? Sorry. I was just testing you. And you were so sweet about it all, not a word of reproach.'

'You were never sent away?'

'Of course not. But she always threatened to send us when we were naughty.'

'Where did the "fathers" come in?' I ask. 'Or was that another kind of test?'

'No, that's the gospel truth. They were part of Mom's strategy for survival, I suppose. She did get married twice, but I think that was the only way she could get what she wanted out of them. The others who came in between, the unofficial dads, were the more interesting ones. Stephen and I must have been the two most spoilt brats in Port Elizabeth. Some of them went for the male bonding thing, treating Stephen to every ball game and outing in town.' A brief pause. Her voice deepens very slightly. 'Most of them thought I was fairer game.'

'You were not' – I find it hard to say – 'abused?'

She takes a swallow from her glass, changes position. 'Let's not go into all the gruesome details. I promise you, most of the time I could twist them all around my little finger, and I did too. Only once – maybe twice . . .' She falls silent.

'And your mother did nothing?' I ask after a long while.

'My mother didn't know.'

'You didn't tell her?'

'What? "Our little secret"? She wouldn't *want* to know. And if you ask me, if she did find out, she'd have blamed it all on me.'

'But what did it do to you?'

'Oh, I survived. I suppose one learns to get out of it what you can while the going's good. I don't think I'm so much the worse for wear.' With a hint of playful coquetry: 'Do you?'

'I haven't seen all your scars yet.'

'There are no visible ones. Except I have a ring in my navel.' Her eyes gleam with mocking glee. 'I actually considered something more daring, but then I got cold feet.'

'Praise to God in the highest,' I comment. But the image she's conjured up makes me uncomfortable. Is she deliberately trying to arouse me? How can I know that anything she has told me is to be believed? If she lied the previous time, why shouldn't she do so again? I stare at her intently, but her face shows nothing. She looks entirely serene.

Impulsively I say, 'You could be a Fra Filippo Lippi madonna, you know. If it wasn't for the short hair.'

She laughs. 'I don't think I have anything blessed-art-thou-among-women in me.'

'Ah, but Lippi was different. Don't you know? He used to slip out of the monastery at night to cavort with his merry mistresses, and then afterwards they'd cover their nakedness in a blue robe and pose for him as the madonna.'

'Sounds like a lark to me,' she says.

'What do you do with all your memories?' I ask, thinking of mine.

'I don't have all that much time for what's over and done with. Just too bad, isn't it? I'm more into what's happening here and now.' A twist of her lip. 'Perhaps after I'm thirty I'll start thinking about the past.'

'What would you really like to do?'

She draws herself into one of her favourite postures: knees pulled up, propping up her chin, arms around her legs, empty glass dangling limply from one hand. 'Whatever it may be, it *won't* be a cherished husband, three and a half children, a mortgage and shooting lessons on Saturdays.' She twirls the wine glass between her fluid fingers. 'I don't really care what I end up with, as long as I get to the top.'

'Whatever that may mean.'

'For one thing, I want to be stinking rich,' she says. 'Under my own steam, not with anybody else helping me. I want to show my mother I can do it. And then I'll travel, I'll be in New York today, in Tokyo tomorrow, in Milan the day after.'

'All the places you went to with your lawyer?'

'He always promised to take me, he never actually did.'

I do not know how to react; she mustn't get the impression that this is an inquisition. So I say, 'Sounds like running away to me.'

For a moment it seems as if she may be stung into a tart retort. But then she says, 'I may be running *towards* something. Don't you think?'

'I don't know you well enough.'

'Do you realise this is just about the second conversation we've had and already I have the weird feeling that you know me better than most. At least I don't feel threatened by you.'

'You mean I'm old and harmless?' There may be more reproach in my voice than I intended.

What could have been a tricky moment is defused by the exuberant outburst of her laugh. 'And I am young and dangerous? You're not scared of me, are you?'

'I think I ought to be, but I'm not.'

'What *are* you scared of?' she deftly changes course.

'I'm not sure. The past? The future?' I try to make light of it: 'Sometimes I think the past is my only future.'

'Oh come on,' she laughs. 'That's too bloody gormless.' She swings her feet down from the couch . . . 'You know what? I'm famished. We just drank and smoked and argued tonight, I never had time to eat.'

'Magrieta left some bobotie.'

'Super idea.'

She accompanies me to the kitchen to warm up the food — at least I'll be able to face Magrieta in the morning — and take it back to the study for a midnight feast. And all the time we talk and talk. I tell her bits about my life in this house and further back — about university and meeting Riana; and the religious indignation of her parents when they heard she was pregnant; and how they later forgave us because they couldn't face the idea of being separated from grandchildren; and how they slowly took control of our lives again. From there I grope back even further, to my childhood on the farm, and my brothers, and my father; deliberately trying to keep it light, steering away from darkness and doubt, for the mood is relaxed, favouring an easy osmosis of memories.

'What kind of man was your father?' she asks.

'I thought you weren't interested in fathers?'

'Not in mine. He disappeared too early. But what was yours like?'

'He was a difficult man. And sad. I don't think I ever really knew him.'

Memories stealing back to haunt me, like old ghosts. I've tried for so long to lay them to rest but they have a way of coming back. Poor Pa. He was never meant to be a farmer, but he had no choice. He was the only son; his own father, known with good reason as Goliath Olivier, dirt poor, had postponed marriage until he thought he could afford it, then became desperate at seventy-three, took to wife a forty-year-old widow from a neighbouring farm, and between the two of them they managed to propel my father, Stoffel, into the world. An introverted child whom not even old Goliath's legendary harshness could prise from his shell. This weighed like a divine reproach on the massive shoulders of the old man, feared far and wide for his size and strength and volcanic temper.

Stoffel spent his days in the veld, tending the goats as he watched for the rare train to draw its thin trail of smoke on the horizon, allowing both his thoughts and his flock to scatter, which earned him a nightly thrashing. More often than not old Goliath administered the beating even before he'd counted the goats. Stoffel's dream was to go to where the trains came from, to become a teacher, the only profession more or less within reach that offered some shine of accomplishment, of 'higher things'. But he was needed on the farm which, as the only son, he'd been predestined to take over; and so, after only five years of education, he was hauled out of school to work his way toward the hapless future his father had plotted for him. Stoffel spent his youth waiting for the old man to die so that he could abscond; but Goliath lived to a hundred and two, by which time it was too late for his son to realise his dream. Moreover, two years before his death the old patriarch had ordered Stoffel to get married and produce an heir; he'd even chosen the bride, Helena Hattingh, a pretty girl of nineteen from a neighbouring district who'd become a burden to her parents because no man would touch her after she'd been 'spoilt' by a city slicker. She brought the promise of a reasonable dowry, which meant at least some reprieve from mounting debts.

Legend has it that after the wedding the old man ordered the couple straight to bed to proceed with the business of procreation. In the old tyrant's terminology it seemed to have 'taken', and nine months later they had their first son, my oldest brother. Goliath, fired by a belief that women served only one function in the world, would permit of no respite. Ten months after the first birth the second son made his entry into the wretched world. But God was merciful. Before my mother's second pregnancy had run its term the terrible old man was thrown by his horse on a hunting trip and died.

Stoffel, nearly thirty and burdened with a family, qualified for nothing else, was too old for a new start. He would bear a grudge against life to the day of his death. His wife's health, seriously impaired by the two early pregnancies, had declined so alarmingly that she was more or less permanently bedridden. In spite of this, probably in a night of desperation and no doubt inspired more by the brandy which had become his mainstay than by desire, my father sired a third son six years after the second. That was I. Helena expired at my birth. That left Pa alone with his unresolved rage against the world. And much of it — how could I blame him? — he took out on the three of us, who in his eyes permanently represented all the injustice and perversity of life.

'What a bitter man he must have been,' says Tessa. 'And what a life for you.'

'Yes, he was bitter,' I admit. 'And yet . . .' There was always something ambiguous in our relationship. He made no secret of the fact that he held me responsible for my mother's death; yet I doubt that he'd ever loved her. She had been forced on him, or he on her; she'd always been a reminder of his subjugation to his father, of his ineptitude, his shame. Only after her death did he begin to idealise the woman she had been, probably to compensate for his own problematic feelings about her. And on the rare occasions when he would recognise in me the child he himself had once been – a studious boy, a dreamer, driven by an ambition to explore the secret world of books beyond the confining realities of the Old Testament, of rocks and goats and thorn trees – there would be a singular, sharp closeness between us. He'd never learned to express his feelings, to translate into words the deep thoughts that troubled or inspired him; but the urge was there and I think I responded to it in my own tongue-tied way.

But I also had a surrogate father, the wizened old Griqua, Outa Hans, who told me stories. Most of them, I believe, had been handed down to him by his forebears, or by the Tswana labourers on the farm. Others he'd read off the rock paintings on the overhanging rock to the back of the farmhouse. Still others, for want of evidence, I'm sure he'd made up. He shared them with me whenever the two of us could find a pretext for being together. I would tell him about my book stories: the travels of Don Quixote, the adventures of Gulliver, the voyages of Sinbad, the three musketeers. In exchange, he would offer me stories about men transformed into rocks or trees or animals (eland, oryx, leopards, elephants), the spirits of young drowned women returning in the shape of birds, bottomless holes in the earth from which, at night, crept curious creatures from the underside of the world. Above all, ghost stories: the ghosts of dead Bushmen crawling from their unmarked graves to plague whoever had unwittingly trodden on them; the ghosts of the murdered returning to bring the perpetrators to justice or drive them to their death; the ghosts of ancient warriors, black and white, rising from forgotten battlefields of the past to haunt the living who tried to grow mealies or pumpkins or whatever on the blood-drenched veld; ghosts of people hanged for crimes they had not committed.

'And Outa Hans's stories were backed up by the Old Testament,' I explain. 'Pa still clung to the old High Dutch State Bible, which, he firmly believed, was written in God's mother tongue. I'm sure he had as much trouble as the three of us understanding it, but that was part of the package. Religion was not *meant* to be understood.'

Pa needed such ceremony, such unchanging formulas, to bolster him. Behind them, I caught desperate glimpses of a lost and lonely man, old before his time, bewildered in the world, threatened by God and Devil alike, fearful of death, certain only of failure.

The care of the farm was left more and more to my brothers, assisted by a host of wretched, indigent black labourers, while Pa simply wandered about in the veld or withdrew into the barn where he hid his Melowwood and did his carpentry. This was the one thing he really was good at and over the years he produced some exquisitely crafted pieces, but he never thought of selling anything and the furniture just multiplied under tarpaulins in the barn until my brothers began surreptitiously to cart the chairs, the inlaid tables, the intricately joined cupboards off to town, where they got quite a flourishing business going. David, the elder of the two, became an auctioneer; Jacob drifted to Johannesburg, where he set up as an 'agent', but exactly what that meant we never found out.

My own future had been decided from that first day when Pa had forgotten me in the town library. And he supported me, though he hardly ever spoke about it directly. When it was time for me to go to university, he took me to the bank and made me sign some papers already drawn up. Only then did I discover that over the years he'd saved the money to make this possible. It was all signed over to me: a convoluted process, as I was still a minor and a sympathetic teacher had to be found to act as a shield. A few months later the farm was sold to pay off accumulated debts; but my money was safe – probably the only dishonest act he'd ever committed in his life.

Pa moved into an outroom on Jacob's property in Johannesburg, in Booysens, where he tried to earn an income from carpentry – until, wasted by disappointment and depression he took a bus to Park Station one morning and jumped in front of a train. He was fifty-nine, but the last time I'd seen him, which was about eighteen months earlier, he looked a badly weathered eighty.

'I'll never forgive myself for not having visited him more,' I confide to Tessa. 'I always had the feeling that we were both straining desperately to reach out, but we never broke through. There were all sorts of excuses, mainly money, difficulties at home, we'd started our family, that sort of thing. But none was good enough. If only I'd known.'

'At least you tried.'

'Not enough,' I say. 'Never enough. Otherwise he wouldn't have chosen that way to die.'

'You can't hold yourself responsible.'

'Where does responsibility end, or guilt, or complicity?'

'This whole guilt thing,' she says, shaking her small head. 'We're all fucked up in this country, aren't we?' She stands up with her empty plate, puts it on the tray and comes to collect mine. For a moment she seems to hesitate, then leans over and briefly puts a hand on my shoulder. I can sense an extraordinary togetherness, a feeling of being brought closer by every new detour or contour of our conversation.

I glanced at my watch, tugged between this moment with all it had gathered within it, and tomorrow, which was as yet unpredictable. The obvious move to make, the sensible decision, would be to say goodnight and go to bed. But I still resisted the finality of such a choice. And I sensed – I wished, I hoped – that she did too.

She went with me to the kitchen; we washed up together – that would certainly score points with Magrieta in the morning – and all the while our talk continued unrestrained. What mattered was not just what we spoke about, but the slowly gathering weight of the unspoken. It meant watching each other, especially after we'd returned to the study with the luxuriously purring cats, the fire newly coaxed into flames, the dark red gleam of the wine in the glasses: watching for signs of that silent territory of which our words were trying to draw the map – rivers of tentative feeling, ranges of desire, nothing named yet, as I held back, held back (dare I presume that it was the same for her?); but all of it possible, rising closer to the surface, a barely sensed presence already acknowledged but not yet uttered.

And so we spoke about her day at work, and mine at home and

in the library, about the house, the street, the suburb, the dangerous city; about her mother and my sons; about shows and concerts; about the signs of the zodiac we were born under (I, Leo; she, Virgo); about the death of Johnny MacFarlane, and justice done and injustice seen to be done; about Magrieta.

'How long has she been with you?' she asked.

'A lifetime.'

'Do you think she'll accept me?'

'Magrieta is unpredictable and possessive. But I'm sure she'll like you.' I began to tell her stories as the memories came back to me, from the long road the two of us had travelled together, Magrieta and I, since the day she'd become part of the deal when we bought the house. At the time she'd been married for some eight years and she already had three children; her husband Andries was a fisherman at Hout Bay. There were tough years ahead for her. First, Andries was killed in a freak accident at sea; then her in-laws claimed the children and went off to Lambert's Bay with them. Magrieta remarried, this time to a carpenter, Barney; but then came the 'clean-up' of District Six and they were resettled on the Cape Flats, among the bare dunes, in the wind. We did all we could – Riana doing the frustrating rounds from one office to the next: under-secretary to secretary to deputy to minister, while I wrote letters and drew up petitions and made representations – but, if anything, our interference made the authorities more intransigent. Magrieta and her family had to get out.

'I'll never forget the day of the bulldozers,' I told Tessa. 'We were with Magrieta and Barney in their small sitting room when the police came to turn us out with teargas and dogs. We held out for as long as we could, but it was useless. In the end we had to run for our lives and the bulldozers flattened the house with everything in it.'

('Bloody white kaffirs!' a pimply youth in uniform had yelled at Riana and me.)

Possibly as a result of all the upheaval, Magrieta lost the child she was carrying. And Barney was fired from his job. He'd had a good position with one of the major contractors, but after hearing about their resistance to eviction the man – James Hepworth, an eloquent

English liberal — prudently decided that they couldn't afford to be involved with agitators. We approached friends and colleagues and acquaintances for help in providing odd jobs: Barney was more than a craftsman, he was a real artist who could make a piece of wood sing in his hands. To myself, I admitted that in finding work for him I was trying to atone for the old guilt about Pa.

In the long run the odd jobs were not enough to keep Barney going. We redoubled our efforts. A week after we'd finally landed him a permanent position with a large firm in Bellville he fell from a two-storey-high scaffolding and broke his neck. It was Antje of Bengal, rather than Riana or I, who pulled Magrieta from that particular valley of death.

This time she steered clear of men for several years before Antje finally approved of Reggie. Who was a driver, with his own bakkie, earning a steady income making deliveries all over the Peninsula. In 1972 their son Mannie was born, followed two years later by Mabel. Just when they seemed set to prosper Reggie was carried off by the flu in 1978.

Three months later Magrieta had a stillborn child. the shock for Riana was almost as bad as for her. She prevailed on Magrieta to move in with us. As a result their children were brought up in this house. At that time our boys were already in their teens, Johann fifteen, Louis thirteen. Quite a houseful. Fortunately Antje was there to keep them all in check.

But Magrieta had a thing about independence. By the time our sons were at university she'd found a couple of rooms with a cousin in Manenberg. That was a serious miscalculation. In his mother's absence Mannie became involved with a gang. For the last seven years she's never set eyes on him. Mabel followed a different course. We — and then I — saw her through school and into UWC. But since her early high-school days there was tension between her and Magrieta: she'd become ashamed of the uneducated, backward mother who'd sold out to the whiteys.

It isn't easy to retrace it all. The cousin and her husband were getting fed up with Magrieta's kids, especially the gangster Mannie. After one particularly violent confrontation Mannie brought his gang home in the night to trash the place. Magrieta moved back to Papenboom Road, but from then on she left no stone unturned to find a house of her own. The new government, she argued, would take care of that: hadn't they promised to do so in Mandela's elections? I just had to put in a word. Dead end. Because if she'd been too black for the old government, who'd thrown her out of District Six, she now turned out to be not quite black enough for the new people in power.

That was the time – coinciding with my own crisis at the library – when the crunch came with Mabel. There was an awful confrontation when she turned up here one weekend accompanied by an earringed boyfriend, who lammed into me with quotes from Marx and Engels, which soon progressed into threats about lessons to be taught to 'fucking Boers'. I tried to keep my cool, but Magrieta was the one who sent them packing and forbade them ever to set foot in the house again. Shouting after Mabel, 'You no longer my child, I don't know you no more, you can jus' fockoff.'

'Our children are our children, Magrieta,' I tried to reason with her afterwards. 'Just be patient. You gave her a good background, she'll come back to you.'

'I don't want to be nuggeted with a child like that,' she shut me up. 'And I don't want Meneer to get mixed up with it either.'

Easier said than done. The episode was particularly painful to me, fraught as it was with memories of Mabel as child. The bright little pigtailed girl who'd followed me everywhere over weekends, or curled up on my lap to listen to stories; and when I was working at my desk she would sit cross-legged in my deep chair drawing pictures or reading the books I'd brought her from the library, until Riana, hypersensitive about my fondness for the girl, would come to shoo her out. (The constant recriminations: 'You have more time for Magrieta's child than for your own.' Ah but they were boys.) How could a few short years have forced us so far apart?

Magrieta took the showdown with Mabel very badly, as if *she* were to blame for it. It made her all the more anxious to find a place of her own. I wrote scores of letters, made endless telephone calls, eventually engaged a lawyer. And after almost a year we managed to secure an unprepossessing little place in Mandalay. At least it was her own.

Eighteen months after Magrieta had taken possession of her house I suffered my angina attack. A pretty scary experience. Magrieta immediately offered to move back here to look after me, but I refused. It would make me feel like a useless invalid, I told her. The real reason was that I simply couldn't do it to her. I don't think she was entirely unaware of it.

And then Tessa and I shifted into the final movement of the night. Now it becomes even more difficult to remember coolly, clearly, in sequence.

'You're a good person,' I hear her voice floating from the shadows.

'Don't say that!' I'm surprised by my own vehemence. 'All my life I've done too little. If you think of what others have achieved . . .'

'Why compare yourself to others?' It amuses me, and touches me: this young woman who sounds so wise. As if she's lived much more than I. And perhaps, it occurs to me, she has. Today's young people.

'If one has lived alone for so long you can't help wondering about others,' I try to explain. 'Whether you still measure up to a changed world.'

'But you've been happy here.' The unflinching stare of her eyes. (An unexpected thought: perhaps she is staring so intently simply because she is myopic and cannot see clearly.)

'Happy? It's a word one uses too easily. Content, perhaps. But only because I've stopped expecting things. It comes with age, I suppose.'

'I feel terribly old sometimes,' she says. 'Like now.'

'Because you're with me?'

'No. Because you make me realise I've never really had a chance of just being young, a child, irresponsible and carefree.'

'Because of your mother?'

'Because of the world.'

There is silence now, a silence that stretches, then eases, sagging into an absence of care or concern. I am aware only of the two of us together. She so young – how young she is – and I, for a brief spell, redeemed from age.

We were both reluctant to make the slightest move – perhaps I'm projecting this on to her now, remembering; I know *I* was – because there was no way of knowing what might happen. I'm not sure I *wanted* anything to happen, not even the simple decision of saying goodnight and going off to bed. But in the end it was I who moved. I got out of the deep chair, involuntarily pressed a hand against my lower back, went over to the couch and took her hands to help her up. She rose easily, lightly, but lethargically. We stood very close together. I remember placing my hands on her shoulders, feeling their concise definition under the black sweater.

'Thank you,' she whispers. 'It's been good to be here with you.'

I hear myself saying, 'Don't go. Not now.'

She briefly allows herself to lean against me, and raises her head to look up at me. Her lips touch mine, the flutter of a small bird's wing.

'Goodnight, Ruben.'

I hold her against me. 'Please stay.'

She doesn't say anything straight away. I haven't really expected that she'd accept and the sudden thought that she may makes it difficult to control my breath.

'Do you think it's a good idea?' she asks.

'I desire you,' I say against her cheek.

For a moment she presses herself against me. I am conscious of the hardness of her body, its warmth flowing into mine.

'I'm tempted,' she whispers.

'Say yes.'

But then she closes her eyes and almost imperceptibly shakes her head against my chest.

I feel the warmth draining from me.

With a serious little smile her lips move against mine. 'Goodnight.' Then she slips from my arms, bends over to pick up her boots and goes out. The creaking of the old floorboards marks her passage as she moves further and further out of reach on her bare feet. Will Antje of

Bengal be hovering somewhere in the dark, waiting? In the cavernous distance I hear her door close. There is no satisfaction in having escaped from temptation. All that is left of her is the blood-smear of the red scarf spilled on the chair.

The night was old and I was no longer young.

I imagined her preparing for bed. I imagined her body. For a brief moment it had seemed real, now it was no longer part of the possible. I thought: strange word, *remember*. To put the members together again, to reconfigure. The past passing through one's heart. There was a dull, undefined ache in my chest, which had nothing to do with a need for nitroglycerine. I thought of poor old Doctor Faustus, abandoned by the ghost of Helen. *O lente, lente currite noctis equi.*

I thought: It is 22 June; tonight is the longest night of the year.

# 2

It was not without trepidation that I went to the kitchen the next morning. It was earlier than usual, soon after I'd heard Magrieta come in: I wasn't sure which I dreaded more — discovering that Tessa had already gone off to work, or having to face her again after the night before. It had been, once again, a bad night. Not that I hadn't slept, but all the time I'd been conscious of trying to recapture in dreams every fold in the fabric of our conversation; and every nuance of gesture and expression that had given them texture. It was an effort to reach beyond the easy undulations of the surface and grasp, however incompletely, what might have hidden in the shadows behind.

I still felt no closer to understanding when Magrieta's presence in the kitchen filtered into my consciousness and I woke up with a more powerful morning hard-on than I'd had in years. I waited for it to subside, while fondly wishing it to remain; then padded to the bathroom for an urgent pee, brushed my teeth, pulled a comb through my unruly hair, fumbled my way into the reassurance of the old gown, and ventured down the passage to the kitchen.

What would there be in Tessa's eyes when she looked at me? Reproach, diffidence, a grudging reminder? Or would they merely be veiled, feigning civility? I wasn't sure which would be worse.

I need not have worried. When she looked up from the kitchen table, where she and Magrieta appeared to be in deep conversation, her eyes were quite unclouded, clear as a sky untroubled even by wind or a flight of birds. There was recognition in them, acknowledgement, brightness; no hint of the judgement which comes before or after.

'Hi,' she said. 'Slept well?'

'So-so. And not enough, I'm afraid. You?'

Her unconditional broad smile. 'I had a wonderful sleep.' She looked as if she'd had a night of eight or nine hours, not the miserly two or three we'd been left with.

'Meneer want some coffee?' asked Magrieta, leaning forward to push herself up.

'I see you've already made it. I'll help myself.' I looked at Tessa again: 'You two discussing serious business?'

'I just telling her about our Antje,' said Magrieta.

'I think she was on the prowl again last night,' added Tessa. 'Just after I put out the light. I didn't actually see anything, but there seemed to be something moving through the closed door.'

'That poor girl is so restless,' sighed Magrieta. 'There must be something she want to tell you.'

'She certainly has enough to tell.' Tessa leaned forward towards Magrieta. 'I was asking Magrieta about those two slave men, Adonis and Cupido. Ruben told me something, but there must be more.'

Magrieta frowned, offended perhaps by the familiarity of the way she referred to me. 'Meneer know all the old stories.' She looked pointedly at me.

'What is it about Adonis and Cupido?' I asked, leaning back against a cupboard as I sipped my coffee.

'If Meneer don't mind us talking when there's work to be done . . . ?'

'You know I love to listen, Magrieta.'

'Well, as I was telling Madam . . .'

'Please, Magrieta, I'm nobody's Madam. Just call me Tessa. You could have been my mother.'

Magrieta grinned. 'Not really, hey. But OK, if Miss Tessa want me to . . .' She shifted her weight. The chair creaked in protest. 'So, the way I heard it from Antje, she was mos just a girl when she came here to Papenboom after Willem Mostert boughted her. En she was scared en all, she didn't know what was going to happen to her, with a new baas, and also with his wife, that Nooi Susara, who had a temper like a devil straight from hell. En then, for a slave girl like her, it was hard to come into a house with other slaves already there, en always hard on newcomers. There was the four women, that's Fatima en Sabina, who was Malay, en the two Masbiekers, Trijn en Bella. From the first day they was always at her with a harsh word here en a snub there, en a slap in the face every now en then. But Antje was such an obedient girl, she tole me herself, that all this badness soon stopped. Specially Fatima became like a kind of mother to her, teaching her what to do in the house, but also showing her — if Miss Tessa will forgive me — all the things a woman must know to please a man. Fatima, as Antje explained to me, Fatima knew these things like no one else. She done them to the baas himself, long before Antje ever came here. En to other men also, workers en slaves en even white men.

'So all these things Fatima tole her, en soon Antje had no more trouble with the women slaves. But now there was the two men also. In those days all the slaves had to sleep together in the outbuilding, except now for Sabina en Trijn, who was the house girls, but the others, men en women, slept all together, en that's never a good thing. But in a way Antje was lucky. Because Adonis, he was the young one, he was already with Bella, en she kept a kwaai eye on him. So that left only old Cupido. En that was now really something of a sad story, Miss Tessa. Because Cupido was a old man. How old, I cannot tell you, in those days people got old faster than nowadays, specially from the hard work, summer en winter, from before sunup en until long after sundown. That made Cupido old before his time. En also because he had a wife in the beginning, came to the Cape with him when they was still young, but then she was sold separately to another baas, en she tried to run away back to Cupido, but they caught her en gave her a beating that she died of. Well, that was that, en Cupido was now a old man, en a sad man. Antje says he opened his heart to her from the very first day she came here. He was like a big old watchdog that tried to protect her from all kinds of harm. If Nooi Susara came to beat her, Cupido took the blame en the stripes. If Adonis tried to show her the snot sjambok when Bella wasn't looking, then Cupido was there to stop him. If the other slave women got difficult with her, Cupido was the one to put in a word for her. He even stole tobacco from the attic to buy them off. Looked after her like you can say he was her own father.

'There was only one thing Cupido could do nothing about en that was Willem Mostert's horn. There was no beginning or end to that man's itch for Antje. En whenever Nooi Susara got in the way, Cupido was the one who must help out. He's the one who must find a ladder when the baas got red ants in his arse to get into attic or bedroom. Unlock a door here, open a window latch there. So the baas could get to the child. En it almost killed old Cupido. Because the thing was this, you see: Cupido had mos his eye on Antje too. He tole her so. You can now say he was old en all, but he was darem a man too, he had the feelings of a man. En for him she was like a bucket of water to a man who's dying of thirst.

'She never allowed him to drink, that she tole me many times. She didn't have the right feelings for him. Quite a cheeky girl, all in all. He was too old, she said. Look, I'm not saying anything against Antje, the two of us are close. But she had her airs, I can tell you. When it came to the baas, it wasn't for Antje to say yes or no – en anyway, as she tole me, it was always yes with her. The two of them was like a sickness in the blood. So it made no difference that she had no right to say yes or no. But where she had the choice, she kept her legs closed. En she kept them closed for Cupido. Not that she treated him badly, God knows she was thankful for everything he done to help her. But she said he was mos like a father to her, en there's things one don't do with a father. En also, she didn't want to cause him trouble with the baas. Because suppose she said yes and Willem Mostert found out, then Cupido would be a dead en buried man.

'Right, en that's how Cupido then became the good old watchdog who looked after her en took her to the baas when he needed her. En it was only much, much later, as Antje tole me, that she found out how it killed him to wait outside with the ladder at night while the baas was having his doings with her. But by then it was too late.'

'And when at last it all came out and Antje was taken to court?' asked Tessa.

'I don't know if they talk about this in Meneer's books, but what Antje tole me was that in the end it was Cupido who went to tell the court people about her. Everybody thought it was Fatima that betrayed her, but Fatima en the others only started talking after Cupido already done the damage.'

'But *why*, Magrieta?' asked Tessa, visibly upset. 'You said the man loved her.'

'Who will ever understand the secrets of a man en a woman that's in love?' said Magrieta solemnly. 'Miss Tessa knows what the Word says: There be three things which are too wonderful for me, yea, four which I know not, en one is the way of a man with a maid.'

'All those years he looked after her,' said Tessa, 'all those years he kept her and Willem Mostert's love going . . .'

Magrieta nodded with a surprising expression of smugness. 'That's so. En when at last it was all over en Nooi Susara was killed en the way to Willem Mostert's bed was open . . . what did he do? He threw her out en tole her he wanted nothing more to do with her.'

A new understanding appeared in Tessa's eyes. 'And then Cupido thought his chance had come, but Antje refused him?'

Magrieta shrugged. 'You can say the man chose the wrong time. But in these things one mustn't go for the easy answers, Miss Tessa. There's things between a man en a woman that must maar better stay between them. All I can tell you is that it wasn't jus' a matter of taking her en she saying no.'

'You've never told me this before, Magrieta,' I intervened.

'Meneer is a man,' she answered without looking at me. 'En that's why I'm saying.' It was a while before she looked up, more at Tessa than at me. 'That girl's heart was broken is all I can say. Committed murder en everything for Willem Mostert. She went to cry on old Cupido's shoulder. He was the only one she could go to. En like he done all those years he took her in his arms en let her cry her heart out en let her talk all the talk she had in her.' A deep sigh.

'And then he took advantage of her?' asked Tessa, clearly shocked.

'Perhaps it wasn't quite like that, Miss Tessa.' It took some coaxing to extract the rest from her. But in the end she complied. It wasn't just that Antje cried on Cupido's shoulder, Magrieta explained. There was a kind of madness that got into her. She took off her clothes, she threw herself at him, she more or less forced him to take her, to hurt her. How could he resist after he'd been burning for her inside for so long? She gave him no choice. And that, honest to God, was what Antje said.

'No woman would do a thing like that,' objected Tessa, quite vehemently.

'Antje done it,' said Magrieta with an air of finality.

It was silent for quite a long time. Then, shaking her head, Tessa said, 'No wonder she's still around.'

'To take revenge?' I asked. 'To look for justice?'

'She doesn't sound like the kind of person that's bent on revenge. And there's not much justice in the world anyway.'

'Then why should she still be haunting this house?'

Magrieta shrugged. 'Just to tell her story, perhaps. Isn't that enough reason?'

# 3

IT IS EARLY evening. It's Saturday. She is having her bath. In an hour we'll be going out. It is only a fortnight, yet it feels as if we've known each other for ever. On our long walk through Newlands Forest this afternoon she threaded her fingers through mine; in a clearing among the trees, high up the slope, fragrant with the smell of pines after the morning's rain, she leaned her head against my shoulder and I held her lightly against me, gave her a chaste kiss on the forehead. It seemed the most natural thing in the world; the two or three people striding past at a furious pace, the family group with small blond children, the panting jogger, might have thought we were a father and his daughter. (Fortunately none of them had dogs with them, or we wouldn't have made any progress at all: on the way up Tessa had stopped to greet and nuzzle every canine passer-by, from dachshunds and chirpy little Maltese terriers to waddling bulldogs and stiff-legged Dobermanns and even a sinuous Afghan swaying like a landau in slow motion.)

Our shared life in the house is limited to late evenings and early mornings. There has not been a repetition of that first Monday night's closeness. Impossible to say if this is coincidence, or whether she has cannily avoided it. In a sense it has taken the edge off for me too. There is no urgency; it is enough to know she is around. Yet I do not think it unreasonable to wonder if tonight may be different. We'll see a film, go 'somewhere' afterwards, all her idea. I'm not pinning any unrealistic hopes on it; for the moment, while I'm still glowing from the unusual exercise of the walk, it is no more than a possibility that need not be discounted.

\*     \*     \*

Is it shameful to confess that I bought a packet of condoms one morning this week? I drove into town for it as I felt embarrassed about buying it from my regular chemist. Haven't done this for decades. The girls from the agency bring their own and often, if I request only a 'pelvic', we don't even use one. Not that I need them at all, I had a vasectomy years ago, after Riana lost the baby and we knew it would be dangerous for her to get pregnant again. But with all these newfangled risks Tessa might insist if it ever came to such a pass, and it would be distressing to see an opportunity lost for a silly reason like that.

I found that condoms, too, have changed. Quite a bewildering experience, in fact. The first time I was so confused by the selection on display (in my time they were still sold from under the counter) that I only bought a tube of toothpaste and walked out again. The lurid colours, the textures, the knobs and polyps and ridges and fringes and flanges and fragrances, were enough to boggle a mind used to simpler pleasures. When I returned the next day, braced for the worst, I asked the pharmacist for advice and told him it was for my grandson. He kept a very straight face. I settled for the most no-nonsense kind on offer.

For the time being the little packet lives in my sock drawer. I feel like a freedom fighter keeping sticks of dynamite in his room. God knows what Magrieta will think should she chance upon it, and I'm sure that in the long run nothing escapes her vigilance – or Antje's prompting. I may as well confess that when I came home I peeled off the wrapper and proceeded to try one on. The readiness is all. The mere prospect caused me to sprout a most reassuring erection; but in the fumbling to sheath myself it lost its vigour and soon shrunk into wrinkly insignificance. Afterwards it took me more than half an hour to flush the damn thing down the toilet. Like the corpse of a saint it kept returning to the surface. In the end I had to fish it out again and stuff a well-worn bar of soap inside to get it down, but I'm not sure that once the soap has dissolved it may not come back to plague the inventor. Next time, like Don Quixote trying on his helmet, I shall rely on faith alone.

As if to atone for something she didn't even know about, I bought

Tessa two bunches of poppies (having suppressed my first impulse to buy roses) after coming from the pharmacy. But when I got home Magrieta was hoovering the passage and she immediately eyed my floral tribute.

'En what's this flowers for?' she asked.

I felt too guilty to admit that they were for Tessa. 'Just something to brighten up the house,' I mumbled. 'I'll put them in a vase.'

'I'll take them, Meneer will just make a mess.'

When Tessa came home in the late afternoon I avoided her, still uneasy about the clandestine condoms. As it happened, it was one of the evenings she went out and that made it easier to live with the knowledge of my morning excursion, persuading myself that the merchandise need never be used. They were, after all, just a precaution, and for her sake, not mine.

During the day she is at her work. Sometimes, when I enquire about it, over breakfast or an occasional nightcap, she talks about the job again. She does not seem to have changed her misgivings about the magazine, but she is resolved to 'give it a go'. I admire the grit with which she sticks it out. In a way it makes her even more alluring.

Buying the condoms has also sent me back to my library in town instead of the one at UCT, where I've been doing my research over the past few years. (I managed to obtain a card through a staff member in history whom I'd come to know while I was still a librarian.) I need to get away from my books sometimes, but apart from the rare outing to a concert there has been little distraction from beyond my study walls in recent months. Previously, at least, there used to be my regular chess evenings with Johnny MacFarlane – how I miss the man – but now I'm mostly confined to my study. I have many projects, of course, but I doubt I'll ever get round to writing anything substantial at my age; it'll go the same way as all the articles I've been making notes for over the past number of years without ever producing one. When I was still working in the library I used to publish a fair amount of my research. It was part of the job description. But since Riana died I've lacked the stamina to complete anything, even though I still go through the motions, the stages of hunting and gathering. Since 'my' library decided to make me redundant even that pretence has fallen away. And it's only been to force a small measure of variety into my long days that I made the move to UCT.

A strange feeling, on Thursday morning when I left the pharmacy with my tube of toothpaste and decided to put the trip to good use and visit my library again. I'd just stroll by, I thought. Enjoy the greenery in the gardens. (Though that, too, appears to be changing. More hobos about, importunate youngsters smelling of spirits. I'd forgotten about all the reports of muggings and worse in these lanes and byways. Not that I felt particularly vulnerable. Who would be interested in accosting a slightly unkempt, perhaps dotty old stroller like me?) And then I was there, and without thinking about it I went up the stairs, past the tall columns, and entered the building where I'd spent so much of my life. For a while I just stood there, looking about at the shelves, up at the high ceiling. I've been happy in this place, I thought. An unqualified and simple, unquestioning happiness. If I look back one day, I'm sure I'll decide that those cloistered years in this place were actually the most rewarding of my life. Including Riana? Well, perhaps. But there's no need to choose, is there?

'Can I help you?' a young black girl asked from the circular counter.

'I'm just looking . . .' And then I said, 'I'd like to see Siphiwo Mdamane.'

'Mr Mdamane is no longer with us,' she said. 'Is there anyone else I can call?'

'No, I don't think so.' I gave her what must have been a silly grin. 'I used to work here, you know. Mr Mdamane took over from me.'

'I see,' she said, without showing any interest, nor the slightest sign of recognition. Of course not. I belong to a different world now. I'm a stranger to the place that has made me what I am.

'I'll just use the opportunity to look up something.'

'I need to see some ID.'

All I had on me was my tube of toothpaste. Nothing else. Except my life, except my life, except my life. And so I turned and left.

'Weren't you too young to retire?' asked Tessa as we were having breakfast in the kitchen the next morning. I'd just told her about going back to the library. Keeping silent, of course, about the visit to the pharmacy which had brought it on.

'I was. Sixty-two. Still had over two years to go.'

'Then why . . . ?'

'Because the times they are a-changing,' I said. I told her about the retrenchment.

'Did they at least give you a proper package?'

'Not bad. But money was the least of my concerns. Riana's parents made sure we'd always have enough, and after her death it all came to me. A hell of an irony, because it was to get away from their money that we got married in the first place. But I'd have been happy to stay on at the library for a pittance. And if they'd fired me because I'd done a bad job I'd have accepted it too. But I know it had nothing to do with competence. I got booted out just because I'm white and male.'

'For a long time people got booted out for being black,' Tessa reminded me as she wiped her mouth, leaving a red smudge on the white serviette.

'I know it was high time things changed,' I said heatedly, 'but you can't solve a wrong with another wrong.'

'You believe in a moral world?' she asked lightly.

'If I can't believe in a moral world I'd rather bow out altogether.'

'Is it really so serious?'

'*You* don't think it's serious?'

'I just don't think life was meant to make sense. If you look for the big words, for morality, for meaning, for God, whatever you want to call it, you're just asking to get fucked.'

'You think God made a mess of it?'

'I don't presume to believe in airy-fairy stuff like God.' A radiant smile. 'But you know, I've always thought that *if* there were a God, he must have felt so ashamed of the balls-up he made of creation that after the sixth day he just backed off. People keep saying he rested on the seventh day. But if you ask me, he put his tail between his legs and ran like hell. Leaving it to us to salvage what we could.'

'You think it's all a big joke?'

'Not necessarily. But if you take it too seriously you just end up getting mangled by a windmill. Like you are right now.'

'Can you blame me for being bitter? It's not just that they took away my job, but I loved that place. I care for it, dammit.'

'You can still go to libraries.'

'As a reader, as a researcher. Not as someone who *belongs* there.' I smiled, even if it felt a bit strained. 'I suppose I'm a sentimentalist. The world doesn't have much patience with my kind.'

She pushed her chair back and got up. In her disarmingly spontaneous way she kissed me on the cheek. 'I must run. We'll talk about this again later.' Once again I had the impression that she was the grown-up, I the child.

We did talk about it again. It came up in the forest, on our walk this afternoon. We spoke randomly about many things on the way. Just beyond the clearing where we'd stopped and I'd briefly relished her closeness, the rhythm of her breathing, I remember quoting to her a line from Heidegger which has always struck a chord in me, 'When we go to the well, when we go through the forest, we are always already going through the word *well*, through the word *forest*.' She gave no direct answer. What she did was to pluck a eucalyptus leaf from a branch, and squash it in her hand, and press her fingers to my nose, and say, 'Here's the forest.' And then we went higher, to where the trees broke off and there was a view of Devil's Peak, rearing up a dark blue against the wintry sky, a few wisps of cloud drifting across the mountain face.

'You spoke about God abandoning the world the other day,' I reminded her. 'You thought he opted out because of the mess he'd made on the sixth day. But if that is so, then this is why: he spent so much time making everything, making it so beautiful – I mean, just look at that – that he simply had no resources left when he came to humanity.'

'You believe in God?'

'Certainly not,' I protested. 'He gave up on me when I was very small, so I gave up on him.'

'How did he give up?'

'I told you. He made me kill my mother. He gave me two brothers. He made a mess of my father. He put us on that farm.'

She put her arm through mine. 'Was it really such an awful place?'

I looked at her. God, those eyes. 'I don't mean it was ugly. There was something utterly and terribly beautiful about it. Everything was so endless, everything was so essential, nothing redundant at all. Every stone, every brittle stalk of grass, every tortoise, every thorn tree reduced to what was strictly necessary. It's just that we were too ill-equipped to deal with it. We didn't belong there. And I still don't belong.'

'These last two weeks,' she said, 'for the first time in years, I've had a sense that I belong somewhere. You and your house are good to me.'

Without premeditation or calculation we embraced. This time it was passionate. There was hunger, and assuagement, in holding her, feeling again − but now without restraint − the definition of her breasts against my chest, her hands on my shoulders, her lips and tongue exploring mine.

When it was over, she said, 'That was good.' Then, looking up, 'What's all this heavy breathing?'

'You must forgive an old man. It's not as if this sort of thing happens to me every day.' The memory, I found, was still disturbing. I'd been suppressing it for so long. 'The last time it happened,' I told her, 'I nearly had a heart attack.'

'How come?'

'I was with a girl. We made love. And then, suddenly, I had this terrible pain in my chest and a kind of tingling in my mouth. She got a fright and ran away. I had a blackout.' I stopped and shrugged. 'As it turned out it was only angina, but it gave me a hell of a shock.'

'Have you been seeing the girl since?'

I shook my head, for a moment too embarrassed to look her in the eye. 'She was from an agency. I'm sorry, I shouldn't have told you this. I'm just a dirty old man.'

'For God's sake, you were lonely.'

'You mean you don't blame me?'

'Why should I?'

'These hang-ups have come a long way with me. It's not easy to let them go just like that.'

'Let me take care of them.'

I held her in my arms again. This time it was less urgent, and less passionate, but in a way, I think, it reached more deeply into me.

# 4

AND THEN THE frontier itself. Crossed, not crossed? Nothing appears easy or straightforward any more. If last Saturday night was a limit, if we traversed it, the country on the other side was certainly different from anything I could have expected.

We went to Cavendish, she in a black polo-neck sweater and matching tights and a red-checkered mini-skirt, to the film she'd chosen for us. I remember very little of it, although I go very seldom, which means that something of the early magic of cinema – 'bioscope' in those days – is still unspoilt for me. In my childhood we hardly ever went. First, the farm was too far away and we were too poor. And by the time I reached high school, and was boarding in town, Pa came to fetch me home over weekends: he needed the extra pair of hands. I cannot recall seeing more than three or four films, all told, in those days. But already they were joined in my mind to the journeys of my reading, the dingy hall where they were shown became an extension of the library, a place of miracles. (Although, if I had to choose, I believe I'd still have opted for the books because the images on the screen left the mind less free to go off on travels of its own.) Later, at university, I went more regularly, but even then those evenings remained special occasions. The hush when the lights went out. The very advertisements had something out of the ordinary about them. Sometimes I went with a girl. Once my date had a dazzling white dress on. It was a particularly romantic film and we were both very much in love. I think it was her birthday. And when we came out she bore on her left breast the imprint of a chocolate hand. Somebody pointed, girls giggled. She burst into tears and ran back to the residence, and never spoke to me again. It was that kind of university. I was thinking of all that as I sat next to Tessa. During the advertisements I told her about my chocolate girl and she burst out laughing so loudly that people looked round at us. After that we were more contained. But I rested my hand on her thigh and she held it there, occasionally moving her fingers in between mine, and once or twice resting her head on my shoulder.

Afterwards we went to a pub in Observatory. I'd already made a reservation in Wynberg and told her so, but she pulled a face.

'We can go there next time,' she said. 'I've heard it's rather posh, isn't it? And I feel like just having a good time tonight. Let me take you to a place where I like to hang out. If that's OK with you?'

Of course, my heart sank a bit because I wasn't sure what her idea of a good time might be. Most likely at odds with mine. I'd always been wary of rowdy places, extroverted people, boisterous music; worst of all, places where there might be dancing, something I've never learned.

There was, thank God, no dancing, but the pub she'd chosen was a surreal place, whirling dizzily like a space capsule through a blue haze of smoke, brimming with people squashed together, some sitting, most standing, drinking, feverishly talking, with music pulsating through one's very bones.

'We'll never get in here,' I shouted above the din, rather hoping she'd give up.

'Come on.' She laughed. Light glinted on her teeth. She grasped my hand and ducked into the fray. I still don't know how she managed it, but somehow she found us two rickety plastic chairs in a corner, at a table already occupied by three other people. I nodded perfunctorily in their direction, but Tessa immediately struck up a conversation with the man wedged in next to her. He was Tony, an architect. Opposite him a film producer, Zach, with a fake American accent. And between them, Debbie, a willowy young woman clothed in little more than wild make-up and tangled blonde hair. I couldn't make out who she was with; and in the course of the evening she indiscriminately French-kissed both the men who flanked her.

'And I'm Tessa. And this is Ruben.'

'Hi, Tessa. How you doin', Ruben?'

Within ten minutes we knew about most of the projects Tony was working on or contemplating in the near future, Debbie's meteoric rise in the world of pop music and 'shows', Zach's recent dashes across the globe in search of deals and contracts; in exchange, Tessa dazzled them with a hilarious account of her recent ventures in publishing, show business, advertising, plucking each new item like a pigeon from a magician's hat and holding it up to their admiring view. Most of what she told them was wholly new to me. And her magazine did not even rate a mention. I was as spellbound as our tablemates. And it jolted me when the blonde-tressed nymph turned to ask, 'And what are you into, Ruben?'

'Ruben is from the world of books,' Tessa proffered before I could even think of a reply.

'A writer?' our three acquaintances chanted in unison. 'How great.'

'Ruben divides his time between writing and travelling,' said Tessa. 'He's been all over the world. Even to places which exist only in the mind.'

'I'll drink to that,' said the blonde, raising her glass and shaking her breasts at me. One of the nipples seemed to wink.

'We need something too,' said Tessa. 'I'm parched.'

'We'll never . . .' I began.

In a moment she was right on the table, waving towards the bar counter. As she raised her arms above her head her sweater pulled up, uncovering the seductive curve of her stomach, the end-of-quote apostrophe of her navel pierced by a thin golden ring with a small red stone. She was now cupping her hands round her mouth, shouting, 'Hey, George! Over here! Two beers.' Glancing down at me. 'That OK with you, Ruben?' And turning back towards the invisible George without waiting for my reply: 'And some eats.'

She came down to our level again.

'Cute navel,' said Zach.

'Thanks.' Tessa briefly flashed her belly at them once more. 'It's the only good thing my mother gave me.' She straightened her top and sat down. I didn't look at her.

'I met a girl in New York last week,' said Zach. 'She had her clit pierced.' He placed a hand on her shoulder. 'You're wasting your talents, my girl,' he said. 'You should be modelling or acting.'

'Want her to throw real pearls to fake swine?' asked Tony.

'Not my scene,' said Tessa smartly. 'I like the wheeling and dealing side of things.'

'Then speak to me, baby,' said Zach.

'I am speaking to you,' she said.

'Here's my card,' he said, playing it like an ace. 'Call me.'

'Right on,' she said, slipping it into her tiny, shiny bag.

'You'd better give me your number too,' he suggested.

'Sure.' She looked at him. 'Don't phone me at work, they're a suspicious lot.' She turned smartly to me. 'Give them our home number, Ruben. I haven't memorised it yet.'

Zach turned two narrowed eyes to me and scrutinised me very intently as if he hadn't really observed my species before.

I didn't feel like obliging at all. But I was out of my depth here and all I could do was stiffly to recite the number, which he jotted down with a fat fountain pen on the back of one of his own cards.

We were interrupted by the barman with our beers and two plates of what turned out to be chilli con carne, so hot it brought tears streaming down my cheeks. Tessa smiled and tweaked my ear, then dug into her own food with relish. No one else noticed my discomfort. And slowly, as the night wore on, as more beers were brought, I began to ease up, to let go, just sitting back to watch and listen as the noise, the insistent throbbing of the music, and the toing-and-froing of conversation at our table washed over me. I wasn't there, it didn't matter. I no longer felt resentful or insulted or excluded, nor jealous when I saw how freely and easily and beautifully she went with the flow of the others.

At some stage we moved elsewhere — not to people she knew, as I first thought, but to a young couple with a dog near the door. Why anyone should bring a dog to a place like that was beyond me. It was a nondescript little mutt, some eight inches long and most of it tail, and it lay quivering on the young woman's lap, blinking non-stop in the smoke. Tessa's radar had picked it up; and as on the mountain earlier that day she homed in on it, knelt at the table, took the wretched little creature in her arms and pressed her face into its hair. Unfailingly, her overture to the dog brought an introduction to its owners; once again, in an act of prestidigitation, chairs materialised and we joined people who only minutes before had been total strangers. He turned out to be a lecturer in Russian, she a visiting linguist from Finland. It was their first date and my impression was that they'd more or less exhausted their possibilities of conversation when Tessa descended on them; but she wonderfully rekindled their interest, not only in the two of us but in each other. Once again phone numbers were avidly exchanged before our ways finally parted.

'Straight to bed,' commented Tessa approvingly as she looked after them.

I was ready to do the same, but by now she'd recognised two friends through the thickening cloud of smoke – in those dingy conditions her sight seemed singularly unimpaired – and she insisted on joining them for a last drink. 'And a cigar,' she proposed.

The friends, and the acquaintances they had with them, turned out to be an unusual bunch. By that time I was too far gone to concentrate, but if my impressions were to be believed one was a magician, one a sculptor working only in smoke, another an artificial inseminator of cows. Which was which I found increasingly difficult to distinguish, and perhaps it didn't matter much. They'd probably invented themselves anyway, just as Tessa had reinvented us. This time she turned into a fashion photographer, I was introduced as a bookbinder specialising in erotica. My mind was in a daze, but the early feeling of being an outsider had by now completely dissipated – perhaps I was simply too exhausted to care any more – and I can only remember sitting back and benignly allowing the night to reel on as it chose.

It was ten to four when we finally staggered through the crowd, which was still partying vertiginously, and stopped for a while outside to brace ourselves against the sudden exhilarating cold. Which was, literally, a sobering experience. I was in a mellow, glowing mood. In the car, on our way back to Newlands, she drowsed with her head on my lap. I wondered whether I'd have to carry her over the threshold when we reached home; but she sat up in the garage, yawned and stretched, and smiled at me.

Yes, I thought, like Molly Bloom, yes, I thought, yes.

'I'm too tired to sleep,' she said limply when we came inside. As if by instinct she turned into the study.

The fire I'd made much earlier had died down, but its mild afterwarmth still lay in the room like a sleeping cat. As she sat down on the couch and languorously leaned back, I spent some time coaxing a semblance of new life back into the flames. When I got up again I thought she'd fallen asleep, but her eyes flickered open, gazing peacefully at me.

'Something to drink . . . ?' I asked.

'Just sit with me for a while.'

I sat down beside her. She gave a little sigh of contentment.

'Happy?' I asked.

'Very.'

'All those people,' I said. 'I've never seen anyone pick up strangers so effortlessly. You're like a dog with fleas. How do you do it?'

'People are fascinating,' she said with closed eyes.

'I think you *make* them so,' I said. 'You make yourself fascinating.'

'What do you mean?'

'Those stories you told them about yourself. Are they true?'

'I can no longer remember.' A little laugh. 'Does it matter?'

'You're a riddle to me.'

'Good.' Another impish smile and this time, briefly, her eyes opened. She put out a hand and touched my face. 'Thank you for taking me.'

'It's all your fault.'

'Did you like them?' she asked.

'Some.' I hesitated. 'I have my doubts about one or two. That Zach person, especially. I'm not sure it was a good idea to give him your number.'

'Don't break your head about that. He won't ever follow it up.'

'How can you be so sure?'

'He's the type.'

'For a little while I was jealous,' I confessed.

'No need for it.' Her hand moved across my cheek, pressed against my lips, dropped back.

'I'm not any more,' I assured her.

I can't remember what else was said; the words seemed slowly to dissolve into the half-dark of the room. I cannot even remember when I began to caress her. My hand on her face, following the contours of her forehead, her temples and cheeks, a finger tracing the outline of her lips, which she puckered in a small kiss. Then down along the vulnerable whiteness of her throat, over the curve of a shoulder, settling tentatively on a breast. Under the finely textured wool the nipple reacted. Again her eyes half-opened. She started to say something, but didn't. I moved both hands in under her sweater, pushed it up, bending over to kiss her navel. When I gently moved the top further up there was a moment of hesitation, but she seemed too lethargic to resist. She wasn't wearing a bra. I touched her nipples with my lips, conscious of my member stiffening as they rose to my caress.

As I prepared to bare the rest of her she laid a hand on one of my wrists.

'I'm not sure,' she whispered.

'May I look?'

The flicker of a smile. 'It's my secret.'

'Can I share it?'

'There's nothing unusual to see.'

But for me there was. She'd shaved her mound. It lent an exquisite vulnerability to the exposed sex, a convolution of petals tightly tucked in between the outer lobes.

Cupping my hand over it, I whispered, in thrall to the moment, 'The intricate and folded rose.'

Here I must interrupt myself again. NOTE ON TESSA'S SECRET. The only way to hold on to the memory now, so much later, is to find words for it. But how sadly inadequate, perhaps even shameful, this recourse to language to say what was then immediate to the view, to touch and taste. A confusion of syllables to replace the simplicity of a moment so intense it brought tears to my eyes.

Am I reduced then, as the old poem says, to a naming of parts? The secret of the moment was precisely what could *not* be named. Yet what did I have except words? Even in that very instant, as I bent over her, in the immediacy of discovery, I was already thinking, without wanting to, of the words by which I would recall it: *convolution*, *petals*, *lobes* . . . I was trying to reach for something different. *Sex* is so bland, so general and impersonal, so evasive. *Vagina* I've always found vaguely offensive, like calling a beautiful flower by its botanical name (even Johnny would agree with me here). Besides, I have moral objections to 'vagina' — a 'sheath', a 'scabbard' — as if there is an emptiness at the core of a woman's physical being which only comes into its own if it functions as the repository of a man's weapon. Several other terms I discarded as well, ranging from the offensive to the inane — obfuscating reality by comparing it to a small feline creature or the diminutive of a Spanish ventilator, or by resorting to synonyms for gashes, trenches, wounds. And *cunt*, for my generation, my disposition, has a connotation of shock, of scandal, although at least it offers neither euphemism nor avoidance. But it remains a word and words do interpose themselves between the world and us; they make us realise how, literally, 'out of touch' we are with the real. It is both their appeal and the despair they bring with them. They leave perhaps a dent on memory, but ultimately a secret remains a secret.

And so I said, 'The intricate and folded rose.'

And Tessa asked, 'What's that?'

'It's from a poem.'

'You have a quote for everything, don't you?' she said with what might be either amusement or light reproach.

I moved the open palm of my hand across the rounded shaven mound. How innocent it was to the touch. I leaned over to outline with the tip of my tongue the small fold of flesh that sheltered her clitoris. I felt her hips tauten as she responded to the caress.

And then, in a sudden movement, with no warning whatsoever, she quickly folded the red skirt down again and sat up.

'Please don't,' she said, and took my head against her breast.

'But why not?' I pleaded in confusion. Considering desperately, ludicrously, to propose a condom from my sock drawer.

'I just don't think we should.' She held my head against her for a long time. She was breathing deeply. My erection was still throbbing with furious insistence. There was a white noise in my ears.

'I don't know if you'll understand,' she said against my ear. 'I'm not sure I understand myself. But if we make love you'll just be another man. And I don't want you to be that. It's always the beginning of the end, it never lasts. And I can't bear to see that happen to us. Does that make any sense?'

'I don't think it does,' I said. But I was calmer now and the throbbing was beginning, very slowly, to subside. I took a deep breath. 'But if that is what you want, if that is the only way I can be with you, then so be it.' A kind of confused resignation remained. But it was not emptiness, not numbness; it wasn't that feeling of irredeemable age that had possessed me the previous time. It was, perhaps, concern; it was care. Care for *her*, this lovely stranger in my house who'd come from the night, like some dark moon, to invade my occluded life, to expose my vulnerability, to grant me no mercy, yet to show me a way to love.

I went with her to her room. On her doorstep I held her again, my hands cupped lightly on her breasts. This time there was nothing urgent about it.

'I wish I could sleep with you in my arms,' I said.

'I wouldn't trust myself with you tonight,' she said with a wry smile, and gave me a quick consoling kiss and went inside. The door clicked shut behind her.

That night I had a disquieting experience. The kind of visitation, I can imagine, which might have troubled an old desert hermit like St Anthony. I'm not sure whether it was a thought taking shape in my conscious mind, or a dream; but it had the feel of a story, something I was reading in a book. It was about myself, I was intensely involved in all of it, yet at the same time I had the old feeling of distance, as if with a cool and untroubled mind I was considering the merits of the story as a piece of writing. I saw myself ten or twenty years older than now, on the verge of decrepitude, in some old-age home; and then you come visiting, out of the blue, out of the radiant day outside, in the fullness of your beauty. You've heard I was living there now, you say, and have come to look me up. You kiss me, fondly but placidly, like some distant relative, and sit down opposite me and someone brings a tray. Coffee for you, rooibos for me. We speak for some time like two old friends, and discover, distressingly, that we have very little in common after these many years. But as you prepare to go, I say in my croaky old man's voice:

'There's something I must tell you. Something that has marked my life for ever. So much has happened since then, I've been going downhill all the time, there's no joy in growing so old, you know. But that one thing you did has made all the difference. I know I'm a sentimental old fool, but it has made life bearable and lit up my memories. Because of it, when I die, I'll be able to say, "It's all been worth while after all."'

'What on earth could that be?' you ask, that little frown between your eyes.

'It was that moment,' I say, 'when you lay on the couch in my study and allowed me to kiss your pussy.'

And you continue to gaze at me, the little frown still in place, and ask, 'Did I?'

It was past noon yesterday, Sunday, before I heard her moving about in the house – while Barenboim was playing 'Les Adieux' in the background, I'd been working on Saturday night's notes in my study, waiting, listening – and joined her in the kitchen. I knew I was bleary-eyed, but she was as radiant as a sunflower. I had no idea of what kind of reception to expect, and I was uneasy, self-conscious about my movements. The only way to deal with it, I decided as I sat down opposite her, was to go straight to it.

'About last night,' I said.

She stretched a hand across the table and touched mine. 'We had a fabulous time, didn't we? I have no regrets.'

'I don't know what came over me,' I said clumsily.

Her unreserved and generous laugh. 'You were a very normal human being.'

'It's no excuse.'

'Do you think I'm a tease?' she asked.

'No.' It was hard to find a way of saying it without sounding like an agony column for young single women. But I plunged in anyway. 'It is *your* body, Tessa; it is you who decide what to do with it, and when, and with whom.'

'Thanks, Daddy.' Her merry eyes.

'It's not funny!' I flared up. 'I'm just trying to understand.'

'It's not that I'm turned off by sex.' Her eyes became frank and clear. 'On the contrary. But I'm scared to risk it with you. I couldn't bear to lose what I have with you.'

'I've been thinking a lot about it last night,' I said. 'Perhaps I'm beginning to understand that part. But there's something you have to understand too.'

'And that is?'

'I can't pretend that I do not desire you. I'm prepared to try it the way you want to. Because what I feel for you I haven't felt for anyone in years. If ever. But it's not chaste and sexless and all-soul-no-body. You have made me discover my body and its needs again. Look, I promise you need never fear anything from me. But one thing you've got to know is that I cannot deny the fact of my body. Or of yours. Can you live with that?'

Her hand pressed mine. 'I'd hate it to be otherwise,' she said. She dropped her head. 'And the strange thing is that it's the same with me. I desire you too. But let's not go too deeply into that.' She looked up with what in the circumstances must have been a brave smile. 'Then it's a deal?'

'Here's my hand on it,' I said with playful solemnity. Suddenly it all seemed very lucid. Not simple, not by any means; but lucid.

# 5

THIS IS WHERE, as they say, the going gets tough. Because without
warning, and hardly allowing me any time to live up to our resolve,
only four days later, the Thursday evening, it all changed. There had
been signs, I suppose. But I ignored them. The phone calls. When
I answered, no one responded. I could hear the receiver being put
down at the other end. Wrong number, I assumed. Twice a man's
voice asking to speak to Tessa. I thought I recognised it, I could swear
it was that smooth film man, Zach; but he didn't give his name. Once
he declined to leave a message. The second time he said, 'That's OK,
I'll get her on her cell.'

'But she has no cell.'

The man merely laughed and rang off.

'Do you have a cellphone?' I asked her when I saw her again.

'Why?'

'Someone called today. Left no message but said he'd call you on
your cell number.'

'As it happens, I got one two days ago. Can't do without it in my
kind of job. Also, I don't want you to be disturbed all the time.'

'By the way,' I said, rather disingenuously, I'm afraid, 'has that man
– what's-his-name, Zach or something, the one we met in Obs and who
threatened to call you – has he ever got in touch with you again?'

She gave me a quick, quizzical look. 'Oh yes,' she said non-
committally, 'he called to say he had some prospects he'd like to
discuss. But I'm not sure I want to see him.'

'A smooth operator.'

'And very insistent.' Her smile. 'But I can handle him.'

And then, on the Thursday evening, someone came to pick her up. He didn't bother to come to the door, just hooted in the street outside.

'Bye, Ruben,' she called from the passage. 'I'm off.'

'Will you be late?'

'Don't know. It may go on for a while. Please don't wait up.'

I retired soon after eleven, but remained reading – or at least lying with a book against my drawn-up knees – for another hour or so until I heard her key in the front door. It was the sign to relax. But then, my hand already reaching for the bedside-light switch, I heard voices and tensed. I assumed someone was taking leave and waited for the door to be closed. It was done. But then I heard them coming past in the passage. A muted murmur of voices. A man's voice? Nothing wrong with that, I told myself. She'd obviously invited her friends – there might well be more than one – for a nightcap.

After a while I turned off the light and opened my bedroom door. The house was dark. They hadn't gone into the lounge. Once more I calmed myself. Why shouldn't she have guests? That was what she had two rooms for.

I closed my door again, but remained listening from the inside until my back was getting cramped from the bent position. It was ridiculous to stay there like that. I put on my gown and went to the kitchen to brew a cup of rooibos. Still I could hear nothing, not even after the hiss of the boiling kettle had subsided. Should I knock at her door, play the host, offer to make them coffee or whatever?

There was no light under her door.

The visitors – or the single visitor? – had probably left, unheard, while I'd been making my tea. I returned to my room without putting on the light, and looked through the window but could see nothing outside. Gone, I decided, relieved. Now go to sleep.

Half an hour later I got up and went to the front door, opened it as quietly as I could and went out on the stoep, down the steps to the front gate. There was a strange car parked in front of it. A large white BMW. I was aware of my heart fluttering.

Back to the stoep. There, on an inspiration, I decided to take a walk round the house. Make sure that everything was in order. Sensible precaution in these troubled times. I had to take care not to trip over roots or get entangled in shrubbery as I picked my way through the dark; there was only a thin sliver of a moon and a few street lights obscured by trees. Everything in the house was dark, her windows too. I stood below her bedroom, straining to listen. Unfortunately – or perhaps just as well? – there was no ladder near by.

And then a light in her bedroom went on. My heart skipped a beat. A small spot against the curtain. Her bedside lamp, most likely. Again the low murmur of voices? Impossible to make out. Most probably my imagination. Another light. Bathroom. It struck me that she might decide to go and boil a kettle in the kitchen, or even, for whatever reason, go to my study – in which case she would find the front door open. Breathless, cursing my own recklessness, I hurried back, tripping over stones that had once marked the borders of flowerbeds. But the passage was still dark. Chastened, but still with a thumping heart, I withdrew into my bedroom again. For God knows how long I kept vigil at the dark window, but nothing happened. It was from sheer tiredness that I finally passed out on the bed, still in my gown and slippers. A sleep of fits and starts. Only towards morning did I really doze off and when I woke up the visitor had left. I knew because I immediately went out to the front gate and found the BMW gone.

Tessa was in the kitchen, finishing her breakfast. I could hear Magrieta in the scullery.

'You're late,' said Tessa through the last mouthful of apple. 'Sleep well?'

'Not really. You?'

'Oh yes. Not enough, though. But that's par for the course, isn't it?' She pushed back her chair and picked up the lunchbox for her bergies. 'Got to run, you must excuse me.'

But I followed her to her room. As she opened the door she looked round with questioning eyes. 'Anything wrong, Ruben?'

'That,' I said, 'depends on you.'

'Meaning?'

'You came in very late.'

She tweaked my nose. 'No daddying, right? I thought we agreed on that.'

'I can't help worrying about you.'

'You can see for yourself I'm safe and sound.'

Careful now, I berated myself. But I couldn't help it. 'You had visitors?' I asked.

'My friend just came in to make sure I was safe.'

I looked straight at her. I could see how, slowly, defiance crept into her eyes.

'There was a car parked at the front gate all night,' I said.

She drew in her breath. Then said, with a suggestion of just-controlled anger. 'I didn't know you had ambitions to become a spy, Ruben.'

I felt my face flush. 'Tessa, I didn't mean to. I swear. But can't you see I *care* about you?'

Perhaps her anger seeped away; it was hard to tell. But she still sounded tense when she said, 'The other night . . . You said you respected my right to say no. Something like that, anyway.'

'I did.'

'But you don't accept that I have the right to say yes?'

'Even if you get hurt in the process?'

'Who the hell says I'm going to get hurt?'

'It's easy for a man to take advantage.'

'You ever heard of consenting adults, Ruben?'

'Please don't misunderstand me!'

'I don't think we should be having this conversation,' she said. 'If this is the way it's going to be every time you happen to think I'm with someone else, you'll make it impossible for me to stay here.'

'I don't want you to go.'

'Are you jealous?' she asked, a blow in the guts.

'Yes,' I said, just as straight.

She gave a small strained laugh. 'But we agreed that what there is between us can have nothing to do with having claims on each other, with possessiveness.'

'I can only say it's harder than I thought it would be.' I looked at her. I didn't want to pursue this, I knew it was outrageous, but I heard myself asking, 'You did make love last night?'

She appeared to hesitate, then returned my gaze and nodded.

I saw in my mind again what she had allowed me to see, only a few nights before. The memory brought back a sense of – yes, at my age I can say it – awe. But it also sharpened the edge of an almost uncontrollable jealousy.

'Was it Zach?' I asked.

To my surprise, she burst out laughing. 'Of course it wasn't! Ruben, I hardly know the man.'

A wave of illogical relief washed through me; illogical, because surely it could hardly make any difference to what had happened. Yet I was, unexpectedly, prepared for almost anything now.

'It was Alex,' she said easily. 'Brian's partner. I've known him for ages. We've been quite close.'

'So this was the man Brian accused you of fooling around with?'

'Sometimes things just happen, Ruben. I didn't plan it.'

(Had he brought a condom? I had to nip this line of thinking in the bud.)

I said what perhaps I should have said much earlier: 'Forgive me, Tessa.' I knew I was in dire need of forgiveness. And I took her hand and pressed a kiss to it.

She did a strange thing. (Why should I think anything 'strange' that has to do with her?) She said, 'Will it help if I tell you something?'

'It depends.'

She came to me and placed her hands on my shoulders. 'I want you to know that I haven't been as close to any other man as I was to you the other night. And another thing. I haven't had an orgasm with a man for more than four years.'

# 6

It is time I brought some order to the scattered jottings of the past few weeks. Not a day has passed without the urge in me to write, yet I have eschewed the moment of facing the notebook or the computer screen. It is too definite and definitive. Yet I cannot postpone it any longer and risk losing touch with it. (*Alison's mole.*)

When she went out on the first Saturday evening after our discussion about Alex, she didn't come back before mid-morning the following day. This time I managed to control my feelings. Over and over I told myself what I'd already told her. If I had any respect for her freedom it had to start by granting that I had no claim on her. What we shared was possible only if we could do so with no obligations and no expectations. It was hard – and made harder by being reminded by my own body how I desired her – to acknowledge that desire and then to free my desire from the humiliating urge to have and to hold. On the simplest level of all it was hard not to be worried that something might have befallen her, a worry – I told myself – I would have felt for any relative, any friend, in fact for Magrieta if on a given day she shouldn't turn up for work.

But I learned. Oh yes, I learned. And that interminable Saturday night was a step in the process. Even though I knew I had a very long way to go. Certainly, I did not foresee the high drama still in store for us, for me.

I did not run to the door when, halfway through the Sunday morning, I heard the car stop and the front gate squeak on its hinges. (Something else I must attend to. I've already had the roof fixed, but there is so much more to be done. The whole place needs a shake-up.) I did freeze behind my desk, feeling numbness creeping through my body. But I contained myself; I was not going to ask any questions.

She came into the study. She was alone. The whole of Handel's Hallelujah chorus exploded in my mind.

'Hi, Ruben,' she said.

'You're back.'

She came round the desk and kissed me. I held on to her, pressing my head against her to contain my emotion; I did not want her to know how upset I was. I'm sure she knew anyway, but there seemed to be an unspoken pact between us not to overstep a boundary we must both have sensed.

'I think you need some coffee,' I said, and got up.

'That'll be wonderful. And then a bath. And a long sleep.'

I took her elbows. 'Can we make an agreement?' I asked. 'I'm just as anxious as you are not to repeat what happened last time. I promise never to ask questions about where, or why, or who with, or whatever. And you need never feel under any obligation to tell me. But *if* there's anything, ever, you wish to talk about, then I'll be here for you.' Was I doing any better than Polonius?

'That's fair enough,' she said.

'Now go and run your bath. I'll bring the coffee.'

Her workroom door was open when I arrived with the tray; so was the door leading to the bedroom. There was a sound of running water from the bathroom and steam billowing from it. She obviously couldn't hear me when I called. I hovered on the doorstep between the two rooms, unsure of where to leave the tray. She had made a few changes, I noticed. I hadn't been there since that first night when her boxes and suitcases had cluttered the floor. Much of the stuff seemed still untouched: clothes and drapes and towels bulging from boxes or trailing across the floor, books in haphazard little piles topped with cushions or bric-à-brac. But the bed was covered with a multicoloured oriental spread, there was a large vase with dried sunflowers, a new set of curtains – too short for the window – had been hung, and there were a few pictures on the walls: in the workroom, prints of Rothko and Arcimboldo, a travel poster of Tibet; in the bedroom, another travel poster (a village in France), prints of Andy Warhol's Marilyn Monroe, an Egon Schiele a trifle too bold to my liking, a lavish Klimt, and a large softboard square to which clippings, cards and photographs had been pinned. Most of those must have been taken at parties or get-togethers with friends, of little interest to the outsider, although I found myself scrutinising all the male faces. Unexpectedly, among the social scenes, there was also a nude of a girl with long black hair flowing over her shoulders; it took me a minute to realise that it was Tessa. It made me feel like a voyeur, yet I couldn't turn away.

In the top right-hand corner of the board, old-fashioned and faded into grey, the face of a young man stared straight at the camera. There was something familiar about the eyes, perhaps the mouth, but I couldn't place it. Until she said behind me, 'Oh that's my father.'

I looked round. She was wrapped in a white towel which she clutched between her breasts.

'A woman appeared to me,' I declaimed.

'What is that supposed to mean?'

'It's Dante, from the *Divine Comedy*. When he first recognised Beatrice.'

'I'm in great company today.'

'It's still a good read. The Sayers translation. And at moments like this it comes in handy. By the way, I brought your coffee. And a double portion of love.'

She took the tray. 'You're a darling.'

'Now go and have your bath,' I ordered sternly, 'while I can still control my wayward flesh.'

The tone of light banter, I found, was the only way to manage what would otherwise become heavy, melodramatic, impossible to handle. Although it was severely put to the test in the weeks that followed. (It's already late August.) She didn't sleep out often; even more rare were the occasions when she brought someone home. We didn't discuss the particulars; but once or twice, usually late at night in the study when we were alone in the flickering half-light of the fire which I supposed inspired confidentiality, she did share some of her thoughts or concerns with me.

'Alex is going through a difficult time,' she would say. 'He just needs someone to unburden to.'

'He's not using you, is he?'

'Who can tell? He's fun to be with when he's not depressed.'

'Why should he be depressed?'

'He's not sure that he's in the right job. Deep down I think he's a frustrated writer. And his wife is a real bitch.'

'He's married?'

'Yes, haven't I told you?'

'That's a real complication.'

'Not necessarily. I mean, they've been sleeping in separate rooms for ages.'

'Says he?'

Her disarming smile. 'Says he. But we've got to take each other at face value, right?'

'I'm old-fashioned enough to hope for some integrity in love.'

'I read somewhere that love is only a symptom of a serotonin deficiency.'

'You think there's a chance a pill could cure you of Alex?'

She laughed. 'I'll just take my chances.'

'Aren't you playing with fire?' I asked in a gruff voice, 'This is your father speaking.'

'Playing with fire is nothing new to me. I've always been some-thing of a pyromaniac. When I was small I often set fire to things, especially my mother's. Books, papers, photos. Once a rather expensive dress.'

'What did she do?'

'Beat the shit out of me.'

'And then you stopped?'

'No. The next day I poured meths on her bed and set it alight. That nearly burnt the house down.'

'Didn't she kill you?'

'No. She handed me over to the current stepfather instead.'

'He beat you?'

'He knew how to handle me,' she said cryptically.

'Is there any chance you might set fire to this house?'

'Not unless you misbehave.' Her cat-eyes shining in the dark.

'And to Alex?'

'It depends.'

'If he hurts you?'

'He won't hurt me.'

'How can you be so sure?'

'Because I won't let him.'

'Isn't that easier said than done?'

'Oh I've learned to protect myself, don't worry.'

No, it wasn't easy to live with. And yet it settled into a kind of pattern, disturbed only rarely. I'm thinking of one Saturday morning in particular, after her guest had slept over again. Under the impression that he'd already left, I was on my way to the kitchen when I met the advertising man, Zach, in the passage.

'Hello there,' he said in mock joviality, his fake accent thick enough to slice.

The old jolt to the heart again; a feeling of nausea. But I tried to keep a straight face. 'Coming or going?' I asked.

'I came twice, now I'm going,' he said.

I didn't escort him to the door, but I did go out on the stoep when I heard him drive off outside. A dashing red Porsche. After a while I turned back and was about to go into my room when I became aware of her at the end of the passage, barefoot, so soundless that for a moment I thought she was a ghost.

For a while each waited for the other.

'I see you've met again after all,' I said with some effort.

'Rather unexpectedly.'

She remained where she was, wearing a short shift, her arms folded protectively over her chest. I came towards her. Did she back up slightly against the wall? I said nothing. She kept her eyes on me until I stopped in front of her. I still remained silent, for no reason except that I had nothing to say.

I went past her into the kitchen to turn on the kettle.

'I thought you were going to hit me,' she said behind me.

'Would that have helped?' I asked, my back still to her.

'You're angry with me.'

'Tessa.' I bowed my head, struggling against myself; then turned to face her. 'I told you long ago I'd never ask and never reproach you. You make your own decisions.'

'But you disapprove.'

'Do you *want* me to disapprove?'

She came to me. Suddenly she was in my arms. 'I couldn't bear it if you did.'

'Are you sure you're doing the right thing?'

'It's not a matter of being right or wrong. It was just . . . kind of inevitable, I suppose.'

'As long as you don't have to regret it.'

'He may be offering me a job if I decide to give up the magazine,' she said unexpectedly.

I could feel my face flush with indignation, but she stopped me.

'I promise you that sleeping with him had nothing to do with that. Nothing at all.' She stared fiercely at me. Why did I have the painful feeling that she was actually pleading with me? But she said nothing more. In silence she walked over to a cupboard, took out the ground coffee, tipped some into the filter of the percolator and brought it to the kettle.

As she stood with her back to me, keeping an eye on the kettle, she said, 'Actually it was pure curiosity. There's been this kind of electricity between us right from the start. I wanted to find out whether there was anything in it.'

'And was there?'

She shrugged non-committally. For a while she continued to busy herself with the coffee things, retrieving mugs from the dresser, milk from the fridge, warming it in the microwave. There was a kind of mock domesticity about it. But the silence wasn't altogether reassuring. And without wishing to I remembered what I'd kept stowed out of reach for years now: those devastating silences in my marriage with Riana. When for days on end she wouldn't speak. But

I angrily stifled the incipient thought. It had been a happy marriage. It *had*. For God's sake.

When at last she poured the coffee I tried gently to nudge the conversation back on track. 'So no regrets?'

She smiled across the mug. 'Actually it was better than I'd expected.'

She probably hadn't meant to be provocative at all, but I couldn't help feeling stung. 'The long-awaited orgasm?' I asked accusingly.

She didn't answer immediately. Then she said quietly, 'Not quite. But very nearly.'

It must have been four, five days later — certainly less than a week — that the Porsche was back at the front gate. Had it been anyone else, I might have resigned myself to what surely was inevitable; but Zach was more than I could bear. And although I knew, with absolute certainty, that there was no deliberate provocation from Tessa's side, the thought of that man in my house drove me to distraction. I tried to persuade myself that it was she I was concerned about, but ultimately I knew it was my own sense of self. Nothing to be proud about. But after so many humiliations this was no longer much of a consideration anyway.

I made my usual nocturnal rounds about the house, inside and out; I explored every nook and hideout in the garden. Just before two o'clock, in my gown and slippers, I ambled all the way up to Newlands Avenue. (If I were to have a heart attack right here in the road, I thought to my almost perverse satisfaction, no one would even bother to stop.) The night dragged on, interminable. Perhaps the low-life bastard was trying to improve on his past performance. *Actually it was better than I'd expected.*

It was when I came back at my front gate (still sagging on its hinges) and let fly with a furious but wholly futile kick at one of the front wheels of the Porsche that the idea struck me. An outrageous and criminal idea, but by that time I couldn't care less. Leaving my slippers at the front door to minimise the noise, I stole barefoot to the kitchen and drew the largest carving knife I could find from the drawer. In the passage I stopped to listen for sounds, but it was deadly silent except for the din of the blood in my ears. Not even the sound of springs. *Built to last*: God damn the maker of such beds.

At the front gate I waited for what must have been ten minutes to make quite sure there was no one on the prowl. (Johnny MacFarlane's murderer was still abroad – what was his name? Vuyisile something, Vuyisile Mthembu – and might, with my kind of luck, choose this night to return to the site of his crime. Well, I was ready with my knife. But, of course, so had Johnny been.) Once a shadow flitting across the street made me catch my breath. But it was only a cat. 'Tis now the very witching time of night when churchyards yawn and hell itself breathes out contagion to the world.

Glancing back for one last time – there was a rustling in the trees: perhaps Antje of Bengal breathing down my back? – I huddled down at the nearest wheel and made a stab at the tyre. The knife bounced back. Clenching my teeth in rage I lunged forward again, with the same result. I went to one of the rear wheels. It made, of course, no difference. How on earth did the culprits that so regularly make the newspapers go about slashing tyres?

Another stab; another mortifying failure.

I skulked back into the house, down the passage. This time there came a sound from the back part of the house. I stopped. If that Zach were now to materialise in the dark passage before me, I swore to God, I'd castrate him. But the sound was not repeated. Perhaps it was Tessa, calling out something in her sleep; or her long-awaited orgasm.

In the dining room I poured myself a tumbler full of whisky and tossed it back in a few large gulps. Leaving it brazenly on the polished table (if Magrieta dared to complain about a ring on the wood, I resolved, I'd blame the visitor), I repaired to my study and slumped down behind the desk. I felt like crying with disappointment. There was little rage left in me, only bottomless humiliation. A cat came to settle on my lap. Amadeus. I stroked him absently, feeling the futility weighing on me like the night itself. I rose to put on a record, but this was not the time for it. From the far side of the desk I turned back and surveyed the senseless spread of papers and books and objects. I picked up a paperweight and put it down again. Then my hand found

Pa's old pocket knife and suddenly I felt my fingers bearing down on the cool, indifferent metal. The blades worn to thin slivers of steel. The corkscrew. The broken screwdriver. And then the peg he'd used on the horses' hooves; once, I remembered, he'd stabbed a wounded blesbok to death with it. Just where the skull joined the vertebrae of the neck.

The anger flooded back, but this time mixed with pure elation. This was it.

I returned to the front door and went out on the stoep, down the garden path. The cool knife was slowly assuming the warmth of my body. There was an uncanny luminosity in the moonless night. I looked down at the dark spike protruding from my hand. Is this a dagger which I see before me? This, my friend Zach, is a knell that summons thee to heaven or to hell.

I was shocked by the loud hiss whooshing from the tyre the moment the peg stabbed through the reinforced rubber wall. It sounded like an old engine letting out steam. I scuttled back to hide among the nearest shrubs in the garden. Surely this would wake the whole street. But nothing happened. And I was too possessed to care much. I'd finish this job if the whole police force were to converge on me now, sirens blaring. Within a minute or two I was back at the Porsche. One, two, three more furious stabs. This will change the course of history. And each time the peg penetrated – this was becoming wholly surreal – I thought: This is for you, Pa. No one is going to shit on an Olivier again.

At last it was done. Came four times, now I'm going. Without waiting for the last sibilant emission to subside I ran back to the house, drew the front door shut, wiped the knife on my gown – one more stain would only add glory to the rest – meticulously replaced it on the desk and returned to my bedroom. I felt extraordinarily calm.

I slept more soundly than I had in months. Yes, I did wake up from the commotion in the house in the morning, as doors were opened and closed and opened once again, and footsteps scurried to and fro between the house and the front gate, and voices spoke on the phone in the passage; and afterwards Magrieta arrived to add to the pandemonium, until much later several car doors slammed outside in the street. (That was the only time when a brief flush of fear moved through me; but when I went to peep through the window I saw only men in overalls, presumably from a garage; no police. So I returned, unperturbed, to my bed.) But then I actually dropped off to sleep again and woke up when it was almost time for lunch.

Magrieta relayed the whole event to me in a great show of theatrical flair. But no one else, certainly not Tessa, has referred to it again.

Afterwards – yes, I freely admit it – I felt ashamed. Deeply ashamed of having being so utterly childish. But I did not feel sorry. If anything, I think of it as something of an achievement. It did not solve anything; I cannot say that life is any easier. But the simple knowledge of knowing that I was capable of doing such a thing gives me a sneaky glow of satisfaction.

# 7

THERE HAVE BEEN difficult moments on other fronts too, this past month. They involved Magrieta. I've been neglecting her. Not just in the house, but in writing her into this account. Her relationship with Tessa remains unresolved. Where it concerns 'woman things', as Magrieta curtly informed me when I dared to enquire, they get along very well; and Antje of Bengal contributes to it. I've often overheard them discussing her – not as a spectre, a figment from the past, but as another woman in the house. What annoys me is the way they exclude me. As a man, but even more significantly as someone operating on a different level, from which the access to theirs is barred: here I am, they make me feel, with a ghost in my own house, yet the only way in which I can gain access to her is vicariously, through books, through the notes I've made over the years based on journeys of exploration through the libraries, the Archives, even the old books of the Groote Kerk. (That was where I'd chanced upon the *Memorie* of the Reverend Le Boucq on his last confessional session with Willem Mostert; subsequently I'd put young Dugmore on to it, and then of course he put it in his book.) They have shown interest in the 'book story', Magrieta's term, and Tessa even read the Dugmore article; but their real involvement in Antje comes from Magrieta's personal encounters with the ghost woman, and from the few occasions Tessa herself has sensed, however fleetingly, Antje's presence on her soundless way through the house.

But these are also the events that trouble Magrieta's relationship with Tessa. If she is relieved to see me out of danger, as she believes, the 'doings' (her word again) between an unmarried girl and men who come and go in the night are not acceptable to her devout Christian scruples. In the beginning I tried, with Tessa's blessing, to present Alex as her ex-fiancé who was trying to make up; and this placated Magrieta to some extent. It wasn't quite as good as matrimony, but at least it signalled moral intent. But when Zach entered the picture most of the devils in hell were let loose. What intrigued me was that it began just after Zach's first visit, even before the commotion about the slashed tyres. And since at that stage Magrieta had not even set eyes on the new lover, I was mystified when she cornered me in the study.

'So that one got a new man to sleep over.'

'How can you say that? I'm sure it was just her fiancé.'

'Meneer can talk until Meneer is blue in the face, I tell you it was another man.'

'How do you know that?'

'A man smells,' she said firmly. 'En no two men smell the same.'

'Now come on, Magrieta, you don't expect me to believe that.'

'Why is Meneer trying to come up for her? What is she to you?'

'She's like a daughter to me.'

'There's daughters en daughters. Meneer can ask me, I know.'

'I'm telling you it's all in your head, Magrieta.'

That was when she squared up to me, arms on her formidable hips. 'Is Meneer now trying to tell me that Antje is a liar?'

'What has Antje got to do with it?'

'She tole me. She sees everything that happen in this house.' I couldn't stop a chill from rippling down my spine. 'En it was Antje who tole me that one's doing things with two menfolk.' A weighty pause. 'She also tole me that not one of them is her fiancé. So.'

'Will you take a ghost's word over Tessa's?'

'I take the word of a woman who knows what it is to be sucked out by a man like a orange en then throwed away. Because she was a slave en because she was coloured en because she was a woman they all treated her like shit. I can't let that happen in her house.'

I changed my tack. 'If that is what is happening – and mind you, we can't be sure – then Tessa should be helped, not condemned. Today's young people are not like you and me.'

'Right en wrong is still right en wrong, Meneer.'

'Jesus said a sinner must be forgiven seventy times seven.'

This time, I knew, I'd won. But Magrieta was beginning to brood on it; and I knew her well enough to expect dire times ahead. The *casus belli* was Tessa's family of bergies. We'd never met them before and all we knew about them was that they continued to receive their generous daily bread from Magrieta's kitchen. It had settled into an easy routine that bothered no one. Until, a few days after my nocturnal onslaught on the Porsche, I arrived home from the library early one afternoon to find five or six strangers round the kitchen table gorging themselves from a huge bowl of macaroni with the fervour of a colony of silk worms on a mulberry leaf. The kitchen was rank with their smells.

I stopped in consternation. No one paid the slightest attention to me, not even when I spilled some of the books I'd brought home on the floor. Flabbergasted, I just stared, not sure whether I should retreat, attack or phone the police. What paralysed me was a feeling of panic at being invaded, as if, suddenly, the whole unruly world out there had taken over my intact space in here. It was no longer my home. I had no control over it. They were simply here as if they belonged here; if anything, *I* was the intruder. And it was terrifying. While I was still aiming this way and that Tessa came down the passage.

'Hi, Ruben,' she said blithely. From the door she pointed at the three dishevelled strangers at the far side of the table: 'Those are Ruiter, Terrie and Salmiena. They're the family I take food to in the mornings. Now an uncle has died and these relatives have come over from Worcester for the funeral and they haven't had anything to eat since yesterday. So I brought them home. They'll be off again in five minutes.'

'Where's Magrieta?' I asked.

'I don't know.' I didn't trust the innocent look on her face.

The five minutes she had promised stretched to rather more than an hour before the visitors left, leaving behind a smell of methylated spirits and a nauseous variety of more human and more obnoxious odours. Tessa accompanied them to the front gate. Even before she returned Magrieta erupted from one of the back rooms, where she must have ensconced herself to sulk. She threw open windows and

doors and started spraying insecticide in such quantities that I broke
into a fit of coughing.

'What's going on?' asked Tessa from the door.

'Miss Tessa want to know what's going on!' Magrieta exploded.
'Bringing that blerry bunch of skollies in here to stink us all the
way to hell! En before we know where we are they carry off the
whole house.'

'They're not skollies, Magrieta,' said Tessa in a soothing voice.
'They're just poor people who haven't eaten all day.'

'This is not a soup kitchen,' said Magrieta. 'Is Meneer not saying
anything?'

I cleared my throat. 'Yes, I'm afraid this wasn't such a good idea,
Tessa,' I said.

She looked at me in surprise. 'You disapprove?'

'I do. Not because you gave them food, but that you brought them
home. We really cannot have that. You may know some of them, but
what about the others?'

'Before we know where we are the whole of the Cape Flats will
be begging at the door,' interposed Magrieta. 'En one morning when
we open our eyes we'll all be murdered in our beds like that poor
Mr MacFarlane.'

'Now that's ridiculous!' exclaimed Tessa, flushed with indignation.

'Not entirely,' I stopped her. 'These days one really cannot take
such risks.'

'They're friends!' she protested.

'Half of them you don't even know, Tessa,' I pointed out as
reasonably as I could. 'The rest get food from you every day. Which
is fine by Magrieta and me. But I hardly think you can call them your
friends.'

'I just can't bear people to be lost and lonely,' she said, subdued.

There was a pause. Her face was still flushed, but after a while
she nodded with an expression of resignation. 'All right then, I'll tell
them tomorrow.'

'Miss Tessa think it will all be fine, jus' like that?' sneered Magrieta.
'You wait en see.'

And I'm afraid she was proved right. For a week after that, at the most unexpected moments, even in the evening, strangers would now turn up at the front door and ask for money, allegedly to buy food. If Magrieta opened she promptly turned them away. Once or twice I relented and offered them bread or fruit or whatever until Magrieta caught me red-handed one afternoon. She said nothing, but she took me by the arm to the study and pushed me towards the window. 'Look!' she said. And sure enough, as the beggar reached the front gate he disdainfully flung the bread I'd just given him into the street; then looked back at the house over his shoulder, raised one leg, clasped the seat of his tattered pants and uttered a loud farting sound through blubbering lips. I wanted to believe that it was an exception; but I no longer dared to go against Magrieta's furious injunctions.

As suddenly as it had begun the influx stopped. When I asked Magrieta about it she feigned innocence. But in the end she admitted, 'It's our Antje.'

'How did Antje get involved?'

'I know these people, Meneer,' she said. 'They'll jus' go on pestering us until something bad happen. So I tole them they better be careful, we got a headless woman in the house. They just laughed at me en shouted ungodly things at me. So then I asked Antje to help en the next time they knocked I sent Antje to the door. Carrying her head under her arm.' She couldn't stop the grin. 'They won't bother us again, Meneer.'

A semblance of peace and order returned to our lives. But only on the surface. The image of that alien gang in the kitchen would never completely dissipate in my mind. My home had been invaded; it could happen again, at any moment, in any of a thousand unimaginable ways. The *thought* would remain and it would haunt me.

And of course, even on the level of practicalities, what had happened didn't improve relations between the two women. In fact, on the day after the incursion of the famished visitors, Magrieta announced that she was no longer going to clean Tessa's rooms. A mutual agreement, Tessa assured me when I asked her; but Magrieta evaded the question, mumbling something about 'a person's got her pride'.

\* \* \*

But in a way Tessa has been the least of Magrieta's concerns. I became aware of it soon after my criminal action on Zach's car. During the preceding week relations between the two of us had been particularly good, aided no doubt by the new interest I'd begun to take in the house. First there had been the roofer to replace the tiles Tessa had discarded as useless on her first reconnaissance. Then I'd called in a plumber to fix two leaking toilets and fit a new washer to the kitchen tap, which Magrieta had been complaining about for months. I even summoned a chimney sweep, as I'd noticed during our evenings by the fire that lumps or clouds of soot would come hurtling down at unexpected moments; and I also wanted to make sure that the chimney in Tessa's room was in good working order. In the garden I'd had a tree removed which had begun to incline at such an angle that any day now it might come down and destroy the boundary wall. I'd also arranged for a gardening service to pay us a weekly visit; mindful of what had happened to Johnny MacFarlane I was wary of hiring a gardener off the street.

Magrieta had taken due note of these actions, which she acknowledged with a number of very generous lunches and, when she was in particularly good spirits, even a special dish for my and Tessa's supper.

But on this Friday morning in early August it was clear from the outset that something was wrong. She came in late, almost two hours after her usual time; and Tessa had slept out, so I suffered from a double anxiety and there was no one to share it with. This was quite foreign to Magrieta's ways. I don't think she's been late more than, say, ten or twelve times in the thirty-eight years I've known her. When I heard the key in the door I hurried down the passage, not yet sure which of the two it would be the greater relief to meet. It was Magrieta.

She came in without attempting to greet me, her large bulk waddling right past me, practically shouldering me out of the way. I followed her.

'Magrieta, are you all right?' I asked in the kitchen. She dumped her voluminous black bag on the table, took off her heavy red overcoat, vigorously shook the rain from her umbrella (this, too, was something she would normally never do inside), retrieved her housecoat from behind the door and started buttoning it up. She kicked off her shoes, rubbed her feet, which were riddled with corns and bunions, and pushed them into the shapeless slippers with their large, obscenely pink pompoms which stood waiting next to the dustbin behind the door. The whole kitchen was dark with the blackness of her mood.

'What's happened, Magrieta?'

She turned to face me. 'They going to kill me,' she said.

'Now come on, it can't be so bad.'

'They going to murder me dead.'

'Who?'

'Those skollies.'

'I'm worried about you, Magrieta,' I said, trying to mollify her. 'Please tell me.'

It turned out to be much worse than I'd expected.

Magrieta had been in the small lounge of her house the previous night, entertaining visitors – her niece Violet and the young woman's husband – when there was a commotion outside. Her township can be quite rowdy, she often complains about it ('especially now they got those black people also moving in en squatting en disturbing the peace'); but this was clearly out of the ordinary. Knowing from experience to be prudent, she quickly turned off all the lights in the house and the three of them watched through the window as a bunch of young kids armed with pick handles, hatchets, spades, kieries and knives set upon a young black woman. They'd already torn all her clothes from her body and she was streaked with blood, all the while screaming for help. There was light in the windows of the house directly across the dirt track ('Meneer will understand now why I switched my lights off'). The woman ran to it and started hammering on the door, screaming like a stuck pig. Someone opened. The young woman fell into the house. Outside the attacking boys were baying for her blood. Then the door was opened again and the occupants bundled the woman out. 'You can't blame them,' explained Magrieta when I tried to protest. 'If they catch you with a witch they burn down your house en everybody in it.'

'What's this nonsense about a witch?' I asked.

'That's what they kept shouting, Meneer, all the time, all the time. They said she put doepa in a old man's food and killed him.'

'Food poisoning?'

'No, he was run over by a car.'

'But Magrieta . . .'

'En they said there was another girl who tried to take away this woman's lover-man, so she killed the girl. Also with doepa, which made the girl mad so she jumped from a roof.'

'But you can't take such things seriously.'

'Witches is serious,' she said curtly. 'I'm not saying it's true en I'm not saying it's not true. All I'm saying is that these kids said she was a witch, so they got to kill her.' She took a crumpled handkerchief from the ample front of her dress and blew her nose. 'En they killed her right there in front of my door, en they cut off her head to go en burn it.'

'You saw it all?'

'With these two eyes, Meneer. There's mos a street light right there on the corner. I can see everything that happens. But it's not like I *wanted* to see.'

'What about the police? Didn't anybody try to call them?'

'You think we all want to get killed?' Her bosom heaved like an ocean swell. 'En that's jus' the beginning, Meneer.'

'Did it get worse?'

It seems that as the butchering was going on the victim's lover, alerted by persons unknown, had arrived on the scene and tried to intervene. He pleaded with the kids, said he could prove she was innocent. But they were in such a state — 'like they showed on the TV, Meneer, a pack of wild dogs' — that they turned on him too.

That was when Magrieta's niece decided to send her husband Michael out for help. He's a teacher from Bonteheuwel. It would be too risky to call the police; but at least he might try to get an ambulance, some paramedics, before the slaughter became a massacre. (That was while the woman outside was still showing feeble signs of life.) Magrieta tried to hold him back, but he broke free and slipped through the door while the attention of the crowd was focused on the 'witch'.

The problem was that the teacher couldn't find a single telephone in working order in the whole of Mandalay. Everything had been smashed in the gang wars raging through the Flats over the last God-knows-how-many months. It took him two hours to find a phone — and that was in a police station.

'He promised us he didn't tell the pollies. He jus' used the phone.' But the police came anyway, dropped him off a few blocks from Magrieta's place so that he could scamper back on foot, and then they went to investigate. By that time there were two dead bodies in the street, one headless, both hacked to pieces. The perpetrators had long gone, but here and there in the dark a few of them were still lurking, like scavengers, to keep watch. Two of them spotted the teacher knocking at Magrieta's door and being let in. They started shouting like lunatics, immediately linking him to the police and threatening dire revenge.

'We didn't close an eye all night,' said Magrieta. 'The sun was already up before Violet en Michael could leave. Their car was parked at the garage, six blocks away, as they always do.' She shook her head. 'But my house is now a marked place, Meneer. Those kids will be coming back, I know them.'

'You can move in here. At least for the time being.'

'En leave my house to the skollies?'

'Your life is worth more.'

'All my life I been waiting for that place of my own.'

'Please, Magrieta. Let us sit it out. The police will arrest the murderers. In a week or two everything will be calm again.'

'That pollies?' She snorted in disgust. 'They all crawled up the gangsters' arseholes. En even if it wasn't, I know I won't see my house again.'

'You're in a state of shock. Everything looks worse than it is.'

'I know what I'm talking about,' she insisted.

'My God, Magrieta!' I groped for words, but couldn't find any.

She took a cue from my expression of despair. 'We can pray, Meneer,' she said. 'The Lord goes with us all the way to the valley of death. But there's one place he won't go en that is out there on the Flats. When the white people dumped us there all those years ago they made that place hell. En God won't set his foot down in hell. He's jus' too scared. En you can't blame him either.'

I made Magrieta some coffee. Under normal circumstances this wasn't something she would permit, and the fact that on this Friday morning she had no objection – she gave no sign of even being aware of it – confirmed the extent of her distress. I honestly didn't know what to do. Worse than anything else, I think, was the sense of the distance that separated us. There was only a kitchen table between us, but we might have been creatures from different worlds who just happened by the purest coincidence to be sharing the same space. She, the large mother from the townships, in her shapeless housecoat and her slippers with the pink pompoms, harbouring somewhere inside her global body the violence and the rage, the raping and killing and burning of her everyday world, its poverty, its meekness and patience and suffering, its anger and rebellion and despair, its affirmations and denials, its witches and witch-hunts; in her ears still the shouting of a lynching mob, the screams of a victim; on her retinas the imprint of a hacked-off head; in her nostrils a smell of smoke and blood. I, secluded among books and music and cats, disturbed at most by images of unrequited lust, my concern a leaking tap, a squeaking gate, a girl not yet returned from her night abroad. How could I ever reach out from my world to touch hers? No way, no way at all. And yet, in my own street, barely three months ago, a man was murdered. I'd passed his broken body on the way and had not lent a hand. But it was only when I read about it in the newspapers afterwards that it penetrated. Now I had the disturbing sense of that world out there, that other world, coming closer. First the invasion of the bergies, now this. My own space was shrinking, retracting from its early easy frontiers. And here we were now, fixed in this space like two flies trapped on the same sticky strip.

I looked at her. I tried to read the lines of her face. What did I know of this woman who'd shared my life for almost forty years? What did I know of her world? She was as unreal to me as any ghost. I reached out and put my hand on hers; it was cold. She looked back at me, but if her eyes conveyed anything it was commiseration. But how could she feel sorry for *me*?

'I'll take you home in the car,' I said at last. 'You can go and pack a few things, and afterwards I'll bring you back here. You can move into the empty room next to Tessa's.'

'Miss Tessa didn't come home last night.'

'How do you know that?'

'I can mos feel the place is empty. It was not slept in.'

'That's neither here nor there.' I was annoyed at her easy way of reaching past all my defences. 'Come now, we must go.'

She didn't budge from her chair. 'You not taking me to that place.'

'We have to fetch your things.'

'If they must be fetched I'll fetch them. It is not safe for Meneer to go.'

'Magrieta, I've taken you home many times. It's not like the old days any more.'

'Some days it is safe, not today. What do you think they will do if they see a white man bring me home? After last night?'

'But what are you going to do?'

'I was thinking a lot on my way in the bus here. First I'm going to the Slams to get something. There's doepa he can bury at my door so they won't burn my place. I don't know if it will work, but I can try. Then I'll bring my things here in a taxi. But first I must wash the dishes and clean up.'

'I can do the housework.'

'You go to your study.'

I stood up, chastened, then looked at her as if for help. 'Magrieta, what is happening to us?'

'We getting old, Meneer. That's all.'

I went to my study. It was almost noon before she was ready to leave. I phoned a taxi and gave her money for the fare there and back. But how inadequate, how useless it all felt. My mind was in turmoil. There was no point in going back to my work, such as it was. More and more I was numbed by the futility of it, this everlasting collection of material for articles I'll never write. An end in itself, a dead end, a chasing of footnotes to little treatises composed in my head, on this and that. That might be my epitaph one day. *He died chasing a footnote.* Yet how could I not do it? What would happen to me without my comforting blanket of notes? And even as I was thinking it, I already knew the thought would make no difference. I would still go on. When the next cold front moved in I'd reach for the threadbare blanket.

NOTE ON OLD AGE. When I think of death I think: acquiescence. I think: space. I have no fear of it. Or very little. I certainly have no fear of what comes after. Why should it concern me if ever since my childhood the real itself has been unreal? Those plains without end, those limestone ridges emerging from the hard earth after running underground for God alone knows how far, those outcrops of rock still smouldering from the heat down below, those skies with all colour bleached from them, yet at sunset gaudily streaked with red like the slaughtering slab in the backyard after a sheep or a goat had been killed. What mattered to me were Outa Hans's stories, the imaginings of little long-ago men painted on the hollow cliff, the travels of Gulliver or Don Quixote. These it would be sad to give up. But I've had them for long enough and I bear no grudge against the idea of leaving them behind. What upsets me is not death, but dying, the getting there. The indignities and ignominies of being betrayed by the senses and the functions of the body, the dependency on others (already I've taken the first step, giving in to my children). The aches and pains. The problem is they creep up on one so unnoticed. A stiff back in the morning, a momentary dizziness, a flickering in the memory; the virile jet of piss reduced to a dribble, a dull ache in the eyes after a long bout of reading, some loss of appetite, less need of sleep. The little, little things, almost unnoticed in themselves. Until one day you're there. Sans teeth, sans eyes, sans taste, sans everything. And all the preparations: after the angina attack, all the cleaning up, throwing away useless old files and papers and journals, even books, planning for disability and death, going into town to see lawyers, accountants, insurance people. Now it's nearly done. Except for the emotional drain. I'm much better at planning for death than at planning my life. So be it. Yet it's ridiculous. For God's sake, I'm not old. I'm sixty-five. Johnny MacFarlane, a great booster of confidence, once told me his father had given up tennis at sixty to take up bowls; but at seventy-five it started boring him so much he reverted to tennis. Only the other day the conductor Simon Rattle insisted that, 'Conductors only start to get competent at sixty.' Was it Clemenceau who, passing a young beauty in the street at seventy or thereabouts, exclaimed, 'Oh to be sixty again?' And Charlie Chaplin became a father again at ninety-something. My own grandfather was thrown by his horse at a hundred and two. Life in the old dog yet. But that's no comfort. The decay has begun. *Dying is born with me*, wrote the old Dutch poet Jacob Maerlant in the Middle Ages. My body has not really let me down yet. Except that once. But I'm old inside. *We're getting old, Meneer, that's all*. You're as old, they say, as you feel; in which case I may be verging on a hundred and thirty-two. I am older than my father was when he died. I'm older, my God, than Don Quixote.

I thought, when Tessa first moved in, she would rejuvenate me. Old goats and nibblesome leaves. Not so. It ages you faster. No diminution in desire, there's the rub. It's as fierce — much fiercer — than before; because there's less time to waste perhaps. And less occasion for relief, let alone satisfaction. What will it be, lovely? — a pelvic or a full house this time? Satisfaction guaranteed. And then I went and died on the poor girl. Or practically. Now I cannot even risk phoning the agency again, too dicey for all concerned. Intimations of mortality. Tessa, Tessa.

# 8

ON ANOTHER DAY I would not have done it. I might not have become inured to Tessa's nights out, as little as to her occasional guest staying over; but at least I'd made my peace with it, particularly after the brief satisfaction provided by my childish revenge on the Porsche. But on that Friday morning, after the upheaval caused by Magrieta's drama, the house could not contain me. I had to talk to someone. In the old days I could have gone over to Johnny MacFarlane's. He always had good intuition in such matters. A clear head. Tessa? I'd never made a note of her cellphone number. I had the number of the magazine written in my pocket diary long ago – that first time I'd procured the address from Telkom to drive past the place, just to acquaint myself. Now I dialled it. Only to put the phone down again just as it started to ring. This was not on, as she might say. I shouldn't invade her space. I took a stroll through the garden – coming on nicely, getting tidied up – watched a squirrel rippling across a path, went round the house to inspect the cracks in the boundary wall, then decided to brew a cup of tea. But I left the kettle boiling to return to the phone. This was not invading her space, it was an emergency. I had to talk to her about Magrieta. And find out whether she was safe after her night out. My love, my love. I remembered how she'd looked, leaving the house the night before: her navy-blue calf-length dress, buttoned up to a high collar, long narrow sleeves, some kind of jersey cloth, clinging to her, flaring gracefully around her legs. A classy look. A lithe and long-limbed lovely look. Nothing like alliteration when you're in love.

'Hi there, this is *Woman*. What can I do for you?'

'I'd like to speak to Tessa Butler.'

'Tessa Butler?'

'Please. I believe she's in publicity.'

'You sure you got the right number?'

'Absolutely.'

'Is she a temp perhaps?'

'No, no, she's been there for a couple of months now.'

A pause. 'I'm sorry, sir, but we don't have a Tessa Butler.'

'Are you quite sure?'

'Look, I just . . .'

I put the receiver down.

Perhaps she'd given instructions not to be interrupted. Perhaps I'd had the wrong magazine. Perhaps . . . I retrieved the directory from the lower rung of the telephone table and began to page through it, then put it down again. It was no use. I knew I'd heard the name right. Then I remembered the night in Obs, the wild account she'd given of her life, with no mention of *Woman* at all.

Back to the directory, going for broke. I'd call the law firm where she'd been before. But it struck me that I didn't know its name. Nor did I have a last name to attach to Brian or to Alex.

Zach? She might still have his card somewhere. It would mean searching her room. I hesitated. But surely this *was* an emergency?

I stopped at her door, looked round, feeling like a guilty schoolboy. Then I drew a deep breath and went in. It was like arriving at a railway station, waiting for a train, but not knowing the timetable, not even my destination. For a few minutes I wandered through the workroom, looking at the surfaces of chairs and couch, the table she used as a desk, a blind computer humming on it (she never seemed to turn it off). I turned on the anglepoise lamp, startled by its glare, flicked desultorily through the papers scattered about, too agitated to concentrate. All I could do was rummage about, more conscious of my heart jumping in my chest like a slaughtered fowl than of what my hands were doing.

I turned the light off again, stood for a while with a bowed head trying to muster my courage and then went through to the bedroom. The place was in a mess. The bed had probably not been made for days. A crumpled shift and a pair of flesh-coloured panties lay on the mat. I picked them up and involuntarily pressed them to my face before folding them meticulously and placing them on the bed. Next to it, on the small cabinet, were three or four copies of *Woman*.

Almost mechanically I bent down to open the narrow top drawer. This was intolerable; and yet I could not stop. A box of tissues. Vitamin tablets. A few loose pieces of jewellery – earrings, a broach, a bead necklace. Tampax. A small purse of ostrich skin. Two cigarette lighters, one empty. When I pulled the drawer further open there was a small collection of condom packets, of the more lurid and extravagant kinds I'd rejected in the pharmacy. I withdrew my hand. There should have been nothing unexpected about the find, but it left me feeling sick. I caught my thumb in the drawer when I hastily closed it and turned away.

As I stood sucking my stinging thumb, my eyes were lured by the pinboard on the wall. They sought out, and found, again, the small perfect nude. The familiar face staring straight at me, the unfamiliar beautiful hair, the dark pubic patch. How curious that she should look more naked like this than when I'd seen in the flesh the cleft and shaven mound. But there was another face I could not avoid. The greyish photograph of her father. (Why was it here, displayed so prominently, if he was the bastard she'd said he was?) His faded stare, even more than her eyes which gazed at me in such unselfconscious candour, confirmed the extent of my intrusion. It was more than I could bear.

And then I heard a sound behind me. Briefly, I closed my eyes, supporting myself with one hand on the cabinet, then I turned round to face the worst. The door was pushed open. A woman came in. But it wasn't Tessa. It was a stranger, a young coloured woman in a long old-fashioned dress, and she was carrying her head under one arm.

The hallucination, if that is what it was, lasted for no more than a few seconds. Then she was gone, the door was closed and my sight was restored. I left the room precipitately. In the kitchen the kettle was whistling furiously, nearly out of steam. Magrieta had been pestering me to replace it with the type that switches itself off. I turned the noisy thing off and took refuge in my study without bothering to make the tea.

I sat down in my deep chair, breathing heavily. There was something at the door. I jerked my head up. It was only a cat. Not Amadeus, one of the others. I laughed out loud with relief, then sat forward to cup my face in my hands, elbows on my knees. It must have been about ten minutes later — the crazy throbbing of my heart was slowly returning to normal — when I heard a sound at the door again. This time it was Tessa. She was still wearing the long graceful dress of the night before, now somewhat the worse for wear; and she was carrying her boots in her hand.

'Tessa!' My voice caught in my throat as I jumped up, sending the cat scuttling with a startled mew. 'Are you all right?'

'I'm fine. Sorry I'm late, but I had to hitch a ride back from Camps Bay.'

'Couldn't your friends' — I pointedly chose the plural — 'have brought you home?'

'There was some kind of misunderstanding.' She gave a weary smile and allowed me to fold her in my arms. I suddenly became conscious of the smell she exuded and turned away in a brief onset of nausea. Seemingly unaware of my reaction, she dropped her boots and sat down in her favourite spot, the sofa. 'Jesus, I'm bushed.'

'I was on the point of phoning you at work,' I said stiffly.

'You must never do that,' she said. 'They're very pissy about taking private calls.'

I steeled myself. Come what may. 'Tessa, I actually phoned. The receptionist said there was no one with your name on the staff.'

She gave no sign of hesitation. 'Was it Michelle you spoke to?'

'I didn't get her name.'

'Well, she's new, and she's absolutely hopeless. So please, don't even try again.'

'What's happened to you?' I asked.

She didn't seem to hear. She just lay back, closed her eyes and appeared to drop off to sleep. Then, her eyes still closed, she asked, 'You ever tried crack?'

'You mean . . . ?'

'Ja, the drug.'

'Tessa, don't tell me . . .'

'One's got to try everything before you're thirty. And I have barely a month to go.' With what seemed like a considerable effort she gave me a fuzzy smile.

I still don't know why that should have been the moment I snapped. I've been mulling over it so much since that morning. All I can come up with is that there had simply been too much happening in too short a time. I'd seen her lovers come and go in the past, I'd seen her stumbling dishevelled and languid from her room with the flush of sex and sleep on her face. But it had never been as blatant as this. I'd never smelled another man on her.

'What's the matter?' she mumbled through her dwaal.

'I don't think I can take this any more, Tessa,' I said.

She opened her eyes, squinted at me, made an effort to sit up. 'Why're you so snotty all of a sudden?'

'You can take your time to sleep this off,' I said, my jaws very tight. 'But when you wake up I want you to pack up and go.'

'You're actually throwing me out?' She turned even paler than she had been, but her eyes were ablaze.

'I never thought it would come to this,' I said with a kind of deadly calm that caught even me unprepared. 'I never thought I could do this. But even a worm must turn.' I choked on the words and stopped to catch hold of myself. It was difficult to see straight.

From the door I looked back at her. She was still sitting motionless, staring at me. It took all I had not to turn back and fold her in my arms. If she'd thrown something at me, or shouted 'Fuck you!', or said anything at all I might still have coped. But her silence was unbearable.

I went outside into the coruscating light and started walking. At Johnny MacFarlane's gate I stopped and clutched at the railing to steady myself. The friend I'd betrayed twice. Once by not stopping for him on the road. The second time by being too cowardly to tell him about it when I visited him in hospital. I always thought, 'Later, later . . .' And then it was too late. There were strangers living there now. The whole world was strange. I let go of the railing again. I walked and walked, blindly. High up in Newlands Forest I finally came to a standstill, my breath burning in my throat. There were birds in the trees. I didn't want to hear them. The most overrated noise in the world.

I spent the whole day just sitting there, off all beaten tracks. I didn't want anybody to see me. I needed, urgently, to think it all through. But right then thinking was beyond me. What assailed me – incoherently, tempestuously, madly – was a random welter of images, emotions, memories. Dark and infuriating at first: her lovers and her lies, her deceptions (where was she, what did she do, the nine-tenths of her daily life I was no part of?), her disappearances, her maddening disregard for my feelings, her invasion and manipulation of my life, her ridiculous, adolescent naïveté, her arrogance, her bitchiness, her untouchability. There was an almost exquisite pain in piling it all up, flagellating myself, lapidating myself, immolating myself. But different recollections began to take over, blending into the others, gradually imposing themselves. The sound of her laugh, the abandon of it. Her waif-like first appearance from the rain. The cool assurance with which she went to work in the mornings. The packets of food she took out to 'her' beggars en bergies. Her eager sessions with Magrieta. Our nocturnal conversations, Amadeus purring on her lap. Never had I spoken so much and so unrestrainedly about my own life to anyone. The quicksilver of her own confidences. What in anybody else might seem suspect, outrageous, crossing all boundaries, became in her the natural and spontaneous extension of her passion for life – even if shaded, so often, by that hint of a well of sadness, that elusive loneliness in her. Her enthusiasm and exuberance. Her confusion and curiosity. After some time I gave up trying to impose any order on it; I knew I'd find no sense in it. It was, like so often in the past, a naming of the parts, a missing of the whole. A missing of her, the woman I so stupidly, foolishly, desperately, shamelessly, maddeningly loved and had sent away because I was too hopeless to offer her the only thing she needed from me, refuge, sanctuary, a moment of repose.

The sun had gone down behind Devil's Peak before I began to walk back. My unfit body was aching from the unaccustomed exercise.

The front door was ajar when I arrived home. My first thought was that Magrieta had returned, but there was no sign of her. Nor of Tessa. If I'd expected – hoped? – to find her still sleeping, in the study or in her room, I was clearly mistaken. I sat down on her bed to face the blank walls.

Only after a while did I realise that at least some of her possessions were still there, stacked in random bundles on the floor against the far wall.

To my shame I must admit that a surge of hope rushed through me.

But in the workroom, on the table she'd used as a desk, I found the note she'd left, clearly scrawled in haste.

*Ruben: I'll be back for the rest of my stuff as soon as I've sorted things out. Sorry. Tessa.*

Nothing hit me quite as hard as that *Sorry*.

# 9

THE DAYS ARE slowly but noticeably lengthening. It's late August and there are signs of spring, but I'm still numbed by what happened. The time after Tessa left was the closest to hell I've known. In the background of my life Magrieta continued to come and go; her gloom pervaded the house, marking the contours of my solitude. But it was Tessa's absence which defined my days.

I tried to persuade myself that I'd done the right thing, the only practical thing. If she'd stayed any longer, I would have bored her to death, and she would have driven me insane. I'd also done the most honourable thing. A man has his pride.

Precisely! That, when it penetrated, was what stung the most. That I could have sunk to the level of any wretched macho swine whose woman had dared to stand up to him. And it was not even that: she hadn't 'stood up' to me. She'd simply followed the rules we'd agreed on. From the very first night she'd moved in here the boundaries between us had been set. There was no uncertainty, no grey area, no ambiguity. I was permitted to love her – neither she nor I could do anything about that – but not to impose myself on her. What there was between us might be unusual (but unusual, surely, only in terms of the rules of my obsolete world), but we had mutually and freely, happily, agreed on it.

In the first few hours I still tried desperately to rationalise; to assure myself that I'd really had no other choice. Even if it meant admitting that I'd been too weak to keep our pact, at least I'd been strong enough to admit my weakness. How could I possibly have gone on bearing whatever pain or punishment she chose to inflict on me?

Wishing her back to resume her hold on me would turn me into the most despicable kind of masochist.

But I'm afraid I didn't buy my own argument. In spite of all my efforts to suppress the thought, I knew I'd made one of the most stupid mistakes of my life. Nothing she had done had been designed to 'punish' me. As for wanting her back, it was not punishment I was looking for, but – perhaps – understanding.

NOTE ON THE RITES OF DESIRE. In the dark heart of everything, the conundrum of desire. The spur of movement, the urge to taste the bittersweet forbidden fruit; the motion from what is towards whatever is not yet. So far so good. Except that it is the age of rights and demands: if we live, and move, and breathe, we claim the *right* to live, to move, to breathe. If I desire, I may well claim the 'right' to desire. But once a right is acknowledged, how does one demarcate its territory, define a content and a consequence? It 'has' no territory as it is constantly on the move; it can have no content, because the moment it contains something, that implies the possibility of fulfilment – and fulfilment is the end of desire, attainment its self-immolation. So where does desire take me: where does it have the 'right' to take me? If I claim desire as my right and its nature lies in motion, its motion towards the other, does not my right to desire invoke the right of the other to refuse me? And does that not make a mockery of 'right', as much as of 'desire'? The most I can claim for desire is the right to be frustrated, to be denied, otherwise it self-destructs. If there are rights, yes, then I suppose desire has a right to be. But that does not give me the right to demand rights for desire. I desire, ergo I am? But only if 'I am,' in this equation, becomes wholly conditional upon 'You are'. And where does that leave desire?

Magrieta returned from Mandalay township in the early evening, lugging a hefty old leather suitcase. I tried to take it from her, but she sidestepped me and carried it down the passage to the room she was to occupy.

'Is this all you brought?' I asked.

'Couldn't find no taxi today,' she muttered, clearly in a foul temper. 'The drivers are fighting again. I must go get more stuff later. If the house is still there.'

'Did you find someone to look after the place?'

'I asked the neighbours. En my niece will look in every day. From tomorrow night one of her friends will sleep in the house.'

'Did you find out anything more about last night?'

'Nobody knows nothing, Meneer. They even washed away the blood from the ground where they chopped her up. I won't be nothing surprised if that woman's ghost start walking in the streets from now on.'

On an impulse I said, 'I saw our ghost this morning.'

'Meneer?' She turned round much more quickly than one would expect of a person her size.

'Antje of Bengal.'

'Where did Meneer see her?'

I was trapped. How could I possibly tell her that I'd been rummaging in Tessa's room? 'Just down the passage,' I lied with as straight a face as I could muster.

'En Meneer says it was this morning? In full daylight?'

'Just after you left. It was the first time in nearly forty years.'

'Ag, the poor thing.' For a moment I wasn't sure whether she was referring to me or to the ghost; but then she added, 'That Willem Mostert should never have done his thing with her.'

'You told me she was in love with him. There's no way one can stop love.'

'I suppose Meneer will know better.' She turned away and started unpacking her things into a wardrobe.

'What is that supposed to mean?'

'That is not for me to talk about. All I can say is I think Miss Tessa is bad news.'

Did she know anything, sense anything? I'd kept Tessa's door firmly shut. I felt my face go cold. I wasn't ready to discuss what had happened in her absence. Perhaps for that very reason I couldn't keep the pique out of my voice: 'You've had something against her from the first day she came here.'

'I got nothing against her!' she flared up. 'I'm not saying there's something wrong with that jentoe. But it's from the day she came that Antje is doing the rounds again. That can't be a good sign.' Adding righteously, 'En Meneer has got a heart en all.'

'You sound just like my sons.'

'They know what they know.'

'I already told all of you there's nothing to worry about.'

'But if something happens I'll be the one to get the blame.'

'That's why we took in a lodger.'

She sniffed in contempt. 'What's the use? She's never here when one need her. Where she been today?'

Some quick thinking was called for. 'Tessa has gone away for a few days. On business.'

She looked hard at me with her probing eyes, which never missed a thing. But if she suspected something, she obviously decided not to let on. Just as well. I wasn't in any state to withstand much of an interrogation.

That night, I confess without shame, I spent in Tessa's bed in the half-emptied room. I remained in my study until very late; Rachmaninov was raging in the background, but turned down very low. At one stage Amadeus entered with an air of unspeakable disdain. I patted my lap, but he superciliously bypassed me, and went to the sofa where he used to lie with Tessa. It felt like a double rejection. Only when I was quite sure Magrieta would be asleep did I tiptoe down the passage to the back – not even bothering to undress, or wash, or brush my teeth – and slip into the dark room like a ghost. I didn't want to put on a light, couldn't stand the idea of seeing what was there, what was not. I wonder now whether behind the urge to wrap myself in whatever remained of Tessa – a faint, departing scent, a lost warmth, elusive memory – might have been the unreasonable hope that, at least, spending the night in her bed would summon Antje of Bengal back to me. But she never came. And her absence, like Tessa's, was harder to bear than her presence.

Before the first birds began to twitter in the oaks outside I stole back to my own room. The bed, of course, was cold and empty, confirming the worst I could expect in my world. This loneliness, forsaken even by Antje, was even more pervasive, if memory was to be trusted, than the guilty misery I'd felt after Riana's death. If only Tessa would come back I swore I'd go on my knees to ask forgiveness. But there was no sign of her all day, nor on Sunday. On Monday, to avoid Magrieta and the house, I spent hours in the sanitised world of the library, staring blindly at the pages of a book I'd taken randomly off a shelf.

That evening, in spite of all my previous resolutions, in spite even of Magrieta's presence in the house, I actually went so far as to telephone an agency. This was, surely, the rock-bottom of despair. (And what would happen if I had another attack spreadeagled on the body of an unsuspecting young woman? Or was that what, secretly and perversely, I was wishing for?) When the inevitable monosyllabic handler dropped the takeaway girl at the front gate I went out and paid him his due, offered her a wad of notes as a tip, and promptly sent them off again. She snarled something like, 'Impotent old fart!' in my direction. (Could I blame her? – to be rejected by an unappetising old scarecrow like me!)

This time I sat up in the study all night, scared of going to bed. Feeling – what? Just old. And much more so than before. Time to wear the bottoms of my trousers rolled. I was snubbed once again by Amadeus, whose restlessness all day had not escaped me. I did not even put on music: Johnny would have approved, no doubt.

The next day, unable to face the pale green interior of the library again, I drove through the streets of Claremont, Newlands, Rondebosch; then into the city centre, cruising past every office block, submitting to the furious jabbing fingers and the obscenities shouted at me by countless motorists and pedestrians. Then back to Claremont, where I spent an hour in front of the elegantly renovated premises of *Woman*. I even pressed the bell at the gate and asked for her, just in case she had been right about the receptionist the last time. But of course I met with another blank denial. Street upon street upon street, once again. And home in the late afternoon to face, guilty and exhausted, a deeply troubled indignant Magrieta. Throughout the previous days she'd studiously avoided all forms of probing – which made it all the more obvious that she knew very well what was going on. But it was clear that she, too, had reached the end of her tether.

'Where you been so long?' she asked.

'I was looking for Tessa.' I was too tired to avoid the issue.

'Why she gone?' she asked, hands on her hips.

'It was just getting too bad, Magrieta,' I said lamely, finally mustering the courage to look her in the eye. 'I had to ask her to go. But I never really thought she would.'

'Meneer tole her to go?'

I nodded wearily.

'Ag shame,' she said. 'En now what's happening to the poor girl?'

'I thought you'd be relieved to see the last of her,' I said pointedly.

'Miss Tessa need someone to look after her, mos. We can't throw her to the vultures like that.'

Was it the unexpected show of female solidarity, or simply the accumulation of desperate moments during the day (all those brief glimpses in the street: the flare of a skirt, the toss of a head, the long-limbed gait of someone in jeans) that made me crack up? I scuttled past her and fled into my study. It was unthinkable to let her see me in that state. It had never happened before, not even when I'd come home to Riana's funeral. (Or had I cried when she'd lost the baby? But even then, surely, I'd have hidden it from Magrieta. From my earliest childhood, this was what Pa and my brothers had bludgeoned into me: men don't. Not ever.)

I remained sitting, my face pressed against my open hands. It took a long time to subside. Only when I'd recovered sufficiently to blow my nose like a trumpet did I become aware of the cloying closeness of Magrieta's cologne. Pretending she hadn't noticed anything, she emphatically cleared her throat and announced, 'Food's ready when Meneer is.' Then marched off, leaving me to straighten up.

She'd set the dining-room table — which marked it as a special occasion — where she made me sit down to a gargantuan meal she had prepared, and which was just about the last thing I could face right then.

That night she didn't retire to her room but sat up in the kitchen, ostensibly to darn my socks; but I knew it was because she didn't want me to be on my own, in case I needed company. And, curiously, when at last she came to the study to order me to bed, I dropped off into a sleep more sound than any I'd had in weeks.

I had given up on ever seeing Tessa again. Together with Magrieta, as if I needed a witness, I went through the things she'd left behind and found nothing absolutely indispensable. There were clothes she could still wear and books and papers that could undoubtedly be used; and the pictures stripped from the wall might readily adorn another room. Arguably, the guitar, dilapidated as it was, was still a prized possession. But the way I'd come to know her she might easily decide she could do without all of that, and not return at all.

But what about the message? No big deal either. She might have thought better about it by now. Good riddance, she'd probably decided; why stir up old shit?

Magrieta dismissed my lugubrious conviction. 'Miss Tessa need this stuff, she got little enough as it is, Meneer must jus' wait.'

'She can get along fine without it, Magrieta. You know it as well as I do.'

'Antje tole me not to worry. So please get on with your work now. Meneer is getting on my nerves en I got things to do.'

Late on the Thursday afternoon, it was the sixth day, she came back. I was sitting on the bench on the front stoep, where I'd begun to spend most of my time at home watching the street, when the red Porsche drew up at the gate. It was like waking up as a child and suddenly realising it's your birthday. (As it happened it was a mere three days before mine.) But the car stifled all joy like a sob in the throat. Insult to injury.

I stood up, ducking behind a pillar, ready to flee what, suddenly, I couldn't face. Then I saw her coming up the path alone. At least he'd had the decency not to get out with her; or perhaps she'd told him to wait.

She clearly wasn't expecting me there. Her face looked drawn.

'My darling,' I choked. It just came out.

'Ruben.'

'Dear God,' I said, 'you're back, I missed you so.'

There was a slight quiver at the corner of her mouth, but she stood her ground. 'I've just come for my stuff. I'm sorry it took so long, but it wasn't so easy to find a place.'

'Where have you been?' (What I meant to ask, but couldn't, was, 'Have you moved in with Zach?')

She shrugged. 'Here and there.'

I put out my hands. Somewhat to my surprise she took them. And there we stood, unmoving, at arm's length, unsure about whatever to do next.

Then Zach blew the horn, three angry, insistent blasts. He must have been watching us.

She swung round. 'Oh fuck off!' she shouted. At that moment it sounded more glorious than the 'Ode to Joy'.

'Please stay,' I said.

No doubt Zach had heard her. He drove off like Michael Schumacher.

'I never thought it was possible to miss anyone so much,' I said.

'You had every reason to throw me out,' she answered calmly. 'I made your life a misery. I didn't mean to, but that was the way it turned out.'

'It was still better than being without you.'

Then something curious happened. The cats came out on the stoep from inside. Every one of them, Amadeus hovering in the back. In a purring and gently swirling motion they surrounded her. The rites of love. She knelt down to greet them and for a while they were all over her, which made her laugh as in the old days. Only then did Amadeus, who'd been proudly surveying the scene from behind, deign to approach, uttering a throaty sound which left them in no doubt. They withdrew with as much dignity as they could, leaving the stoep clear to the undisputed *primus inter pares*. Tessa scooped him up, fondled him, addressed him in a low voice. It took quite a while before she put the cat down and came past me into the house, Amadeus still gliding around her legs. They settled down together on the sofa in the study.

'Can I have some wine?' she asked.

It was, perhaps predictably, another of those conversations that went on for much of the night. At one stage, as I refilled her glass, she said, 'We can't afford to be emotional about this, Ruben. If you really look at it objectively, don't you think we'll just be going into a slow spin, getting back to the same point time and time again, and losing something every time? I couldn't bear that.'

'It won't happen again.'

'How can you be so sure?' Her desperate candour.

'When we first made our deal, I accepted because it was the only way to keep you. This time it is my own choice. I have seen the alternative, and I cannot bear it. I want you to stay. But only on your own terms.'

'And if it becomes unbearable again?' Her steady and relentless gaze.

'It can't become unbearable if I know exactly what I'm choosing. I have no illusions about it, Tessa.'

'But you still love me?'

'I do.' It sounded very solemn. 'For better or for worse, and all the rest.'

She rose to put her glass on the small chess table in the corner. On the way back to the couch she stopped to kiss me.

'I'd like to be here for your birthday,' she said simply.

'I'm too far gone to have a fuss made about birthdays. I'll be sixty-six. Add another six and it'll be the sign of the Beast. Let's save our celebration for yours, which isn't so far away either. You said you were a Virgo, didn't you?'

She smiled, wistfully it seemed. 'If ever there was a misnomer.'

# 10

It's SEPTEMBER ALREADY and once again I have been avoiding my notes for too long. Every time I attempt to retrace my steps, ours, the memories begin to run and merge – a confusion complicated by the constant pressure of what was happening to Magrieta. It was a threat I could do nothing to avoid; yet when I try to recover these past weeks, remembered from where I am now, it is Tessa who remains most urgent in my mind. And all our conversations flow together. The talk we had that evening when she came back, and others in the weeks that followed. One on my birthday, another on a freezing Sunday when she insisted on going to Hout Bay for a walk on the beach, yet another in front of the fire during a sudden cold spell, while she was sitting on the floor, painting her toenails an assortment of colours, like small perfect Smarties, with little wads of cotton wool wedged between her toes. Not that the sequence of the conversations matters. Below the orderly passing of the days there was a timeless flux in which we simply went on talking.

Of one recollection I'm sure: my birthday. She brings me a present in a little box and the smallest card I've ever seen, the size of a postage stamp. The card, she explains, her eyes lit up with laughter, is because I refused to have any fuss made. The box contains a simple golden ring with a small red stone set in it.

'A ruby?' I ask, taken aback.

'Genuine glass,' she assures me gravely.

'But the ring? It won't fit any finger.'

'It's the one I had in my navel,' she says. 'I took it off for you.'

'Won't it leave a scar?'

'Just a couple of pinpricks. They'll soon fade away. I thought I'd better get past the things of a child before I strike the terrible thirties.'

'Balzac,' I say, 'believed the woman of thirty was on the verge of her greatest decade.'

'We'll soon know.' She kisses me. 'In the meantime I wanted you to have the ring to remind you of my pristine youth.'

'You'll be pristine until you're ninety.'

'We'll see about that when I get there. By which time you'll be well into your second century.'

'And still standing to attention whenever you enter the room.'

And then – or does this happen on the beach? in the garden, or the kitchen, or my study? – we speak about that pristine youth, about how we lost our virginity. She tells me about the young man, Andy, a neighbour, whom she approached when she turned seventeen to ask him quite formally whether he'd be so kind as to deflower her. Virginity had become a burden to her, all her friends had achieved the rites of passage and she was beginning to feel left out. She'd known this Andy for years. In fact, he'd been struck with her ever since she was twelve, but she'd kept him firmly at bay. ('I know all about being kept at bay,' I assure her.) Now the time had come. Her mother was off on a business trip, having forgotten about her daughter's birthday, the brother was bribed into sleeping out, and Tessa prepared the nuptial bed, in her mother's room, in style. She'd even bought (forging her mother's signature) a set of luxurious embroidered sheets for the occasion.

'Did it work?' I ask.

'Technically, yes. In all other respects it was a mess. It hurt like hell and I bled all over those new sheets, and the earth didn't move, only the bed fell in – slipped off its frame or something – and Andy was so upset it took hours to get him hard again. Also, he was trying to be terribly considerate, he'd bought a whole dozen of condoms and everything' – I know, I know – 'but I told him I wanted all or nothing, he could take it or leave it, and that made him droop again. So it was quite a schlep, ending in something of an anticlimax, you might say. But it got done and that was all that mattered. I remember marching into the kitchen in the morning and baking about a million muffins and making a huge pot of coffee, and if Andy hadn't stopped me I'd have run out into the street trailing the sheets after me.' At last the wry, wise smile. 'All of that for so little.'

And then – or is it on a different occasion again? – I tell her about my own initiation, when I was lamentably miscast as Lord Peter Wimsey in a student production of *Busman's Honeymoon*. For four weeks, on a winter vacation tour through the Karoo and the Free State, in the interests of more convincing acting, I tried to bed the equally hopeless actress who was playing Lady Harriet. Without success. And then, on the penultimate night of the tour, when all the other students had already gone home from the show, I found myself backstage in the company of the girl who played Miss Twitterton. The only reason why it hadn't happened earlier was that she was too beautiful for me: but she had just broken up with her boyfriend, and before we knew where we were that was it. In due course she became my wife.

'Happily ever after,' says Tessa in a mocking voice.

'Not on your life,' I retort. 'Her parents couldn't stand the sight of me, they were rich wine farmers and I was trash. They tried everything they could to wreck the relationship. Once they realised we were serious they even sent her to Bloemfontein for a year, where she retaliated by failing every subject she sat for.'

'What did you do?'

I pick up a small smooth pebble and hurl it away. (It must be the day on the beach then.) 'I'm afraid I acted despicably,' I confess. 'I tried to forget her by sleeping my way through an improbable number of other girls.'

'Did she find out?' asks Tessa.

'I told her as soon as she came back.'

'How naïve can you get?' she asks, amazed. Then curiosity takes over again. 'But she did take you back?'

'Only because we were young enough and sufficiently in love. But I've wondered since then if the real reason wasn't that we needed each other in the fight against her parents.'

'But in the end you did get married.'

'After a long battle, yes. You wouldn't believe the lengths they went to — stand-up fights, lies, slander, emotional blackmail, threats to disinherit her. Once her father became so mad he thrashed her.' I pause. 'But it was only a few years later, when we discovered that she was pregnant, that they finally gave in.'

She presses on. 'But once you were together it was a happy marriage. That's what you told me.'

'Well, I suppose so.' I struggle against myself. 'We had our differences,' I admit at last; it feels like a betrayal, but her eyes leave me no choice. 'I've always found it hard to share. And Riana could be quite opinionated. Which I suppose was why I fell in love with her in the first place.'

'Were you ever unfaithful to her?'

I've never spoken about this to anyone. But I find it hard, when I'm with her, to hold back. I tell her about that day, after Riana had lost the child, when Magrieta was summoned by Antje of Bengal to interrupt my tryst with Alison.

'Did you confess to her again?'

'I wanted to. It would have made things easier. For me. But I told myself I couldn't hurt her again, especially not at that time, when she was still so frail after the miscarriage. The truth, I suppose, was that I was too much of a coward.'

'She never found out?'

'No. Because there *was* nothing to find out.'

'Did it ever happen again?' asks Tessa.

I look away, then back. 'Only once. At the very end. The day Riana died, in fact.'

She takes my hand. 'How did she die?'

'A car accident. She was crossing Main Road down here in Newlands when a delivery truck jumped a red light. While I was away at a library conference in Pretoria. I'd met someone there, one of the organisers. Her name was Tania. We were actually in her hotel room that afternoon, making love at the very time Riana was killed. I got a call that evening. Just as we were conspiring to slip away from dinner for another secret get-together.' I sigh. 'Do you understand why I blamed myself for it?'

'It was coincidence, Ruben.'

'Morally I was to blame.'

'You've already paid a hell of a price,' she says, patting my cheek. 'I think you've had a lot of guts to face what you did.'

'Guts didn't come into it. It was purely desire. You are much more courageous than I ever was.'

'Courageous? What makes you think so?'

'Just the way you live. On the edge. And somehow you bring it off quite gloriously.'

Was that what I said? 'On the edge'? I couldn't have known, then, how close to the mark it was. She was going through a brief bad spell earlier this month. For the first time since she arrived that stormy night in June, she became moody, temperamental. She had a stand-off with Magrieta. She was looking pale, but when I asked, she shrugged it off: she was just having a tough time at work, she said, but it would soon be sorted out. Probably made worse by PMT. Yet her previous periods had passed without any sign of it.

It was late last night that she came here to my study. She hadn't been out at night for a week. There were dark patches under her eyes.

'You must tell me what's wrong,' I said.

She came to look for comfort in my arms, like a small, frightened girl. We ended up on the sofa. 'Please love me,' she said. 'Don't ever stop loving me.'

'Why are you so emotional?' I asked.

'I need you, Ruben,' she whispered in my ear.

I misunderstood. I thought she meant it sexually. I began to remove her top, paused to kiss the sweet and already almost unmarked navel.

Without trying to resist, she just asked in a voice almost too whispery to hear, 'You really want to?'

'Please don't say no.' This time, I felt, this time, at last, it was going to happen.

I began to undo the rest of her clothes. It was like seeing a landscape once seen in a dream: except I wasn't sure whether the dream had happened before and was remembered now, or was happening now to be remembered later. I was looking at her and thinking the words: expose, bare, uncover, discover; and I recalled the winged word by Montaigne to whom 'discover' and 'invent' had been synonymous, *Our continent has just invented another.* This was *my* new world, *my* invention.

She was lying very rigid below my hands. Her eyes were closed. It was hard to be sure in the uncertain light, but I thought I could see a shimmering of tears through her lashes. It hit me in the guts.

'What is wrong?' I asked.

'I'm pregnant,' she said. 'I need to have an abortion.'

# Three

# 1

MONDAY, 14 SEPTEMBER. This is unimagined territory and still unimaginable. It is now, it is here. Yet I cannot grasp it. She lies on the narrow white hospital bed in a sleep beyond my reach, further removed than ever by this experience which excludes me, the male, the old man. I've been sitting here with my notebook on my lap, its pages dazzling in the spring sun, ever since the brisk little wisp of a nurse with the faintly disapproving air came to the waiting room to tell me, 'You can come through to your daughter now, Mr Olivier. But she is still drowsy from the anaesthetic. It was very light, but it's better to let her sleep it off.'

'Did everything go all right?'

'She'll be fine.'

I wanted to ask her what exactly it is they do, what the procedure involves, how they go about it. But I sensed it was not my place to ask such questions. I followed her down the green corridor. Everything here is very bright. It is a private hospital. I insisted on taking care of all the arrangements and expenses; I wouldn't let her go to one of those public abattoirs with crowds of chattering visitors hanging about, the lifts and corridors littered with crisp packets, Coke tins, crumpled plastic bags among the blood and vomit stains; cleaning staff sprawled on chairs intended for patients who are forced to stand, leaning against the filthy walls, holding their own drips. I saw enough of that when I went to visit Johnny MacFarlane after his first attack; and when I mentioned it, outraged, to Johann in a telephone conversation, he replied with a harsh laugh, 'Now you see why we left, Dad.'

In the doorway to the room at the end of the corridor I stopped, my throat constricted. The nurse went off. Tessa's small dark head lay against the stark white of the pillow. I said her name. She opened her eyes and gave a difficult little smile, making a half-hearted effort to raise one arm.

'Ruben,' she said, 'don't go away.'

'I'll be here.' I pressed her hand to my lips. 'How are you feeling?'

She said drowsily, 'A little sad.' And drifted off, the wan smile fading into sleep.

That must have been more than an hour ago. I'm still sitting here, watching her, every slight movement of her mouth and eyelids, occasionally a twitching of the hand on the covers; sometimes she makes an almost inaudible whimpering sound. How very far away you are, my darling. But I'll be here when you wake up, if you need me, and even if you don't. I'll be making my notes. Scribble, scribble, Mr Gibbon. It is my only remedy to help me hold on, to concentrate the mind. But concentration is the one thing I feel incapable of right now. My thoughts keep scattering. Like the bugs on the dingy walls of that small hotel in the rue du Dragon in Paris, where Riana and I stayed on our first trip so many years ago. Ostensibly to celebrate our togetherness. It was more to try and make the marriage work again. So much had gone wrong. Her unhealthy, growing attachment to her parents. My attempted infidelity. But Alison had been only a symptom of it. Ever since Riana had lost the child it had not been the same between us. I don't want to think about that now. But what has happened – is happening – to Tessa relentlessly brings it back, forces me to face it. How will she be changed by it? *A little sad*. It will go deeper than that, my love. It has a way of lodging in the most unreachable recesses of mind and memory. I know. What I need now, perhaps, is a long frank talk to Magrieta. The practical, matter-of-fact, busy, brusque, understanding Magrieta.

I didn't tell her why I had to bring Tessa to hospital this morning, of course. Except to assure her it wasn't serious, 'just a small woman thing, you know, she'll be back in the afternoon'. She grunted. She may well guess, in her uncanny way, more than I'd like her to suspect. But she knows when to be silent.

There have been more silences between us than usual over the past month or so and it worries me. Not just about Magrieta's life, but about its implications for my own. Over the years she has constantly kept me – or us when Riana was still alive – informed about what was happening in her world. But after our attempted intervention in the forced removal from District Six it has never again threatened to invade our own in the way this killing of the 'witch' has done. I tried to imagine how Riana would have handled it. I knew she would have approved of Magrieta moving into the house, at least for the time being; but was that enough? And the very awareness of such questions unnerved me. I'm not used to dealing with this kind of thing. If my life was a desert, at least it was my choice to withdraw into it; and if that made me a hermit, so be it. Like those scruffy, rather unsavoury lot of early ascetic saints. St Simon Stiletes, St Jerome, St Anthony, and their ilk. Except, of course, that even in the desert temptation would not let Anthony be. Monsters, lunatics, murderers, amphibians, naked women, greed, lust. I should read up on him again.

About a week after the killing of the 'witch', just after Tessa had come back, Magrieta returned to the township to fetch the rest of her transportable belongings, arriving back in the late afternoon in a badly battered taxi loaded to the roof with all she'd chosen to salvage. Shoes and clothes, her TV set, a box of her most prized kitchen utensils, a sewing machine, blankets and pillows, two pink lamps with frilly shades, portraits of her late husbands and of Mannie and Mabel as small children, even – quite touching – a framed photo of Riana and me taken many years ago. (What, I wondered, would I salvage if I were suddenly given a day to clear out my home?)

I helped her unload while the taciturn driver sat smoking behind his wheel.

'Is this all?' I asked, as we staggered from the taxi with the last bundles.

'It's all there was place for.'

We carried the stuff inside to the bedroom she'd moved into, and while I was helping her to stow it in and on the wardrobe and the large yellowwood chest of drawers, Tessa also came home.

'Good,' she said. 'I was worried about your things left in the township.'

'Ag, the world is a dangerous place, Miss Tessa.' Magrieta cocked her head like an oversized spaniel. 'Mind, it's only for a little while that I'm staying here, hey.'

We chatted for a while, but when I started filling Tessa in on what had happened in her absence, Magrieta quickly found something else to do. It was the first of many evenings she spent long hours at her sewing machine, often well into the night. She couldn't sleep anyway, she explained, so she might as well do something useful, rather than work up a headache lying awake.

Which would leave Tessa and me alone again. That is to say, if she spent the night at home, which wasn't all that often. It was like a game of musical chairs among the three of us. In an inexplicable way it was as if we were waiting for something to happen, something still in the process of taking shape and untouchable as yet. It seemed to start moving in a more definite direction when, after about three weeks, Magrieta announced she was moving back to her own house. 'I can't go on living like this,' she said. 'Meneer was good to me, I appreciate what you done for me. But this isn't my place no more. I better go back to my own house.'

'But it's dangerous, Magrieta!'

'We been waiting for three weeks now en nothing happened. Perhaps it is all right now. Maybe I was just too upset in the beginning because of what they did to that poor witch woman.'

I did all I could to dissuade her, but once Magrieta had something in her head there was no reasoning with her. For the first few nights after she left I hardly slept a wink. And then, gradually, just as it had happened after Johnny MacFarlane's murder, the anxiety began to fade. We are a resilient species. Every time you adapt to the changed world; every time you review your definition of the 'normal'.

And when my children telephoned – Johann (or more often Cathy) from Sydney, or Louis from Johannesburg – I kept on assuring them: there was nothing to worry about; everything was just fine.

'But we've been reading about the violence in Cape Town getting so bad,' said Cathy.

'You know the newspapers just go for sensation, my child. I *live* here. Our suburb is peace and quiet itself.' I chose not to tell them about Magrieta's experience or the incident with Tessa's bergies. 'And anyway, I'm not on my own any more, remember, there's the lodger.'

'How are you getting on?'

'No complaints. We get along fine.'

Louis was the one who became facetious: 'No marriage prospects yet?'

'I'm too old for that kind of thing,' I said gruffly, surprised at the jolt it gave my heart.

He was not to be put off so easily. 'A lodger is no long-term solution, Dad. We'd feel so much more relaxed if we knew you were looked after on a permanent basis. Once we go to Canada, especially, it'll keep on bugging us.'

'Are you still serious about going?'

'Of course. Before the end of the year. Or early next year at the latest. There's no use putting it off once one has made up one's mind.' And then, after a pause. 'How about going with us, Dad? Janet and I were discussing it last night.'

'What about Magrieta?' I trumped him.

A surprised laugh. Then, with an audible effort to indulge me, he said, 'We can arrange a pension for her. It's time she retired anyway. But you're the one we're talking about now. Don't change the topic. Think about it, Dad. We'll discuss it again later. We want you to come and visit before we leave, OK?'

'I'm not sure I'll have the time, Louis.'

'You just have to. There's so much to talk about.'

'We'll see.'

He concluded with a show of joviality, 'Well, say hi to the lodger for us.'

Back to the three of us. Would anyone outside understand the dynamics of our relationship? The three of us. Four. He'd forgotten to mention Antje of Bengal.

But today, here in the sterile isolation of the hospital, Tessa is the only one that matters. Fitfully sleeping. And I here at the bedside, with my notebook on my lap, waiting for her to wake up.

'Would you like to talk about it?' I asked her that night when she first told me.

'What is there to say?'

I knew it had to be asked sooner or later; whether either of us was up to it yet I wasn't sure. But I had to try. 'Whose child is it?'

'Not yours,' she said with an incongruously bright smile.

'More's the pity.' I made the old, inevitable gesture, placing my open hand on her still bared stomach.

She folded her jersey down, but made no attempt to remove my hand. 'Will it shock you very much if I tell you that I don't know?'

I know I briefly closed my eyes. Yes, it was hard to bear. But this was not about me.

'It's obviously either Alex, or Zach.'

She didn't answer. I tried to suppress the feeling of sickness her silence provoked.

'Have you spoken to them?' I pressed on after a while.

'Zach is in the States somewhere. He'll never come back if he knew.'

'And Alex is married.'

'Yes. But I told him.' She rested her hand on mine, the fabric of the jersey between us.

'How did he react?'

To my surprise she said, 'He wants me to keep it.'

'You sure you don't want to?'

'Of course not. I can't have a child under these circumstances. The world is a messy enough place as it is.'

'Was he upset?'

'Terribly. All pro-life and everything. He even offered to divorce his wife and marry me.'

'Did you consider it?'

'Marriage is not an option.'

'It could be a starting point. For the baby.'

'For how long do you think Alex would stay with me? I'm not

trying to blame him. He's a man. And in the end they always let you down. It comes with the job description.'

'Not all men, not always.'

'Would you have stayed with me? For ever?'

I looked down at the bulge my hand made under her jersey. Her thighs were still bare. 'Would you care to give me a chance?'

'You know it can never work, Ruben.' The challenge of her eyes: 'It didn't really work with Riana either, did it?'

'I told you we were happy.'

'Yes. You told me.' She said no more, but I'd seldom felt so exposed.

'If you can't consider marriage,' I pressed on, 'what about adoption?'

'If I bring a child into the world I must take responsibility for it. Don't you see?'

'I suppose I'm just a very old-fashioned man.'

'My sweet love.' She sat up and stroked my cheek. 'Do you find this horrible, unbearable?'

'Not horrible. And hard to bear, yes, because I'm concerned for you; but not unbearable.'

'I've let you down.'

'All that matters now is to get you through this and not to hurt you any more.'

'I'm not sure you can call it hurt,' she said. 'In a strange way I feel very detached. Perhaps I just can't believe it yet. It's all so different from the way one thinks about it.'

I remembered, as she spoke, the distant moment when she'd allowed me to bare her secret for the first time. The frankness of it. But that was in another country, and besides the wench is dead.

And now we're here, sharing another intimate moment, but you're oblivious to it and my own mind is wandering. Grasping at every possible means of escape. Anything but this — even if, right now, there's nowhere else I would rather be. Every time I look up from my notes to gaze at you, that sleeping lovely face with its disconcerting innocence, I feel the threat of here and now. It's like the morning I searched your room and looked at your nude photograph, except that your sleeping face is more naked, and infinitely more vulnerable, than the image of your body. I write 'vulnerable'. But it is not the right word. As you lie here in the white bed — Snow White sleeping off the poison — you harbour no secrets. You *are* your own secret; you 'have' none. True mysteries are hidden in the light: Jean Giono. Your serene face. The almost inaudible coming and going of your breath. Your body, white and clothed in white, bathed in the gentle white light filtered through white curtains. The image of chastity, haunting me, stalking me as surely as any ghost. I desire you.

While this poor, passionate, mountebank body has arms to hold you and lips to say, 'I love you': the flamboyant overstatements of Lord Peter Wimsey in *Busman's Honeymoon*. The fumbling love scenes with my Lady Harriet on stage. And then the surprise discovery (that word again) of Miss Twitterton. The course of a life decided in a touch of hands, after the performance in the school hall, when she borrowed my comb for her unruly dark hair. We looked at each other, fingers still touching, in one of those amazing moments of mutual discovery when the world becomes a different place; and she asked, presumably because like me she could think of nothing sensible to say, 'Do you like Chopin?' I said, 'I don't know much about music,' and she said, 'Then it's time you got to know him.'

There are few places quite as desolate as a stage after a performance. It was made worse by the tattiness of the set, showing all the wear and tear of our long tour. In the small glare of the prompt light, which to avoid being discovered was the only one we dared turn on, Riana opened the upright stage piano and started playing. Chopin. The ballads, as I learned afterwards, one by one. Between the third and the fourth we made love.

Music was her subject and her passion. That first night I was more enthralled by the play of the light on her dark hair, and the incredible nimbleness of her fingers on the yellowed keys, than by the music itself. But after that it became the dimension in which we moved and kept in touch.

'And then you lived happily ever after,' you once mocked. And I played along. How could I tell you the truth? I'd never looked it in the face myself. Only now, as you lie there absent in sleep, can I return to it and try not to be repulsed. Not because it was so horrible, but because it was so ordinary.

The opposition of her parents was bad enough, but we could handle that. It even added a sense of adventure. The feeling of doing the unacceptable, of challenging everything they represented, all the thou-shalt-nots of her father's respectability and power, in society, in church, in politics. We could not know that our escape would be by a circular route, ending up where we started from. What else should we have expected? In exchange for all the quid they lavished on us we were inevitably required to pro quo. And Riana, more daring than I, more beautifully outrageous in her rebellion, ever more radical in her rejection of constraints in those heady early days (the quiet determination with which she flunked every exam after her father had sent her away to Bloemfontein; the way she told him from her bed after he'd given her that humiliating thrashing, 'If you ever touch me again I shall get up at the next biduur and tell God in front of the whole congregation that you sleep with the coloured girls on the farm') – Riana was the one to return more absolutely to the fold.

Admittedly, the fact that her father had a stroke a year or so after their confrontation played a decisive role. More and more she began to be plagued by the memory of her own earlier revolt; in his decline she was discovering increasingly the hand of God. Perhaps she'd always had this urge towards excess; but I'd only ever seen the one extreme and was caught unawares by the backswing of the pendulum. I was still willing to follow where she led, ignorant of what should by then have become obvious. When she insisted on making our peace with her parents, I acquiesced. My happiness was conditional on hers, and if she could only be happy with their blessing it seemed a small price to pay. If I look back now, with all the acrimony and guilt and regret, and all the clarity of disenchantment lent by distance, I know I was simply too blinded by desire. To have her, as I then believed possible in my youthful male myopia, wholly, entirely, unconditionally; the music with which she could churn my feelings into a frenzy, and then caress them into serenity – Mozart, or the 'Appassionata', the 'Tempest', the Rachmaninov Preludes, and always back to Chopin – and then the deep alto of her voice, her carefree walk, the way she tossed back her long hair, and carried her body, the body itself which she'd shared so extravagantly with me, for ever and ever, amen.

With the new religious doubts filtering into her to turn opaque the once translucent clarity of her mind, came all kinds of fears and suspicions about sin and sex. For a while I still managed to persuade her; but the pregnancy that forced us into marriage became for her a sign from heaven that branded us with a mark as irredeemable as Cain's. From that moment whatever we might attempt together was doomed beforehand by our 'insult' to God and common decency.

Matrimony, then, for a quarter of a century. And for eleven years, since her death, I have clung to the memory of a happy marriage. It was the only way, in retrospect, to redeem those years – my life – which otherwise would have been wasted. The only way to keep faith in myself. Today, in this precarious moment of truth granted me by your sleep, it seems more like a purgatory. But I must not overstate it. We did have times of happiness together, when like the brief flare of a match in the dark her passionate nature would reassert itself and something of our early joy would be recovered. But the odds were stacked ever higher against us. Perhaps I should have pretended more, in matters of less consequence, like religion. But having once rejected Father, Son and Holy Ghost, way back on the bare plains of the Kalahari, and finding my resolve finally confirmed by her parents' hypocritical attachment to the Church, I couldn't go through the motions any more, not even for her sake. While she turned ever more desperately to God and his team of heavies, especially after the children were born.

Johann. Then Louis. Both names chosen from her family. Father, grandfather. I wasn't particularly set on having my own father commemorated, but the point was that I wasn't even given the choice. Our relationship, which had been founded on rejection by her parents, more and more became the property of her family. And her father's stroke, which had marked the turning point, did not prevent him from living on to over eighty. After which all their possessions passed into Riana's hands and at her untimely death, by default, into mine, before she'd had time to establish the trusts for our sons and their children through which she had schemed to keep me out of her testament. Perhaps there is a God after all.

No, no, no. I must not yield to bitterness. I never knew I had so much of it in me. As if the mere sight of you lying there in sleep has brought it all to the surface; perhaps there is so much unresolved, forever unresolvable between you and me that I turn instead to Riana, to blame it all on her. I know it is too easy, and it solves nothing. But how insufferable she was, all those years.

Her obsession with cleanliness. It wasn't enough that Magrieta hoovered the whole house every morning; every cursed evening before we went to bed — even when we'd been out to a concert, or to friends — Riana went over every square centimetre herself again. 'Suppose one of us dies in the night, what will people think if the house is in a mess?' Or, more directly, 'What if God comes in the night to find us living like pigs?' Imagine what dear God would do, I thought venomously, if he were to surprise us in something really wicked, like sex? It happened seldom enough, but just suppose he got lucky? And then, of course, in the end it was exactly what happened, only the woman turned out to be a girl from an agency, not my lawful wife. Enough to make God turn in his grave. Let alone poor Riana.

On weekends it was particularly aggravating. It was usually the only opportunity for some closeness. But Saturdays were the culmination of the whole week's cleaning rage (in preparation for Sundays, rigorously set apart for God, even though I'd long given up accompanying her and the boys to church). An obsession she might well have inherited, at least in part, from her father. Idleness, he had impressed on her, was the Devil's pillow. But for him it was a purely pragmatic urge. 'In a land like this, surrounded by a sea of blacks, we whites have got to work that much harder, otherwise they'll lose respect.'

In his eyes I was precisely the kind that invited swamping by the black masses. The smugness with which they'd impressed on me my social inferiority. They need not have bothered. Riana had a lifetime to perfect it. Not as crudely as they had done, to be sure. But much more efficiently. Simply by demonstrating at every turn how inconsiderate I was ('Can't you have a shower without messing up everything? Now *I* have to do the cleaning up again'), how unpractical ('You can't even fix a plug, Ruben'), how bad a father ('You're always hiding away in your books when you should be playing ball with your sons'), how boring ('Please, Ruben, promise me, when the guests arrive, you won't start rattling off pointless quotations from books no one has even heard about'). And then the casual, throwaway reminders of what she'd sacrificed. 'I see Mynhardt is going to perform with the City Orchestra. Can you believe it? There was a time when he turned the pages for me.' Or, 'I wonder whether we shouldn't sell the Bechstein? It's just gathering dust.' And I couldn't help thinking of Olive Schreiner's remark about her mother as a grand piano now used as a dining table. A quote I was careful never to mention in Riana's presence. And yet I'm wrong to call it a purgatory. Tessa, all the time I loved her. I desired her.

It was unfair perhaps (and unfair of me now to think of it that way) that someone as rigid and humourless as Riana had become — after those few magical years of madness, and fun, and music, and laughter, and love — should have remained so beautiful. Not only for me, as I grew older with her and learned to forgive my own failings and stumblings and signs of mortality by acknowledging them in her; but for others too. And she knew how to use it to prime effect. 'You know who I ran into at Cavendish today? Gerrie Henderson and his wife. Turns out he's a director-general of something. Still cuts a dashing figure. But then, he's always been a handsome man. Remember at university, when he was so madly in love with me? And he actually had the cheek, when we were alone for a moment, to invite me for a drink at his hotel tomorrow. I said no, of course.'

I don't know whether she ever said yes, Tessa. I don't think so. But there was a time when she derived some kind of dark satisfaction out of keeping me wondering. Always, in the end, she would cite her 'principles' as the reason for refusing to give in to temptation. She knew how to play the moral card, the religious card. But how much of it was real? How much merely designed to provoke or humiliate me? Perhaps the pretence was enough for her — it certainly was painful enough for me — to know how that would stoke up my desire, the better to frustrate it afterwards. 'Not now, my angel.' She had a habit of resorting to the most intimate terms of endearment at the moments of firmest refusal. (The worst, by far, were those occasions when she called me 'my Rubinstein'.)

The problem is that this kind of deterioration, like ageing, invades one's consciousness so slowly, you tend to miss the moments of revelation. Especially if you resist the knowledge, if you refuse to admit it exists. As I have tried to do more and more desperately over the years, even more so since she died and left me with the guilt. But if there was a point of no return it must have been the loss of Helena.

It is the name our daughter would have had if she'd survived. My mother's name. (That, I confess, was the official version. More privately, it would also have been my secret sanction of little Lenie.) For once I had insisted. Riana could decide about boys, but if there was a girl the choice would be mine. And rather to my surprise she'd accepted it. Perhaps, for her too, there was the hope that a daughter might be our salvation.

It had been a difficult pregnancy from the start. At three months, and again at four, Riana went through alarming experiences of contractions and bleeding. On the second occasion the doctor took me aside from her hospital bed to warn me. 'Ruben, you'd better prepare yourself for bad news. I'm not sure she's going to keep this baby. If she does it may do a lot of damage, perhaps more than she can take right now. We'll know in the morning.'

I sat beside her bed all night, holding her hand even while she was in a fitful sleep. At about five in the morning she unexpectedly opened her eyes, with a smile as frank and untroubled as when our world was still bright in the discovery of Haydn's first 'Let there be light'; and said, 'Ruben, I'm not going to let this one go. I owe it to you.'

At that stage, of course, we didn't know yet whether it was going to be a boy or a girl; in those days we didn't have today's prenatal probings. We were just unspeakably close together. I was crying. She smiled and held my hand very tightly, like a mother comforting her child. And when the doctor came on his rounds he shook his head and said, 'Don't ask me to explain this, but I think she's made it.'

For another six weeks. But then she lost it after all. I very nearly lost Riana as well. And after that it seemed impossible ever to recover what had been taken from us. I think – now, too late – that what we needed most, particularly after we knew that there was no hope of further children, was simply to talk; to find some kind of mutual reassurance: that we *could* survive, that we had in ourselves enough resources to go on together. Perhaps each of us was afraid of what the other really felt. We dared not look one another in the eye because we couldn't face ourselves, darkly, in the mirror.

In desperation, I tried to introduce a new beginning by taking her on a trip abroad, a second honeymoon (we'd been too poor for a first), leaving the boys at home with their over-eager grandparents. (But was it out of concern for Riana, or to run away from the memory of Alison?) It helped, up to a point. Even if in the end we came home several weeks earlier than we'd planned to because she couldn't bear being away from her home and children any longer. From then on her obsession with tidiness became uncontrollable. The poor kids had an even worse time than I. I'm afraid I withdrew more and more into my work, spending hours longer than necessary in the library, doing research, or simply reading, reading, filling reams of foolscap paper with notes. The most effective way of getting away from Riana, from the endless cleaning and nagging, the noise of children growing up.

I began to go away more often, to conferences, symposiums, annual general meetings of the Library Association. A self-generating thing, as I then became elected to committees, panels, organising bodies. Until that last congress in Pretoria. Where I met Tania. So young, so carefree, so head-over-heels, so everything-that-Riana-no-longer-was. And we spent that one afternoon making love while Riana was run over by the green delivery truck.

It won't be long now before you wake up. Light movements have begun to invade your body. I want to be here when you return from wherever you have been. Not a mere, physical presence, but really be here, and with you. One of the rare moments in my life when I had the experience of being fully present was that night behind the set of *Busman's Honeymoon* when Riana played Chopin on a piano half of whose notes were off-key and three or four were stuck. And then, surely, that night when you allowed me to discover your body. Even its repetition, in such a minor key, when you said, as I bent over you, 'I'm pregnant. I need to have an abortion.' And perhaps now, here, as I sit watching you while you return from sleep?

You didn't want me to come to the hospital with you. You were most emphatic about it. 'This is something I've got to do alone.'

But I went on arguing; I was just as adamant.

'It's not even your child,' you reminded me.

'What has that got to do with it? At least I can hold your hand.'

'You make it sound like a major operation, Ruben. It's no worse than a D and C. I'll be in in the morning and out in the afternoon.'

'I wasn't just thinking of the physical bit.'

'I'll be all right.'

'That's what Riana thought too, when she lost the baby.' I hesitated. 'But maybe this is not the time to talk about it.'

'The difference is that you both wanted the child and to lose it must have been a hell of a shock. But I have chosen this, I know exactly what I'm letting myself in for.'

'There may be hidden hurts. A kind of post-traumatic stress.'

'Then we'll deal with those afterwards.'

'In the meantime,' I said in my strictest paternal tone, 'I'm going with you.'

'They won't let you. You're not a relative.'

'As far as they are concerned I can be your father.'

That was when you smiled and said pensively, 'I think I'd like that.' And kissed me on the forehead.

# 2

To LIVE FORWARD and understand backward: Kierkegaard. When I think back to that day, a week ago, when she woke up in the hospital, there is little understanding. Somehow I had expected an experience of some moment. But all she said when she opened her eyes and grasped my hand was, 'It's bloody sore.' After that it took a while before she spoke again, looking quite forlorn. 'It's gone,' she said.

Years ago, Riana, crying uncontrollably: 'I lost it, I lost it, I lost it. Oh God, I'm so sorry. It must be God's punishment, I know it.'

'Don't talk now,' I said, to Tessa; to Riana.

Neither paid attention to me. Riana was hysterical and soon had to be sedated again; Tessa spoke with what sounded like controlled anger.

Tessa said, 'I don't know how the hell it happened, Ruben. I was trying to be so careful.'

Riana: 'I've made a mess of everything. It's all my fault.'

'What was it?' I dared to ask.

'I don't know,' said Tessa. 'It was too early to see on the sonar. I didn't *want* to know.'

'A girl,' said Riana. She had just been told. I felt my stomach contract. 'The one you've always wished for. I so much wanted to give you a girl.'

'It's all so weird,' said Tessa. 'Even when you brought me here this morning I couldn't really believe what was happening. It was only when they pushed me into the theatre and did the sonogram and then explained the whole procedure so graphically – that was when it hit me. My God, I actually have a small live thing in me and they're going to take it out.'

'How far was it?' I asked her.

'Six weeks. A little tadpole, that's all. But it was alive.'

'There was no other way,' I assured Riana. 'The doctor said if there's a miscarriage it means it couldn't go any further. The child itself didn't want to be born.'

Riana was still sobbing uncontrollably. That was when the sister came and gave her the injection.

Tessa was speaking compulsively. 'It was only on the safe days. Otherwise I insisted on condoms. Even so it happened.'

'It's over now.'

This will never be over, I thought, looking down at Riana's face, drawn even in sleep. This will haunt us for the rest of our days.

'Thank you for coming with me,' said Tessa. 'I never thought anyone could do it.'

A nurse, one I hadn't seen before, came in with a tray. 'I brought you some tea and a biscuit, Mrs Butler,' she said. Did I imagine her stressing the 'Mrs'?

'I'm feeling quite spacey,' said Tessa, pushing herself up. 'I haven't had anything since eight last night.' Her mouth formed a small grimace of pain. But with something mischievous in her voice she asked the nurse, 'Have you met my father? Mr Olivier.'

'Nice to meet you, sir.' She turned back to Tessa to ask, 'How's the pain?'

'Bad.'

'We'll give you something before you go.'

'I must look terrible,' said Tessa. She turned to me. 'Will you find me my make-up? It's in my bag, somewhere in the front, I think.'

I reached for the small dark red satchel she'd left on the floor.

She seemed to have thrown all kinds of odd, last-minute things into the bag. Among them the already dog-eared photograph of her faded father. I found the brightly coloured little cosmetics bag, then sat watching her as she pulled faces in the pocket mirror; a bewitching little ritual. (I stowed in my mind 'bewitching', 'ritual'.)

Half an hour later the same nurse and a colleague returned and sent me out into the passage while they gave her a final check-up, then drew the curtain so that she could get dressed. It took a while as she still had pain and was feeling dizzy. She held tightly on to my arm as we shuffled down the long green passage to the light outside. No Haydn this time.

'I don't want to go home,' said Riana on the day she was discharged. 'Why can't I just die?'

'Everything will be fine, you'll see. Johann and Louis can't wait for you to come home.'

'I can't face them right now.'

'I'll put some Chopin on for you.'

'I don't think I can stand Chopin right now.'

'Something else then. Anything you like.'

'I don't want music. Just let me be.'

'Wait here, I'll get the car,' I said to Riana, with a sinking feeling.

'Wait here,' I said eagerly to Tessa, 'I'll get the car.'

There were small beads of perspiration on her forehead, and she was very pale and clearly in pain.

We drove home slowly; I tried to avoid all sudden stops and swerving, which wasn't easy in the Cape Town traffic. Neither of them spoke on the way home.

'It'll be like a new start,' I said as I carried Riana across the threshold, a dead weight in my arms.

'If only one *could* make a fresh start,' she said and started crying again.

'Somehow it does feel like a new beginning,' said Tessa as I carried her into the house, which amused her hugely. 'You're stronger than I thought.'

'You're lighter than I thought,' I said with some surprise. 'I can count your ribs.' To Riana I said, 'We'll soon have you back to normal. You just rest, I'll take care of everything.'

'Leave it to Magrieta.'

Magrieta was there, as always. Food for Riana, food for Tessa. She was needed and that was her element. Through all the years food had been her most effective articulation, and her instrument of peace. She knew the favourite dish of each one in the house – my bobotie, grilled galjoen for Riana, pumpkin fritters for Johann, borriepatats for Louis – and could resolve the most uproarious quarrels by preparing the right food at the right time. Only once, as far as I can remember, did she make a mistake, but that was with the best intentions. It was soon after Riana had miscarried. The boys had spent some time with her parents on the wine farm to take them off her hands, and when they came back they brought a piglet with them which Johann had won at a church bazaar and refused to give up. Riana was livid, but too weak to impose her will as she would otherwise have done; all she exacted from them was that they would take care of the animal and clean up any mess it might cause. It lived in a box in the kitchen. Within a week or so, of course, the novelty had faded and they started neglecting the little pig. Riana began to mutter unchristian threats, but by that time I'd become curiously attached to the little creature. It would follow me around wherever I went, and squealed heart-rendingly when I left for work in the morning. This attachment probably went back a long time: I remember when I was very small, about seven or eight, Pa had designated a young pig to be slaughtered for Christmas. I was horrified at the idea. Why, I don't know. There were always fowls and animals slaughtered on the farm. But for some reason I must have chosen this one for a friend. The day before the execution I managed to steal the piglet and hid it in a deep disused dipping tank about half a mile from the farmhouse. Every day I would smuggle leftovers for it and spend an hour or more consoling the lonely little creature. It must have lasted for about a week before one of my brothers followed me there and discovered the pig. That was the end of it, and very nearly of me too.

My attachment to the little animal the kids had brought home soon aggravated all the tensions in the house. Riana hardly spoke to me any more. Then came my birthday and we were served suckling pig for dinner. Magrieta's well-meant attempt at solving a situation none of us could manage any longer.

This time, for Tessa's welcome, we were offered the same thick, rich oxtail soup Magrieta had prepared for Riana's homecoming. And the explanation was similar too, 'Nothing heavy. But Miss Tessa needs her strength.' The house was quieter this time, there were no children around. But just like years before we retired early, soon after Magrieta had caught her taxi to Mandalay. I left Tessa with a book, a glass of water and a small bell to ring if she needed me in the night. We left the door open. Riana wanted hers shut, she couldn't wait to be alone.

Some time deep in the night I was awakened by a sound. Unable to sleep, Riana had felt her way along the walls down the passage from the spare room into which she'd moved so as not to disturb me (or because she couldn't bear me near her right then?), and was playing the piano in the dark. Not on the baby grand in the lounge, where she used to play when she was serious about it, but in the room at the back of the house where she gave her lessons on the little upright; the one which is now Tessa's workroom. It was an eerie, hollow sound in the dead of night. Chopin's Funeral March. I broke out in a sweat. For almost an hour I listened before I dared to go to her and lead her back. She followed quite meekly, as if she'd been walking in her sleep; and perhaps she had. It wasn't the last time.

Some time deep in the night I became worried about the silence. I went to Tessa's room. I'd been unable to sleep, trying to keep myself busy by reading in bed, making notes in the study, putting on records, the Bach Brandenburgs, the volume turned down so low that the music was a mere melodic whisper in the dark; but I was thinking of Tessa all the time. Would she be awake too? Plagued by memories, by guilt, by God knows what? Or in pain? I did not want to disturb her, but I couldn't let her suffer on her own either. And so in the end, it was past three, I felt my way along the walls in the dark, down the passage, to the old music room. I paused at the open door to listen. It was all quiet. I went through to the bedroom and stood looking at the bed before going closer.

I bent over her, listening to her breathing as many years ago I'd used to do beside the boys' little beds when they were ill. I always found it easier to indulge my feeling for them when they were not boisterously awake.

She was asleep. The curtains were open and a pallor of the night outside – a hint of moonlight, a street lamp shining obscurely through the oaks – illuminated her face. Serene, distant, an innocence that caused my heart to ache. *Have you met my father?* she'd said. And much earlier, *Yes, I think I'd like that.* My darling. Ring the little bell if you ever need me.

# 3

THE NEXT DAY was the worst. (With Riana, the next several months.) Tessa got up early and we had breakfast together. But she looked pale and still felt some discomfort, and it didn't take Magrieta much of an effort to send her back to bed. I worked in the study, but went to check on her every hour or so. Sometimes she was asleep, but more often she just lay with open eyes. I never saw her cry. When I asked how she felt she said, 'I'm OK. Don't worry about me.'

'Would you like me to sit with you?'

'No, I'd like to be on my own for a while.'

'Anyone I should phone?'

'No, please don't.'

Back in the study I thought: She'll probably be turned off from men now. At least for some time.

It might even change her way of reacting to the world. Nothing had seemed to touch her deeply before. Gliding along the surface of life with the flair of an Olympic skater, taking the most awful risks yet remaining singularly uninvolved. Except this time. And it was hard to tell how it would mark her, what scars would remain. (Even after all our endless, probing conversations, what did I really know about her? What had I known about Riana, after a lifetime together? Had I ever cared enough to find out how it had all affected her?)

In the evening, after Magrieta had left, she rang the little bell for the first time.

'Do you have anything to do right now?' she asked.

'I was just reading.'

'Could you do it here?'

'Of course.'

'I'm feeling a bit lonely.'

I brought my book and moved a chair to her side of the bed.

'Sit next to me.'

For a while I sit beside her, the book closed on my knees. She shifts to rest her head against my arm. I'm beginning to think that she has drifted off to sleep, but when I look down I see her gazing quietly at me.

'This has been a tough day for you,' I say.

She nods. 'Not so easy. But I'll be OK.'

'I wish we could just undo all of this and wake up tomorrow morning and find it has never happened.'

'That's a strange thing to say. If it happens it means you've got to face it. Even if it's tough.'

I take her hand. 'Don't you sometimes wish you could go back to wherever you were before you had your first boyfriend?'

'Good God, no. I'd hate to be back there.'

'And yet you shave your pussy,' I say. 'Isn't that a way of wishing you were still a little girl?'

'No. I just feel more in touch with my body that way.'

'What happened to your first love?' I ask. 'For how long did that last?' I was prepared to ask her anything, merely to give her a chance to speak, to get rid of whatever she'd been hoarding inside.

But she remained singularly controlled. 'Andy? Not long. It became kind of boring. By the time I left for university it just sort of petered out.'

'Then you met someone else?'

'After a year or so one of my lecturers became interested. And that was rather good. But then he had to do a stint at some American university. Six months. And when he came back he gave me one look and said, "You've been fooling around with someone else."'

'Was that true?'

She chuckles. 'It wasn't as if *he*'d been all that monogamous.'

'So that was that?'

'We still saw each other from time to time, and then it was OK. I just didn't want to feel trapped again. One's got to move on.'

'Since then you've been on the move all the time?'

She shakes her head against my arm. 'There's no pressure. I can skip sex for months. Before I met Brian I didn't have a man for over a year. Many friends, but not lovers.'

'How serious were you about Alex?'

'He was good to be with. And I knew it couldn't get out of hand, what with him being married. He was rather lonely, I already told you his wife is a bitch. Alex is quite sensitive. He *cared*.'

'You had something going with him while you were still with Brian?'

'It wasn't planned. Brian was overseas, one of the trips he promised to take me on and never did. I felt pissed off, Alex was feeling low, so it happened.'

'You told me once before that Brian accused you falsely.'

'I didn't know you well enough.' There is no hint of contrition in her voice.

'And now, you said, he's changed?'

'He just became terribly possessive when he heard about the child. Like it was his sole possession, not something I had any say in.'

'What about Zach?'

'Zach's all right. Always on the go, one never knows what the next move will be. And I knew from the beginning he'd never settle down, so there was no danger.'

'No chance of breaking your heart?'

'I never let my heart run away with me. My mind is always in control.'

'It sounds terribly calculated.'

'That's not what I mean. I can go with the flow. But I won't get caught, I know when to pull out.'

'This time you got caught.'

'By getting pregnant, yes. Not by losing control. And I doubt if I'll see Zach again. I feel there's so much that belongs to the past now. Perhaps with the birthday coming up I'll really become a staid old maid.'

'What will you do for sex?' (She once brazenly asked *me*. The very first night she met me. When perhaps I should have shown her the door. How much quieter my life would have been then. How much more meaningless.)

'What I've always done,' she says. 'I don't *need* it, I've never felt desperate. And after all, there are ways around it. I have a mean hand.'

Impulsively, playfully, I take her hand and kiss the fingers one by one. 'Do give my love when you visit again.'

She laughs, a soft but deep sound. 'You know, if it had been your baby I might have decided to keep it.'

'I'm out of the running, I told you.'

'I'm sure you'd be a great father.'

'I was a hopeless father. As Riana never stopped reminding me. To be a good father you must be able to invest yourself in others, unconditionally. Perhaps I'm just too selfish, or too insecure. I'm always aware of holding something back.'

'You've never held back with me.'

I smile. 'I don't have to. *You* are the one who keeps me at a distance.'

'Not emotionally.'

'No,' I admit. 'Not emotionally. But sometimes it's bloody hard to know you don't mind sharing your body with others, while it's off-limits to me.'

'You know why I cannot.'

'Because I'm old. And you are young.'

'No!' She seems really dismayed. 'Ruben, I told you. It's because *we* matter to me.'

'Does that mean that the others don't?'

The familiar little frown returns to her brow. 'You know what? I have an idea that I might never have had anything to do with Alex or Zach if you hadn't been here.'

I feel my face go numb. 'You don't mean you wanted to spite me? Or "show" me?'

'Of course not!' She is quite indignant. 'I'd never do that. I promise you. It's just that because you were there I think I felt a kind of stability in my life, like I've never quite felt before; and that gave me the confidence to have other relationships. I knew I wouldn't stray too far, you would be there to hold me.' She looks at me. 'Does that sound crazy?'

'I suppose there is some kind of sense to it. But it doesn't exactly make things any easier for me.'

'You make me feel safe and the only reason I feel safe is because you don't demand that kind of involvement.'

'I may not demand it but I certainly desire it.'

'I told you. If we do make love I know it will be the end. I couldn't stay here, I couldn't trust you. Above all, I think, I couldn't trust myself. You must believe me, Ruben.' She sits up beside me, flinching briefly with pain, then presses herself against me. I can feel her breasts through the old blue T-shirt she's wearing.

'You mustn't let this happen again,' I say in an onrush of urgency, holding her against me.

'No fear of that.'

It is getting late. But when I move my legs off the bed she grasps my arm in a kind of panic. 'Don't go, please.'

'You need to rest.'

'I don't want to be alone tonight. Last night . . .' She takes a while to compose herself. 'I think Antje visited me again.'

'Did you see her?'

'It was too dark and I was in a kind of daze. But I'm sure she was here. Standing at the foot of my bed, staring at me for I don't know how long.'

'Did you try to speak to her?'

'No, I daren't. And I can't face her tonight. Will you sleep here with me and just hold me?'

Throughout that long night I lay next to her, her back pressed against me, one of her breasts in my hand. I didn't dare to move, not even when my arms got pins and needles and my neck went numb. It was one of the most uncomfortable nights of my life, but I wouldn't have missed a minute of it. There was nothing neutral about it. Desire permeated me, but desire without urgency or need, a kind of lasting, low-key orgasm that suffused me with satisfaction. If I think back now, it was like Pachelbel's Canon — or, even more intensely, the Adagio from Beethoven's Sonata number 32 — though the music has more urgency, a swelling and a gathering of sound moving to fulfilment: mine did not *seek* fulfilment, it *was* fulfilment; I didn't even have an erection, and was conscious of that in a way which brought me profound contentment. Whatever might happen after this, I thought, however far from each other we might stray, whatever distances, misunderstandings, estrangements might yet come, this night was ours; and no one dead or alive could take it from us.

# 4

JUST AS WELL. Because so much has changed since then. It is early November already, the weather is dry and hot, with a raging south-easter, and the discomfort is replicated in the mind. It does not bode well for summer. There are spells so beautiful that one is tempted to believe life is worth while after all; but on days like today the mountain oppresses me. I miss the endless parched plains of my youth. I've never gone back, not even with Riana. As if I knew it had become a space closed off to me. There was a time when people believed the earth was flat; in the Kalahari it has remained flat. No amount of science has changed it. It is arid and archaic, and the Bushman paintings mark it as they did millennia ago. I'm often aware of an almost physical pang of nostalgia in me to go back. But there is no entry possible into a flat world from a round one. My present world is marked by mountains. I've always been a stranger here. (But did I feel any less of a stranger on those flat plains?) After almost forty years in this house I'm still a guest. I don't really live here, at most I haunt it, like Antje of Bengal. In the early days, when Riana and I first moved in, we went from room to room to make love in every one of them; even on the kitchen floor, in the pantry and the scullery, the passage, the storerooms, to leave our imprint everywhere, to mark like cats or dogs the extent of our territory. But all that has faded now, except for sudden, piercing, fleeting memories, like Antje's unpredictable appearances. My world is getting more penetrable.

All I really care about, I must admit, is Tessa. And she's the least predictable element of this little world, more achingly beyond my

reach than ever. In the week or two just after she'd come back
from the hospital it seemed to be changing. She spent more time
with me, went out less. It was not that I was beginning to hope
our relationship might change – that had been firmly ruled out. But
within the frontiers we had come to accept there did seem space for
growing. If not in width, at least in depth. Now I'm not so sure.

I gave her a gold chain for her birthday, a few days after she came
home from the hospital. A very finely wrought, delicate little thing;
and vastly expensive, but I didn't think twice. How much longer will
I need my money – Riana's parents' money – anyway? I took it to
her room on a breakfast tray, very early, even before Magrieta had
come in. A bottle of Veuve Clicquot, two glasses of orange juice I'd
freshly squeezed, muesli, soft-boiled eggs, toast, some strawberries
I'd found at the farm stall in Constantia. A small round vase with
three nasturtiums. And the meticulously made up little parcel.

Tessa was still asleep when I came in and opened the curtains. She
mumbled something and gazed at me in some confusion. Only when
she sat up did she discover where she was.

'I thought you were my mother,' she said. 'She always came to
wake me by opening the curtains. But she never did it so gently. She
used to jerk them open with a kind of sadistic vigour.'

I sat down on the bed with the tray. 'Happy birthday, my love.'

'You remembered?'

'How could I not remember? This is the watershed, isn't it?
Thirty.'

She shook her head. 'I can't believe it. People shouldn't live to be
so old.' And slid under the blankets again with a groan. 'I can't bear
it. I think I'm going to stay in bed for a week.'

'I'm more than twice your age,' I said. 'One tends to survive.'

'There's nothing left to do for the first time,' she said. 'I think
that is the worst.'

'There's bungee jumping,' I said. 'And skydiving. And climbing
Everest. And taking a walk up the mountain on a path we've never
taken. And going to Machupicchu. And making love to me.'

'There's something in that. Where shall we start?'

'I can make a suggestion.'

She sat up again. The worn old T-shirt had slipped off one shoulder and she didn't bother to pull it up. 'Perhaps I'll live just a little bit longer after all.'

'Age cannot wither you,' I declaimed, rather predictably I fear, 'nor custom stale et cetera. Shall we drink to that?'

She slipped into a mood as effervescent as the bubbly. And she was delighted with the chain.

'When I go to bed tonight,' she said, 'I promise I'll wear only this chain and nothing else.'

'Can I come and check on it?' I asked lightly.

Narrowing her eyes for a moment in her lovely, myopic way she said, just as lightly, 'Of course.' And with a flash of impulsive generosity, 'I'll keep it for tonight, then you can come and put it on for me.'

I'd hoped to take her out for a private celebration, but in the evening she went out with friends. A carload of young women came to pick her up quite early; they drove off into the dusk like a whole tree of chattering birds. I waited up, of course. It was the first time she'd gone out since she'd been to the hospital and I was worried she might get tired. (At least there didn't seem to be men involved. O brave new world.) Later I fell asleep on the easy chair in my study with Amadeus on my lap and only woke up when I heard her key in the front door. The Mozart clarinet quintet I had put on must have come to an end hours before. It was five o'clock and outside the birds – real birds – were twittering.

'Ruben!' She stopped when I appeared in the door. 'You haven't waited up, have you?'

'No, I was working. I got quite carried away. Chasing a footnote.'

'You're lying.'

'Did you have a good time?'

'It was wonderful to get out again. I'm afraid I'm totally pissed.'

'I can put you to bed.'

'I'll just about manage.' Then, unexpectedly, she remembered. 'But you can come with me to put on my chain.' She gave a befuddled and endearing smile.

It was almost too much to believe. But I went with her, her arm ceremoniously hooked into mine, like a bridal couple down an aisle. In her room she kicked off her shoes, went to the bathroom and after a while emerged again. The smooth integrity of her limbs. No sign of what had happened only days before, the darkness traversed, the moments — surely — of loneliness, uncertainty, perhaps terror; no scar at all on body or mind. Even her memory, it seemed, untrammelled. I was the one who still lay awake at night, concerned about her, or wandered through the dark house, listening at her door to find out whether she was perhaps crying, moaning, in need of something or of me. While she just glided through the days, intact, smooth, untouchable, entirely beautiful.

With a voluptuous sigh she slid her legs in under the bedclothes, remaining seated, uncovered from the waist up. She pulled open the drawer of the bedside cabinet and took out the small black velvet box, leaving the drawer open. Scattered inside were all the odd objects I remembered from the last time. But this time I wasn't shocked, not even by the more scandalous ones. Not because I'd seen them before, but because this time she was there and in her presence they made sense. She deftly removed the chain from the box and held it out to me. 'Will you do the honours?'

I'm afraid my hands were trembling and it took me a while to drape it in a delicate glittering loop between her nippled breasts.

'Good,' she said. 'Now I won't ever take it off again.'

We kissed, she pulled up the blankets, I turned off the light and closed the door. Since then she has indeed been wearing the little chain every day.

# 5

OUR PRIVATE CELEBRATION had to be postponed because of a new
crisis in Magrieta's life. She came in late – it was the day after Tessa's
birthday – but this time, at least, someone had telephoned to alert
me. No reason was given, but I had that awful feeling. And when
I heard the gate – it really is time I do something about it, but it
is quite useful as a warning signal – I immediately went to the door.
She was still fumbling for her keys when I opened.

For a moment she just looked at me. Then she broke down. 'Ag,
Meneer,' was all she could say as she fell in my arms.

It was quite a weight to sustain, but I stood firm. And the sobbing
didn't last long. With a show of vexation – from embarrassment
more than anything else – she broke away from my hold, took out a
tissue, blew her nose energetically and came past me. I followed her
to the kitchen.

'So it happened,' she said, dumping her bulky bag on the table.

'Not the house?' I asked, aghast. 'Don't tell me they came back?'

'This is what I got left today,' she said, grabbing the bag and
slamming it down again. 'Naked I came into the world and naked
I go. Praised be the name of the Lord.'

I pulled out a chair for her and tried to make her sit, but she
resisted. 'Tell me what happened, Magrieta.'

'They burnt it down. There's nothing left, jus' the black walls.'

'The same crowd?'

She shrugged. She stood opposite me like a boulder buffeted by a
hurricane. 'I think it was. How do I know? Same difference.'

'Did they say anything? Didn't they give you any warning?'

'I saw some of them there in the streets the last few evenings when I came home. Coming, going, hanging around. I spoke to the neighbours en they said yes, they seen those young skollies about. But how can one be sure it's the same ones? Then early last night there was suddenly a lot of them in front of the house. Shouting at me to come out. *Impimpi* they called me. That's what the black people mos call someone who goes to the pollies. I jus' stayed inside, I didn't answer. I had no lights on. I was there with the woman who sleeps there nowadays. Paulina. I heard some of the neighbours telling the kids to go away, but they didn't listen. I looked through the window, standing to one side so they couldn't see me. Then I saw them bringing the plastic cans. Petrol. I know, I saw that mos in the bad times when they did the necklacings. En then I got out.'

'How on earth did you do that?'

'I was lucky, Meneer. I had my back window fixed last week en they haven't put the burglar bars back on. These skollies didn't know that. So while they was singing en making their noise in front, the two of us we got out.'

'You jumped through the window?' I stared in some disbelief.

She broke into a smile resembling a rictus. But it didn't last long. 'Don't ask me how I got through with my body. But I did.'

'Where did you go?'

'We went to the garage en there we got a man to take us to friends in Bonteheuwel. They brought us back this morning to look at the house, but it's gone now. Only the walls.' And then she surprised me. 'Now I can sleep again in the night.'

'What do you mean?'

'I no longer got nothing to worry about, Meneer. The worst has now happened, what I was always afraid of. Now there's nothing to fear no more.' She opened her bag and took out a bible that seemed to be falling to pieces. 'I jus' brought God with me.'

I clutched the back of a chair and closed my eyes for a while. 'But why did they wait so long? It's over a month. We thought they'd given up.'

'That's what they waited for, Meneer. But I knew mos it was coming.'

'How can one live like that?' I asked, more to myself than to her.

'One lives when one must live.'

'What shall we do now?' I said, desperate.

'I must find a place to stay. There's friends. The ones in Grassy Park en others in Bonteheuwel.'

'You have to move back in here, Magrieta. There's room enough.' She didn't answer.

'Can't we get in touch with Mabel?' I asked.

'Mabel turned her backside to all of us, Meneer. You know that.' With a flush of anger she added, 'Jus' as well her father didn't live to see the day. He'll shit in his grave.' She became more subdued again, but below the calm on the surface I sensed all the suppressed rage. And for once she allowed it to break out. 'What's happening to this country, Meneer? I thought I knew the place, but I no longer do. I no longer know myself. We had the bad days when the whites ruled us like Pharaoh and the Egyptians did with the Jews. Then they tole us it was now a free country, Mandela will bring us peace.' She turned to the window and made a helpless gesture. 'Is this what a free country looks like? That poor Mr MacFarlane killed here in our street. En that poor woman they called a witch. En now my house. En all this is just a drop in a very big bucket: what about the thousands en thousands of other things that happens? Every day of our lives. En up there in parliament they just get richer en smarter with their big cars en their cellphones en their stuff. No one even hear us when we cry. We are too common for them to hear us. Is this now the freedom they brag about so much?'

'It takes time,' I offered lamely, avoiding her eyes.

'How long they expect us to wait?' she asked. 'Have they not milked us dry enough yet? Have they not killed enough of us? I'll be seventy-two next year, Meneer. En what can I show for it? This!' She slammed her bag down again.

'I'll look after you, Magrieta,' I said, shot through with the futility of every word. 'We two will take care of each other.'

But she wasn't even listening. She was unpacking her bag. It was like a scene on some stage, which I watched from a darkened hall.

Every item, ludicrous and exposed in its nudity, its incongruity, its hopelessness, was placed separately on the scrubbed surface of the table: a powder compact, a comb with missing teeth, her tortoiseshell glasses in a scuffed plastic case, a packet of tissues, the broken-off heel of a shoe, the pocket bible, several lengths of string, an assortment of little boxes, some with pills, others empty; a screwdriver, a ballpoint pen, an empty Scotch-tape holder, some used bus tickets, a pair of scissors, a horseshoe, large coloured beads from a broken necklace, keys, a purse, a little green ID book, a single yellow knitting needle, a broken glass paperweight the boys had given her one faraway Christmas and which had once contained a miniature snowstorm, a pink pompom from a slipper, two safety pins, a child's shoe, the small framed photograph of her two children, a pocket watch that had stopped going years ago, a half packet of acid drops, a pair of rusty pliers, a brass doorknob, a glass pendant earring, a pipe with a broken stem, a glittering brooch that had lost most of its stones, a blackened toothbrush, a few rubber bands, a smooth round pebble from some unknown beach, several hair curlers in assorted colours, an empty perfume bottle, a baby's bottle-teat, a post-office savings book, a tin of Koo tomato soup, an egg whisk, a half set of dentures, a life.

# 6

IT WAS NOT until two or three days later that we had time for our private, belated, birthday celebration. Magrieta had to be taken care of first. In spite of all my attempts to coax her into staying, she insisted on moving out to her friends in Bonteheuwel. If it didn't work out, she promised solemnly, we could discuss the matter again; but I knew it was only her way of placating me.

Tessa wanted sushi, so we went to Sea Point; but the place she'd had in mind was full. I've found out that as a matter of principle she refuses to book in advance as she prefers to make up her mind at the very last minute. On this occasion, as on others, we had to look for an alternative. It was a pretty nondescript place, but what mattered was the talk, not the food. It was as if, on the very first night she'd come into my study and my life, we'd boarded a train of conversation; from time to time we'd get off at a station to explore the surroundings and then board another train to be carried off to whatever stop came next, with no inkling of a destination, no wish ever to arrive for good. The going was all.

While we talked I became aware, from time to time, of other people looking at us; men especially. One elderly man having a meal with what must have been his wife – they never exchanged a single word – stared at me with open, hostile envy. I could almost hear him thinking, *Lucky fucking bastard*. (And I thought: Lucky, undoubtedly, my friend; fucking, no.)

We were both still preoccupied with Magrieta.

'It is not good enough to let her go,' said Tessa. 'We have a responsibility.'

'But she refuses to listen, Tessa.'

'Perhaps if I weren't there she might agree to come back.'

'I can't think of living without you.'

'That's purely selfish,' she said and pressed a finger to my lips.

'Perhaps. But at my age I'm entitled to it.'

'What will she *do*, Ruben?'

'I'll try to find out about another house. In a different part of the Peninsula, where those skollies won't find her.'

'She is so vulnerable. I know she puts on the great motherly act, but behind it all I think she's a terribly lonely person.' She disposed of a few mouthfuls of fish, chewing in a pensive way. 'We had a long chat yesterday. You know how much you mean to her?'

'She's been part of the family. But this country makes it hard to win.'

'It's no use thinking of "this country" as if it was some great abstraction, Ruben. It's all of us. If *we* don't make it work . . .' She was becoming more and more intense. 'And there's no point in just complaining. The country is not just crime, and corruption, and failure, and whatnot. We must believe there's something more to it, something larger than all of us, a kind of hope, a kind of potential. It's something like Antje of Bengal: even if one doesn't see her, we must be prepared to believe in her. Otherwise her whole life would have been in vain. Magrieta knows that better than you or me. And Magrieta is as good a place to start as any.'

'Magrieta has never known another life except with us.'

'What do you *really* know about her, Ruben? What do you really know of what she feels about your house, about you?'

'We talk all the time. She knows I'm there for her. But Magrieta has a sense of propriety that keeps a certain distance between us.'

'Magrieta *cares* about you.' She looked at me. 'Like I do.'

'I've never deserved that from anyone.'

'Not even Riana?'

It was suddenly very hard to talk about her. 'Ever since you had the . . . ever since you went to hospital, I've been thinking about our married life,' I said at last. 'It was so different from the bliss I'd forced myself to believe in. I made her life a misery.'

'Your infidelities?'

'Just by not caring enough. But the infidelities too.' I took her hand across the narrow table. 'I once told you she never knew about Alison. But she did.'

'Did Magrieta tell her?'

'Magrieta was discretion itself. She was shocked, of course, but she'd never discuss it with anyone. No, there was a letter from Alison. After what happened. To say how sorry she was and that she still loved me. The old sitcom situation: it was in the pocket of a jacket Riana took to the cleaner's.'

'She confronted you with it?'

'No. She only put it on my desk and never said a word. And I was too shattered and too ashamed ever to bring it up myself. Not just about being caught out, but because of something Alison had made me discover about myself. That I was *not*, in my heart of hearts, the model husband, the good and upright citizen, but that I had things in me I hadn't known before, a capacity for lust, with little regard for the straight and narrow.' I sighed and emptied my glass. Then waited for the waiter to clear our plates away. I ordered dessert, Tessa a cheese platter.

'How did you meet Alison?' she asked.

'She was a music student. She played the flute. It was pure magic. I could listen for hours when she played the Mozart sonatas. Riana had met her at the conservatoire in Stellenbosch and brought her home. We soon became close, but we were very firm about keeping our emotions in control. When Riana lost the baby and went to her parents' farm to recover, we were suddenly both very vulnerable. And then it happened.' I smiled wryly. 'Or didn't happen. Thanks to Magrieta, and Antje of Bengal, of course.'

'Antje has played a major role in your life, hasn't she?'

'For such an absent presence, yes. I only saw her once, you know.'

'Yes, you told me.'

'You don't know how it happened.' This was a precarious moment. But it was another of our nights when there was a need to tell all. 'That night you spent in Camps Bay . . .' It brought back so much,

I couldn't go on straight away. But I mastered myself. 'I was frantic with worry the next day, about you and about Magrieta. That was when I tried to phone you at work. Then I remembered Zach had given you his card and I went to your room to look for it – I can't tell you how ashamed I was, but I could think of nothing else – and then the door opened and Antje was there.'

It was almost a relief when the waiter came back. While he was refilling our glasses, we made small talk. About cheese, I remember. Camembert specifically, which was her favourite. I told her what I'd heard about the processes of maturing it, turning it upside down in the dark and all that. Then the young man left and we resumed as if there had been no interruption.

'Why did you tell me you worked for *Woman*?' I asked.

'I suppose it was just to impress you.' The candlelight flickered across her high cheekbones, the fullness of her mouth, made shadows on her temples, around her small ears. 'Also, I was scared that if you knew what a measly job I really had you'd never let me have the room.'

'Where *did* you work?'

'After I was fired from Brian's firm I got a job as Girl Friday for a small computer outfit in Claremont.'

'Even if you had no money I'd never have turned you down.'

'I was a total stranger and I must have looked like a tramp that first night.'

'You were utterly beautiful.' Like often before, I kissed her fingers; and in my mind sent unspoken messages.

'By the way, I'm starting in a new job on Monday,' she announced. Before I could ask, she said, 'Production assistant with a film group. It's a local company working with an American outfit.'

'Sounds glamorous.'

'More hard work than glamour, but it's a start.'

'How did you land it?'

'Zach,' she said.

My stomach contracted. 'Have you been seeing him again?'

'He's back.' She relished a piece of cheese on the tip of her fork. 'I haven't seen him, but we spoke on the phone.'

'Did you tell him about . . . the hospital?' (I still couldn't bring myself to say the word.)

She shook her head. 'It's water under the bridge.'

'You really want to see him again?'

'Nothing serious, I promise you. But I can't deny that he's exciting in a way. Never-a-dull-moment sort of man.'

'You hardly know him, Tessa.'

'I spent at least two years with him one night.'

'You think because you're thirty you're mature enough?'

'I've also been turned upside down in the dark.'

'I just want you to be careful.'

'I've learned the hard way. You can trust me.'

'What you need is someone to pee on your toes.'

She burst out laughing so loudly – that deep, gathering, erupting laugh I can never hear enough of – that everybody turned to stare at us, the old codger in the corner with ferocious hostility. 'What on earth does that mean, Ruben?'

I told her about my early years at school. The merciless winters on those exposed plains, where it seemed there was nothing between us and the Antarctic. The earth, hard as stone, white with frost. And most of us dirt poor, going barefoot; and there was the special ritual which obliged the boys to hold back until we got to school, where those of us who had favourites among the girls overcame our habitual inhibitions to seek out the chosen one and pee on her feet, as that was the only way of warming them, a demonstration of the truest love. I looked through the candle flame into her magical face. 'Little Lenie was the only one on whose feet I ever dared to pee,' I said.

'I won't invite you to pee on me,' said Tessa. 'But if I was little Lenie I'm sure I'd have been most honoured.'

'It was probably the closest I came to worship in those days,' I said. 'Real religion never stood a chance. Even if I'd been inclined that way my brothers, who were always holier than thou, would have beaten it out of me.'

'My religion was also nipped in the bud,' she said. 'Mainly by my mother. My one memory of Sundays is of how we always arrived at the church in the vilest of spirits. There would be so much fighting and bickering and snarling and slapping going on to get us there on time and in the proper clothes and with the right collection money that we had nothing but hate and shit in our minds by the time we sat down in those ghastly, uncomfortable pews.'

'That is where Magrieta puts us both to shame,' I reflected. 'She probably has more reason than either of us to have been totally turned off by religion. And yet she is in church every Sunday. And singing hymns while she makes the beds and polishes the floors. And reading her Bible mornings and evenings.'

'Which was probably why our colonial ancestors brought religion with them in the first place,' she said. 'To keep the natives in their place and make them bear their cross with joy.'

'It's supposed to have changed.'

'It's for us to make the change,' she said again, like before.

'Kafka wrote somewhere,' I said, '"There is hope. But not for us."'

'Kafka is dead,' she said. 'We are here.'

Then the waiter came with the bill and I paid; as we left I stared straight back at the man who'd been glowering at us all evening. When Tessa passed me at the door I caught a glimpse of the little chain around her neck, between the wide lapels of her elegant charcoal jacket. And in my mind I could see her going to bed as she had on the night of her birthday, how she would slide in between the cool sheets and how the thin line of gold would lie like a sign of victory between her breasts.

Lucky bastard.

# 7

Two DAYS AFTER our evening out Tessa left for Johannesburg with her film group. She was to be away for three weeks. The house became as empty as a barn. Amadeus slunk from to room, mewing mournfully. Magrieta, bless her soul, moved back for the time being. Which made me wonder whether it was purely for concern about me or whether there was something about Tessa's presence which had indeed become offensive to her. But if so, what? In the weeks since the bergies had swamped us, and particularly since Tessa had come home from the hospital, she'd been a model of virtue. At least as far as I could tell. When she went out it was invariably with other women, or in a group; and except for that one night of her birthday, which surely was understandable, she never came back too late. She certainly never had sleepover guests again. So all I could think was that, without being asked, Magrieta had decided I shouldn't be left alone.

Something of the old confidence between us was restored. And however much I missed Tessa – there were times, especially at night, when it was unbearable, an almost physical pain – Magrieta's presence brought a certain consolation. Even before Tessa left I'd begun to spend an inordinate amount of time trying to set in motion the complicated process of finding Magrieta a new house. My preferred mode of contact, writing a letter, turned out to be wholly useless; no one even bothered to respond – and it was immaterial whether I sent it by ordinary mail, fastmail or registered mail. The second step, still at a safe distance, was the telephone. But I'd forgotten just how convoluted the process was. It took days of enquiries to find a starting point, a friend of a friend of a friend who could provide the name of a person dealing with housing. Local government, provincial government, even central government. Back to local. From one secretary to the next, one department to the next, involving waits of ten or twenty or forty minutes at a time, listening to bad music on the line, interrupted by a canned voice assuring me that my call would be answered and how much it meant to them. Then I would be cut off. Even when one got on track, it was all too easy to get lost again: the person who answered the telephone today would never be the one I'd spoken to yesterday and wouldn't have the slightest idea of what had been discussed or promised before. All the particulars had to be given again, often to someone at the other end who had difficulty writing down the simplest information. ('How do you spell *Daniels*?' 'What's the address again, Mr Oliver?' – Not Oliver, Olivier, with an i-e-r.)

But in the end I did locate the right section of the right department. I made an appointment to visit the office in person. Right place, right time, no official. Out on a call. No, sorry, we have no idea when he'll be back. His cellphone is switched off. Could you call again tomorrow?

Tessa's three weeks were almost up before I actually tracked down the elusive kingpin, Mr Jacobs, and even then I had the impression it was pure luck: having forgotten that I was coming in he'd failed to make a getaway in time. And although we'd spoken about it on the phone three times, he'd mislaid the file and we had to start once more. He suggested I take the papers home and submit them the next day, but I insisted on completing everything there and then. I knew there was a long way ahead and that more than time and patience would be required. But at least a beginning had been made, however painful I found these personal meetings. I'm simply not cut out to face such situations.

Magrieta accepted the news with equanimity rather than pleasure. It was clear that she had even fewer illusions than I. But there was no alternative to playing the game. After every phone call and every excursion the two of us would have a session at the kitchen table to evaluate the progress or lack of it. From there we would branch off in all directions. We would retrace the courses of our children's lives, of her three marriages and my one; we would review the newspapers, to which she would add her own observations on events from her world. She had much to say about the family she was living with in Bonteheuwel. The man was out of work: he'd been a builder all his life, but had been laid off when contracts dried up, so for the time being his wife, Jessie, was the only breadwinner. She worked in a delicatessen in an upmarket mall that had recently been renovated, which meant that the rent was almost doubled and working hours increased. Instead of five days a week, from eight to six, Jessie now had to put in seven days, until nine in the evening (noon on Sundays), with only every other Saturday free. The changed schedule brought no extra pay, and when Jessie and her colleagues complained, the delicatessen manager curtly explained that he couldn't afford the rent if he had to pay them more; if they didn't like it they could lump it, there was no shortage of people looking for jobs. Whereupon the staff joined a union which charged them exorbitant membership fees and then ignored them. (Two of the union leaders had recently been arrested for embezzlement but were soon released for lack of evidence; it was known that they had relatives in parliament.) Jessie managed to gain one concession, and that was that her daughter, aged seventeen, Beulah, a student at UWC, could stand in for her on Saturdays. Which worked well until the weekend before Magrieta told me about it, when on her way between the bus stop and her home, a distance of less than two hundred metres, Beulah had been abducted, dragged into the ruin of an old shop and gang-raped by five men, after which they had slit her throat. When Jessie telephoned her boss at the delicatessen the next morning to explain what had happened and ask for the day off she was told that it wasn't her free day and unless she clocked in within the hour she'd be fired. If one started making exceptions employees would be playing truant for any reason whatever.

'What I'm scared of,' Magrieta confided in me, 'is that Stanley, that's now her husband, he's so angry he's capable of doing something very bad en what's going to happen then? That girl was the apple of his eye. It's a upside-down world, Meneer.'

Not all Magrieta's accounts were violent or depressing. There was a constant stream of reports on celebrations, christenings, weddings, school sports, bus trips to Strandfontein or Cool Bay; on people pricking the bubble of arrogant officials in any of the innumerable offices where one's life was decided; on getting by with stolen electricity or water, paying an account with a bag full of cents, outwitting a traffic cop, harassing an inept policeman, heckling a visiting politician. Otherwise she'd simply resort to retelling me the many stories about her family I'd already heard in so many variations over the years – stories told by her mother, who'd heard them from her grandmother, and so on, all the way back to an ancestor first brought from East India as a slave. In the course of many retellings this matriarch became, predictably, a contemporary of Antje of Bengal. Her name was not known, so it was impossible for me to fill out any details from archives or books. But somehow we settled on the name of Maria of Tutucorijn, for no other reason than that its music appealed to us. Mere facts were never an impediment to Magrieta's powers of imagination and her stories about this foremother were entertaining enough to hook even the most sceptical listener.

Somewhere in the succession of generations other, local ingredients must have been added to the bloodline, as several of Magrieta's tales showed undoubtable influence from Khoisan sources – a monstrous water snake carrying a diamond on its forehead, water maidens luring unsuspecting men into their stream to possess and drown them, tales about chameleons, and hares, and the moon, and a hunter-god commemorated by cairns of rock in the hinterland – and even a hint of Xhosa. What intrigued me was her easy appropriation of it all; what had mesmerised my sons, who'd been brought up on Magrieta's stories, was the verve of invention with which she told them.

The house became, as it had been long before, a place of talk and imagination; but it was also a lonely place, an empty pod in which Magrieta and I rattled like two desiccated old seeds. Tessa's absence lay on me like a physical weight. I had hoped that it would help me to sort out some of the intricate and incongruous twists in my relationship with her – the fierce sexual urge and the curious consolation of abstinence, the need to have and the satisfaction of doing without, the fatherly instinct to protect and the compulsions of the lover. But as it turned out her absence was so numbing that instead of allowing the thoughts to flow more smoothly it made the process more lumbering and laborious. And, of course, Magrieta didn't overlook a thing.

'You missing that girl,' she would say, if I came into the kitchen for the third or fourth time of a morning.

'I got used to her. The place is not the same.'

'The place was the same for many years.'

'Don't you miss her?'

'One get used to missing people.' A sudden twist: 'You perhaps thinking to marry again?'

'I'm too old for that. Tessa is too young.'

A grunt of what sounded like relief. 'At least Meneer is not quite mad yet. But you got the fever in the blood anyway, I can see that.'

'There's nothing one can do about it.'

'You can keep busy instead of walking up en down en getting under my feet.'

I felt the need to make a clean breast. 'Magrieta, I love that girl.'

'You just said you too old for that.'

'Too old for getting married, not for love. And I'm scared if I think of everything that can happen to her. The world is a dangerous place.'

'We all live in it.'

'But one can try to make it easier for others.'

'Make no difference. Years ago when you en Miss Riana tried to stop the bulldozers what came to take us away, what happened?'

'We *tried*.'

'The bulldozers came anyway. They still coming. En no one can do nothing.'

'You want me to stop loving Tessa?'

'I loved my husbands, Meneer. All three of them. I loved my children. If I could, I'd give my own life to save theirs. But where are they now? And where am I? That's all I'm saying. En leave the rest to God.'

More perturbed than I'd been before the conversation, I would resume my aimless wandering, with one of the cats, usually Amadeus, twirling round my legs. Sometimes, usually in the evening, I tried to telephone Tessa, but the cellphone invariably put me on voicemail. Twice she phoned me, very brief calls, just to reassure me that she was all right; and afterwards I'd spend hours recalling every syllable, every small nuance. It was more frustrating than rewarding, but at least it confirmed that she was there, that the absence was temporary, that she'd be back.

I never dared to enquire outright about her days and nights, except perhaps to say, 'Please don't overdo it', or 'I hope you manage to have the odd early night?' But she never gave straight answers. Not that she sounded evasive; there were simply too many other things she wanted to talk about. What kept me sane was the conviction that after what had happened she would not easily take the same risk again; with some luck she might even change her lifestyle altogether. But that might be wishful thinking. And then all the wild imaginings would return to torment me.

To work at home made it worse. Every corner held some memory, some fleeting shadow, of her. And Magrieta became exasperated with my restlessness. When we weren't talking she wanted to get on with her work and I was in the way. I started using the time to make detailed lists of the work that needed to be done around the house. The cracks in the boundary wall had to be repaired, there was a chimney pot to be replaced, the garage could do with a coat of paint, the shutters on the bedroom windows needed stripping and revarnishing. I started on some of these projects, then found them too frustrating. I'd rather wait till she was back. And so I took to going to the UCT library more regularly. It was another form of returning home, even if this library was too clinical for my liking, not sufficiently lived in, lacking the atmosphere, the age, the loftiness of the one that had shaped my life. A place of safety, 'as real as paper and as bracing as ink' as Alberto Manguel described it (a man after my own heart). A return to a place where everything can be named again, where order can be found for the disorder of the world. Not that it necessarily bestows certainty; but at least it brings the reassurance that the wilderness of emotions and events *can* be held in check.

I had nothing specific to work towards. But the old habits were compulsive. It was good just to work steadily on some of the many topics I'd been filing away in my mind for future consideration.

A fitting interruption here: NOTE ON ST ANTHONY THE ABBOT (AD 251–356). I have now had time to look up *Butler's Lives of the Saints*, edited by Herbert Thurston and Donald Attwater, vol. I (Burns & Oates, London, 1956), pages 104–9. The paintings of Bosch and Brueghel – or, more recently, James Ensor and Max Ernst – might lead one to expect a more colourful life. But one would have to be a believer, and preferably Catholic, to find Butler's dry account illuminating. The saint, one hundred and five when he finally gave up the ghost, certainly was an exemplary old geezer as far as the contemplative life is concerned. Devotion, ascesis, deprivation, fasting and prayers, you name it, in all respects Anthony was a model of virtue. But not my cup of tea. (I find him more appealing when conflated with Anthony of Padua, patron saint of lovers, of women in confinement or distress, of objects lost, and of lost causes.) Still, in his later years he did perform the odd endearing miracle, like curing a girl possessed by demons. Born near Memphis in Egypt, the son of wealthy parents who kept him at home and never allowed him to go out into the world, he was left at the age of not yet twenty in possession of a sizeable fortune as well as the care of his younger sister. But listening to a sermon about Jesus's advice to a rich young man to sell all his belongings and distribute the money among the poor, he was moved to do just that himself. He also, conveniently, packed off his young sister to a 'house of maidens' (To a nunnery, go!) and withdrew into the desert.

For more than eighty years after that Anthony avoided society, moving from one near-inaccessible retreat to the next in his obsession to escape the devout, who were clamouring to benefit from his reputed wisdom. In the process he founded several monasteries without settling in any of them himself (although he regularly visited them, in one instance – the monastery of Fayum – by swimming through a crocodile-infested canal).

In the end he foretold his own death and on the appointed day stretched himself out as if to sleep, announced to the two young disciples he'd summoned that he was now ready to go and drew his last breath. He had never been ill, notes Butler (who may or may not have been an ancestor of Tessa's), his sight remained unimpaired, and he still had all his teeth when he died, which must have been quite something in those days. And that was that, at least as viewed from the outside. All the rest is pure interiority. And the few signs traditionally identified with him – the small bell, the book, the T-shaped cross, the pig – cast little light on the enigma of his mind. For that, one should go back to the early *Vitae Patrum* or the life by Athanasius, because clearly there was more to the man.

What does prod my curiosity is the brief passage about the Devil, who was so fascinated (I use the word advisedly: *fascinus* being, as I once read, a word for 'penis') by the hermit's denial of the world that he couldn't let him be. He tried one temptation after another. But unlike Oscar Wilde, who so famously asserted that he could resist everything except temptation, old man Anthony (I'm afraid I cannot ever visualise him as a young man) stayed firm. Some of the temptations must have been particularly alluring, notably the arrival of a young nude woman sent to seduce him but resolutely turned down – not, I was relieved to find out, without a desperate struggle against his natural urges. In the Bosch triptych she appears in a hollow tree, very smooth, very white, very naked, with a hand on her hairless mound – but whether it is to shield her genital cleft, or draw attention to it, or even to masturbate, only Bosch and perhaps St Anthony can tell. Other visitations were frightening, particularly the arrival of a black man who came to instil the fear of hell in Anthony, but was converted instead. On the whole I find the paintings more enticing than the written accounts. I never fail to be enthralled by the riotous fantasy of the Lisbon triptych (now in Brussels), which according to D. Bax in *Hieronymus Bosch: His Picture-Writing Deciphered* (A. A. Balkema, Rotterdam, 1979), might well have had to be removed from the chapel where it had first been hung because it was deemed too sexually provocative. But the later Bosch painting (which it seems is nowadays attributed to someone else) can also keep me in its spell for hours: here everything is much more muted, attenuated and dominated by the fixed, other-worldly stare of the hermit. I'm afraid I would not have made the grade. And there are moments when I wonder whether Anthony himself would have remained as firm if the naked temptress sent to him had been Ms Tessa Butler. Suppose she had permitted him to gaze upon the Mystery of the Mound – and then denied him entry? There's the rub. Hagiography might have taken a different turn altogether.

# 8

I MET HER at the airport, two days ago, when she came back. I was an hour early and the plane was late; so it was quite a wait. To see her coming down the stairs and across the tarmac, her short dress flaring in the light breeze, made me catch my breath. She was even more beautiful than I'd remembered. It was as if the whole day suddenly slotted into place: here, now. Hodiernal Tessa.

But there was something else too. Something I couldn't pin down, in the way she walked, or carried her shoulders, or swung her little bag from its long strap. And I remembered what she'd told me of her early lover, the ardent academic, coming back from the States and giving her one look, and saying, 'You've been fooling around with someone else.'

I felt ashamed even to think of it. After all the time I'd had for soul-searching, after all the firm resolutions to respect the boundaries and conditions we'd set, here I was, at first sight, ready to succumb to jealousy again. Not saintly material, that at least was clear.

There was no question of asking her directly, of course. But it was there, in the background, all the time. On the way back home, through the extravagant welcoming meal Magrieta had cooked, later that evening in the study, with Amadeus purring on her lap, relaxed for the first time in three weeks.

She spoke non-stop about her work. Knitting the local production group into the LA team, finalising the planning for their first joint production, doing the provisional budgeting, working with the scriptwriter, streamlining proposals for casting, locations and the myriad of other preliminaries, most of which were beyond me.

She was carried away by her own enthusiasm, her large eyes glittering, the small furrow between her brows coming and going, her gestures energetic, eager, emphatic.

'This is definitely my line,' she said. 'I should have made the switch long ago.'

'So you had a good time?'

'Hectic. But great. It was like cramming an hour into every moment.'

'I hope they're giving you a bit of time off to recover?'

'Two days. Then it's all systems go.'

'Met any interesting people?'

'Tons. It was just amazing. Some shysters too, though.'

'Nothing unpleasant, I hope?'

Her carefree laugh. 'Nothing I couldn't handle.'

'Did Zach show up?' I ventured.

She met my look without a hint of discomfort. 'He looked in once or twice early on. Then he had to dash off again to Paris. We're hoping to get a French company involved too.'

'You'll soon be a globe-trotter.'

'I hope so. But I'm only a very small cog right now.' She glowed with satisfaction. 'At least I was noticed.'

'I don't doubt that for a moment.'

She beamed. 'You're a darling.' Leaning over to touch my hands. 'And I did miss you. Just to talk things over, to share ideas, to calm me down when I got too carried away.' For a moment she seemed very serious. 'I think I needed this, Ruben. To discover just how important you are to me.'

'No other candidates yet?'

That was when she showed the slightest hint of hesitation. But she was clearly not going to avoid anything. 'There was one who got quite interested. The scriptwriter, Derek.'

'Any lifelong commitments?'

'No, I'm sure it won't ever go so far. He's just come out of a long relationship, so he's still very fragile.' Her eyes. Oh God, those eyes. And I knew before she said it: 'We spent one night together. We were both very cautious, neither of us can afford to get committed right now.' Holding one of my hands between hers. 'But it was good. I want you to know that. It was good, and he was very gentle and understanding. You know, after what happened I was feeling pretty low. I wasn't sure I could ever . . . So I needed this and he was the right person. Is it OK with you?'

'I think you're right, that you needed to find your feet again. And if it worked out that way . . .'

'There's no one else I can discuss it with,' she said.

We were quiet for a long time. How utterly strange it was, I thought; and yet, in spite of everything, I felt a kind of profound comfort in her frankness.

'Will he come down to join the group here?' I asked at last.

'Well, he's the scriptwriter, he'll have to. But there's nothing lined up, if that is what you mean. We'll just play it by ear.'

'And how did Zach take it?'

'He left before it happened. But he was a bit pissed off with me because he was keen for us to get together again and I said no. In fact, I decided to tell him about the abortion after all. That certainly brought him up short.'

All is for the best in the best of all possible worlds.


We talked again yesterday morning. It was the first wholly windless day for a week and I suggested we go to the beach. We went to Muizenberg.

We walked away from the brightly painted bathing cubicles, barefoot, hand in hand. I see it again as I write about it. Past the cubicles she stops to strip down to the small red bikini she's put on under her clothes. I steady her while she hops on one foot to kick off the jeans, and then carry the small bundle for her. Because it is a weekday there is hardly anyone else about.

'When it was like this in the Eastern Cape,' she says, 'Andy and I would drive to one of those endless beaches, near Kenton, and take off all our clothes and walk for miles, and stop to make love, and then walk on again. Once we fell asleep and when we woke up the incoming tide was already at our feet. I wanted to make love once

more, trying to time it so that we'd come together at the moment
it washed over us.'

'Did it work out?'

'Not quite. I nearly drowned and he came too soon. But it was fun,
so totally carefree, reckless, crazy. It will never be like that again. I'm
too old for that now.'

We walk on, she speaks without interruption. I look mostly ahead,
or at the sea. Although I am aroused by the litheness of her wind-loved,
sun-loved body in the small bikini, there is something relaxed about it
all, a naturalness and a spontaneity that both baffle and please me. It
is – it seems to me now – like seeing something the moment before
it happens, when the world is not yet real, and not entirely known,
and any unexpected movement may make it all vanish.

It lasts only a second or two. Then, already, in my old distracting
way, I begin to imagine how I will remember this tomorrow, or a
year from now, ten years; how I will look back and doubt whether
it could possibly have been true, and yet it will have been. I try out
the words with which I can hold on to the experience, but there is
nothing to set it apart, make it unique. And yet it is, I know it is.

We reach a deep inlet between two dunes where the receding tide
has washed out a whole shoal of small silvery sardines. They are still
flopping about frantically, dancing like particles of refracted light on
the glistening sand. She runs towards them and starts scooping them
up to toss them back into the sea. Most of them are too weak to swim
by now and are washed out again, limp and barely stirring. She starts
running in deeper with every wriggling little fish she catches, which
slows down the process.

'Come and help me!' she calls over her shoulder from where she
stands bent over, legs astride, looking up urgently in my direction.
But I am too mesmerised by her liquid movements to obey. Bending,
swaying, swirling, throwing, all the poetry of motion, her body quick
and shining as silvery as the fish.

'Come and help me!' she calls again, turning this time to face me,
one weakly struggling little sardine in her hand.

'There's no point, Tessa,' I try to reason. 'There are thousands.
Even if you throw back a hundred, it won't make any difference.'

'To this one it does,' she says and hurls the little fish far into the lapping waves.

And this, I know, is what I shall remember: all that shimmering morning captured in a single line of sound. Briefly, glistening, almost translucent, she is for my eyes only, and the world is a wild and distant, improbable place indeed. And what I suddenly know is this: I am where I am. For once I'm not looking at something through a glass darkly or through the filter of past or future, of wishful thinking, regret or guilt. I am here, with you. And I remember a line by the old Dutch mystic Ruusbroec quoted next to a reproduction of *The Temptation of St Anthony* in one of the books on Bosch: What we are we gaze at; and what we gaze at we are.

I shall remember. Because that night, last night, it changed. She'd told me earlier that she was going out and just before eight two of her girlfriends came to pick her up. I stayed behind, as usual, in the study. In the afterglow of our morning on the beach, and soothed by Schubert, I felt relaxed; there was no need to be concerned about anything. But then a little nothing happened which unduly upset me. I'd written a letter to Louis and Janet in Johannesburg (it was too serious, I felt, for e-mail), trying to explain once more why I didn't think it was such a good idea for me to come up for a visit before they started packing for Canada – there were no good reasons, but I just couldn't face the idea of such disruption – and was rummaging through the drawers of my desk for an envelope when I came across the little box in which I'd kept the navel ring Tessa had given me, so playfully, for my birthday.

I quite forgot about the envelope. In my easy chair I sat, fingering the delicate little ring, rubbing with my thumb the small red stone, 'genuine glass', until Amadeus appeared from nowhere and jumped on my lap. I dropped the ring. It rolled a little distance and disappeared under the small inlaid chess table, into a chink between two floorboards. I'd long meant to have the floor repaired.

I brushed the cat from my lap, pushed the little table aside and went down on all fours to look for the ring, but it was gone. Such a small thing, but I had a hollow feeling in my guts. This was bad news. Something was going to go wrong, I knew.

It surely wasn't irrevocable. Even if I had to get a carpenter in to rip up the floor, I thought grimly, I would see to it that I got it back. The thought brought a measure of calm. I replaced the chess table, went to the dining room to pour myself a Scotch and then returned to settle down in my chair again. But something of the unrest persisted. I went to bed disconsolate.

It was very late, at least two o'clock, when I heard her coming in. She was not alone. They went down the passage speaking in low voices. Once she stifled a laugh, that laugh. She had a man with her.

I lay awake all night, but towards morning I must have dozed off because I jumped up with a start when I heard the front door. I was too late to catch a glimpse of the visitor, but just in time to see the red Porsche drive off from the gate.

# Four

# 1

I'm BEGINNING TO lose faith in making notes. Or is it just in my ability to face them, once made? For so many years I have done this to obtain a hold on my world, on the treacherous water of life running through my fingers. Frost's momentary stay against confusion. But the downside is that once it has been written down, irrevocably, on paper, one cannot pretend it has not happened. Even if the account is not reliable – or perhaps *especially* if it is not reliable? – it compels one to face it. And the course of events these last three weeks or so has been hazardous enough to keep up with; confronting it in this way threatens what little remains of my peace of mind.

Already we have crossed the threshold into December. Everything is so unsettled. It's like when I was a child and after the rare rains the flying ants would come out. Hundreds of them, thousands, the whole sky rustling and thriving and quivering with them. I'd rush about trying wildly to catch them. And missing them. Unless I focused on one at a time, it was hopeless. Like Tessa's little fish, that transparent, heartbreaking day. That is how I must try now to capture the elusive thoughts. It is the only way.

First there was the shock of Johnny MacFarlane's case, which finally came to court. It was Mrs Lategan, the neighbour who'd originally reported seeing the murderer coming from Number 23, who came over with the news one morning. She'd been summoned to appear as a witness. If it hadn't been for her I wouldn't even have known. I offered her a lift to Wynberg; Magrieta also went. All for nothing, because when the case was called after we'd been kept waiting for two hours, there was no sign of the accused, Vuyisile Mthembu. A warrant was issued for his arrest, but we all knew what the outcome would be.

'It won't surprise me one bit if that poor Mr MacFarlane's ghost now also starts walking in our street,' Magrieta said solemnly on our way back.

'Don't say such things,' Mrs Lategan reprimanded her, nervously rearranging her fiercely floral hat. 'It brings very bad luck.'

As bad luck went, Magrieta continued to have her fair share. I remember her coming in on the Monday morning after the weekend when Zach had come back into our lives, with the news that the household in Bonteheuwel she had moved into was 'blown up'. On the Saturday – which was the only opening Jessie had in her week, it being her once-in-two-weeks day off – they'd buried the raped and murdered girl, Beulah. The whole of Bonteheuwel was there and the people were angry: no arrests had been made yet; clues provided by members of the community had not been followed up. Expecting trouble, the police had pitched up at the funeral in force; but in spite of the grief and rage, the situation remained under control. The only problem was Jessie's husband, Stanley. He went berserk and several people had to restrain him when he tried to prostrate himself on the coffin as it was lowered into the grave. From the cemetery the crowd marched to the police station to demand that something be done, and soon. Only after that did they return to the house of the bereaved for the funeral meal; Magrieta had been cooking for it all week in our kitchen.

When Jessie left for work in the mall on the Sunday morning Stanley insisted on going with her. She tried to talk him out of it – he was dressed in his dirty overalls and she knew her boss would be offended and might turn nasty – but he assured her he wouldn't go to the delicatessen with her; he was just 'going shopping'. She was still uneasy; there was something smouldering in him, but he refused to talk about it. Anyway, she had no choice. And at Claremont Station he left her, heading for Lansdowne Road, which made her breathe more freely.

It must have been an hour later when he suddenly burst into the delicatessen, brandishing a crowbar. 'Where's that fucking bastard that runs the place?' he shouted.

The manager came from his office. 'What's going on here?'

'You the boss here?' asked Stanley.

'What do you want? Who are you?'

'You the one who force people to work when their children is murdered?'

The manager looked at Jessie. 'Has this man got anything to do with you?' he asked.

'You fucking blerry cunt!' shouted Stanley.

The manager backed away and ducked into the office, reaching for the telephone. But before he could pick it up Stanley tackled him from behind. They rolled about on the floor. The manager was unarmed and Stanley had the crowbar. It was a miracle that he didn't kill the man. If the staff, and a number of passers-by attracted by the rumpus, hadn't intervened so quickly there would most likely have been a murder on the premises. Someone called security; within minutes – it's a posh place after all – the police arrived, and an ambulance. The manager was carried out on a stretcher; Stanley, still kicking and swearing, was frogmarched off to the waiting police van. In the general consternation Jessie took her bag and quietly went home.

'Now there she is,' said Magrieta. 'She was the breadwinner en now she got no job no more, en Stanley is in the tjoekie. When it's real skollies they get bail so they can start killing en raping again soon's possible. But when it's a man what got mad because his child was murdered en his wife insulted, then he must sit. En what is going to happen next?'

What happened was that Magrieta asked me – ordered me – to put a lawyer on the case. I was reluctant to get drawn into a quagmire which concerned me only indirectly, but how could I turn my back on her? They were her friends, they'd offered her shelter and companionship, and that extended her responsibility to me. Two days later Stanley was indeed granted bail (which I had to pay), but his trial was still pending; and it had done little to ease Jessie's distress.

There were other repercussions as well. Presumably as a result of probing questions asked by the lawyer, and transmitted by the magistrate, about the police handling of Beulah's rape and murder, a member of the Good Livings gang in Manenberg was arrested. The crime, rumour had it, had been part of an initiation rite for gang members. The youngster's parents, God-fearing people and respected in church circles, put in an impassioned plea for their son, who was granted bail; but for once the amount was so high that it seemed unlikely his family and friends could afford it.

That was when Stanley made his second move. Before Jessie or Magrieta had any idea of what he had in mind, he'd set up a collection in the community of Bonteheuwel, and scraped together the R5000 needed to free the young gangster. Accompanied by a crowd of neighbours and acquaintances he set off for the magistrate's court where the boy had made his appearance. The bail was paid and the accused released into the hands of his supposed benefactors. Who promptly dragged him off and gave him the beating of his life, after which they castrated him and then hacked him to pieces.

Within days, four other gang members were taken in by the police; in the meantime Stanley and some of his helpers had also been arrested. For once, nobody was granted bail.

For the first time in as long as I could remember, Magrieta took a week off. She was the only one who could keep Jessie's household going.

My own household, I realised, needed taking care of. In many ways. There was Tessa. There was the house itself. There was the need to find Magrieta a new home. At the earliest opportunity I contacted Mr Jacobs again.

This time it took only three telephone calls to get hold of him and then some extensive explanation to refresh his memory. Even after he'd located the file it was clear that he was hedging, though his tone was quite friendly. I proposed another meeting, which he did not find such a good idea. I too wished, even more fervently than before, that we could manage without it and arrange everything in a civilised manner, by correspondence; but I knew that would be the end of the matter. So I refused to be shaken off by mere promises; the saga of Bonteheuwel had been getting on my nerves.

In the course of our discussion, when I now think back, I must have said something like, 'Mr Jacobs, this is very urgent. Mrs Daniels has gone through deep waters. I can personally vouch for her. And between you and me I can assure you that money won't be a problem.'

It was probably a rash thing to say; and only much later did it dawn on me what he might have read into it. What matters is that he promised, with a new tone of commitment in his voice, to call me back, which to my surprise he actually did within days. He had something to discuss, he announced. Preferably not on the telephone. But as it happened he was coming out on a business call to my part of town. Could we perhaps meet at Rondebosch Station, in the parking lot? I found the request unusual but gave it no special thought; the important thing was that there seemed at last to be progress of one kind or another.

It nearly turned out a wild-goose chase. After waiting three-quarters of an hour I discovered that there were two parking lots at the station, one on either side of the railway line; and as I came up from the subway, panting, into the second lot Mr Jacobs was just getting into his car to drive off. Looking pointedly at his watch, he invited me into the passenger seat.

Look, he said without much of a preamble, there was a new state-subsidised housing scheme at Delft. There had been a hash with the waiting lists and there might be an opening for Magrieta. The only thing was that it could take a long time, unless some money could be produced up front to untangle some of the red tape which might come up. 'And since you said money was no problem . . .'

Even then it took a while for the penny to drop. I could have got out of the car in disgust. But that, I knew, would have buried Magrieta's hopes of finding a house.

He assured me he would do his utmost because it was clear that the two of us mos understood each other. We were practically old friends by now, were we not? The problem, he explained, did not lie with him but 'further along the line'. If it depended on him . . .

'How much?' I cut him short.

He seemed somewhat taken aback by the brusqueness of the

interruption and first launched into a long and abstruse new explanation, concluding with the abrupt remark, 'Five grand for starters.'

'And after the starters?'

That was difficult to say at this stage, he replied, unfazed. But he didn't think there would be too many problems remaining. Anyway, he could assure me that he would do his personal best to keep costs as low as humanly possible.

'Shall we shake on it?' he proposed.

We solemnly shook on it. I'm afraid my smile was rather perfunctory. But what else could I do?

'When shall we two meet again?' I asked. 'In thunder, lightning or in rain?'

'Oh, I'm sure we're in for a spell of good weather,' he assured me.

It turned out, not altogether to my surprise, that he would be coming out this way again the very next day. So how about meeting at Rosebank Station? At the entrance to the ticket office.

That was where we met. I was tempted to ask for a receipt when I handed over the padded envelope, but fortunately thought better of it; Mr Jacobs was not given to spurious humour.

There the matter rested for two weeks. I telephoned a couple of times to enquire, only to be told that 'these things take time' and that the matter was 'receiving attention'. On the second occasion he pertinently advised me to be patient. Don't call us, we'll call you.

It was not until two days ago that I heard from him again. Good news, he announced, sounding as if he was conveying tidings about a funeral. Progress had been made. There were just one or two last hitches.

'When can I come in to see you?' I asked.

'I'm not phoning from the office,' he said. 'Can you make it tomorrow morning at ten?' A pause. 'Same place as the first time?' His voice had a muffled sound. Although he was probably using his cellphone, I preferred to imagine him in a public booth, cupping a hand over the receiver, as he added with great solemnity as if announcing the names of the pall-bearers, 'Same amount.' And then he rang off.

A slight feeling of nausea crept up from my stomach, but I swallowed it back. It was not the kind of money I was used to throwing about; and certainly not in this manner. But if this was what it took – I tried to visualise how Magrieta would react to the news of the house (all information about the means of securing it carefully suppressed) – maybe I should just take it on the chin like a man. She was still overwhelmed with the events engulfing Jessie's family. A few days earlier our lawyer had finally secured bail for Stanley after the police had been forced to admit that they still had no hard evidence against any of the individuals involved in the lynching of the rapist, the whole community of Bonteheuwel having clammed up in an impressive show of solidarity. There was still no prospect of a relaxed Christmas, but at least the family would be together again. Except for Beulah, of course.

And yesterday morning I met Mr Jacobs again in the parking lot at Rondebosch Station, money changed hands and, as we shared another conspiratorial handshake, Mr Jacobs said, 'Look, it's December now, things are moving a bit slowly, but I think we can sign the papers just after the holidays, early in January.'

'Will there be any further unofficial costs?' I asked, this time without attempting a smile.

'Of course not!' he exclaimed, as if it was a personal insult. 'I told you, Mr Olivier, if it was up to me you'd have had the house in no time and at no extra cost. It's just these other people.'

'Further along the line,' I said.

'That's right.' He seemed to appreciate my understanding.

I came home, not exactly with a song in my heart but with a feeling of cautious relief. At least I could now give all my attention to the work still to be done on my house.

As soon as possible after losing Tessa's ring I had consulted the *Yellow Pages* and called in a carpenter to open the floor in my study; it took four days before he finally turned up, by which time I was frantic. Finding the lost ring had, ridiculously, become vital to my mental equilibrium, something to hold on to as the world became more and more slippery. Apart from the unnerving events in Magrieta's life there was more than enough happening to Tessa to keep me in a state of near despair.

Magrieta was perplexed and annoyed by the whole enterprise. I couldn't possibly tell her why I needed to have the floorboards ripped up. The pretext I offered was my fear of damp rising from under the floor and endangering my books.

'We never got damp in the study,' she said. 'Where shall it come from so suddenly? In the dining room, yes.'

'Then we'll open the dining-room floor too. Anyway, I can *feel* the damp in the study. I work there every day of my life. You don't want me to develop asthma or something, do you?'

At last, on the Friday, the carpenter came, a scruffy-looking character with a missing thumb, black fingernails and the lean and hungry look of a mangy fox. It took him two hours to saw through the four boards I'd indicated; in the process he badly scarred two others and nearly wrecked my easy chair. Suppressing a strong desire to send him scuttling to his rickety bakkie with a kick in the backside, I dispatched him to the dining room, where he could continue his ravages under Magrieta's relentless supervision. As soon as they were both out of sight I lowered myself into the basement of the study with a strong torch which I'd bought specially for the purpose.

There was no sign of damp. Nor of the ring. On hands and knees I crawled about in the dark, in ever-widening circles, conducting an archaeological exploration of about four square metres below the spot where I'd lost the ring, searching through the sand and dirt and rubble. I brought to light a number of coins, two ballpoint pens, paper clips, a nail clipper, three broken razor blades, chocolate wrappers, a few lucky-packet charms (probably dating back to little Mabel), and a variety of other odds and ends that had found their way through the chinks over the years; but not a gleam or a glimmer of gold, real or fake.

I sat down on my haunches and pointed the torch to the floorboards above my head. Perhaps the ring was still stuck somewhere. But no luck. Although it was unlikely, if not impossible, that the ring could have rolled some distance across the uneven ground, I proceeded to explore the entire surface of the basement, but the only result was that I wrapped myself in grey sheets of cobwebs and gritty dust.

With frustration throbbing like physical pain in my temples I returned to the jagged hole the carpenter had cut and hoisted myself back to the study floor just as Magrieta made her entrance.

'That man is jus' looking for trouble,' she exclaimed, flicking a dust-cloth at me.

'At least there's no damp here,' I said, avoiding her reproachful look.

'I tole you.'

'Let's check the dining room.'

The destruction wrought there was even worse than the mess he'd made in the study. Several boards appeared so badly splintered that they'd probably have to be replaced altogether; and I knew how hard it would be to match the brashness of new wood with the patina of the old Oregon pine. (Riana would have had a fit.) Yet the wretched little fox sat beaming at me from the scene of his demolition with the satisfaction of a dog that had just retrieved a stick from a scrap heap. He seemed most confused when I summarily thrust a few notes from my back pocket into his filthy paw and told him to get the hell out of my house.

A wasted morning. It meant going back to the *Yellow Pages*. But that was where Magrieta resolutely stepped in. Stanley was a builder, wasn't he? Well, he had contacts with all the best artisans in the Peninsula. If I would leave it to her, she'd make the necessary arrangements through him and his colleagues, then we could tackle the whole house and get a proper job done once and for all while we were at it. Frankly, I wasn't too eager to get more deeply involved with that family – even though I was shamed by my own reluctance. But I had little chance against Magrieta.

Given the deplorable turn of events during the following weekend, which was when Beulah was buried and Stanley went on the rampage, it took another few weeks before anything could be done about the house; but then a whole contingent of builders, bricklayers, plumbers and carpenters turned up one morning to start working on a thorough overhaul of the whole place. To my surprise they even managed to find some ancient floorboards to replace the damaged ones in the dining room. They also made a proper trapdoor, and below the floor an extractor fan was fitted to control the damp.

The only room I designated out of bounds was my study. I did not even want the ripped-up boards replaced. When Magrieta protested I explained quite curtly that this was my sanctum, and enough damage had been done; I'd placed the four removed boards back in position to cover up the hole made by the fox, and spread a small Isfahan prayer mat over them. 'Better to keep it like that, then I can check for damp from time to time.'

'There *is* no damp,' she reiterated.

'There may be one day,' I said. 'One can never be sure with these old houses.'

What I did not tell her, nor did I want to, was that I could now go down into my basement every night when the house was quiet and resume my solitary search. It had become a compulsion to find that little ring which had once adorned Tessa's navel. I knew – even though by all the laws of reason it was nonsense – that once I'd found it there would be light in the gloom that had settled, as far as I was concerned, on Tessa's life. And night after night I descended into my own private little hell to resume my exploration. I started in the corner nearest to the spot where the ring had disappeared, and with a baking sieve sifted through every cubic centimetre of dirt and rubble below my floor, working systematically over the whole area, feeling more and more like an old mole of a prisoner digging a tunnel from his dungeon to the freedom of the world beyond. It might take months. I didn't care. I felt I owed it to myself. And perhaps even more urgently, if more obscurely, I owed it to Tessa.

I can no longer put off writing about her. How can I avoid it if everything I've done and thought during these weeks has been invested in her? – her coming and going, and the coming and going of her mysterious and ever more menacing nightly visitors. I hardly sleep at night, keeping my shameful vigil in secret, in bedroom or study, waiting for her to come in, listening for the muffled voices in the passage that will confirm the presence of a companion, tormenting myself with visions of lust and depravity. If there is no Everest that love cannot rise to, there are no ignominious depths either to which it cannot stoop.

And it is so unfair of me. There has been nothing secretive about her actions; she hasn't tried to hide anything from me. Nor is she ashamed of anything. On the contrary, there is a touching frankness in the way she discusses her life with me whenever we have the time, as if our closeness around the hospital and its aftermath removed a last barrier between us. What am I to her? Father Confessor, confidant, accomplice? There is no word for it. She knows I do not attempt to deny the body, nor does she: but she accepts implicitly that I will not overstep the boundaries so painfully agreed on. She will go about in the house, when Magrieta is not here, wearing only a T-shirt and panties. There is no suggestion that she is trying to provoke or tease me; it is, rather, I think, I hope, an expression of trust. She will kiss me and cuddle up against me, she will call me 'My love', or 'Darling'. More than once she has fallen asleep on the old sofa in my study, her head on my lap; and once, when I could not suppress an erection, she even acknowledged it with a smile and a gentle brushing of her knuckles against it, assuming – knowing – that there would be no claims staked and no demands made. On a few occasions when I overslept on a weekend morning, a rare enough occurrence, she has brought me coffee in bed and settled down cross-legged next to me for a chat; once, in a sudden cold snap, she crawled in under the blankets with me and stayed there for hours, talking in her almost breathless, carried-away manner. There is a sense of liberation in our undefined and indefinable relationship, even for myself, after a lifetime of deprivation which has caused me to accept, both in rage and resignation, what Lawrence once wrote about being 'crucified into sex'.

She does wifely things for me: takes me shopping (which I hate on principle) to buy me new clothes, and goes through my wardrobe to throw out what she regards as ridiculously old-fashioned. (Only the threadbare old dressing gown am I allowed to keep; I believe she's become as fond of it as I am.) She does motherly things, even if she is less than half my age: makes sure that I take vitamins and other nutritional supplements, that I take my pills regularly, that

I do not read in bad light, that I tuck in a serviette so as not to mess on my shirtfront. She does sisterly things: berates me for not telephoning or writing to my children regularly enough, cuts the bristles in my ears, reminds me of things I once told her about and have since forgotten. She does loverly things: ruffles my hair with her fingers, strokes my back, kisses my nose, parades for me when she has brought home new clothes on appro and changes from one dress into another unselfconsciously, allows me to paint her toenails, thrusts her breasts against me when I hold her in my arms.

She goes out very often, her new work is obviously more demanding socially than the old. Three times she's gone away with the film crew for five, six, eight days – to Johannesburg, up the west coast, into the Karoo. These trips are almost unbearable; the shadow of her absence falls over the whole house. And yet it is a curiously luminous shadow. Because when she is not here I can imagine her more perfectly than when she is with me. And there is always a return to look forward to. Every time she brings me back something: aftershave with a special fragrance, the brightly coloured feather of a bird, a perfectly round pebble. I keep them religiously. Not one of them will get lost through a chink in my floor.

Twice in her absence I go to concerts in the City Hall. Some of the old magic of live music is recaptured, but deep down I'm aware of a restlessness that will not be stilled. How I miss my chess nights with Johnny. Two, three times I even go into my old library in the city, but there is nothing to hold my attention. I wonder where Siphiwo Mdamane has drifted to. Perhaps, under different circumstances, we might have become friends. I don't know. The whole exercise was such a failure.

There is little else with which to while away the time in Tessa's stark absence. On lonely nights, and most of them are lonely, I go down into my basement like a hermit into his cell: not to escape visions of temptation, but to conjure them up in my search for the small magic ring, which seems to have evaporated into the stale, dusty air of my underfloor world. The piles of sifted earth increase steadily, but digger's luck still eludes me.

When I come out again it is always with a sense of regret: down below there is, at least, the hope of finding something someday; up here are only the intricacies of a world in which I feel less and less at home.

Except, of course, when she is around, but that is rare and becoming ever more so. When we do have time together we talk. It begins on that first morning after Zach has leaked his oily way out to the red Porsche. I do not know how to broach it, feeling it would be an unacceptable intrusion even to refer to it. But to my surprise, and my intense relief, she brings it up when we have a salad lunch together in the newly habitable garden.

'I hope Zach didn't wake you up last night,' she says. 'I told him to be quiet.'

'I heard you come in. And I heard him leave.' Should I mention this? – of course I should. 'At least he was less obnoxious than the first time he stayed over.'

She raises her eyebrows. 'How so?'

I may as well plunge in. I tell her what he said that wounding morning, months ago, about coming twice and going once.

'Zach can be a real shit,' she says, more vehemently than I would have expected. Then smiles disarmingly (of course). 'At least this time he had nothing to brag about.'

My turn to ask, 'How so?'

'He wouldn't use a condom, so I refused. I won't take that kind of risk again.' The sudden eruption of her laughter. 'You'd be amazed to hear the excuses men come up with to avoid wearing one.' She starts mimicking, '"I want to make it better for you." "I'm allergic, it makes me come out in spots." And the jackpot: "I am too big."'

'I'm surprised that Zach should take no for an answer.'

'Oh, he blew a gasket all right. Slept on the floor. But he refused to leave. He obviously thought he'd wait until I was asleep and then take his chance.'

'And did he?'

'Sure he did. But I turned him down again. He was totally pissed off by the time he left.'

'Do you think that's the end of Zach?'

'I'd be surprised.'

And she's right, of course. Barely a week later he is back for another night. But this time he leaves quite soon, barely an hour after they have come in. And he slams the front door. When I go out into the passage she comes from the back of the house, her face flushed, wearing only panties and clutching a crumpled top to her chest.

'I'm sorry,' she says, out of breath. 'The bastard.'

'Are you all right?' I ask, my hand on the doorknob, ready to pursue the malefactor into the depths of the night. The old quixotic syndrome.

'I'm fine.' And suddenly her laugh again, the full glory of it. 'I'm afraid *he* isn't, though. Shall we make some coffee? I'm wide awake now.'

'So am I.'

The condom argument has come up again she says, while we're waiting for the water to boil. He came up with his old excuse, 'I am too big.' Whereupon she produced some extra-large ones she'd bought, which then turned out to be too big for him. She burst out laughing, which in the circumstances was probably the worst she could have done. The scene rapidly turned nasty. Beside himself, he hit her. She felt constrained to use a knee on him and threatened to scream, and then he stormed out.

'I think this is the end of the road for Zach,' she says, seating herself on the kitchen table; for the sake of propriety she has thrown the crumpled top over her.

'I must admit I'm not sorry to see him go.'

'I'm sure you aren't. But it's a pity you saw only his worst side.'

'He also brought out the worst in me.' And now I'm stepp'd in blood too far to turn back. 'I even slashed his tyres.'

'*You* did that?' She stares at me in amazement. And breaks into a carillon of laughter. 'Well, bully for you.'

'It was nothing to be proud of,' I confess, 'but I cannot say I was sorry.'

'I've been making your life miserable, haven't I?' she asks with such genuine contrition that I know I can forgive her everything, anything; and come back for more.

'Shall we drink to the future?' I propose.

She solemnly clinks her mug against my cup. Then bites her lip. 'My only worry is that he may now try to get me fired from my job.'

For a while at least that doesn't happen; Zach must be wary that she may publicise the truth. However, as it turns out, Zach is not my only cause for concern. Only four or five days after his histrionic departure, she starts bringing home other visitors at night. Only one? I do not know. I no longer really want to know. Yet when, as usual, Tessa brings it up I cannot muster the courage to stop her. I find it painful, yet I'd rather know what is happening than be left in the dark; and in a way her confidence is flattering too, sometimes moving in its spontaneity. Even if I'm beginning to wonder if an alarming sense of vicarious gratification isn't creeping in. (Or has it been there from the beginning?) Disgraceful. Revolting. The dirty old man at large again? *Homo sum*, whatever.

'I've been thinking a lot about my life, Ruben.' Raising her gaze to meet my eyes. 'I mean about men.'

'I've been noticing the odd stranger around,' I say, trying to keep it light, but conscious that my smile is strained.

'You don't approve.'

'My only concern is *you*.' I pause. 'It's not that I'm not jealous. But that is not at issue.'

We are in my study, it is late; she has been out with her girlfriends and has just come in, slightly sozzled. 'Ruben, I really, really assure you there's nothing to be concerned about.'

'Do you want to talk about it?'

'If you want to know.'

I look at her, awaiting the inevitable.

'I've been seeing Derek, the scriptwriter. I told you about him. He says he loves me and I think I can believe him.'

'Do you love *him*?'

'And do you know what?' she says, with a charming show of shyness, and ignoring my question. 'I actually came last night.'

Down, down, green devil. 'If this is what he does for you it can't be all bad.' Then my age asserts itself again. 'As long as you're sure it's not a way of escaping. From yourself, I mean. From what happened.'

'Somehow abstinence just doesn't seem the right thing to me just now,' she says. 'It's hard to explain. I'm still not ready to get involved – perhaps I never will be. At the same time . . .' She stops abruptly. 'Would you rather not talk about it?'

'No, tell me.' Briefly, in our weird, comradely way, I press her against me.

'After what's happened, I have an urge to find out things about myself. Can you understand that? It's not an obsession or anxiety or anything, just a kind of eagerness.'

'To see how far you can go too far?' I sigh. 'Another quote, I'm afraid.'

'Perhaps it's just a kind of curiosity,' she says. 'About myself. About men. I sometimes feel a need for another body close to mine, you know, a male body. I cannot think of it as wrong, as some kind of flaw in my make-up. I mean, is it wrong to desire a male body, to find it beautiful, but also carnal? It's not just lust. And it's not sort of ethereal love. But it's *there* and I don't see the point of denying it. Perhaps right now I need it.'

What I need, I think, would best remain unsaid.

There were others after that. Other lovers, other conversations. If, in the process, the relationship between us was intensified, it also brought problems on other fronts, deepening eventually into crisis. Magrieta has been in a volatile mood lately. At the slightest provocation she flies off the handle. Not with me – the habits of a lifetime are too deeply ingrained – but in a way her sulks are worse; and suppressing whatever anger she may feel when she is with me exacerbates her tantrums when she has to deal with Tessa.

At the root of her temper lies her precarious position in her friends' household. She feels she cannot impose on Jessie and Stanley any longer: they're going through a tough enough time without having to cope with a lodger; but at least she brings in some desperately needed money and her presence in itself helps them to deal with their avalanche of legal and domestic problems. But that, in turn, saps so much of her energy that she finds it difficult, physically and emotionally, to cope here in Papenboom Road.

'I don't know what's happening in this country' has become her stock phrase. 'In the ole days things was bad, but this is worser. No one is safe no more. Meneer should jus' see what happened at the bus station this morning. En there's no respect for old people.'

I would wait to hear more, but usually she doesn't care to go into detail. Every day there is something new from the townships and she brings it into the house with her as surely as Tessa once brought her bergies home.

And yet the news has not been all bad. Stanley's trial on the assault charge took an unexpected turn, due mainly to the spirited performance of our young lawyer. Magrieta attended the trial, of course; so, to my surprise, did Tessa. But I really did not see my way open; I'd just started making notes on a new project. And just as well I didn't take the trouble because as it turned out they had to repeat the performance no fewer than three times, since the case was postponed twice – once because someone had 'mislaid' the file, once because the investigating officer was, allegedly, ill. The lawyer, Mike Coetzee, made some pretty acerbic comments on both occasions. At the trial itself, when it finally happened, Tessa reported he was in great form. He did not try to condone Stanley's attack on the delicatessen manager: it had happened, he said, it was inexcusable, Stanley was deeply remorseful; but the question he placed before the court was *why* it had happened. And then he went into an eloquent exposé of the malpractices in the delicatessen over many months: the working hours, the wages, the contraventions of the labour laws, the unconscionable exploitation of the staff, even the abuse and attempted abuse of younger female workers. He had witnesses to substantiate every allegation. It was astounding – and moving – to see how Jessie's colleagues were prepared to lay their own jobs on the line by testifying for her. So devastating was the accumulation of evidence that just after the lunch recess the plaintiff's lawyer announced that his client was withdrawing the action against Stanley. Jubilation among the family's supporters; but disappointment too. They'd been robbed of a climax. Mike Coetzee did score a final point, however, by persuading the magistrate to refer the evidence against the manager to the police for investigation.

'Not that anything will come of it,' he told us afterwards. 'The bastard will no doubt buy off the officers and that will be the end of it. But at least he may be a bit more careful in the way he treats his staff from now on.' (As it turned out this was somewhat optimistic. A week after the trial all three staff members who'd testified against the manager were fired on accusations of misconduct that had nothing to do with the case.)

In the meantime Stanley's murder case has not made it to court yet; there is every indication that it may be dropped for lack of evidence. Not that I feel entirely easy about this development.

'From what you yourself told me,' I told Magrieta, 'he did collect the money and led the procession to bail out the rapist. He was involved in the killing.'

She shrugged. 'It's now up to God, Meneer,' — as if that made the matter sub judice — 'en if Stanley must go to hell for it, then jus' too bad. All I'm saying is that if skollies can get away with rape en murder, en if the pollies don't do anything to stop it, then the people must do what they think best.'

'But such a mob can kill innocent people too, Magrieta. If you hadn't escaped through your back window the night they came for you, you'd have been dead. And all those people would have said you were guilty.'

'God helped me to get out,' she said piously. 'En he didn't help the little shit what raped Beulah. So that just shows, doesn't it?'

'What would happen if everybody just took the law in their own hands?' All the old, obvious, moralistic arguments. To me they still matter; perhaps I can still afford to think in such terms.

'En if there is no law?' asked Magrieta. 'Then what?'

'The law is still there,' I persisted. 'Look at what happened in Stanley's assault case.'

'You got a good lawyer there, that's all,' she said. 'There was no lawyers that day when those animals raped Beulah en cut her throat like she was a chicken.' She shook her head. 'No, I'm sorry, Meneer. I know my Bible en I pray to God. But if there is evil in the world we got to pluck it out. If no one will help us, we must help ourselves. En jus' look at the way all those people stood together. You won't find one single man or woman or child who will point out the ones what killed that good-for-nothing raping murdering shit.'

There was no way to reason with her. Upset and confused, I dropped the argument. But Magrieta's state of mind was fraught with such rage and frustration that I was getting deeply worried about her.

'Don't you want to take a few weeks' holiday?' I suggested once.

'En what will happen to the house?'

'I'm sure Tessa and I can manage.' I added hastily, 'Not as well as you, of course. But we'll keep it going.'

'That one will turn the house into a pigsty. Look at her room. A pigsty en a brothel.' I didn't even think she knew the word. (But she did pronounce it to rhyme with 'hotel'.)

'You need some time out, Magrieta. I'm worried about you. You're not a spring chicken any more.'

'I'll retire if I got a place of my own again.'

'I'm working on it,' I assured her. I hadn't updated her on my more recent dealings with Mr Jacobs, as I didn't want to raise her hopes too soon – for all I knew he could drop out again at any minute, having pocketed what he extracted from me, and then we'd be back where we started. But I didn't want her to think that the matter had stalled either. 'I saw a man from the Department again yesterday. He thinks there may be something early in the new year.'

'I won't believe it before my eyes seen it,' was all she said.

'But in the meantime you may just as well take some time off. There's very little to do right now, and perhaps I'll be going to Louis and Janet in Jo'burg for a while. They keep on nagging me about it.'

'En who's going to look after the place when you gone? Those skollies will come breaking in here soon's you turn your back.'

'Tessa will be here.'

'What can she do against a whole gang of them?'

I must confess that the idea horrified me too. But I was thinking of proposing to Tessa that she should invite a friend to stay with her while I was gone. Even if it had to be a man. Perhaps her loving scriptwriter. I broke out in a sweat just thinking of it; but was that really so much worse than what was happening under my eyes right now? This, of course, I dared not mention to Magrieta. But she guessed.

'She bringing men in here while you gone?'

'She's a grown woman, Magrieta. It's for her to decide.'

'That poor Antje haven't got a moment's rest no more. Already she is walking day en night.'

'She lived almost three hundred years ago, Magrieta.'

'En she still see the same things happening what happened in her time.'

'Antje was a slave, Tessa is a free person.'

'What woman is free, Meneer? You tell me.'

'I think Tessa is as free as anyone can wish to be.'

'Meneer don't know what Meneer is talking about.'

'You're under stress, Magrieta. You won't get so upset once you've had a bit of holiday.'

'You want me to go?'

'You know very well I can't do without you. I need you. But I can see things are getting too much for you. Your nerves can't take it any more.'

'En where will the nerves go if I stay with Jessie en them? You think I can have a nice holiday there?'

'I know it's hard on you, Magrieta. But you're trying to do two full-time jobs at the moment. It's too much for flesh and blood.'

In spite of herself, I could see, she was somewhat mollified; the idea must have been tempting after all. And in the event the continuing tension with Tessa helped her to decide.

Every time Tessa harboured a guest for the night she confessed to meeting Antje. These encounters were seldom unequivocal. 'I'm not sure I actually saw anything,' she would tell me. 'There was just a hint of something, a shadow flitting by. And perhaps not even that: no more than a feeling, as if a door had been left open and a breath of wind came past.' Also, there was no fixed routine. Sometimes the ghost would be in the passage to welcome Tessa and her guest when they came in; more often she would make her presence known when they were in bed, when the man entered her; the night when Tessa had her rare orgasm with Derek, she felt Antje's breath between her shoulder blades as she straddled him and that was what triggered it. Once or twice Antje only showed up when it was over, when the man opened the door to leave; and then there was a kind of melancholy feeling about the event, something like remorse, regret.

Once, once only, Tessa had the impression that Antje spoke to her. But she had difficulty describing it. It was one night after a lover – not Derek this time – had left early. She went to the bathroom. When she came back Antje was sitting on her bed. This time she quite clearly saw her visitor, although she could also see right through her.

'I wasn't sure what she expected of me,' said Tessa. 'One thing I do know is that I didn't feel scared at all. It was as if one of my girlfriends had looked in, nothing extraordinary about it. I thought I should ask her something, but I couldn't actually find the words. And when she answered, it wasn't in a voice I could hear either: it was as if she kind of insinuated the words into my mind, like telepathy.'

'What did you talk about?' I asked, thoroughly bemused.

'She asked me about the abortion. She was sad about my losing a child. It reminded her of her own miscarriage after the flogging Susara had given her. I told her there was nothing for her to worry about, I knew what I was doing and I was sure it was the right thing. And then I asked her about herself. You know, about Willem Mostert. I've never stopped thinking about what you told me that first night – about how he went to more and more extremes, making love to Antje in his bedroom, even on the bed right next to his wife . . .'

'Did she answer?'

Tessa didn't answer immediately. It was as if she was gazing right through me, at something behind me in the distance. After a long time she suddenly looked back at me.

'Suppose,' she said out of the blue, 'suppose it wasn't he who dragged her into his bedroom, into his bed, to make love under the eyes of his wife?'

'What do you mean?'

'Suppose it was *she*? Suppose that was the condition she set: that she'd only make love if his wife was present?'

'That's perverse! It's preposterous.'

'Any more than the other way round?'

'Was that what she told you?'

'I told you I couldn't be sure it was she who spoke. It was just a feeling. But it felt real enough. What I really wanted to know about was the relationship between her and the old slave, Cupido. That's something that hasn't stopped nagging me.'

'Did she say anything?'

'She told me how she'd gone to him after Willem had rejected her and begged him to sleep with her.' She paused. 'I'm still confused about this. Remember, I couldn't *hear* her. But I got the impression that she practically forced herself on him. Which is what Magrieta told us, right? But then Antje went further. She told me that when it was over − this is the weirdest part of all − she ordered him to go to the Council of Justice and tell them it was she who'd killed her mistress. Cupido refused. But Antje made him go. She said she could not go on living after what she'd done, and all for nothing because her lover didn't want her any more. I suppose the only way she felt she could have some kind of justice done was to pay for it with her own life.'

'There's nothing of that in any of the books,' I said. 'Not even in the pastor's *Memorie*.'

'Of course not. No one but Antje and Cupido knew about it.' She shook her head. 'And anyway, it's just a bit too spaced out for a historical document, don't you think?'

Something occurred to me. 'But if Antje's execution was really her own wish, then why should she go on haunting this place? Ghosts are supposed to wander about because they still have unfinished business in this world. And hers was done.'

Tessa shrugged. 'How must I know? Maybe she isn't here for herself but for us.'

'What do you mean?'

'Perhaps,' she said cryptically, 'perhaps we need our ghosts as much as they need us.'

# 2

TOMORROW I'M OFF to Johannesburg to spend three weeks with Louis and Janet. I have, finally and reluctantly, ceded to their persistence. It will be the last time I shall see them before they're off to Canada. In blacker moments I think it may well be the last time I shall see them, full stop. And Christmas seems as good a time as any. I really don't want to go, but I'm not sure I can stay here right now either. It comes at a moment of crisis, one that seems to involve everything. Magrieta. The house. My life, my world. Above all, Tessa.

However long it might have been coming, when the moment arrived, yesterday, it caught us – me, certainly – unprepared. It was one of the rare occasions when Tessa had a visitor overnight during the week; usually, by design or not, this tended to happen during weekends when Magrieta was in Bonteheuwel. So this in itself was probably enough provocation. But, certainly as far as Magrieta was concerned, there was an aggravating circumstance. The visitor was black.

The two of them were having coffee in the kitchen, with some of the rusks Magrieta had baked the day before, when I came in. I knew that Tessa had had someone with her in the night, I never missed that; but I didn't think he was still there. For some reason I thought he'd slipped out quietly before daybreak, as her visitors tended to do. But there he was.

'Ruben,' she said, crunching a rusk between her strong teeth, crumbs sticking moistly to her lips, 'this is Zolani. He's a cameraman with our outfit.'

'Hi,' said Zolani, waving from the far side of the table. 'Not a cameraman, sweetie, just an assistant.'

'He will be soon,' said Tessa. 'He's very good. And he does stills too. He wants to do a shoot of me.'

'I'm sure he does,' I said.

'Can I pour you some coffee?' she asked, rising. She looked mellow, lived in. She was wearing her faded T-shirt and not much else. I imagined that she hadn't slept much.

'I can help myself,' I said.

Then Magrieta arrived and immediately there was electricity in the air. She didn't respond to Zolani's hearty greeting and immediately started bustling about at the sink with such a clattering of dishes that talk was impossible. That must have contributed to Zolani's departure only minutes later.

Tessa saw him off at the front gate and then came to my room. She didn't knock. I was sitting on the bed when she came in.

'You not feeling well?' she asked, seating herself next to me.

'Not particularly.'

'Another bad night?'

'I never sleep when you have visitors,' I said, feeling no need to dissemble; she knew me well enough by now anyway.

'That is naughtly,' she said, 'and you know it.' She swung her legs up in her irresponsible way. Oh that this too, too solid flesh would melt.

'I'm not saying this to blame you, I'm only stating a fact.'

'Zolani is lovely,' she said happily. 'His name means "The quiet one".'

'I didn't know you understood Xhosa?'

'I picked it up in the Eastern Cape.' Her unrestrained smile. 'But they say one never knows a language before you've made love in it.'

'He passed the test?'

'He was great.'

I wondered: Should I or shouldn't I? I decided I should: 'You came again?'

'I did. How did you know?'

'Your face.' I touched it with the flat of my hand. 'And did our Antje show up?'

'Shamelessly,' she said. 'She was on the bed with us. I actually got a kick out of it.'

'So you'll be seeing him again.'

'I certainly hope so.'

I looked at her, taking my time, studying her as one might inspect a painting; her eyes were on me, not waiting for a verdict – she must have known in advance what it would be – but simply taking note. My examination left no imprint; once again I was amazed by the way her smooth surface deflected any gaze, or simply let it through, unrefracted, as if she were no obstacle to light.

'Have you ever read Browning's *Pippa Passes*?' I asked.

She shook her head. 'Should I?'

'He must have thought of you when he wrote it.'

'Then I definitely won't read it.' She swung her bare legs back over the edge of the bed. 'I must go. We're shooting in the Cedarberg today. We'll probably only be back tomorrow.' A kiss on my cheek, and she was gone.

I mouthed the words, 'Take care,' without saying them aloud, knowing it was no use.

Now there was Magrieta to contend with. She was still washing up, but she hadn't touched the mugs on the table. The kitchen was heavy with her massive silence. I put the mugs in the foaming hot water. She moved away immediately, wiping her hands on her apron.

'What's the matter, Magrieta?' I asked.

'I don't wash those things,' she said with quiet emphasis.

I stared at her in dismay. Yet why should it have surprised me?

'Zolani is a very nice young man,' I said, anxious no doubt to persuade myself as much as Magrieta. 'If Tessa likes him it's not for us to complain.'

'I'm not complaining, Meneer. I'm jus' saying.' She went out, and I could hear her slippers slapping down the passage to my bedroom to make the bed. A minute later she was back, filling the doorway, hands on her hips. 'If it is still all right with Meneer, en seeing that Meneer is now also going away to Louis en them, I'll maar take that holiday.'

When she left early last night, having given the whole house

– including, surprisingly, Tessa's rooms – an almost mind-blowing cleaning, I paid her for December, with a sizeable Christmas bonus thrown in. We arranged for her to come back on the first Monday after New Year. And then, suddenly, I was on my own, with a feeling of being abandoned like the sole survivor of some apocalyptic catastrophe. As I had done so many times in recent months, only more desperately aware of the surrounding emptiness, I walked from room to room. In Tessa's bedroom I sat down on the bed. Magrieta had changed the sheets, but pressing my face into a pillow I could still imagine some lingering scent. I stood again before the pinboard. The photos had been rearranged. The faded portrait of her father was now in the middle, the exquisite little nude had disappeared. Given as a memento to some nocturnal visitor? Lucky fucking bastard.

It reminded me of my own memento, the slender little navel ring. Which sent me back to the basement below my study. For an hour, two, maybe three, I absorbed myself in my excavations again, in the blinding glare of my torch, turning molehill after molehill of earth and dirt into a mountain. Unsurprisingly, I had no luck. Exhausted, I half-rose to stretch my back. And dropped the torch. It promptly went out. Medieval darkness wrapped itself around me like a hermit's shroud. It didn't last long; a dull glow from the study above filtered down through the rectangle of the opening in the floor; but there was a brief moment of terror before I could breathe more easily again. I felt a dull ache in my ribcage. Like a fire dying in my chest. Not the heart, I assured myself. Not the heart. This ache was behind the sternum. A slight dizziness. At most a light recurrence of the angina. And no wonder, given the stresses of the day.

It was unworthy and I knew it. Yet how could I not wonder about it? – Zolani is welcomed into her bed, but I am still denied? The darkness of my sepulchral cell made it easier to recall detail. Her body, every limb and moment of it. That first instant of revelation: *There's nothing unusual to see.* Her exasperating and prodigal beauty, distributed like alms among the poor. Only I remained denied.

It was as if some force beyond myself had caused me to levitate, to look down on myself from the trapdoor above – in the dark my body below seemed to glimmer spectrally, like ectoplasm – and then hurled me down again in disgust. All I could feel was weariness. Almost literally unto death. I lay down on the uneven ground: not seeing the dirt made it easier to succumb to exhaustion. I didn't care any more. Zolani was young. I was old, old.

I must have fallen asleep, or passed out. I woke up to find something crawling over me. It was terrifying. Unable immediately to remember where I was and how I'd got there, I wondered in a moment of fanciful imagining if this might be hell; if the stirrings and scuttlings about my body were those of demons come to torment me, in the shape perhaps of frogs, of huge hairy spiders, gnawing rats. I groped for, and found, the torch. In its sudden beam of light I caught a glimpse of a small furry creature scurrying away. If that was real, everything else might have been.

This is not an interruption, but more of an extension. NOTE ON ENDINGS. I'm trying to recover those hours in the basement. My thoughts. It is not so much death I have to confront as the idea of an ending. All my life there has been this sense of the need to avoid, to sidestep or transcend an end. I've never had God or religion to give me confidence in another world, whether better or worse. This is it. And yet that is what is most difficult to accept. And it gets worse. In childhood one just assumes everything goes on for ever. Until something happens. In my world it began with little Lenie. Less than a month after our breathless game in the barn among the sweetly pungent lucerne bales, her mother left the farm, taking the children with her, to relatives somewhere in the northern Transvaal. We never saw them again. Years later news filtered back into the district that Lenie had died. Diphtheria, Pa said. 'Carried off by diphtheria.' For a long time I thought of Diphtheria as the name of an angel or devil. You'd better be good, or Diphtheria will come and get you. She carries you off to some place you never return from. The word, with its meaning (as I learned much later) of 'sudden disappearance', remained imprinted on my mind for ever as one of the most unspeakable in the dictionary. And one of the worst aspects of the experience was that I gradually came to doubt my own memories: had my brothers really tried to coax her into taking off her yellow panties that far-off day? If so, had I perhaps joined them in their exhortations? Could I trust the memory of that day of discovery in the barn? I needed her to confirm it, but she was no longer there. With her disappearance, an ending that failed to resolve anything, I'd lost a vital part of myself.

How many of my memories were left unfinished by Riana's death? How many were buried with Pa? The unborn baby girl was too young to carry part of me off with her. And yet I'm not sure. No conscious memories, of course. But how much of faith and hope and love, possibilities for the future? It all ends. Love ends. All those flowers that sprang up on the dead plains after a rainstorm in spring: they ended. Sometimes, in one of his more exuberant or desperate moods, Pa would go out in the veld and sprinkle brandy on the daisies to make them drunk so that they wouldn't feel the pain of shrivelling up and dying. That's how he tried to explain it — which sounded to me like peeing on the girls' feet on winter mornings — but that was little comfort.

Perhaps most of what one does is aimed at getting past the sense of an ending. The stories we tell, the work we do. The procreation of children, stillborn or alive. The lust that goes into the making of them. The love, if you're lucky. I think of Dante's lovers in hell, Paolo and Francesca da Rimini, in the Sayers translation, hand in hand on the dark wind drifting go. As I know I approach my own, I still don't know what happens *after* the end. What comes after the thousand and one nights when Scheherazade falls silent and there are no stories left to tell. Poor Antje on her never-ending cryptic passage through the house, down the centuries, to keep her story going. What happens when Magrieta and Tessa and I are no longer there to listen to her? And what happens to my own story?

Maybe it is purely a problem of my own making. Someone like Tessa, I'm sure, wouldn't even give it a thought. To her — that, at least, is how it seems to me — everything is already so imbued with ending that an alternative is not even thinkable and so she needn't waste any time over it. It may be the secret of her survival.

Sadder, but hardly any wiser, I dragged myself back to the trapdoor, a bag of bones. I barely had the strength to hoist myself up and

face the house. A desert landscape under a dark moon. It was
almost enough to send me back to my hideout. This, I thought,
was how it would be from now on. So dark, so lonely. If only
Johnny had still been round. For years our chess sessions and long
conversations had kept me going. Now those, too, had ended, like
so much else.

I wandered through the dark house. What made me turn into the
lounge, I don't know; I hardly ever go there any more. I stopped at
the Bechstein, a gift from the Hugos, stroked the unrelenting glossy
surface, absently pressed middle C. I'd never learned to play; but
merely to press, randomly, whatever note my finger came to rest
on, trying to imagine the riches that might flow from it had I known
the secret, the key to the riddle, held me in thrall. Another note.
Another. I remembered the rickety, off-key little upright backstage
in the school hall long ago, where it had all begun. The light on
Riana's dark hair, her fingers rippling across the yellowed keys. How
could I have done to her what I had done? The worst betrayal of
all: to distort her memory, now that she was no longer here to
correct it. Was it not I who had set in motion the long decline by
making her pregnant to persuade her into marriage, then aggravated
it by withdrawing into books when she yearned for a living man? In
cherishing my own suffering down the years, what had I ever, really,
tried to understand of hers? Like Antje, she too had a story. If only
I'd allowed her to tell it. Now it was too late. I was left behind,
alone. What I had most feared in my life was slowly coming true.

At the moment it was still provisional. Riana was lost to me.
But Tessa would be back, Magrieta would return after her deserved
break. But not for good. Nothing was for good any more. Soon
they too would be gone and I would remain behind, a ghost in my
own house.

And now was the time to start facing it. I had to shut out of my
mind Magrieta and her world, which lay beyond my grasp and my
wish to understand. More painful, but perhaps more necessary right
now, was the need to forget, or pretend to forget, that somewhere
in this unreal night, among distant jagged mountains, entangled in a
sleeping bag with a new lover, was the woman I loved. In the weeks

ahead my reality had to be defined by my son and his wife, and an unknown number of unruly children. That, if nothing else, should sober me up.

It was time to take my capsule.

# 3

I AM BACK from Johannesburg. I could not cope any longer with Louis and Janet and their tempestuous household – their projects and their plans and their talk of Canada, and the daunting walls topped with razor wire surrounding the Alcatraz they call their home. Whether I can continue to face what awaited me here today, in what *I* used to call home, is something else again.

I changed my ticket to fly back earlier. One can take so much and no more. Had I known then what I know now, would I still have come back this afternoon? A futile question. Would Adam have wished undone the eating of the fruit?

She is sleeping now. I am sitting here in my study, listening to Wanda Landowska playing the Scarlatti sonatas, the volume turned down to a silvery-grey rustling in my ears. I was tempted to go down into the basement to make my notes there; it would feel much more protected, but it would be awkward to sit on the ground and write on my drawn-up knees. Still, in my more irresponsible moments I toy with the idea of moving a chair down there, even the small chess table, and perhaps a light on an extension cord. I can turn it into my private bunker, safeguarded against all the threats of the outside world. If I have a proper trapdoor installed – after the builders' holiday I can ask the carpenter from Stanley's team of unconvicted murderers to do it – I can close it after me when I'm down there and no one will be any the wiser. With a safe retreat like that, poor Johnny might well have survived. He got murdered; I'll get a murderer to make my house safe.

Perhaps I can abduct Tessa into my stronghold and keep her there, happily ever after. *The Collector*, John Fowles. Come into my parlour, said the spider. Rats down there, and all manner of devils. If I found the ring I could ward them off with that. I'm sure it would work just as well as St Anthony's T-shaped crucifix. Sanctified by her pierced flesh. Now healed, with not a scar to show. What surprises me most about her abortion is the ease with which she has come through it. I know I'm irredeemably old-fashioned, but still one would think it must take time, it must return to haunt the conscience. It's not that she is trying to deny it, pretending it never happened. She talks about it, accepts it. And goes her light-footed way untroubled and, it seems, unscathed. I cannot recall ever having seen her cry. (Only that one night, the possible brimming of tears?) Even this afternoon, following the shock of my homecoming, did not unsettle her.

It's not that the fortnight with Louis and his family was an unmitigated disaster. Even the kids were better behaved than I'd remembered them and feared in advance. There has always been a distance between my sons and me, for which I'm willing to take the blame. When they were very small I was delighted with the newness of them; and whenever Riana was ill or tired I was happy to take them over at night. Which was relatively easy as after both births she stopped breastfeeding very soon. I was resolved to take upon me the whole father–son thing as they grew up: do with them everything I loathed, teach them all I didn't know. But at least I'd also introduce them to books, and to music, and the pleasures of being alone with one's thoughts. But there was still the hope of a daughter, one day. It was after Louis's birth that Riana and I began to drift more and more out of touch. For at least two years we hardly ever made love. It was almost unbelievable that from one of those rare and unremarkable entanglements she should fall pregnant. Yet slowly, after the first few months, it began to draw us together again. And then the miscarriage and the discovery that it would have been a girl, a shadow fallen irrevocably between her and me. I began to lose interest in the boys. With Johann, a cherubic and bubbly little creature, I could still make some contact; but Louis, I fear, has always been too much like me, introverted to the point of taciturnity.

Once they were grown up holidays together never exceeded a

week. (Magrieta has firm views on this, in spite of the premium she places on family, especially ours: 'Relatives is like fish, after three days they go off.') We would start by beaming ferocious good will at each other, yet find it impossible to sustain a conversation for more than ten minutes. We would exchange our heartfelt greetings and then disperse, each withdrawing with a book or a newspaper into a different corner.

This time, too, we appeared to settle into the same pattern. But the imminence of their departure – now firmly set for the end of January – brought some of the barriers down. And they were particularly effusive in their praise about how 'smart' I looked, how well dressed I'd become. I tried to smile it off, embarrassed to go more deeply into it. But it did smooth the way. I even accompanied the kids to a terrible Something-on-ice, and to a steakhouse, and on a day trip to Hartebeespoort Dam so that Louis and Janet could spend some time together.

She did much to get us talking. The country was, inevitably, a good starting point. Even though we have always differed on politics, never a topic to excite me. I did watch Mandela's walk to freedom from Victor Verster prison (they'd wanted to fly to Cape Town to be there in the flesh, standing for hours in the merciless sun, but they couldn't get a flight booking); but I did not vote in the much-vaunted democratic elections of '94. Queuing was too tedious for my liking; Louis and Janet spent something like five or six hours for the dubious pleasure of making a cross in a square. Perhaps inevitably, the swing of their pendulum was also larger than mine. From their excessive euphoria not quite five years ago they now cannot find enough words to fulminate against everything that has gone wrong (but the experience of Janet's friend, hijacked and raped, cannot of course be made light of); whereas my feelings range from occasional outrage, as when I was so summarily retrenched, to annoyance or vague irritability. The outside world has simply never mattered to me all that much. I find a mad disproportion in the country, especially when I'm cornered by Magrieta's tales of woe, but except in brief and exceptional moments – Johnny's death – it does not threaten me personally. Or am I suppressing a fear, I wondered during our discussions, of confessing the confusion I feel in reaction to the clamour that seems to come more and more insistently from the space out there? The invasion by Tessa's bergies . . . ? But that, too, had come and gone, and life had continued much as before. Or had it?

My main regret, I told them, was that after having been *against* so much for so long – all the violence and lies of the previous regime, from Malan and Verwoerd all the way down to de Klerk – one would have hoped that in the new dispensation there would at last be the possibility of being *for* some things. Louis differed quite vehemently. To be 'for' anything is just misplaced nationalism, he argued. There are enough bad guys around to fight against without having to invent angels to fight for. 'There is no need to be for,' he insisted. 'To be against is enough.'

I did discover that behind all the bravado about going to a new country and starting all over, they also had to contend with fears and anxieties. Could they possibly sprout roots again? Would they survive in the cold? Could they really leave behind the country they'd come to disparage and to loathe so much, yet which had made them what they were, for better or for worse? That made it easier for me to air some of my own trepidation, my dread of growing old alone.

Perhaps I should not have mentioned it. Because then, after the easy early banter and teasing about the new lodger, they started the attempts to bludgeon me into submission with their generosity: why couldn't I go with them? I had no special ties to a job or family, no truly indispensable friends; I was getting old before my time and emigrating with them might provide me with a new lease on life. I could indulge my love of music, of museums, of libraries. It would be stimulating and rewarding; and I'd still have all the time in the world to do what I liked best – read, research, make my notes and reflect on them.

It kept me awake at night. What could I really offer them, in reply? Usually, I suppose, you simply remain in a country because you happen to be there, the way you stay with a woman once you're married to her. Riana and I. But when, without any warning, you're suddenly given a choice like the one Louis and Janet were offering me, there is no hiding behind habit or superstition any longer. I did not *want* to get drawn into such arguments. Not at my age. There should be no call for it. But how could I shut my eyes to what they had made me see?

I knew I had no sound counter-arguments which would stand up to even the slightest scrutiny. But can you really resolve the most vital moments of choice in your life with 'arguments'? There's beggary in the love that can be reckoned. Had I taken Tessa back after throwing her out because it was the 'logical' thing to do? And suppose I chose not to leave with my children but to remain here – would that be because it is in any respect 'easier' to do so? Unimaginable. This *is* no easy country. It is merciless, it is hard, hard. (And not necessarily hard in a male way but with the kind of hardness I'd come to realise only a woman can have.) Whoever elects to stay here cannot expect to remain unscathed. It cannot care less, it wipes its backside on us and leaves its trails of blood on us. There's certainly nothing romantic about it, none of the old *Blut-und-Boden* stuff. Perhaps it's more a matter of need, of necessity? I do not know.

Maybe it is true, as Louis argued, that things have gone too far already, that in this broken existence there is no hope of repair. But at least it *is* an existence still. And perhaps the only way of attempting to repair it is by remaining part of it. Again, I don't know. Perhaps I just didn't want to choose.

'The offer stands,' said Janet. 'Don't push it, Dad. But promise us you will at least think about it. We really want you to spend your old age in some peace and comfort.'

And this was what got me down in the end. An overdose of kindness. I was not ready to contemplate such a move. How could I admit to them, or to myself, that I will never budge while Tessa is around? Not in the hope of ever changing her mind, of 'winning' her; I've long since given up that hope. We have no 'prospects'. This, now, at such a distance, at last, I was forced to acknowledge unreservedly. But I cannot, will not, leave her. It would be a form of suicide, all the more sure for being so slow. I need her, not for this reason or that, only for a love so irrational, so pointless, so mad, that I would make myself ridiculous even by mentioning it. Stupid old fool. Even in my dotage, grant me this: I love her.

That was why, much to their consternation, I decided to come home a week early. To get away from all the well-meant cajoling; to get back to Tessa.

We had spoken a few times – three – on the telephone. Briefly, to exchange news, talk about the weather, ask aimless questions; and to hear her voice, that deep, full-bodied voice like a dark red wine matured in oak; if possible to make her laugh. The last time she phoned, the day before Christmas, she casually asked, halfway through an account of a film she'd seen, 'By the way, would you mind if I invited a few friends over some time?'

'Of course. There's no need to ask.'

'Thanks, love. You're a star. When will you be back?'

'Day after New Year.'

As soon as I put the receiver down I knew I was going home. Some crisis, I vaguely said to Louis. And when he demanded to know more I invented something about Magrieta. Thrown out by the people she'd been staying with, I explained without batting an eyelid (I'd already told them all the depressing details of her story), and given her situation it might be dangerous for her to move into my house on her own. What with all those skollies and murderers abroad . . . Louis had all kinds of solutions; Janet even offered to fly down with me and help me sort it out, then return to Johannesburg. But I stuck to my guns. In the end it was quite an emotional farewell.

The house was ablare with music when I got out of the taxi at the front gate just after two this afternoon. Not my music, but something unspeakable. I stopped at the front door, which stood wide open, bracing myself before I went in. The racket was coming from the study, but there was no one there. It was the kind of noise the boys had sometimes indulged in when they were in high school or at university, but that was usually confined to the back section of the house and when I had been home there were strictly enforced rules about times and decibels. This wave of objectionable noise came throbbing and thundering and screaming from every corner, reverberating in the very walls. All I could make out were two inane lines, constantly repeated:

*But if you close the door*
*I'd never have to see the day again . . .*

I left my luggage in the passage to cover my ears with my hands
as I picked my way along an obstacle course of unimaginable junk
– bottles, pillows, cutlery and crockery, shoes, jackets, sunglasses –
all the way to the kitchen. What I found there was beyond imagining.
Dishes, cups, plates, glasses of every description piled up in the sink,
on the table, on the dresser, even on the floor; shards of broken glasses
and bottles littered everywhere. There was no sign of life, not even in
her rooms, where the chaos was equally astounding: drawers pulled
out, pillows and blankets strewn across the floor. Even the mattress
had been tipped from the bed. The Assyrian came down like a wolf
on the fold.

A burglary, I thought. Magrieta's ominous prediction had come
true. The place was ransacked. And Tessa, for all I knew, was
murdered. It was all I could do to keep from retching at the thought.
Where would I find the body, and in what state? Howl, howl, howl,
howl, howl.

Back in the kitchen I stopped in bewilderment to look round, then
grabbed a rolling pin from the dresser. Not much of a weapon, but it
least it was something to defend myself with. I couldn't quite carry off
the TV cop act – press my back against a doorpost, look left and right,
raise my weapon and jump inside, legs astride like a dancing Cossack,
bang, bang – but I did look into all the rooms along the passage.
Bedlam everywhere. Mere anarchy loosed upon the world. Among
the familiar objects, in various parts of the house, were discarded
items of clothing, mainly of the female variety. Not Tessa's, thank
God, I knew hers intimately from the washing line. Even my bedroom
had been turned upside down, obviously slept in, partied in, cavorted
in, fornicated in. If it was just a straight burglary I could still resign
myself to it. But this vandalism, this trashing of a place as much part
of myself as my body, was beyond outrage. And still no sign of life,
human or otherwise. Even the cats must have fled.

Someone had been sitting on my chair – eating at my table –
sleeping in my bed.

And then I found her. She was in the study after all, invisible from the door, behind the desk on the floor, a spilled glass of wine at her elbow.

She wasn't dead. She was asleep, snoring in fact. And the music just went on blaring, probably set in a repeat mode.

Only then did it strike me that the music should have put the notion of a burglary out of my mind; but its very loudness had made all thought impossible.

I went to the pick-up to turn it off and discovered that it had been disconnected and replaced by an alien CD player. It took me a while to find the right button. The sudden silence throbbed like a heartbeat in my ears.

She stirred and sat up. Through dazed eyes, with dark patches under them, she stared at me for a while, blinking. I'd never seen her looking so ghastly. Yet I thought: You're beautiful. And knew without a doubt that I was now beyond redemption.

Then she said, in quiet, carefully spaced syllables, 'Oh my God.'

And for quite a while that was that.

After what seemed like the proverbial eternity she spoke again. 'What are you doing here?'

'I was just going to ask you that,' I said. 'In the present perfect.'

She stood up. She was swaying on her feet and had to prop herself up with her hands on the desk, hanging her head. I didn't move. After about a minute she raised her head again, making an obvious effort to focus her eyes on me – the pupils very wide, I noticed – and came unsteadily towards me. She was wearing, predictably I suppose, the faded T-shirt, and nothing else.

'Am I glad to see you,' she said.

Without thinking, I took off my jacket, a dark brown one she'd chosen for me, and draped it round her waist. She made an attempt to hold it in place. It was a blazing hot day, but she was shivering.

I took her in my arms. If I hadn't, she might have lost her balance. She smelled of smoke, and sweat, and alcohol, and stale semen.

'What in God's name was that music?' I asked.

'Good, wasn't it?' she asked. 'An old thing from the sixties. "Some Kinda Love". Group called Velvet Underground.'

'Nothing velvety about it.'

She evidently decided to ignore my remark. 'What day is it?' she asked.

'Sunday. Almost three o'clock.'

'You weren't supposed to find me like this,' she said, trying not very successfully to smile.

'What have you done, my darling?' I asked, finding it difficult to steady my voice.

'We had something of a Christmas party.'

'The few friends you asked over?' I didn't mean to sound sarcastic; it was just beyond my comprehension.

She nodded. 'It must have gone on for a bit longer than I meant.'

'Two days?' I guessed.

'Something like that. But it's so good to see you. Did it go well? How are your kids?'

'Come with me,' I said resolutely, supporting her with an arm under hers. She lost the jacket along the way.

'I'll be all right. I just . . .' A vaguely blissful smile.

'Are you drugged?'

'Right now I'm most things you can think of.'

We stumbled slowly across the passage, through my bedroom to my bathroom. The toilet, like everything else, was filthy. I pressed the lever, closed the lid and lowered her on to it. Still steadying her with one hand, I turned on the bath taps with the other. I'd meant to help her into the bath without removing the T-shirt, but somehow she managed to wriggle out of it.

'Will you be all right on your own or will you drown yourself?'

'I'd like you to wash me.'

'I'm going to get you some coffee,' I said sternly. 'When I come back I want you clean and dry.' Right then I couldn't face her nakedness.

It must have been at least an hour later, probably more, before we settled in the study – she on the sofa, I on my habitual chair – where I'd tried to re-establish some order. By that time I'd already escorted her to her bedroom where she'd said she had some pills that would help; I could only hope to God she knew what they were. She was wearing my shapeless old gown. She gulped down two cups of strong black coffee. I felt like my father dousing the daisies with brandy.

Tessa reacted more positively than the daisies. Before long she was chatting briskly. The dark patches were still under her eyes, but there didn't seem much wrong with her which a solid sleep wouldn't cure. Still I wanted her to take it slowly.

'You sit here,' I told her. 'I'm going to do some cleaning up.'

'Can't it wait till tomorrow?'

This, I thought, was exactly what I would have asked Riana in similar circumstances. Except that we never in all our married years had a house remotely resembling this scene of devastation. I was tempted to let it go: why the hell not? It would be so good, so indescribably good, after two weeks away from her, just to spend a peaceful hour with her, have one of our long, unpremeditated, meandering conversations, hold her in my arms perhaps, watch her fall asleep with her head on my lap; and much later in the night to take her to her room and put her to bed, and go to sleep myself. But there was a touch of vindictiveness in me too, I must admit. This had exceeded all the limits of admissibility and one way or another it should be brought home to her. If she acted like a child it was my fatherly duty to treat her as one.

But if this was so, why did I not simply order her to start cleaning up herself? Why this perversity to punish her by taking on myself what was by rights her sole responsibility?

'We can't leave it like this,' I said calmly. (Riana would have said, 'What will the neighbours say? What would God think if he came in the night?') 'You have a rest. I'm going to make a start.'

'You certainly won't,' she said. 'Not without me.'

'The house can't stay like this,' I said sternly, 'and you're in no fit state to do anything.'

'Try me.'

It was nothing short of amazing to see how methodically and efficiently she did her bit. We began by dumping all the empty bottles on the back stoep, sweeping up the broken glass and cigarette stubs, stacking the dishwasher and washing up the larger utensils.

Then we tackled the rooms one by one, packing away what needed to be stowed, making piles of what had to be returned to various other parties – CDs, plates and bowls, glasses, items of clothing – and going over the whole surface of the house with the vacuum cleaner. We didn't speak much while we worked. In the beginning I thought she was cowed, guilty, crestfallen; but from the few remarks she randomly tossed at me it was clear that she felt no remorse at all. Sorry, perhaps, for the inconvenience; but that, after all, was my own fault for coming back a week earlier than expected. She seemed almost happy as she worked, humming or whistling tunes unknown to me, attacking each new room like a battlefield to be won with sheer dedication, even exuberance.

'We're a good team, you know,' she said when we started on her room. 'You should have come home earlier.'

'I'm rather relieved I didn't,' I said.

'Are you mad at me?'

'I was quite floored when I arrived,' I said. 'I couldn't believe what I saw. Or heard.' I had to make a pause. 'But frankly, I was too worried about finding you dead to give much thought to anything else.'

'I tried to keep them out of your study,' she said. 'I really tried. But after a while I suppose I was getting too spaced out myself.'

'You did go rather overboard, didn't you?' I said, aware of weariness beginning to spread through every bone and muscle in my body.

'You *are* angry with me,' she said – not defiant or accusing, not demure either, just quiet, matter of fact.

'I wish I could say I was,' I replied. 'It would make it much easier. Right now I don't know *what* I am.' I tried to order my thoughts, which wasn't easy with her eyes studying me so calmly. 'Yes, I am mad at you. And yet I wouldn't be anywhere else in the world tonight than here with you.'

'I don't deserve you, Ruben,' she said.

'We've done enough,' I decided abruptly. 'Let's go back to the study for a while. Just to sit. I'm not sure I should offer you anything to drink, though. Except more coffee perhaps?'

'I'd love a glass of cold water,' she said. Then a familiar impish look glinted in her eyes. 'And I have something to offer *you*.'

What she brought to the study was — honest to God — a dagga zol. Which I wouldn't have known if she hadn't told me.

I could only shake my head in dismay.

'You've never tried it?'

'Absolutely not. And I'm not going to start at my age.'

'Just a few puffs. Don't be a nerd.'

I remained wary, but there was something so seductive about her, and I was so relieved to be with her again, that I did what under any other circumstances — and certainly in the daytime — I would have refused very firmly. I think even if she'd asked me to dance, which is probably the worst ordeal I can think of, I would have taken her in my arms and waltzed off with her — or boogied, or jived, or whatever one does nowadays.

I regret to say that it had little effect — even though to please her, and in some annoyance with myself, I finished a joint on my own. All it did was give me a dull headache and a hint of palpitations, no more. While she — after God knows how much more of the same, and worse, over the past two days and nights — became entirely relaxed, a graceful feline reclining more and more euphorically in the half-dark.

'I'm relieved that you survived,' I said through the lazy early fumes.

'It wasn't so bad.'

'I don't mean only the party. The last two weeks.'

'We were shooting until just before Christmas. I was practically working day and night.'

'You still happy with the job?'

'Yes.' She became more pensive. 'And no. The work is fantastic, but some of the people are arseholes. I'm thinking of making a move.'

'Anything concrete?'

'Just beginning to take shape. One of the other women has contacts in the production world. Nicky. Also, she knows somebody with money to invest. And I'm supposed to have the brains. If it comes off it'll be exciting. If not . . .' She shrugged. 'But I first want to see this project through. Apart from anything else, it may involve a trip to Paris at the end of January.'

'Sounds too good to miss,' I said, aching with envy. And suppressing the obvious question: *Who with?* All I dared to ask, as casually as I could, was, 'Zolani doing all right?'

'He's getting better and better.'

'I was thinking of his camera work.'

'He's getting better with everything.' She smiled across the room, through the gentle haze of smoke.

'Do you still see Derek?' I asked point-blank.

'I suppose so.'

'You're not sure?'

'I mean, I'm seeing him. But he wants it to be exclusive and I'm not ready for that. I've been moving about a bit. I'm not quite sure who I'm seeing, Ruben.' She propped herself up on an elbow. The languor had faded, but a sensuousness remained. (I filed the words in my mind, hoping vaguely that the distinction made sense.) 'To tell you the truth, my love life is a bit confusing right now. You know, last night – I think it was last night – I actually slept with two men. I've never done that before.'

It felt like a crude blow with a blunt instrument. Still, I tried to make light of it. 'Safety in numbers?' I asked. But there was a bitter edge which might have been noticeable only to myself.

She seemed to take it seriously. 'It's not that. Not that at all. It's – I'm not sure . . . In a way, you know, I think, to have someone with me, inside me . . . It kind of reassures me. It makes me feel I'm real, my body is real, I'm all right.' And then the inevitable total frankness. 'I think the abortion shook me up a bit. I was no longer so confident of myself. I mean, it was good to know I can have children. But in another sense I sort of let myself down. And now . . . I'm not proud of myself. But I'm not ashamed either.'

I said nothing for some time. She stretched herself out again.

'Did Antje put in an appearance?' I asked.

'For once she didn't,' said Tessa. 'It's strange. Do you think she was shocked?'

'I think there was simply too much noise.'

She chuckled and closed her eyes. I could see the sleepiness taking over. But there were still things to talk about before she slipped too far out of my reach. I made the move over to the sofa and took her hands in mine. 'I hope you'll understand what I want to say, Tessa.'

'You're worried about me.'

'I'm worried about two things,' I said with as much intensity as I could muster through the first intimations of the headache. 'One is that you may get hurt.'

'I can handle that.'

'The other,' I persisted, 'is that you may *not* get hurt.'

She looked hard at me for a long time. I kissed her little frown without letting go of her hands.

'I'm not sure I understand,' she said.

'I'm worried that to walk your tightrope you may have to keep emotion so much out of it that you lose the capacity to feel. And that would horrify me.'

She moved into my arms. In one respect it was extremely chaste, wrapped as she was in my large, shapeless gown (I thought of a description of St Anthony in one of my books on Bosch, 'sheltering in his mantle as if within a cave'); in another it was disconcertingly sexual, because I was only too agonisingly aware, all the more so after our long separation, of just how naked she was within it.

Only the oldest, most useless, most indispensable, words remained. I said, 'I love you.'

She said, 'I have a feeling that I may be going into a period of total chastity.'

'I have hope for you yet,' I said lightly, although I felt more like crying.

'Hope,' she smiled, 'is the thing with feathers, isn't it?'

Then I took her to bed and came back here to catch up with my writing. I don't want to interpret or tease meaning from it, or wonder, or speculate; I just want to mark the paper.

One by one, as the long night has worn on, the cats returned, first Amadeus and then the rest in tow, like shadows, like the mere possibilities of themselves. It is too late now to go into my basement. There will be time tomorrow. The search must continue in earnest. Hope is the thing with feathers.

# 4

WE HAVE EDGED into the new year. An unremarkable transition, overshadowed all too soon by what has happened in the fortnight since. My premonition has come true. Magrieta left late yesterday afternoon. My life seems to have drifted loose from its moorings, such as they were. I wonder whether even Tessa can sound the depths of my present distress. Losing a companion after thirty-eight years. For Magrieta it is not entirely without its brighter side. To me it's like a death in the family. She'll still be looking in from time to time, I know; and I may visit her occasionally to share a cup of tea. But I know it will be different. One limb after another of my life is wrenched from me. It is a long-drawn-out goodbye.

She came back from her holiday on the Monday just after New Year's Day as we'd agreed. It has all gone so fast (perhaps because I'm going downhill anyway). I find it increasingly difficult to keep up. And suddenly, on an ordinary summer's day, I've now lost something which diminishes me.

As she came in that Monday and deposited her large black bag on the kitchen table, she lifted her nose and sniffed the air like a retriever, and asked, 'What's been going on here?'

'What makes you think there's something going on? Tessa has gone to work. I've been back from holiday for ten days or more. We cleaned up the whole house for you.'

'She been turning the place upside down, I see.'

'How can you say that, Magrieta?'

'You perhaps cleaned up a bit on the top, but this place look like a sparrow's nest. She got on the go again while Meneer was gone?'

'Not as far as I know.'

'You never notice nothing, Meneer.'

'I hope you had a good holiday?' I deliberately changed the subject.

'How can one have a good holiday in a house like Jessie's? En now Stanley has started messing her up too.'

'Why?'

'Ask him, he's mos a man, he'll know. Out of a job, lying about all day, it's a good-for-nothing life. There's a heavy load on that house, Meneer. I can't take it much longer.'

'I'm going to phone the people about your house again. Remember, they promised me things would start happening after New Year.'

'Their promises!' She began to put on her housecoat. It seemed more of a struggle than before to make the flaps meet in front. She wheezed with the effort. 'You know how long this been going on now? Ever since the time of District Six, when they chased us out and dumped us on the Flats. Never a day's peace since. Meneer remember the day they sent the bulldozers? Miss Riana was still with us then, shame, the poor thing.'

'I remember very well, Magrieta,' I said. I could have added: For us, too, that was where everything began to go wrong. I was so shattered by what that young upstart had shouted after us. Riana wanted me to do something about it; my only wish was to forget all about it as soon as possible. We quarrelled all the way back here. I promised I'd write a letter of protest. That made her more furious than anything else. 'What's the use? They'll wipe their backsides on it. You don't have the guts to stand up for anything you believe in. If there *is* anything you believe in. You wouldn't even have come along today if I hadn't made you. When I first met you, you seemed scared of nothing. You even took on my father. What's happened to all that? You've got feet of clay like all the others.'

There was no need to be too upset; one constantly says things one regrets afterwards. But those words, added to what the pimply little runt had shouted at us — 'White kaffirs!' — were rooted in my mind. A kind of screen had shifted in between us; and it was sealed for good, it seems to me now, in one of the endless quarrels that followed her miscarriage when, driven to desperation by her constant accusations that I wasn't 'man enough', I hit back with the lowest and most shameful blow I could think of. 'And what kind of a woman do you think you are? You wouldn't even give me a daughter.'

That must be the worst thing ever said between us. It was beyond forgiveness; I couldn't even try to ask, the words stuck in my throat. Not even Alison could cancel them. Neither could Tania, so many years later. All they did was to drive me ever more deeply into my shell. Yes, you're right, Magrieta. That's where it all began, the day of the bulldozers. They flattened me as surely as they did your house.

'We'll get through, Meneer,' she said with sudden sympathy. 'We're mos used to bad times. We'll show them.' (Whoever her 'them' might be.) Taking the vacuum cleaner from the cupboard she shifted the topic: 'And what was Meneer's holiday like?'

'Louis and Janet send their love. And a present. It's waiting for you.'

I turned to go to the study and she went with me. The gift, a pair of slippers – my suggestion – and a sizeable cheque in a buff envelope, immediately mollified her. She tackled the house with fearsome vigour as I withdrew to have my bath and get dressed for the day. After that I tried to telephone Mr Jacobs, but it turned out, as I should have expected, that he hadn't come back from his vacation yet. Not a propitious beginning to the new year.

Yet he surprised me. Before the end of the week, on the Friday, without any further prodding from me, he called me out of the blue. 'Mr Olivier? I got news for you.'

'Don't tell me you found a house for Mrs Daniels?' I joked.

'Spot on,' he said. 'If you bring her round on Monday we can sign the papers.' I was so flabbergasted that for a while I couldn't answer. He asked, 'Mr Olivier, are you there?'

'I'm here all right.' Perhaps I shouldn't have been so stunned. After all, I'd paid him enough. But I'd prepared myself for another delay before something budged. I did my best to collect myself. Clearing my throat, I said, 'We'll be there, you can count on us.' For a long time I remained sitting with the receiver on my lap, until Magrieta found me there.

'Why you sitting like that? Meneer got bad news?'

'Very bad, Magrieta.' It was all I could do not to start laughing like a hyena. 'We're going to sign for your new house on Monday.'

'Meneer is not pulling my leg now?'

'I won't believe it before I see the keys in your hand,' I said. 'But that's what Mr Jacobs just told me.'

As it turned out, it happened four days ago.

'At long last they've wiped out District Six,' I said.

'Don't talk too soon, Meneer,' she warned. 'One don't just buy thirty years back like that.'

I thought: You haven't heard half of it. But I kept my peace. She was quite capable of giving the house back if she heard about the bribes.

'But at least it's a beginning,' she relented, offering me her hand in a gesture of solemnity. 'En it's all Meneer's doing.'

'Mr Jacobs is the man to thank,' I said with a straight face.

Just as well we had that bright moment. Because the rest of these two weeks has not served Magrieta quite so well. Mainly because of Tessa.

For the first few days they treated each other with restrained diffidence. But Tessa was having a hard time at work and she was more edgy than usual. Too cowardly to tackle her head on, Zach was getting at her in roundabout ways; and when he found a pretext to fire Zolani (he must have begun to suspect something there) it all blew up. I'm sure Magrieta aggravated Tessa's volatile mood, as she'd been looking for a confrontation for some time. And when Zolani openly moved in with Tessa for two days while he sorted out his affairs, that was the last straw.

'It's bad enough to spend the night,' said Magrieta. 'But sticking around day and night is too much. They're not our class, Meneer.'

'We just have to be patient, Magrieta.'

She didn't even bother to answer. But I could see her fuse was getting shorter. And on the second morning, at the breakfast table, it exploded.

'Miss Tessa.' Magrieta appeared in the doorway with a duster in one hand. Tessa and Zolani were seated at the table; I'd just come in with my breakfast tray from my room. 'What you bring in here is your own business. But then you mustn't make it other people's business too.'

'What's up, Magrieta?' I tried to intervene.

She planted herself between them and me. 'Meneer must now please stay out of this.' She pulled a small bundle of clothes from under her housecoat and shook it in Zolani's direction. All I could see was Tessa's face glowing with indignation. 'If that one starts asking me to wash his underpants for him, then you making it my business. That's when I say so far en no blerry step further.' And with a histrionic gesture she scattered the underclothes across the quarry-tiled floor.

Zolani had the opportunity to save the situation, but unfortunately he wrecked it all. Tilting his chair back on its rear legs he said haughtily, 'You don't expect *me* to wash them, do you?'

Tessa jumped up and starting gathering the clothes. 'Don't bother, I'll wash them myself,' she said, her face now a very deep red – but whether it was from anger or embarrassment I couldn't tell.

Unexpectedly it was all channelled in my direction. Magrieta slowly turned to face me. 'I'm sorry, Meneer. But this house is getting too small for the lot of us. Now it's for Meneer to tell us: must these two go, or must I?'

'Please, Magrieta, don't . . .' said Tessa from the floor.

Magrieta was still looking straight at me.

'I'm sure you can sort out this whole thing among yourselves,' I said, flustered and distressed, and strode off to my study. In my head I could hear the echo of Riana's taunting words all those years ago.

Only minutes later I heard Zolani hurrying past in the passage. The front door slammed after him. Number one, I thought.

Very soon afterwards it was indeed Tessa who followed. She went as far as the front door, then stepped back, hesitated in the doorway and came into the study. She was pale. I looked up, unable to say anything.

'I'm so sorry, Ruben,' she whispered. As so often, she raked her fingers through my hair and planted a brief kiss on my head. 'Can we talk about it later?'

Moments afterwards I heard the noisy Beetle pull off outside.

I remained in the study, waiting for Magrieta to show up. But in her time-honoured way she waited until noon before she appeared massively in the doorway.

'Meneer busy?'

'I was hoping you'd come.'

'I'm sorry, Meneer. I didn't want this to happen. But Meneer was there yourself.' Adding a barb, 'Until Meneer decided to leave it all to us.'

I felt guilty, but this wasn't the right time to talk about it. All I said was, 'I thought it was better to avoid a free-for-all.'

'I got my self-respect, Meneer.'

'I know that, Magrieta.' Adding with probably a touch of wishful thinking, 'Did you manage to sort it out?'

'I come to give notice, Meneer.'

Slow paralysis overtook me. 'That's not possible, Magrieta,' I said.

'It was not possible before today, Meneer. But I'm not taking orders from a . . . from a stranger.' I knew she'd meant to say something else. 'I'm not his meid, Meneer.'

I got up, very determined. 'I'll talk to him myself, Magrieta. I'll talk to Tessa too. I know she's feeling bad about it, she already came to tell me.'

'I had the whole morning to think about it, Meneer. I decided it's the best for all of us. It comes at the right time too, I now got a house of my own to go to. En you got somebody staying here. It will never work out between me and Miss Tessa. I had a long chat to Antje about it, in the back room, en she also see it my way. It's time for me to take my retirement.'

'Let's give it some time, Magrieta. Even if it's only until after the weekend. We need to sleep on it. We two go back too far to rush things now.'

'I don't need no more sleep, Meneer. I spoke to Antje en that is now how it is. En if Meneer don't mind, I'd rather not wait for the end of the month. I jus' want to finish this week. I'll come in tomorrow, even if it's Saturday, so I can leave the house spotless.'

I kept on pleading. She waited patiently, but I could see that her mind was set on it. It was an unruly day, especially after she'd gone home in the afternoon. For me, as I was to find out, my day had only just begun.

I spent the evening working in my study. 'Work' is hardly the right word, my mind was in such turmoil. I put Telemann on the record player, but it didn't work its usual soothing magic. Then Mozart's flute sonatas, abandoning myself to nostalgia. But that was the wrong choice too because it brought back too many memories. And I couldn't concentrate on the music anyway: I was listening for her footstep outside, her key in the door, her face appearing like an exotic moth out of the night.

After midnight, when the wait seemed fruitless, I went to pull up the four floorboards and let myself down into the basement, carrying the new lamp on its extension cord with me. I resumed my subterranean explorations, the only discipline – I'd come to learn from recent experience – to keep my thoughts in check. So fierce was my concentration that I lost all sense of time. Only when I made the discovery did I look at my watch and register with dismay that it was nearly six o'clock. From far outside one could already hear the morning birds.

What I'd found was not the lost ring, but Antje of Bengal.

By that time I'd covered the entire surface of the basement in my search. All that had remained was the furthest corner against the outside wall, which I'd left for last – because it was the least likely place to look for the ring, the floor sloping upwards in that direction; and because the whole corner area was taken up by a heap of stones of all shapes and sizes, some so large that I could barely move them by myself. I wasn't sure I should even risk it, not with my heart. The Victorian builders who'd moved in a century ago to rebuild the house on its old foundations must have decided it wasn't worth removing the rubble and had left it untouched among the massive walls.

Only when I found the scattering of small bones among the stones did I stop. A chill moved down my spine like a slow, hairy caterpillar. It wasn't exactly fear. Nothing as uncomplicated as that. I immediately knew it was she, even though there wasn't anything to identify her by, not a shred of clothing, nothing at all. Willem Mostert must have stripped her naked before he laid her down here. Unless he'd brought the body from the gallows without clothes. All kinds of obscene possibilities came to my mind, but I tried to suppress them, concentrating instead, in as disciplined and measured a manner as I could, on removing the stones one by one and setting them well aside until the whole skeleton was exposed.

The only true indication of who she might have been was the fact that the skull lay in the abdominal cavity, one bony hand folded over it. The other hand, presumably the one chopped off by the executioner, was the one whose scattered bones had first caught my attention.

She was much smaller than I'd have expected. More child than woman. But that of course fitted Magrieta's description. The only time I'd seen her for myself, when she'd surprised me in Tessa's room, it was half-dark inside, and I was in such a state that I didn't think about estimating size or shape. Of delicate build. Finely shaped wrists and ankles, like the skeleton of a bird.

Dear God. Never before had I been faced with this ultimate essence of bone that both defies and defines humanity. So little left when it comes to this. But so indestructible, so obdurate, so firm, so bony.

Without thinking of what I was doing I began to trace the outlines of the skeleton with a finger: and only much later, when I thought back, did it penetrate my mind that I'd been stroking her in a lover's caress. Except there was nothing left of what would hold the rapt attention of the lover. Here, the instep of a foot, that delicate, vulnerable, miraculous extremity of the body. Here, the exquisite line of calf and knee and thigh. The fineness of fingers, the fragility of a wrist, the sharp point of the elbow. Here had been the ears which had translated the world into sound: whisperings of love, a slave bell clanging at the break of day, Susara's imprecations, the smacking sound of the sjambok. Here the eyes that gave shape to naked light: the beaches and jungles of Bengal, tigers burning in the night, lianas; the violence of a tossing sea, the raptor's eyes of buyers at an auction, Willem Mostert's rampant lust. Here the nose, the sensitive tongue, here the lips. Here were the girl's breasts that tautened under her master's caress. In the bed where Susara lay, asleep or awake in the fear of hell; or on the small mat by its side. Here was the soft stomach, the indentation of the navel, the slight swelling of the lower belly, here the mound sloping down into the cunt. Nothing unusual to see. Only its concave hereness exposed to the touch of a cupped hand. Nothing left of all that. All the suffering, and pleasure, and fear, mere illusion? Here was only the impenetrability of bone. Behold, thou art fair my love; behold, thou art fair; thou hast doves' eyes within thy locks: thy lips are like a thread of scarlet, and thy speech is comely: thy temples are like a piece of pomegranate within thy locks. Thy two breasts are like two young roes that are twins, which feed among the lilies. A garden inclosed is my sister, my spouse; a spring shut up, a fountain sealed. Forever impregnable, beyond my reach. Vanity of vanities, saith the preacher; all is vanity. Or perhaps he was wrong. Perhaps the miracle remains intractable. *Because* it decays, *because* it is mortal, *because* nothing endures but bone. All of it gone, and now forever here and now. For nothing can match the memory of the lover. Nothing is as durable as desire.

I mustn't go on like this; I'm becoming an embarrassment to myself, a prolix old man. I'm trying to use words to worm myself into what was pure bone, unmitigated reality. How I love thee, my beloved. But it is a dangerous love I bear thee. Do not listen to me. Flee from me. Make haste, my beloved, and be thou like to a young hart upon the mountains of spices. Here I go again. Make haste, my beloved.

I left her, for the moment, just as I'd found her. Except for restoring, very carefully and gently, as best I could, the small bones of the severed hand, and returning the skull to the top of the vertebrae of the neck, where it belonged. I couldn't think any more. It had all been too much for me.

With considerable effort I hoisted myself up through the trapdoor. The outside air felt cold on my face. I was covered in sweat. My throat was parched. I needed my nifedipine. I left the hole open. Almost mechanically I went to run a bath. My whole body felt wrapped in a film of dust and cobwebs and death. This, I thought as I came past a mirror and saw my reflection, was what Lazarus must have looked like stumbling from the dead. How surprising that he wasn't sent straight back to the grave. What did a man like that presume to do among the ignorant living?

I had a bath, and shaved and got dressed, then sat on the edge of the untouched bed waiting for Magrieta to arrive.

She stopped in the passage when she saw me. 'What's going on, Meneer?' she asked, clearly worried. 'Something happened?'

'I found Antje of Bengal.'

'Meneer saw her?'

'I didn't just see her. I found her body. Her skeleton. Under the study floor. Come with me, I need your help. We've got to get her out of there so that we can give her a proper burial.'

Only when we reached the gap did I realise it was out of the question to get Magrieta through it. I offered to break out a few more boards, but she stubbornly shook her head. 'I can maybe get in, Meneer. But I won't ever get out again.' I wondered whether it was really the movement in or out that worried her, or whether she was reluctant to face the dead. A ghost was one thing, the reality of a skeleton something else altogether.

I could not stomach the idea of carrying Antje out bit by bit. It seemed indecent. But to go out and buy a coffin and bring strangers in here, and cause a public scene which might well attract the media, was even less appealing.

'If only my husband Barney was still alive he could make her the nicest coffin you ever seen,' said Magrieta. 'That was a man what could use his hands.'

We decamped to the kitchen to discuss the matter. I first made sure the outside doors were locked; the house suddenly felt very vulnerable indeed.

Magrieta refused even to consider the possibility of moving Antje's remains. 'This is her place, Meneer. She'll never have no peace if we take her away en bury her among a lot of strangers.'

'She has no peace as it is, Magrieta,' I argued.

'But Meneer put her head where it belongs?'

Involuntarily I wiped my hands on my trousers and nodded.

'Then she will be in peace now.'

'But all exposed like that?' Now, in full daylight, the ghastliness of it began to overcome me.

'Meneer must cover her up. There's still some of the new sheets in the linen cupboard what you bought for our lodgers. We never used them.'

'And then?'

'Then Meneer can cover her mos up again under the stones.'

The idea still didn't appeal to me. But it was certainly preferable to a public spectacle. Magrieta went to fetch one of the sheets – the virginal white sheets intended for Tessa before I'd even met her – and I spread it over the bones, intricate and delicate as the fossil of a fern. Before I could tuck the sides in, Magrieta called me back to the trapdoor. She was squatting at the entrance, holding her small and much-thumbed black bible.

'I want Meneer to give her this. Put it nicely between her hands, like when you bury a person.'

'But what will you do without your bible? This one you've had since before you first got married.'

An angry click. 'I can mos get another one. En she need it more than I do. The two of us was together for so many years, I want to give her something special of my own. So she can remember me.'

I knew better than to protest. I balanced the bible on the narrow ribcage – Thou art beautiful, O my love, as Tirzah, comely as Jerusalem, terrible as an army with banners – and arranged the remains of the hands on top of it. The previous night, when I'd explored the bones and replaced the skull, there was no sense of reality to disturb me; but this time it was like trespassing, a violation, and I felt distressed. A few of the small bones from the right hand dropped off again, forcing me to redo an awful puzzle before I could tuck in the large sheet, and slowly and meticulously reconstruct the burial mound over her without disturbing or crushing the bones.

When I was done, Magrieta offered me a hand to help me out, and under her sharp eyes I replaced the boards for what I hoped would be the last time.

And the aim of the whole endeavour, finding the little navel ring, was still unrealised. Perhaps, I thought wryly, I might have put it on one of Antje's bony fingers: now we'd both missed our chance.

Magrieta made us an early lunch. Afterwards I went to take a nap. I couldn't sleep, although I was, in a manner of speaking, bone-tired. At least a patch of nitroglycerine helped me to relax. Which was something I needed, as I still had to say goodbye to her. I tried once again to dissuade her from going, but she stopped me very quickly. Her mind was made up.

Neither of us felt like discussing practicalities. She would come in one day next week for that, she proposed, once things had settled down. I promised to have a few pieces of furniture delivered to her new place. There were things to finalise about her pension, scores of little threads to tie up. But every time I mentioned something she'd say later, later, it could wait. There was a time to come and a time to go, a time to speak and a time to be silent.

She made us coffee. With almost ceremonial formality we sat down at the kitchen table, facing each other. It was the only time she indulged in a show of sentimentality.

'All the things we lived through in this house, Meneer. En this is now the end.'

'It'll live on inside us,' I said pedantically. 'It'll never be gone.'

'That day little Louis brought the live frog from the garden en gave his mother such a fright she dropped the whole tray with tea things.'

'That day the dog came in en stole the Christmas joint.'

'That day I got married to Reggie en we had the reception here in the garden.'

'That day they knifed Verwoerd en we all sat here by the wireless. One didn't know if one must cry or say glory to God in the highest.'

'That day the pollies squirted the people with purple paint from the Casspirs en they brought Mannie here. He was crying so much.'

'That day they beat the schoolchildren with the sjamboks, even little Mabel, she was only eight, her whole body was black en blue, en Meneer put stuff on to help with the pain.'

'That day Mabel came here with her boyfriend to tell me she was ashamed to have a common mother like me, en she cursed Meneer so terribly.'

'That day Miss Riana was killed en Meneer was so far away in Jo'burg, en we phoned en phoned for hours before we could get you.'

'That day Meneer en me en Mr MacFarlane sat here watching the TV when Mandela came out of jail, en that woman beside him.'

A whole shared history, private and public, hers and mine, Riana's, our children's, the country's. As if in some inexplicable way it all became focused on this house, like rays of light through a magnifying glass. Until it draws smoke and then gives life to flame. But whether it was a flame that consumes redundancies, or one that only causes soot and dirt, was too early to tell. What I did know, more than ever before, was the way in which this woman had always held my life in her hands, how she'd been the vital if unlikely representative of Antje of Bengal in the flesh, the keeper of my fate.

I don't know where our talk changed course. As we went on, we seemed to turn to more and more intimate things. Antje was drawn into it all. And at a given moment Magrieta said:

'That day when Antje called me en I came home to find Meneer here with that other woman, the pretty little one.' It was the first time in all these years she'd ever mentioned Alison.

'That was a bad day, Magrieta.'

'I always liked her,' said Magrieta.

'But you never knew her?'

'Of course I knew her. Every time she came here with Miss Riana. It was such nice music they made too, Miss Riana on the piano en she on that silver flute.'

'You must have been very angry with me. Seeing that Riana was so sick at the time.' I stroked my hand across my face as if to wipe away the cobwebs of the night before, of many years. 'Losing that baby girl really hit us very hard.'

'That child was never meant to live,' she said with a vehemence that surprised me.

With an edge of reproach I said, 'You could always find comfort in the will of the Lord. I couldn't.'

'I'm not jus' talking about his will,' she said. 'I'm talking about the way he struck her dead. He didn't have anything against the poor child. It was Miss Riana he was aiming for.'

'Don't say that, Magrieta. You know how much I wanted that girl.'

'That girl wouldn't have been your daughter, Meneer.'

I stared at her without understanding.

'I never spoke out of this house, Meneer,' she said calmly, 'but now my time has come to go, so I can just as well speak.'

'What are you talking about?'

'That was another man's child, Meneer.'

'How can you say such things about Riana?'

'God is my witness, Meneer. I saw them with my own eyes, in that room that's now Miss Tessa's bedroom, where Johann en Louis used to sleep when they was small. I wish God had cursed me with blindness that time. She en that fancy music man. The professor. The one who came here so often, usually with his wife, en then sometimes alone.'

She went on talking and talking, but I wasn't listening any more. The first I grasped again was when she said, 'She never wanted that child.'

'Are you trying to tell me . . . ?'

'I'm not saying she killed the girl aspris. But she *willed* her to die.'

'How do you know that?'

'Because Antje tole me.'

I tried to stop her, but she was too deeply into it by now. 'So that time Antje called me back en I found Meneer here with the pretty young one, I was almost glad. I suppose it was a sin, but I thought it was the right thing for Meneer to do.'

'And all the time I believed you'd never forgive me.'

'Forgiving is God's business,' she said in her righteous voice.

I thought: How different it would all have been if Magrieta hadn't found us that day, just as I was undressing beside the sofa, with Alison's musical hand clasping me. (And what was that about her mole?) Because we were in love. One of those things, as Tessa would say, that aren't meant to happen but which do. For months we'd fought against it. And then, that one weekend afternoon when the house was supposed to be free. We'd started discussing the hard step ahead: to tell Riana, to get a divorce. But the way in which it happened somehow changed everything, made it small and sordid. Alison, especially, saw it as a sign. Antje, Antje, how you have avenged yourself through the centuries. Because you were a woman, a slave, not white. I cannot blame you. In the name of how many others have you been wandering about through the years? But what a pity too. So much is wasted with the bad. There's always such a price to pay. Just because we're human.

Soon afterwards Magrieta left. I took her to the station in my car. I held her in my arms. It was like taking leave of a mother. We were both crying.

# 5

AND NOW I'M sitting on the steps of my front stoep, waiting, writing. Sunday, 17 January. I'm shying away, temporarily I'm sure, from my study with the pile of bones below. Tessa went out a few hours ago. If she can get away early enough from wherever she'll be spending the day, she agreed — her own life is not without its crises right now — to go for a walk in Newlands Forest in the late afternoon, as we did once before.

I stayed up late last night, but once again she did not come home. I needed so much to talk to her after the scene on Friday. Unless I was disgracefully misreading her absence, her period of chastity had evidently not yet begun. Hope flies eternal, while the feathers last.

I tried to concentrate on reading. Painter's biography of Proust, which I read in the sixties when it first came out. The print is very small. I rediscover every day, and every time with renewed irritation, that my eyes are not what they used to be.

There was one brief passage that left a sudden little scar. I don't feel like getting up now to check it, so I must rely on memory. Something like: Love is the only feeling that can never be returned. I didn't feel like reading any more after that. And probably from exhaustion I fell asleep. It was high morning before I heard her come in. When I hurried to the kitchen I found her making breakfast for two. For a moment I thought there might be someone waiting in her room, perhaps Zolani, but then discovered to my joy and shame that she was making it for the two of us. I'd planned the night before to be very stern; or distant at the very least. But the breakfast and the carefree kiss that came with it made the firm resolve evaporate.

'Tired?' I asked. She did look strained. Not just — the inevitable tinge of jealousy — the result of sleepless nights, but perhaps something deeper. (Whatever you do, I thought, don't tell me you're pregnant again.)

'Not too bad,' she replied, sitting down opposite me and stirring her coffee.

'I've been missing you.'

She looked up at me. 'These last few days have been total chaos. After I left here on Friday I was ready to freak out. I confronted Zach and shouted things I suppose I shouldn't have said, and then walked out. At least it was better than getting thrown out. And now Nicky and I are not quite organised yet to get our own project off the ground, so it's all in something of a mess. We were working so late on Friday that I just stayed over at her place. Yesterday we continued from where we left off. We're not done yet, but I had to come home first for an oil change.'

'How far did you get?'

'The project is coming on, touch wood.' She laid her hand flat on the table; those inventive and practical fingers. 'But Gavin is a tough customer. He's the guy who has to put up the money.'

'And your job is to soften him up?'

She gave a smile which might mean anything. 'Not necessarily in the way you think.'

'Not necessarily?'

'No,' she said, not flinching in her look. And then changed the subject deftly. 'How are things here?'

'Magrieta left,' I said as quietly as I could.

'Oh Jesus.' She briefly covered her face with her hands. 'It's my fault, isn't it?'

'Not so much yours as Zolani's.' I mustered the last bit of the firmness I'd decided on before she came in. 'I'd appreciate it if you wouldn't let him come here again.'

She nodded, her eyes cast down. 'I'm so sorry, Ruben. I made a total fuck-up of so many things.'

'We've had a fair amount of upheaval here,' I said. And I told her about finding Antje of Bengal.

She was tense with excitement. I had to tell her everything in detail; and then she promptly wanted to go down into the basement with me to see. But I restrained her.

'She's been laid to rest now, Tessa. I think it's better to leave her that way.'

'I wish I could have been here.' The little frown. 'It's curious, isn't it, how one can become attached to someone you don't know at all. Someone who isn't even alive, who lived hundreds of years ago. She could have been my sister. She could have been me.'

'Hardly,' I said. 'You have other ghosts to put to rest.'

'Only my father.' It came out so suddenly she seemed as surprised as I was.

'You've still not made your peace with him?' I stretched out my arm to touch her hand.

She didn't react.

'You still have his photograph on your wall,' I quietly prodded her. 'You even took it to the hospital with you.' It was the first time I'd referred to it.

She nodded, but still said nothing.

'You've never tried to contact him after he left you?'

Her eyes rose to meet mine. 'It's all very complicated, for me at least. You see, I hate him for what he did to us. But in a way I guess I've always admired him for himself, for having had the guts to go for the thing he wanted. I mean, he was a top-notch lawyer and everything . . .'

'I thought he was a professor?'

She stared at me through narrowed eyes for a moment, then shrugged. 'You must remember I was very small when it happened. Lawyer or professor, it was one or the other. The point is, all he really ever wanted to do was paint. And so one day he chucked it all up. Left his family for a set of brushes and a roll of canvas.'

'No other woman involved?'

'No, but it was much the same, don't you think? A woman, painting . . . it was still a question of passion. After he left, from time to time, he continued to send me books. Buying off his conscience, I suppose. The last one came for my twelfth birthday. It had a Paris postmark. I have no idea what happened to him afterwards – if he failed, or died, or made a splash. But he followed his passion.'

'You're not doing too badly yourself.'

'I'm not so sure, Ruben. Perhaps it's just these last few days that have been getting me down.'

'You usually seem to thrive on crises and consternation.'

She was quiet for some time. 'I'm confused,' she admitted at last. 'I think I need you more than ever.'

'My fatherly advice, or me?'

'You.'

'I'm not detached or objective or disinterested enough.'

'That's why I need you.' She became unexpectedly intense, 'Whatever happens, I never want to hurt you. I never want you to think badly of me.'

'I love you too much for that,' I said.

For a while our conversation became easier and less focused. Then she got up. 'I must run a bath and get going. Nicky will be waiting for me, it's a make-or-break day for us.'

'You and Nicky? Or you and Gavin?'

'The three of us. The project.'

That was when I said, 'If you can make it home in time we can go for a walk in the wood again.'

Her eyes lit up. 'That would be magic. I'll move heaven and earth.'

'If the earth moves it'll be enough for me.'

She laughed and went off, leaving me with the breakfast dishes; fair enough.

Before she left she skipped in for a quick goodbye. 'I'll be back before dark,' she promised. 'We both need that walk. Just to make sure the world is still a beautiful place.'

# 6

EVEN AFTER A week it still seems outrageous and improbable. But now it cannot be postponed any longer. Let me try to be as sober and unsentimental as possible. So help me God.

She came home earlier than I'd expected, that Sunday afternoon, 17 January. (What meaning has a date like 17 January? Why do I even bother to write it down?) I was sitting outside with the morning's paper, which I hadn't read yet, catching up on the week's quota of murders, attacks, hijackings, rapes, robberies, miseries. Cape Town, the leader page asserted, was beginning to replace Johannesburg as the crime capital of the country. It all seemed unreal, vaguely preposterous, in the tranquillity of this garden with its dark oaks, its silver trees, its hibiscus and proteas and roses, quite a pleasant place now that Garden Services had taken over. Johnny must be smiling in his coffin. It was just after six. The sun was still high, although it was obscured by Devil's Peak. The almost terrifying heat of the day was beginning to abate, except in patches of sunlight where it would still lie throbbing, ready to snarl at the unwary. Feeling sticky and irritable from the heat, she went to have a shower first. When she came back she was wearing a pair of faded jeans and a white T-shirt, and her trainers. The thin gold chain was visible in the V of her shirt. I was conscious of the light pulsing of her throat in the small nook between her collarbones. And of her breasts. She wore no bra. I note these small things not, as usual, as thoughts to stoke an old man's pathetic desire, but because they are relevant for what followed. I was not the only one to be conscious of her physical attraction.

We followed, as far as I could remember, the same route as before.

Perhaps even the people we encountered were the same, in twos and threes, sometimes a bunch of six or seven. And the dogs. Which, like the previous time, considerably delayed our progress. She had to greet every one of them, fondle them, rub their ears, kiss them. But in the end we did go further than before, I think. Higher. And turned onto a different path, the one less travelled by. There was a strong smell of pine needles. And innumerable more subtle fragrances from the other trees and shrubs, from the fertile black soil itself.

Once I stood her against a tree to kiss her. And she responded with a passion that both moved and provoked me. Her tongue was in my mouth, her hands behind my head to press my face more urgently against hers. Her smell mingled with that of the pines, of bark and gum. We stopped when another couple strode by, returning from the higher slope; and grinned somewhat sheepishly. She waited for them to pass, then briefly and boldly touched my erection through my pants, raised her hand to her mouth and kissed it. I would have loved to linger, but she said briskly, 'Let's go on.' And we continued hand in hand, her fingers locked in mine.

I suppose we were both a bit euphoric. Which was why we went up so far and paid scant attention to the magic and the mysteries of the forest around us. So we never saw them approach. There were five of them, although I didn't think of counting then. Young men, ranging I'd say from the mid-teens to the late twenties. That is what I told the police afterwards. One had a limp, another a scar on his left cheek. One wore a knitted cap drawn down low over his eyes, the rest were bare-headed.

When we became aware of them they'd just emerged from a clump of bushes lower down; their voices and the sharp snap of a dry branch made us turn round. They formed a half-circle around us, cutting across the path we'd come by. Even then we didn't suspect anything. Tessa called out a cheerful greeting. Two or three of them mumbled a response.

We half-turned away to resume our walk up the slope, although by then I wasn't quite at ease about having them behind us. That was when one of them called out sharply. I couldn't hear what he said, but looked round and saw them drawing closer and moving up beside us to close the circle.

Tessa put her hand through my arm. I should have brought a cane, I thought. We don't have anything with us at all. And they – without warning, shockingly – had knives. Flick knives. And one a longer, more fierce-looking hunting knife.

'Is there anything we can do for you?' I asked with some effort. My voice didn't sound familiar to me.

One of them patted his left wrist and grinned.

I tried to grin too, hoping to exorcise any evil intentions he might be harbouring, and quickly tore the watch from my wrist, holding it out to him. One of the others gestured towards Tessa. I gave a half-step forward to shield her, at least partly. She removed her watch too.

The one wearing the cap said, 'Shoes.'

An odd thing to ask, I thought. But if shoes were what they wanted, I'd be happy to oblige. I was willing to give them anything. I tore off my shoes, stumbling slightly as I did so. Tessa undid the laces of her trainers and handed them over too. In a sudden inspiration, thrusting my hands in my pockets I took out all my cash and handed it over with alacrity. *Allegro con brio.* Then turned out my pockets to demonstrate their emptiness.

'That's all,' I said, trying to clear my throat. 'That really is everything.'

They still didn't make any attempt to leave. For the first time I began to feel fear. I put my arm around Tessa and drew her close.

The young man with the cap pointed at Tessa's throat. I glanced at her. Not the little chain, I thought.

'Look,' I said, 'please . . .'

'It's all right, Ruben.' She brought up both hands behind her head to undo the clasp. I caught a slight smell of perspiration from her, even though she'd just had a shower.

She placed the chain in the cupped extended hand of the cap man.

'Now, this is really all we've got,' I said, making an effort to keep my voice brisk and steady and speaking as clearly and reasonably as I could.

I don't know how we moved into the next stage. I remember that one of them laughed, or said something. It still didn't sound ominous. But suddenly my arms were pinned behind my back. Some of them moved in between her and me with a swiftness that caught me by surprise. They'd seemed so lethargic, almost indolent, before. I was pushed back against a tree. Then there was a knife against my throat. I could feel the tip of the blade pricking the skin.

'Please don't,' I tried to say.

'Shut up!' my tormentor snapped. It was the one with the scar.

He pushed my head back against the trunk. I tried to strain against his hold, using all my strength to turn my head, to look at where she was. There were sounds of a scuffle near by. A sharp short cry coming from her, followed by what sounded like a slap. Scarface turned away slightly to look at what was going on and sniggered. They had her on the ground now. She was kicking and fighting like a cornered rat.

'Don't!' I exclaimed hoarsely. 'Don't touch her!'

Like a striking snake the knife was back against my throat. I could see the whites of the man's eyes. I could smell his breath. This time there must have been a cut where the point probed into the skin. I could feel something wet trickling down my throat.

'You talk again,' he said into my ear, 'I cut your throat.'

I could still hear Tessa fighting, struggling, writhing about, kicking. At least one kick must have found a target because I heard one of the attackers cry out. Followed by another resounding slap. She was making choking sounds.

'Don't shout,' one of them said in a furious hiss, 'don't shout. Just shut up or I kill you.'

The knife against my jugular pricked into me again. My head was throbbing. I'm going to pass out, I thought. I must fight against it, I must control it. If I don't they're going to kill her.

And then she screamed. I'd never have thought that such sound could come from her. My first thought, as tears began to break from my eyes, was: They're raping her. They're raping her. But then I realised it wasn't fear or pain that produced the sound. It was mostly rage.

Someone smacked her again. They must be trying to close her

mouth, to throttle her, I thought. But she went on screaming and screaming as if she'd never stop. The sound seem to ring out against the mountains, echoes were coming back. Screaming and screaming.

And they actually let go. They began to back off. Scarface made a lunge in my direction, knife thrust out towards me. I don't think I did anything clever or quick. In a reflex, I merely ducked. But he missed. The hunting knife was stuck a good centimetre into the tree.

Still she screamed.

I'm not sure if that alone could have saved us. They retreated for a few paces, seemed to waver, but then began to regroup. I knew that if they did there would be no stopping them. Tessa was on her knees. Her shirt had been ripped from one of her shoulders. Her jeans were halfway down her buttocks. And she was still screaming, bent over double with the effort.

Then there was a sound of dogs barking. People's voices. From lower down some hikers appeared, running and panting. And the attackers fled in among the trees. In a few seconds there was no sign of them. They'd dropped one of Tessa's trainers, but nothing else. Not the little chain.

She stopped screaming. She just remained bent over, pressing her hands to her face, heaving. I was breathing with difficulty. With a numb hand I touched my throat and stared curiously, in disbelief, at the smudge of blood on my fingers.

# 7

I DON'T EVEN know the names of the people who rescued us. There were four of them, I think, but it could have been only three, or five, or six. Does it matter? Somehow they brought us down the slope again. One of the men had offered Tessa his tracksuit top. They took us to the Claremont police station. We struggled through interminable questions. 'Why aren't you people more careful?' the constable who took down our particulars asked at some stage. 'Don't you know it's dangerous?' Later, in an attempt, I'm sure, to show understanding, he said, 'Anyway, nobody got killed or raped, so it's not so bad.' When I asked him if they would send a patrol up the mountain he looked mildly surprised. 'We don't have a van right now,' he shrugged. 'And they'll be gone already. You know, those people, they live in the bushes, they know the place. But we'll maybe send someone up in the morning, OK?' Then our helpers, two of whom had stayed behind in the police station with us, brought us home in their car. The weather was changing, I noticed detachedly; the wind, which had been a mere breeze up in the forest, was gathering strength and banks of clouds were massing overhead, swirling down from Devil's Peak.

Tessa was very tense, but she seemed inexplicably calm. I was still trembling all over. I sent her to have a hot bath and had one myself. Afterwards, in the dining room, I poured us two stiff whiskies and took them to the study. She came in wearing a full-length off-white dress in a very light material, cheesecloth or something, reaching down to her bare feet, long-sleeved and buttoned up to the clavicle. She'd bought it at Greenmarket Square a week or so before and had come home in a state of great excitement to show it to me.

'You look like a bride,' I said in an unsuccessful attempt at light-heartedness.

'I don't feel like a bride.' She sounded almost curt.

Only then did I notice that she'd brought two joints of dagga from her room. She offered me one, but I refused. She sat down, and began to draw on hers very slowly, occasionally peering at me through the whorl of smoke as if from a great distance. Already what had happened seemed unbelievable, remote, impossible.

I thought of Henry James, somewhere: We can never again be as we were.

I put on a record, but as I raised the pick-up arm I caught her eye. She shook her head quietly. I replaced the arm on its support and returned to my deep chair.

There was a movement at the door. Amadeus appeared on the threshold, tail up like a pennant, surveying the room, then quietly turned back and disappeared into the house. Except for that one occasion when Tessa had moved out I couldn't recall him rejecting either, or both, of us so disdainfully before. But neither of us remarked on it. Even a small thing like that was too precarious to talk about.

For a long time we sat in silence, drained of everything. At least we're still here, I thought. Something terrible could have happened, but hasn't.

'I never thought you could scream so,' I said at last.

'I got that from my mother.'

'I thought he was going to cut my throat,' I said after another silence.

'It looks like a razor nick,' she remarked.

And that was all we could think of saying about what had happened. Later it might, would, catch up with us. Not now.

I was dead tired. She must have noticed it, for she said, 'You must go to bed, Ruben.'

'What about you?'

'I'll just finish my smoke, then I'll turn in too.'

'You sure you'll be all right on your own?'

'Of course. Goodnight.'

She lifted her head for a perfunctory kiss. Fleetingly it brought back the memory of our caress among the trees and I made to take her in my arms, but she did not respond. Through the smoke her face began to dissolve, as if in water. I wasn't sure whether she was still there. Yet she was the one who was smoking the pot, not I.

It was eerily quiet in the house. The kind of silence I'd last been conscious of when I'd come home from Johannesburg and found her here and turned off the music. That irritating song which continued, in unguarded moments, to invade my mind. 'Some Kinda Love'. But if you close the door I'd never have to see the day again.

I went to bed and closed the door. It wasn't quite ten o'clock yet. I tried to read for a while, but Proust's life could no longer hold my attention. Too remote, too sheltered. I put the book away, turned off the light and lay with my arms behind my head: not actively thinking, just allowing thoughts to move unhindered through my mind.

She screamed for help, I thought. She screamed for help, and people heard, and came, and saved us. I haven't even asked their names. But they were there. They helped.

And then the next slow wave of thought unfurled. How many other voices have there been shouting for help throughout my life, shouting for me to help? Riana, more than anyone else, ever. Shouting and shouting, in so many ways. But also my sons. Alison. Perhaps Tania. My mother from beyond the grave, my father from his carpentry shed in Booysens. Magrieta and her three husbands, her children, little Mabel. Antje of Bengal. Johnny MacFarlane, so urgently. My dear friend who lay there in the road, unable to shout, but weakly raising an arm at me as I drove by. Perhaps he'd recognised my car. But he never spoke about it. And I drove past. One doesn't stop for bergies. One doesn't stop. All those cries for help from a clamouring world. While I chose not to listen. I couldn't bear to get involved. Unlike those strangers, this afternoon. I complain, often, like everyone I know, except Tessa perhaps, of how the place is going down the drain. Misery, violence, terror, the lot. All the voices, voices. Yet I prefer not to listen, not to respond. (Even Tessa's bergies were shown the door.) And by turning a deaf ear I help create the very space in which the world can sink into the morass. The mindset that makes atrocity possible. Even old St Anthony, whom I in so many ways despise for turning his back on the world, indulging only in dreams and fantasies, visitations, visions of blacks and naked women – even St Anthony at times ventured into a canal infested with crocodiles to visit his monks. But I just want to stay out of it altogether. The world is too much with us. I cannot bear it. If Tessa had been raped, I would have been to blame. Even had there not been a knife against my throat I would not have had the courage to intervene. I write letters, I make notes. I don't like shouting.

In the end I fell asleep. It was more of a coma I think than sleep. I don't know what woke me. The more I think back the more I'm left with a single possible answer: Antje of Bengal. But Magrieta had said she would now be at rest? I know better. Wasn't there the slightest hint of a shadow flitting past the bed, an obscure moon floating past the window, a female presence? There was more evidence to come.

I put on the light – it is just after two, yet it feels as if I've slept very deeply, and for a long time – and get out of bed, sitting on the edge for a moment to combat the momentary dizziness. My eyes, with some disgust, take in my old man's nakedness, not an alluring sight. The cadaverous legs with bony knees, lean hairy shanks, knobbly feet, the shrivelled penis with its dumb blue head, the belly folds. I put on the trusted old gown. Time to buy a new one, really. This one has served me more than it had ever been meant to.

When I come into the passage I can see that there is still light in the study. That is also when I catch the first whiff of smoke. She lies asleep on the sofa, curled up in a tight foetal ball, a childlike thumb in her mouth. Ash from a cigarette, a zol, must have dropped on a newspaper on the floor, from where the fire is spreading along a pile of opened books I have been working from. The flames are still low and tentative, hardly any damage has been done. Grabbing a pillow from the sofa I start beating down the infant fire. It takes only a few minutes.

I hurry to the kitchen to fetch a dustpan and a brush to sweep up the black and grey cinders. She is sitting up on the sofa, her legs folded under her, blinking her eyes.

'What's going on?' she asks.

'You tried to set fire to the house,' I say lightly. 'Your old mad streak again?'

'Oh shit.' She looks on in dismay. 'Can I help?'

'No harm done.' I stand up with the dustpan, wait for a moment to ease a strain in my back, then touch her cheek with my knuckles. It leaves a black smudge. 'I think you should go to bed for a proper sleep.'

After emptying the pan in the kitchen bin, I return to find her leaning against the study door.

'Can I give you something to make you sleep?' I ask.

Suddenly she starts speaking, very urgently. 'Please, I can't sleep alone tonight. Perhaps I'll really burn the place down this time.' She puts a hand on my arm. As once before, in another world, another time, she asks, 'Will you just hold me? I need someone with me.'

*Someone*, I think — but it is as if I'm observing another person thinking, not myself. *Someone*, not: *you*.

I take her to my room. For some reason I do not try to fathom, I close the door after us. No one must come in here tonight. No murderers, no rapists, no hungry bergies, not even Antje of Bengal. She sits down on the bed.

'I'm thirsty,' she says, like a child preparing to be tucked in. How often did I hear this from Johann and Louis when they were small?

There is a water carafe on the bedside table; I fill a glass and she gulps thirstily, then hands it back to me.

As I replace it on the table she gets up and starts to unbutton the long white dress, an endless row of buttons that reaches all the way down.

'Shall I help you?' I offer. She makes a small shrugging movement with her shoulders. I hesitate for a few moments. From the furthest distance the wail of an ambulance impinges on my consciousness.

I kneel in front of her and start undoing the buttons from her ankles up, while she works her way down. It is a slow and meticulous ritual, performed in silence. We meet in the middle. She is naked under the dress. Reaching up, I put my hands on hers, looking up at her face, into her shaded eyes.

She helps me up, then turns to let the long dress slip from her, leaving it in a small heap on the floor. For the first time I see the dark bruises all over her body – throat, arms, breasts, stomach, thighs. This must be why she has put on the long dress; but now she is hiding nothing. She raises her face and presses her lips lightly to the small, still painful scar on my neck. I bend over to open the bedclothes. She slides in. I cover her and remain standing beside the bed, unsure about what to do.

After a moment she half-sits up again. 'You must take off this old gown,' she says.

'I haven't got anything on under it.'

'I know.' She undoes the loosely tied knot. Like Alison in the distant past she reaches out to put her hand on me. She does not say, 'You're beautiful.'

I turn off the light and get in beside her. She moves closer to cuddle up against me as if she's cold.

'Hold me,' she says.

I'm trying to relax, to keep all thoughts at bay. I cannot dictate to my body how to react, what to do, what not. Nor do I want to interfere. My early urgency gives way to the slow osmosis between her cold and my warmth. I begin to yield against her, adapting naturally to the contours of her back and legs, one of my hands sheltering a breast. The wind outside is turning into a gale, tearing through the trees with crude violence; branches scrape noisily against the roof; but in here it is very still.

She remains tense, easing up a bit from time to time as if forcing herself to let go; but then I can feel the muscles of her back and buttocks tautening again. A light film of perspiration has gathered between us. Once she sits up with a start, a smothered sound in her throat.

I raise myself on an elbow. 'It's all right,' I say in her ear. 'I'm here. I'm with you.'

She moves into a new position, facing me. She no longer pretends to be peaceful. In the dark I can feel her eyes on me. She begins to caress me, not gently, lovingly, but with a kind of unassuageable urgency.

'I can't get it out of my mind,' she whispers. 'The moment I close my eyes it all comes back again. If those people hadn't come . . .'

'Tell me whatever you're thinking,' I say. 'Just get it out of you.'

'I don't want to talk either. What is there to say? You were there, you saw it all.'

'And I didn't help you.'

'What could you have done? They'd have killed you. Oh God, Ruben.'

She is tugging furiously at my penis. I put my hand on hers to restrain her, but she shakes it off impatiently. She sits up again, angrily throwing the bedclothes from us, offering herself to me in the uncertain light.

'Will you make love to me?' she whispers desperately.

'I want you to calm down first,' I say. 'Tessa, let's talk. Or just lie together quietly.'

'Don't you want to?' she asks in a kind of rage. 'Are you disgusted with me now?'

'My love, my love,' I say. 'I love you more than ever.'

'Then help me, for God's sake! Make love to me. Fuck me.'

She grabs my hand and forces it between her thighs. In spite of my distress my penis is rampant, some kind of dumb animal with a will of its own, impervious to fear or grief. I hold my hand tightly on her mound, that perfect thing denuded of feathers. Abandon ye all.

'Tessa,' I groan, 'Jesus, Tessa.' But whether it is a plea – and for what? – or an expression of desire I cannot tell.

'Fuck me!' she gasps. 'Fuck me, damn you!'

She pulls me on to her. She seems possessed by an uncontrollable violence. Is this what I have so passionately lusted for, needed, dreamed of, fantasised about, for months and months? This act of taking, this possession, this fucking? Is this what I have envied the others for, cursed them for, damned them to everlasting hell for?

I press my face in the hollow between her neck and her shoulder. My hands are holding her head, her small head with its wartime stubble of hair, and I feel under my fingers the clear definition of the skull. I imagine the structure of bones beneath the pressure of my body.

Cranium and mandibles. Ribcage, scapula and clavicle, vertebrae, humerus and ulna, the intricacies of carpus and metacarpus; the flare of the ilium, the length of femur and tibia, the delicate bones of tarsus and metatarsus, the phalanges of fingers and toes.

I raise my body and press her down with my hands on her shoulders.

'Tessa!' This time I nearly shout her name.

For a moment her frenzy abates. She stares at me. 'Come into me,' she whimpers. 'Please, come into me.'

'I cannot do this to you,' I plead. 'Do you understand that?'

'You don't want me,' she says through rigid lips. She lies very quietly under me now.

'I've never wanted anyone, or anything, as much as I want you right now,' I hear myself say. 'But we can't do this. Not now. Not like this.'

I remove myself from her. We are slippery with sweat.

She lies unmoving beside me. I sit up, reach down and pull the sheet back over us. We do not speak. The silence lasts and lasts. After a very long time I put out my hand to find hers. For a moment I fear she is going to shake it off, but then her fingers fold over mine, tightly. She still doesn't talk. But I can sense her body relaxing very slowly, the terrible tenseness ebbing from her. Outside the storm is raging, the violent night is hurtling on its way to God knows what or where. We're caught in its eye, in this unnatural calm beyond the reach of hope.

Later still, the birds begin to twitter outside, anxiously, unsettled by the wind.

'I cannot stay here any longer,' she says at last, so softly that at first I am not sure it is she; it is my imagination, I try to think; or Antje of Bengal. It cannot be Tessa. But it is. 'Not after what has happened,' she adds.

'Do you mean on the mountain?' I ask. 'Or here, tonight?'

She doesn't answer, I do not dare to ask again.

Helpless light is moving into the room like a slow tide coming in.

'You must be free from me,' she says. 'I need to stand on my own feet.'

'I don't understand,' I say, feeling numb all over.

I turn my head to look at her. Her terrifying eyes on the pillow beside me.

'How can you ask me to do that?' I ask.

'I cannot do it on my own.'

'I want you to stay,' I blurt out heedlessly.

'It's not only me,' she says urgently. 'It's you, it's everything I touch and everyone I get to be with. I've taken everything from you.' She rests her forehead against my chest. 'I've broken what you had. I made Magrieta leave. I've ruined your world. I've nearly burned your house down. Will you please tell me to go?'

I just shake my head.

'What about what you've given me?' I ask at last.

'Like what?'

Suddenly I'm at a loss. Not because I think I've been mistaken but because I cannot find the words. How can I thank her for a desert space, for loneliness, for anguish, even for despair? How can she understand – how can I myself understand – that a desert holds the promise of flowers, that the dark of a moonless night is a condition of the light, that only in solitude can we discover the need of others, that even after a storm like the one outside the little birds can begin to sing? Yet it is nothing new. It is something I grew up with. The miracle of rain after three years of drought. The flowers bursting from the parched earth. The flying ants. After the violence of my brothers, little Lenie behind the lucerne bales in the barn.

I fix my eyes on her, clutching her hand very tightly as I say, 'Then go, my love.'

Later that morning she left. She came back with Zolani, who helped her to pack and carry out her suitcases and boxes, armfuls of clothing, books and CDs, shoes, lampshades, the pinboard with its assortment of notes and pictures (most of them recent; one very old), the computer, the broken never-used guitar. (Poor instrument, I thought, you don't know what you're missing.)

And then she was gone. The door was closed, I faced the day. I must call a char to come and tidy up; I don't want to go back into her rooms before they have been thoroughly cleaned. There must be no accidental mementoes, nothing under bed or chair or cupboard. I have memories, I can survive.

I am alone now, in this tumultuous desert where Tessa has left me after disrupting the flatness of my old world. But I am also not alone. Antje of Bengal is here. She will help me – and, no doubt, also make it more difficult – to face what has to be faced, what all my life I've tried to turn away from. There is the world outside – how did Rilke phrase it? – which requires me and strangely concerns me. Antje will see to it that I do not avoid it.

I have no doubt about her continued presence any more. When I came in from the stoep where I'd stood that morning to see the old Beetle drive off for the last time in its cloud of smoke, I came into my study to take my seat here behind the desk. And found on it, neatly on top of the pile of books I'd rescued from Tessa's flames, the little navel ring that had been lost, its genuine glass ruby glittering like a small drop of blood. My desire is intact.

# Footnote

THE CHARACTER OF Antje of Bengal has been inspired by Nigel Penn's remarkable essay 'The Fatal Passion of Brewer Menssink: Sex, Beer and Politics in a Cape Family 1694–1722' in *Rogues, Rebels and Runaways* (David Philip, Cape Town, 1999). The historian Geoffrey Dugmore does not exist; most of what has been ascribed to him in the novel comes from Penn. Apart from the sources on the life of St Anthony cited in the text, I have also quoted from Carl Linfert's perceptive commentary in *Hieronymus Bosch* (Thames & Hudson, London, 1972), as well as from the massive study by R. H. Marijnssen and P. Ruyffelaere, *Hiëronymus Bosch: Het Volledig Oeuvre* (H. J. W. Becht, Haarlem, 1987). For some of Tessa's insights she may well have been indebted to Naomi Wolf's *Promiscuities: A Secret History of Female Desire* (Vintage, London, 1998). The remark by Emmanuel Levinas on page 28 is from his 'Enigma and Phenomenon' in *Basic Philosophical Writings* (Indiana University Press, Bloomington, 1996), while Heidegger's comment on page 104 comes from *Poetry, Language, Thought*, trans. Alfred Hofstadter, (Harper & Row, New York, 1971). 'The intricate and folded rose' on page 113 is an image from Judith Wright's wonderful poem 'Woman to Man' (in the eponymous volume published by Angus & Robertson, Sydney, 1949), and the reference to the 'naming of parts' on page 114 comes from Henry Reed's poem with that title in the volume *A Map of Verona* (Jonathan Cape, London, 1941). Lines from Dorothy L. Sayers's *Busman's Honeymoon* are quoted, deliberately from memory, from a student production, over forty years ago, in which I bravely but woefully played Lord Peter Wimsey. (Details about the production itself are, *nota bene*, fictitious.) Sayers's Dante translation, from which quotes appear on pages 125 and 256, is, of course, published in the Penguin Classics. The quote from Alberto Manguel on page 216 comes from *Into the Looking-glass Wood* (Knopf, Toronto, 1998). D. H. Lawrence's anguished cry about sex on page 239 is quoted from 'Tortoise Shout' in Volume 1 of the Complete Poems of D. H. Lawrence, eds Vivian Sola Pinto and Warren Roberts (Heinemann, London, 1964). George D. Painter's *Marcel Proust*, from which a comment on love has been taken, with a crucial phrase missing, on page 288, was (re)published by Pimlico (London, 1996). The synoptic Rilke line on page 306 appears in J. B. Leishman's translation of the 'Ninth Duino Elegy' in *Rilke: Selected Poems* (Penguin Books, Harmondsworth, 1964). For obvious reasons, widely familiar allusions are not acknowledged here. Besides, Ruben Olivier's mind is such a crow's nest of quotations and secondhand references that I cannot claim to have traced or identified them all.

# Glossary

aspris — ('express') deliberately

baas — boss, master
bakkie — pickup van
bergie — Cape Town vagrant
biduur — prayer meeting
blarry, blerry — bloody
blesbok — medium-sized antelope
bobotie — traditional Cape Malay dish of curried mince
borriepatats — sweet potatoes prepared with turmeric and cinnamon
broekie lace — ('pantie lace') wrought-iron decoration on veranda

dagga — South African marijuana
darem — after all
doek — headscarf
doepa — magic potion
dominee — Dutch Reformed pastor
donga — ditch
dwaal — (here) daze

erf — plot

galjoen — Cape fish (*Coracinus capensis*) with particularly delicate
  meat
gazat — (here) trousseau

Groote Kerk — ('Big Church') oldest Dutch Reformed church in Cape Town

harders — mullet

impimpi — police spy, traitor

ja — yes
jentoe — (pejorative) girl with loose morals

kierie — stick, cane
koppie — rocky outcrop
kwaai — angry, strict, fierce

*Landbouweekblad* — 'Agricultural Weekly', major Afrikaans farming journal

maar — but (often used as a conversation filler)
Masbieker — Mozambican
mealies — maize
meid — disparaging appellation for non-white (servant) woman
memorie — memorandum
meneer — mister, sir
middag — afternoon
(to) moer — (crude) to administer a beating
moerkoffie — ground coffee
mos — after all, just so

necklacing — lynching by placing a burning tyre around the victim's neck
nogal — what's more; into the bargain; if you please
Nooi — Madam (from of address for a white woman by her coloured employee)
(to be) nuggeted — to be saddled

outa — form of address for older black man: previously respectful, now pejorative

riem – thong
rooibos – ('red bush') traditional South African herbal tea

sjambok – riding crop
skollie – gangster, criminal, good-for-nothing
Slams – ('Islamic'), Cape Malay traditional healer, often believed to
   have magical powers
snot sjambok – (crude) penis
sommer – just so
spook – ghost, spirit

tjoekie – jail

UCT – University of Cape Town
UWC – University of the Western Cape

vygie – succulent (mesembryanthemum), with dazzling flowers

zol – joint of marijuana